THE
LAST
RADIANT
HEART

DANIEL LANCE WRIGHT

A VIRTUAL TALES BOOK

The Last Radiant Heart

Copyright © 2010 Daniel Lance Wright (www.daniellancewright.com)

Edited by Jake George (www.sagewordservices.com)

Cover artwork by Sheri Gormley (www.sherigormley.com)

A Virtual Tales Book
PO Box 822674
Vancouver, WA 98682 USA

www.VirtualTales.com

ISBN print: 1-935460-38-2
ISBN eBook: 1-935460-40-4
Library of Congress Control Number: 2010935467
First Edition: September 2010

Printed in the United States of America

9 7 8 1 9 3 5 4 6 0 3 8 1

DEDICATION

To my wife, Rickie, for enduring my many ups and
downs while in the process of bringing this story to life.
Without her support and indulgence, it simply would
not have come together.

Also Available from Daniel Lance Wright

Paradise Flawed

Six Years' Worth

Where Are You, Anne Bonny?

Coming Soon from Daniel Lance Wright

Defining Family

Annie's World: Jake's Legacy

WWW.DANIELLANCEWRIGHT.COM

CONTENTS

Foreword..1

Chapter 1..3

Chapter 2..15

Chapter 3..22

Chapter 4..31

Chapter 5..43

Chapter 6..51

Chapter 7..58

Chapter 8..64

Chapter 9..71

Chapter 10..76

Chapter 11..90

Chapter 12..104

Chapter 13..112

Chapter 14..121

Chapter 15..126

Chapter 16..132

Chapter 17..136

Chapter 18..139

Chapter 19..143

Chapter 20..147

Chapter 21..155

Chapter 22..161

Chapter 23..166

Chapter 24..174

Chapter 25..182

Chapter 26..190

Chapter 27..197

Chapter 28..201

Bibliography...207

Author Bio 209

FOREWORD

Whether beliefs are rooted in creationism, evolution, or any other discipline, there is a point everyone will likely agree on: The human mind functions at a mere fraction of potential.

Debate on the subject creates more questions than answers. Although theories are bandied about, nothing has ever been proven. It remains a debatable and interesting topic of conversation.

If two people can agree that the human mind is only using a miniscule portion of that potential then the question becomes: Is there a story out there— a person—that could provide evidence of a brain fully developed? If so, what would it mean? What would that person be capable of?

Theoretically, such a person would set the scientific and theological communities on their ears. Such a discovery might require an overhaul of thinking that has been around for thousands of years. Since beliefs tend to harden with time, changing that thinking might require a large hammer of truth.

Let's explore a possibility: What if a person existed that had full use of every square centimeter of brain matter, not just part of it? Furthermore, what if full use of that gray matter did not constitute an increased ability to think reason or control body parts—or any other function considered primary?

The result could be a projection of power that changes this person's personal universe. In other words, allowing him to physically move from one time to the next, one place to the next, or even one dimension to the next.

Could there be truth in such a story? The popular answer would have to be no. But let's assume the unpopular answer is correct.

Thanks to near-infinite genetic variations, we are amazing creatures, and amazingly different. Some are capable of tremendous feats of ingenuity while others are tragically challenged to perform the simplest tasks.

What if a scale should exist to measure absolute mind capacity? The difference between the near-vegetative human being and the person with the highest intelligence quotient on the planet is indistinguishable on this scale, both near the bottom. The ability to think and reason is common to both. Their assigned position on the scale already indicates how little difference there is between them. Furthermore, we are assuming a scale to measure *absolute* mind capacity.

What if thinking and reasoning were only a tiny part of the brain's planned purpose? What if incremental increases in mental capacity create abilities that compounded with each click of the pointer on our assumed scale?

These extraordinary gifts wouldn't be considered normal or even believable by today's standards. Such *gifts* would be labeled queer aberrations of the human condition. Religions of the world would take it to extremes. Some would assign Christ-like status. Others would call it Satan's work. But everyone would disbelieve until they witnessed it for themselves. It would test all belief boundaries. Therefore, it makes sense that someone possessing such abilities might desire to keep them secret.

Let's consider these for example: telepathy, telekinesis, astral projection, time travel, inter-dimensional travels and a myriad of others, real or imagined. Small, yet passionate, groups around the world believe in such areas of study. A few openly profess to practice these fringe concepts.

Somewhere, in a lonely position high up on this mind-measuring scale is a nonbeliever. He's a man of average intelligence—a man that confines such topics to party conversations. But, what he has believed all his life is destined to become irrelevant.

CHAPTER 1

Jack Dane had to keep in mind that he'd walked into Nikki's office believing she'd be difficult to convince. Even still, living up to his expectation pissed him off.

"Damn it! Don't patronize me," he blurted.

Nikki Endicott recoiled. "Hey, calm down."

Although she was trying to take the edge off his anger, her half smile irked him. Old friend or not, Nikki's advanced degrees in psychology should have clued her that her facial expressions carried meaning beyond her words. He knew her body language. She made no attempt to hide suspicion that her dear old friend may have gone round the bend and seemed to be in the early stages of making a joke out of it. But Jack had to prove that he wasn't a candidate for the funny farm—that's the reason he made the decision to come to her office in the first place—to prove that he wasn't losing his mind.

He sighed and looked to his feet. *I have to be real. If I'm wondering if I'm crazy—why should I be angry that she agrees?* "I'm sorry," he said barely above a whisper. "I've been touchy since all this crap began."

His pounding heart settled. Heat left his face and the kink in his gut went away. There were likely many medical explanations for his problem but none that included the word sane. He had an experience perceived by all his senses and that, for him, made it real. He needed Nikki's expertise as a clinical psychologist to understand how a vision could be so vivid, if that's what it was. Nikki Endicott was the only person he believed he could trust with such a fantastic tale. But, obviously, that brought with it no guarantees.

Pushing to the edge of his seat, he leaned forward, placing hands on the front of her desk. "I didn't mean to snap at you. I'm just rattled. That's all." He pressed his thumb and index finger into the bridge of his nose. "I know it sounds feeble, but I can't be certain it was a dream. It was more of… an experience. I swear to God, Nik, I was there in that time and place."

He studied her expression. It seemed whimsical, as if she waited for a punch line like it was some kind of practical joke and the truth would soon be coming out. Slapping her crossed his mind. Maybe that was how to get the seriousness of his point across that it was no damned joke. She may have been his only shot at expert advice. Taking it slow and keep plugging was all he could do. "I really need your help. I'm beginning to believe I really was in a different place instantly and had no idea how I got there."

She seemed to soften, unlacing her fingers from atop the desk and leaning back. The overstuffed, high-back, button-tufted leather chair engulfed her. The leather squeaked. "Look, we've known each other a long time."

"So?" He sighed, sensing a lecture. Sitting across the desk from her, he felt small and still shrinking, as if looking into the face of a judge. His eyes again fell away to the worn leather of his scuffed shoes.

"I still remember a day you looked at me with dreamy eyes..." She paused and shook her head. "God, the tripe you laid on me." She licked her lips, as if tasting something bitter. "True love you called it. Remember that?"

He kept watching his wiggling toes. "That was a long time ago."

"Stop me anytime you feel that I'm straying from the truth. Isn't that what you told me?"

"Hey. I've already admitted it. What do you want from me? I screwed up. So what?"

Nikki fell forward and dropped both arms on the desk with a thud. He glanced and recognized the body language. She had become the aggressor. Only the desk prevented her from getting in his face. "Then you should also remember I tried talking you out of it. For Christ's sake, Jack, I knew marrying that woman wouldn't work. You didn't listen to me then. Why should I believe you'd hear anything I have to say now?"

His face flushed—this time embarrassment. He nodded almost imperceptibly. She made a compelling case that he didn't always know what he was talking about. She certainly had the first hand memories to back it up. That's when it occurred to him that she was a pretty damned good behavioral therapist. She had just taken his anger and flipped it, transforming him into a defenseless heap in a matter of seconds.

"I thought I was your best friend and you didn't even let me know you were getting married until the decision was already made." She went silent.

Those last words seemed tinged with sadness. He looked up.

She swallowed hard.

Was it a sentimental lump?

"Then you showed me how short your memory was by saying the same thing prior to your second marriage. True love?" She fell back and slapped the armrests of the chair. "My ass! You didn't know what the word meant."

Jack wanted to respond. But the look on her face indicated it might be best to hold comments on that subject for another time. As quickly as his admiration for her professionalism piqued it went away. The conversation had suddenly gone from him to being about her. And he hadn't said a word to make it happen.

Still, she wasn't finished. "By the way, I'm still not sure why I took the time to go to that second wedding. I knew where it was going before it started… just like the first one."

A wild gesture nabbed his attention. He looked up.

"Now this." Her manner took another turn. She snickered. "Jack Dane, you sweet idiot. You might as well be telling me it's true love all over again, because, buddy, I think this story is the product of an overactive imagination, too. You've already proven that you lie to yourself until it becomes your personal truth." She laughed. "Is this just another load of scat?"

And there it was; that sarcastic half-grin he remembered so well from their college days. He wanted to leap up and throw it all back at her, but couldn't. Frankly she was right. He just didn't understand why she'd dredged it up. Was it just to make that point? It was so far in the past he couldn't figure why she'd pull it up and use that for an example. The only reason became unnerving. She still had romantic leanings. He sure as hell didn't want to explore that—not here, not now. *This has to stay about my problem. Screw her childish romantic frustrations.*

"I think there's a whole universe with an epic cast of characters, but each and every one of them exists only between your ears," she said. "They're not real. Not then. Not now. You shouldn't be a small-town newspaper writer. With an imagination like that, you could get rich going after J. K. Rowling's job. I always thought it'd be interesting to crawl inside your head and look around. Jack Dane-world seems like a fascinating place. I just don't think I'd want to stay long."

Anger simmered, but he remained cool. The list of people he could tell this story to was short. Short list? Hell, she was the only one on it. He had to remain focused and not become distracted by her desire to take the conversation in a different direction.

"Look. We awaken from dreams and then…" he blew a puff into his fist and released it into the air. "…Poof! They're gone… nothing left but disjointed events that may or may not create some type of story pieced together from odd memory bits. When fevers break so do hallucinations. Nik, I traveled back. I felt some kind of… transition. Do you understand that? I didn't just wake up. I didn't snap out of anything. I was aware the whole time, from that stagnant cesspool of a lake back to my apartment. It was sudden. All the desolation of that place vanished and I found myself sitting on my aching ass on the shower stall floor, butt naked and scared, shaking like a puppy dog that had just been beaten with a rolled up newspaper. Light intensity, odors, temperature… all changed instantly. My shoulders were sore from swimming and I could still smell the rancid odor of that nasty water."

He stopped talking and hoped candor and directness got through to her. If he kept talking at this pitch, he became certain it'd only add to her conviction that he was out of his mind. So, he shut up. He sought every advantage to make her an ally. But she had to get there at her own pace. Though he considered her a friend, this session wasn't going as he'd hoped. He fidgeted.

Not only did the silence between them become uncomfortable, the ultra clean and modern ambience of her office had the opposite of a calming effect. It would not have been his first choice for a place to talk, preferring a deli or a bar. As a single man, he felt more comfortable in a cluttered environment. Diplomas and awards plus books lining shelves to the ceiling behind her made for an uncomfortable formal setting. Maybe all those volumes simply complemented her doctorate hanging on the wall—a decorating choice. He finally tired of the musing. "Well, say something."

She again leaned back in that gaudy chair, this time with no apparent attitude attached. "Okay. Tell me the story. I suppose I owe you that much." She rested her chin on a steeple of fingertips.

On the outside he worked at remaining calm. A nervous flutter in his stomach threatened the lunch it held because of rumbling excitement that Nikki was willing to listen. "Thank you. Just knowing you'll listen means a lot." He slid back in his chair and paused long enough to collect his thoughts. Then, he recounted the whole story as he remembered it.

"I was naked standing on the shore. But the odd nature of what was happening and what I saw made that unimportant. Stinking and stagnant, the water was murky red with fallen trees everywhere. Lifeless stumps littered the surface. Ahead and to my left a row of gnarled dead trees extended beyond my range of vision in the distance. Some still stood but most had fallen, victims of their own dead weight. It looked like the aftermath of a watery battlefield that the victors had long since abandoned. This view remained unchanged to the far shoreline. I think it was a shoreline. I couldn't quite make it out, blurred by distance and haze. It provided no clues of what this place might be. The waterscape that lay before me reached beyond the limits of my vision.

"The entire scene would have been dead had it not been for the wake left by two swimmers.

"A vision, maybe a waking dream—whatever it ultimately will turn out to be, strangled my senses and continues confounding the way I view the world around me because I'd never seen anything so stark and barren before. I had no idea why I was there or how I'd gotten there. I struggled to comprehend how I came to be in that place.

"Why was I watching my brother swim through muddy water that stunk of decay? I didn't need to see his face to know it was Kyle. Devoured by breath-robbing fear, I could do nothing more than watch my only living relative swim a dangerous distance from the safety of solid ground. I was overwhelmed by helplessness to do anything other than watch. The weight of gloom pressed my heart.

"My dog, Buddy, swam close at Kyle's side, but only for a moment. Even the strong swimming ability of that little guy couldn't maintain the speed with which my brother swam. The dog faltered. The little canine showed signs of giving up. Buddy's head was all I saw. For a short time, he struggled to keep up with Kyle but then slowed, meandered and finally stopped swimming altogether.

"My only sibling moved through the water with uncanny ease, accelerating the farther out he swam. After a time, he moved over the water as a leaf might on a windy day, darting here to there with no effort. The wake he left seemed to indicate mechanical power or, maybe, supernatural power. I don't know. Yet, I was driven to preserve this last surviving member of my family at any price. I reasoned that if I failed, it would be the last time I would ever see him. I couldn't say why I thought this but it was ingrained like hunger because it gnawed at my gut the same way starvation would. Hope dimmed. I couldn't understand why I thought that either.

"The mystery of my presence in that place shrank into the background. My brother's safety and what I might be able to do about it had been suddenly thrust into the spotlight.

"I wrung my hands, twitched and shuffled my feet. I may have even whimpered aloud. I'm not sure. I can't remember details but I do remember making a quick decision on the best course of action. Images that should have had no bearing cluttered my thoughts, like a snapshot of myself soaking wet, covered in whatever slime this water held beneath its murky surface, should I decide to go into it. Or should I drown, I carried no identification. I was totally nude. I shook off superfluous thoughts fueling indecision and slid into the water. Ultimately, I was driven by the need to help family—my brother. Poor chances of success and concern for personal safety be damned. I was suddenly up to my neck in putrid water and queasy from the stench.

"Muscles strained against resistance of the foul smelling soup as I paddled to a swimmer's prone. The water was warm as bath water on the surface but cool—even cold a few inches below the surface where the radiant warmth of the sun had no chance to reach. I fought to maintain a fast pace over its surface.

"As a watery film covered my eyes, I had to shake the blur from them to clear my vision. Because what I thought I saw, I couldn't believe without a second look. At first I thought it might be a trick within a trick upon my mind.

"Or as you might say, Nik, it could have been the product of an overactive imagination. But, I assure you it was not.

"What I thought I saw remained unchanged even as my vision cleared. The partially decomposed carcass of a dog came into view across a fallen tree between its branches, a macabre sight in that it had been fashioned by human hands. All four legs had been stretched and tied. Its midsection flayed, the entrails gone. The mutt was left staring at the sky through rotting eye sockets and a grin suggesting I might be next. A convulsive shiver and gag racked my body. I wondered: What demented thinking caused someone to do that? Was it a threatening message or, maybe, a warning? Was it even meant for me? Perhaps it was designed to help understand something I could not yet grasp. What the hell was it all about? The introduction of each new strange sight became even more confusing and frightening.

"The brutalized animal was only the beginning. Bones and decomposing bodies of unknown origins littered the water. At first, I thought it was submerged branches brushing the underside of my naked body. As I swam over and disturbed the water, bleached white ribs still attached to spines and skulls, some with flesh dangling from bone, swirled to the surface and drifted out of sight into water that had no clarity at all.

"As any mortal might, I thought: *This water must be crawling with disease.* Raw sewage would be as sanitary. Not swallowing the water became a rule I vowed not to break. As I weakened from fatigue, the harder that promise was to keep. I swam on.

"My body ached. A small but not insignificant comfort came over me when I realized Buddy, my ever-faithful pet, would not need to be convinced to return. Self-preservation driven by instinct drove him. He'd return when fatigue threatened his existence. The dog was pre-programmed to survive if possible. I took comfort in that. He would know without having to be called when he reached his limit, turning back before exhaustion pulled him under.

"It was Kyle that concerned me. I could not suppress malignant fear that my best efforts would not be enough. My heart broke as distance separating us increased. Kyle swam with superhuman ease, apparently determined beyond all influence to reach the other side. The gap between us lengthened as he pulled away. Couldn't he see I wanted him to stop? Hadn't he noticed that I feared for his safety?

"I shouted, 'Look at me Kyle. Turn around and look, damn it!'

"I received no response.

"The little dog displayed frustration in his own way. He turned and began the swim back.

"Even as bleak and frightening as my surroundings were, I had swum far enough to glimpse the other side. To my great surprise, it was beautiful. A magnificent forest appeared, yet still some distance away. Tall trees gently swayed to a breeze I could not feel. Where I swam it was hot, calm, bleached lifeless and barren. But there, on the other side, brilliantly colored birds lifted and glided from branch to branch while three deer grazed beneath a tree's canopy. The serenity of it touched me.

"This was no simple view of just any forest you might see in a glossy photograph on the cover of an outdoor magazine or topping a spring month on a calendar. It was a vision of immense power and permanence that induced calm acceptance—a profound sense of peace. It drew me forward, dulling my concern over getting back to where my journey had begun far behind me. I found myself wanting to be there with Kyle. My eyes fixed on its beauty and grandeur. It called for me as surely as if it had a voice beckoning me over. Little wonder Kyle had no desire to stop or turn back. I was more than a little inclined to join him.

"There was no detectable current in the water, yet I felt an unmistakable force push me on and pull me forward. Whatever it was had nothing to do with that nasty cesspool. It pulled me farther out. It seemed I began to move faster toward something I could not understand. As if two large hands were at my back, I was propelled through the water leaving a wake as I went. I stopped questioning my senses. I wasn't swimming. I was no longer under my own power. I sped through the water toward the magnificence of the far shoreline.

"I fought to turn away from the beauty that spoke directly to my soul. Kyle had made it to the other side standing up to his knees in water that had transitioned from this reddish slop where I was, to clear blue water that was surely as cool as it appeared. He did not seem tired, nor did he appear wet as he emerged from the water. Most baffling of all was a look of jubilation on his face. He turned away from me and opened his arms as if inviting whatever might come. He looked back with a broadened smile and began to laugh. But I couldn't hear it. As he walked up onto the bank toward the luscious flora, the grazing animals remained calm even as he approached. He was without clothing, too. It seemed natural to see him that way in that setting. *My* nakedness didn't feel natural at all. Even as I feared for my life, I still felt shame for being unclothed.

"The wildlife seemed totally at peace with his presence. He moved through a ray of light. I clearly saw him wave at me and mouth something in my direction. I can't be sure but I think he said. 'I love you. Goodbye'. By then, it was plain that Kyle had known all along that I was behind him and would not have the desire to make it all the way across.

"I had no more time or strength and began to return to where I'd swum from, following in little Buddy's wake. He was exhausted, too.

"I was compelled to look back one more time. Part of me wanted desperately to follow my brother, to be in that place where ribbons of soft light filtered through trees. I mustered all reserves of energy to fight whatever force it was that moved me through the water. I did wonder if that force was of my own making. I couldn't be sure... still can't. But the desire to get back to safety, and perhaps reality, I was quite sure about, paramount in fact.

"As difficult as the swim out had been, the return proved much more of a problem. The sight of the tortured and dead canine was not the shock it was on the way out, nonetheless disgusting. Fighting for every foot of progress my muscles burned and ached. I resisted the temptation to look back again. Somehow, I knew that if I did it would be as if a fisherman's hook had snagged me and I'd be reeled all the way across despite intent. I had to stay the course—to remain focused. I couldn't seem to get enough air; huffing for more each time my head broke the surface. I didn't know how much more my arms could take. All I thought about was this place, my brother, and why I was here watching him go there—wherever the hell *there* happened to be. These thoughts swirled through my mind. I was losing the battle. I think I began moving backwards, yet never wavered or slowed my fight to swim away.

"Glimpsing Buddy, it occurred to me: Thoughts. Logic. That's the answer.

"My head snapped back as I sucked in as much air as my lungs would hold. My little dog had less difficulty for one simple reason; he reacted only to instinct. I had to take that cue, to shut down my overactive mind, to wipe it clean—free of everything except a strong image of my destination.

"Without consciously choosing to do so, I became determined to talk my arms into finishing the job. 'Hand over hand, arm over arm, round and round they go, taking me where I want to go,' I chanted in time with my stroke. 'Hand over hand, arm over arm. Round and round they go, taking me where I want to go.'

"As images that plagued and confused me faded, my vision tunneled to the safety of where my quest began. Vile things I witnessed vanished. Becoming thoughtless by choice, I was returning successfully.

"Suddenly, my head slammed backwards.

"Had something been dropped on my head? I remember wondering.

"I sucked in water and gagged, coughing to regain breath. I tried to look out ahead, but all I saw was a void, featureless black. I was conscious because every physical sensation was acute. I felt gravity pull at my body, from my head down to my toes. Something pushed the bottoms of my feet, buckling my knees. A sharp pain in my butt electrified me. I became nauseous.

"The black I looked into suddenly went brilliant white, like an exploding flashbulb in my face. Then, even that faded.

"The water was still warm, as it had been, but now it lacked the stench and sprayed down on me from above. I opened my eyes and followed the stream of water up to its source… a showerhead. I remembered where I had been before it all started.

"The nausea was gone. It appeared I had hit the back of my head against the shower wall and collapsed to my rear end. I checked my body.

"I tried making sense of things. But the more I thought on it, the more frightened I became.

"There was no sense to be made of it. None!

"Water pelted my aching body as I sat on the shower stall floor.

"The only thing I could believe was that I had indeed returned—but from where? I can't say.

"I have no idea where I was or how I'd gotten there. The only thing I remembered before it all started was being naked and trying to coax Buddy into the shower with me. It was time for his weekly bath and was much easier to accomplish in a closed stall with me. When, out of the blue, an image of Kyle popped into my head and I wondered how he was doing. It had been so long since I'd seen him.

"Sitting on my ass in that shower stall with a soaking wet dog at my side, I was forced into only two avenues of thought: I'd lost my mind and went totally round the bend, or something that defies all known laws happened. I refused to believe either. Still, even my reeling imagination is not providing plausible answers."

"From a clinical standpoint," Nikki said, "I should consider having legal papers drawn up to have you institutionalized." She paused. With chin in palm she doodled on a tablet with the other hand. She didn't look up. After an awkward silence she tossed the pen on the tablet. "Seriously, I have no basis for believing you won't hurt yourself or someone near you."

At that point Jack had three choices: Run, hurl obscenities, or take her advice. None were what he sought. At this point, he feared that whatever he said might fuel the assessment.

A smile crept across her face. "If someone told me this morning when I came to work that Jack Dane would be walking into my office and telling me such a… a fantastic story, I would've laughed them right out of my office." She twiddled the pen between her fingers. Her eyes drifted upwards. "Although… I've always thought you might be easily swayed in your opinions, I never thought you were anything but level headed."

She held a smile. It was abundantly clear she mulled something, probably spiraling down to some decision. Scooting back in her chair, she sat up straight and grabbed her Mont Blanc pen. She pulled in that yellow tablet and flipped to a clean sheet of paper. "Let's say, just for the sake of conversation that everything you told me is true."

Oh no. Here comes the I-think-I'll-believe-whatever-you-say pitch. He smiled a crooked smile.

She assumed a well-honed professional demeanor that seemed faintly rehearsed. "I'll need more information to understand what I'm dealing… excuse me, what *you're* dealing with. Did you experience any other strangeness? Tell me about the days leading up to that episode."

He became thankful not to have acted on an impulse to yell at her again and storm out of her office. Her tone, now, was different. She spoke evenly—no longer with that condescending ring. For the first time since the conversation began, hope sprung forth that Nikki might want to help.

Beyond a failed fling in college, followed by a more casual friendship, Nikki's day-to-day life since their time at the university had been a mystery—one he had no desire to solve, then or now, even though they'd always lived in the same city. This part of her life had not interested him until weirdness dropped into his lap and, suddenly, he thought about those things. Jack now wondered what made Nikki Endicott tick. He knew she lived alone and that she had this behavioral therapy practice. But that's all. Judging by the trappings, she appeared to be a talented and prosperous practitioner.

Gleaning a spark of sincerity, he seized upon it. "You may find what I'm about to tell you just as difficult to believe as the story just finished. Maybe more so. I don't know. But I have to bounce it off... someone. And you're it." He realized he'd been staring at the floor mumbling. Forcing his eyes up to meet hers, he cleared his throat. "To give you a sense of what this is all about, I'll have to take you back several months. It has been an agonizing journey for me." He wriggled down comfortably in his chair. This story would take a while.

"My life is not exactly stress-filled, Nik, but on one particular day I was running late. It was one of those mornings. You know the type, unable to focus. My mind raced. All thoughts, like bats in a belfry, were random and unimportant. My head seized on every little thing as potentially critical, but none were.

"Occasionally a thought stuck and I'd dwell on it, contemplate it, study the nuances, and then I'd suddenly come around realizing time had passed. It happened repeatedly that morning. Finally, a glance at my watch told me an unacceptable amount of time had slipped by. The race was on. I was late for work.

"I finished dressing and ran through the apartment gulping coffee as I headed out the door. I noticed how beautiful the early spring morning was, sunny and a few degrees warmer than a normal beginning to a March day. Birds flit noisily. But there was no time to enjoy the moment. I ran for the car.

"It was after nine o'clock. I should have already been at the newspaper. A feature assignment was due on the city editor's desk by ten and, of course, it was unfinished. Getting psyched to do a story on a women's organization with no members less than seventy years old was a formidable task. I don't mean to imply it was a difficult assignment. It wasn't. But my lack of enthusiasm made it seem huge. I just didn't want to do it. I had procrastinated until the crap was in the air heading toward the fan. Christ, it was something about a benefit auction, just another formulaic benefit. Putting it off was about to get me in hot water with my city editor.

"These events may seem unrelated but they're important. As you can tell, they didn't support frivolous flights of fantasy. Nonetheless, that was the day it began.

"While driving, I began thinking about the family I never really had a chance to know. Why it crossed my mind, I have no clue. I had so many other things to worry about. But the fact that it did... at that particular time... was strange. I hardly ever think about them, even when my mind isn't cluttered with a job-threatening situation. The timing had only been one strange aspect. Once it popped into my head, it overtook every other thought.

"You see… my mother and father were divorced when I was six. My brother Kyle was less than a year old. Before I turned seven, Mom had remarried. She jumped back in and remarried too soon. Her new husband was a loser—more than that, he was abusive. In fact, Oscar was a certifiable son-of-a-bitch. This is the kindest label I can think of.

"The memory that began playing in my mind was of Oscar coming home one evening and flying into a drunken rage. Mom had not filled the pickup truck with gas, as she had apparently promised to do. He was a hard drinking piece of white trash. Over something as unimportant as that, he hit her with a heavy coffee mug, knocking her off her feet, unconscious before she hit the floor. Blood gushed from her ear.

"I threw myself over her, sobbing. 'Please, don't hit her anymore!' I yelled up at him.

"He growled, 'Get away from her, you piss ant.' Drool streamed in rivulets from his slobbery lips.

"His order only made me hug my unconscious mother tighter. 'You don't understand what you're doing!' I shouted.

"I might as well have kicked him in the nuts. He became enraged. I tried shielding her, but I was only seven. He tossed me aside as easily as he would a wadded shirt.

"He kicked her hard. Even now, I'm sickened when I remember the lifeless wheeze that came from her when he did. 'Don't hit her anymore!' I yelled, crying and hanging on to his leg.

"As I remembered this, I became agitated. It occurred to me I had yelled out, 'Don't hit her anymore!' inside the car. Suddenly, a halo of light brightened, circling my vision, as if a bright spot was trying to develop in my eyes, much like having a camera flash go off. But it didn't blind me. It only affected the limits of my peripheral vision, not the center of it.

"As I looked through the windshield, the road ahead appeared to be framed in a soft white light. I leaned forward slightly. My face broke a plane of some sort. A sudden extreme chill washed over me. My body convulsed. I shuddered and slammed back into the car seat.

"The thought of my mother beaten to death so many years ago ceased to be a memory. It was then a vision, playing out within that circle of light, straight ahead, just beyond the tip of my nose.

"As strange as it sounds, I never lost sight of the road or forgot I drove on a busy interstate. Both realities, one present… one past, were squarely in front of me, differentiated by the ethereal translucence of the past overlaying the present.

"I pondered the likelihood I was having a moment of insanity. Fear overwhelmed me. I thought I might lose consciousness behind the wheel and careen out of control. I remember wondering: Is this the first scene of life flashing before me? Am I about to die? Is that what this is all about?

"The scene played out. I saw Oscar's face. He suddenly sobered realizing what he'd done. He ran out the door. I saw it as plainly as I saw the sixteen-wheeler passing me on the right. As the truck went around, I realized that I played a dangerous game of distraction. Steering the car to the right, to the outside lane, I made my way off the interstate, determined to stop and allow time to figure out what was happening.

"The vision continued.

"I braked hard to a stop, tires screeching.

"I saw my mother's neighbors, an elderly couple, running toward the house. I can't remember their names but their faces I recognized instantly.

"White-knuckling the steering wheel and jaws clenched tight, I perspired. A drop gathered on the end of my nose. I felt trickles down both cheeks.

"'What the hell is happening?' I heard myself scream, pounding the steering wheel with doubled fists.

"In a flash, I realized the extreme agitation had taken its toll. I threw the door open and vomited.

"God as my witness, Nikki, that's exactly what happened."

CHAPTER 2

The diagnosis tumbled from Nikki's lips at a level of expertise Jack expected, but it was textbook talk. She still hadn't figured out that the problem was unknown to academia. She put a worldly spin on an episode Jack was convinced was unearthly. Years of cramming for tests and the rigors of college spilled out of that woman like a nickel slot hitting big. *I should have expected this.* He perceived it as a pre-packaged spiel off some list of standard diagnoses.

"This may sound like I'm trivializing your problem, but I think there's a simple explanation," Nikki said. "Anytime a traumatic experience is left unresolved, such as the violent death of your mother, the conscious mind may not be capable of coping with it, so it's suppressed, maybe forgotten altogether. But that throws the subconscious into overdrive, looking for ways to lay the issue to rest and, yes, creating fanciful scenarios that somehow relate back to it."

She stared at some indistinct point over his head obviously searching the archives of her mind to further the diagnosis.

I bet she's trying remember a paragraph out of one of those books behind her.

She jotted something on the tablet in front of her. As she did, his eyes went back to the shelves behind her desk that extended to the ceiling. He looked up, down, and right to left. Expensive looking volumes and reference books lined each shelf. *Everything out of her mouth probably comes from one or the other of them.* Under different circumstances he might have been impressed.

Note taken, she dropped the pen on the tablet. As it hit with a thud, his scan stopped abruptly on her face. She continued. "It would seem a part of you is fighting to bring this issue to the surface so it can be dealt with. The series of events that put the family back on your mind is probably the trigger, the mechanism that set off an involuntary string of events that seemed quite real… to you."

The comment struck him as simple and benign. It annoyed hell out of him. He raised his eyebrows, sighed, and let his head drop. It was probably a sound diagnosis by known criteria. She just didn't understand the depth and breadth of what he dealt with. He needed answers, not textbook explanations. Irritation escalated.

"Doctor Endicott." Her name tumbled out like profanity. "Excuse me, but—"

She held out a hand. "Whoa. You may not like what I had to say, but you can't beat the price of the session." She laughed and kissed the air between them.

Something new had just been added to this touchy conversation, reminiscent of a time long ago when hairstyles were different and bodies leaner. A capricious air suddenly surrounded Nikki. Even the look on her face reminded him of lighter times in younger days. Professionalism had come to a screeching halt and he saw that flirty nature he remembered so well.

In a flash of enlightenment it occurred to him: *I might have to take a different tack. This isn't working.* "I apologize for the sarcastic tone, but can't you at least pretend I'm a deeply disturbed patient?"

"Oh, I don't have to pretend. You're deeply disturbed all right." She winked and grinned.

"If you'd just—"

"Stop right there. That reminds me of something else entirely... "

On that comment, he sat back and let the conversation go wherever she wanted, coming to believe she didn't want to talk about his problem any longer and likely never did. Besides, he liked her smile and didn't want it to go away.

She laced fingers together and cradled her chin atop them. This time a dreamy far-away gaze emerged. "Why have you been married twice and I never figured into that mix anywhere?"

The loaded question splattered him like a chilled water balloon. "Uh... "

"Answer that one... if you can. I might even accept a well crafted lie." She grinned as if anything he said would be laughable.

Jack raised his eyebrows and held a faint smile. He had no intention of being the fly in that web. His problems be damned. She had another agenda. That lopsided grin stayed fixed. She remained silent and plainly would say nothing more until he offered an excuse. Never having been as quick-witted as she, he had to stay on his toes.

Fortunately, this time an answer came flying his way out of the cosmos. "For God's sake, Nik...why would I want to destroy a perfectly good friendship? You've already touched on how successful marriage has been for me. Now haven't you?"

"Good answer. It would seem you're not totally void of oratorical skill..." She shrugged. "...however nominal, mind you."

He let his smile fade and looked to his hands lying limp in his lap and attempted drawing down the flippancy to get back on topic. "Can we be serious about the reason I'm here?"

"Oh all right. But if you want me to be more doctor-like and less friend-like, it's going to cost you dearly, buddy. The few minutes I had to spare are gone. I have a patient, *a real one*, scheduled to be here..." She glanced at the clock on her desk. "...right now."

Jack swallowed hard. A week's salary from the paper might cover three sessions. But, he couldn't see that he had an alternative. He made the choice to suck it up and pay the fee, if that's what it took. "You'll have to look at me as someone you've just met to see this thing objectively. I really need your help. Please?" She seemed to remain a bit too lighthearted.

"Okay," she said with an exaggerated sigh. With a frivolous flip, she tossed her below-the-shoulder dark auburn hair back. "I'll be with you when you're Jack Dane, loveable small town feature writer. And I'll stay on when you change channels to something a little more supernatural. I believe all guys need tweaking and tuning before they're fit for release into the world anyway." She winked. "I'll just depend on you to tell me which role you happen to be playing at the moment. Okie dokie?"

Not exactly capitulation, but close enough. In so many words she had offered to help. He trusted her. For all her changing moods, he knew that much. That's why it frightened Jack to think she might consider having him institutionalized. Would she follow through on that, too? *Keep the faith, baby. Just keep the faith.*

Although he'd tossed it back, he considered her question on marriage valid—just not one he cared to think on very hard. Why hadn't he asked her to marry him all those years ago? They were inseparable for nearly two years. Maybe she'd made herself too convenient, blinding him to the jewel she was. *Could that be it?*

That's a conundrum he chose to relegate to the idle curiosity section of his mind just below that other burning question: How big is the universe? He began to smile, thinking on something else she'd said. Men do need fine-tuning before being allowed out in the world unchaperoned—too much analysis and not enough heart, and analyzing her was exactly what he was doing at the moment.

"Jack, your hour's up. Now get out." She grinned.

It was impossible to complain. He hadn't paid for the session but felt cheated anyway as he left her office. He hadn't heard what he came to hear. It was an hour of his life he'd never get back. Help him or not, it was his problem, his cross to bear. She would always remain a friend regardless.

His relationship with Nikki had always been rooted in sarcastic banter. But truth between them was a given, spoken or unspoken. She played the game well, talking to him as if he were a bastard stepchild at times. And he almost always let her get away with it. Saying the session was of no value didn't mean he hadn't enjoyed it. The good doctor cared. For now that was good enough. When the chips were down she'd have his back.

But that didn't change the depths of the dilemma. Questions without answers rattled his brain. He sought reason, a shred of understanding—anything to provide at least a few brush strokes in this paint-by-the-numbers picture he called a life. Stepping onto the elevator, he grunted chastisement for using the contraption. Taking the stairs should have been the first choice. The paunch circling his middle hadn't bothered him until he stood before a lean and sexy Nikki

Endicott. Now, the quivering roll embarrassed him. He spent most of the hour in her office holding his gut in. *One thing's for damned sure; I can't swim very far.* As he looked down with a disgusted smirk at his belly, he glanced to his watch and muttered, "Oh crap! I'm late."

Sliding sideways through the parting doors, he raced from the cool office building into the parking garage. The air turned hot and heavy—typical for late June in Springfield. The garage stunk of exhaust fumes.

A car honked—ear splitting in this concrete labyrinth. The noise and heat didn't add one iota of gaiety to his mood, nor did the fact that his car's air conditioner hadn't worked in years. The windows in the aging vehicle stayed down most of the summer. Sometimes he left the keys in it, hoping someone would steal it, but no luck so far. Thieves in Springfield must have had standards he just didn't measure up to.

The day had slipped into late afternoon and Jack became certain he'd be dealing with an irate editor for spending too much time at a so-called doctor's appointment. He pulled open the driver's side door, hinges squawking displeasure. Dropping into the seat, he slammed the door. His dear old friend rattled from headlights to taillights, protesting the disturbance. He patted it on the dash and said, "It's okay, girl. Just get me to work, will ya?" He wriggled on the seat until his butt found that preformed pair of dips that knew his ass better than he did.

Pulling out of the garage, he felt the first blast of a breeze and breathed it in. Even as warm as it was, it comforted him and allowed his mind to go elsewhere. Thoughts ricocheted between securing more time with Nikki and what Gus Landau, his editor, would be saying to him shortly. That little worry shoved Nikki right out of his head.

A crotchety old guy, Gus only wanted Jack to be a good writer. He carried himself as a stereotypical newspaper editor from a bygone era—sixtyish, thinning gray hair, overweight—quite a stout man actually—that wore the same red suspenders stretched over a bulging belly every day. Jack couldn't remember a time he didn't have them on. Gus always had a slimy cigar butt clenched between cheek and teeth. When he walked, his knees didn't appear to bend. He rocked side to side and, somehow, forward progress was made. He used a gravelly voice to his advantage, putting decibels into it when the occasion called for it. Gus Landau was old-school. He had no clue how stuck in the past he was and, likely, didn't care.

In a few minutes Jack would be offering the old guy ample reason to test that gravelly-voiced decibel thing. Gus had two favorite pastimes, jumping Jack's bones and grumbling about no longer being allowed to smoke cigars in the office. The old man derived a twisted sense of pleasure from complaining about everything from global warming to the strong smelling urinal cakes in the restroom. Jack tried to remember a time that he'd seen him happy, laughing, or even accidentally letting something positive slip out. He couldn't.

What the old man might hit him with when he got there was important, but Nikki weaseled back into his thoughts anyway. He had trouble caring too much about consequences where it concerned his grossly underpaid position at a small market newspaper.

There was a time he treasured every available moment with her. But that was two wives and a lot of years ago. He began to understand that if he spent time with her a fire might be rekindled. Maintaining control of his libido suddenly jumped to the forefront as an important detail. Getting a handle on his problem should come first.

If he called her and scheduled another session, she'd put it on her calendar and charge the crap out of him. That made him wonder: *What would she do if I tried to schedule an after-hours session?* The reality was she'd laugh and hang up on him. *But what if I asked her for a date?*

Jack had just stepped into risky territory when that embryonic idea struck him but believed it worth considering. Nikki might have a problem with that approach, too. On the plus side, it'd be cheaper. Money remained a top consideration—had to, because he didn't have any. *I think I can handle dinner and a couple of glasses of wine. But how do I maintain a respectful distance?* "Humph." He scratched his head and thought on that as he drove a few more miles. Finally, he gave up. He steered into the parking lot at The Journal.

He'd reached the point that he saw Nikki's inclusion as an absolute necessity. Weeks ago, he'd become convinced that if there were no one to confide in, insanity would come quickly.

Racing to the front door of the newspaper office, he grabbed one side of the glass double doors and slung it open, barely breaking stride all the way to his desk. His inclination to get to his desk unnoticed turned ludicrous. Although The Journal was a small-market newspaper, it happened to be prosperous, a continuous bustle of activity. This day was no different.

"Hey, Dane, did you take a long nap after lunch?"

Jack jerked his head this way and that, looking for the source of the crass comment that seemed to come from beyond the prairie dogging co-workers over the tops of partition walls of many cubicles. The shout came from the far side of the expansive room. Although noisy, the voice was unmistakable and all too easy to understand, even from that distance.

"It's four o'clock in the freakin' afternoon!"

"No, sir… no nap," Jack called out and grimaced at such an unimaginative response.

"You promised to have that Women's Auxiliary benefit story on my desk no later than three," Gus said loud enough for all to hear. "I bet you a dollar of your money you haven't even started it."

Jack began walking in Gus's direction. "You know as well as I do that any rookie could knock out that piece in less than fifteen minutes."

"Is that right?" The old man took on a defensive posture, hands resting on his chubby waist.

"Well… yeah." *Crap, I think I just lit the old man's fuse.*

He chewed that cigar so fast it spun in a circle at the corner of his mouth. "Good to know." He pulled the stubby cigar from his cheek and spit tobacco pulp in a nearby wastebasket.

Jack watched it fly into the trash and made a face at the slimy brown wad splattering on a piece of paper.

"Then I'll give you the opportunity to show me that you can write faster and better than a freshman reporter. I accept the challenge."

"What challenge?"

"You have ten minutes to have that copy on my desk." He ignored the question and turned to walk away stabbing the air with a chubby finger. "Not a minute longer, Dane. Got that? Not a minute longer."

He walked away and didn't look back.

"Yes sir." Jack rolled a chair under the keyboard at his computer terminal and immediately began typing. Fortunately, he'd done the research and committed considerable information to memory, certain he could do it in less than ten minutes, and did. It wasn't a long piece.

Chore done, he laced fingers behind his head and leaned back as far as the chair allowed, turning his mind over to Nikki Endicott. *You have the opportunity to accompany me to dinner tonight and talk about the good ol' days… or… whatever.* The idea to make the date came fast. Picking up the phone and dialing did not. After a sudden but tiny burst of courage, Jack yanked the receiver up and pecked out her number with a pencil eraser.

She answered after one ring. "Hello."

Surprised by how fast she answered, he froze. An impulse to slam the phone down caused him to pull the receiver away from his ear. Instinct kept that from happening. He stammered, "Uh, Nik?"

A long pause followed. Finally, she said, "Does your mother know you're playing with the telephone, young man?"

Jack rolled his eyes as he heard a snicker and knew that behind that condescending reply she fought to control a belly laugh. He found his wavering courage and fired back. "Cut the crap. I *was* going to offer to buy you dinner for seeing me on short notice today. Now I'm thinking that that might have been a bad idea."

"It most certainly is not. It's an excellent plan."

He tried not to acknowledge surprise of her quick acceptance. "No… no, it's bad timing. I can see that now."

"It's great timing. I insist. You owe me. Pick me up at 7:00. My address is—"

"Don't need it. I looked it up."

Then came a sudden click followed by a dial tone. She was gone.

"Jack Dane, get your ass in here!"

Startled, he swung around to see Gus rising from behind his desk through the glass wall of his office. "Yeah Boss. What is it?" He wheeled his chair back, sprang to his feet and met the old man half way.

Gus marched to him and stopped, his nose nearly touching Jack's chest as the stout little man looked up at him. With a patronizing lack of sincerity, the old guy put his hand on Jack's shoulder. "There's a psychic, a medium, a magician or… whatever the hell he's called, helping the police," he said in a tone reminiscent of an idling diesel engine with no muffler. "They're crediting him with solving a murder and finding a missing boy. With two solved mysteries in such a short time this could be big. I want you to research and write the story."

If he really thought it might merit front-page attention, it would've gone to one of the investigative reporters, not a feature writer. Jack mustered a lame smile.

"His name is Arthur Wainwright. Here's his address and phone number." He stuffed the slip of paper into Jack's shirt pocket, patted it down and slapped him on the shoulder. "I want a good story. Got it?"

"Sure Gus. I'll get right on it."

"You'd better," he barked. "Don't keep me waiting on this one."

The large clock suspended by a bracket standing out from the wall showed it was four fifty-five. *Close enough.* Jack looked once over his shoulder to see Gus waddling back to his desk. That was his cue to head straight for the door. *I figure five minutes of the company's time is a small price since I haven't had a raise in two years.* Excitement ratcheted up at the prospect of a date with Nikki. He hadn't been out socially with a woman since his last divorce over a year ago.

Romance was a bad idea. He'd already come to terms with that. But thinking it and actually putting himself in a situation requiring control of sexual urges might be problematic. *I am a man after all. I don't date. I am heterosexual. And it has been a long, long… long time.*

"Crap!" he muttered. He pounded his head with the heel of his hand realizing he'd just given himself reason and permission to lose control—a whole new line of thoughts to grapple with; hoping degrees of difficulty didn't keep rising until it rang the bell. He had to keep infatuation and sexual tension under wraps until the hard questions had been answered. A vision of Nikki's long auburn hair cascading over her shoulders caused his breath to hitch.

CHAPTER 3

Jack's courage faded as he pulled his finger away from Nikki's doorbell without punching it. Touching his lips with fingertips of that hand, the downsides to entering her apartment played out in his head. There were many. He tried again but stopped, holding it inches from the button wondering if it'd be worth it, or just create a complicated inseparable mishmash of needs and desires.

Willpower had never been an ally and putting himself in a position to be sucked into a romantic relationship with Nikki had to be viewed as a genuine threat. He couldn't be sure he wanted to prevent it, and that was the problem. She wanted it—that was clear enough. But then he remembered how desperate he'd become for answers before he finally caved in and went to see her in the first place.

The extended finger rolled back with the other fingers into a balled fist. That tingle in his groin had to be kept in check or all decisions would be controlled by it. It may have been a cliché but true. Men think with their penises. The relationship had to remain professional or, maybe friends, but that was as far as it should be allowed to go.

Forcing his lips into a thin straight line, Jack grunted frustration and refocused. The time had come to shove that tiny snowball off a snow-capped mountain and pray it didn't become an unmanageable monster. *I can do this and control it. I know I can.*

But he pulled the hand back and dropped it to his side. Although no one witnessed the cowardice, that didn't lessen embarrassment. Like a nervous teen on his first date, his stomach fluttered. Action versus hesitation; each came in short but overwhelming bursts.

God help me, I don't have a choice. He rang the bell.

Nikki's face appeared around the edge of the opening door, lustrous auburn hair waved toward it as she pulled it open. Since he already thought losing control might be a problem, this view didn't help matters at all.

"Give me thirty seconds before you come in." A wry grin came up. "I don't have any clothes on yet." From the tone, she might prefer a slight miscalculation.

Keeping that sexual tingle at bay had just come under attack. He cleared his throat and struggled to maintain civility. "I really thought you'd be angry that I'm late. It's a few minutes after seven, but it looks like I could have shown up even later and still be ahead of the game."

She withdrew her head but left the door ajar. "Oh, no you couldn't. You're supposed to be a gentleman. It's the lady's prerogative to be late." She paused. "Why haven't you come in yet?"

"It hasn't been thirty seconds."

"So?"

That single word spoke volumes. "Fair enough." He took another deep calming breath and slid sideways through the partially opened door as if it might electrocute him if he touched it. He gingerly closed it behind him, making a point not to look in the direction she walked. When he finally did, he blew a sigh of relief. She'd already disappeared into the bedroom.

Alluring perfume trailed her—no doubt expensive, judging by his surroundings and what he knew about her—an elegant apartment and a prestigious career. If he should judge simply by the aroma it could be ten dollars a gallon or a hundred dollars an ounce. It was all the same to him.

The spacious apartment was neat and clean—too much so. It appeared sterile, a place for everything and everything in its place. *Yep. The girl has a housekeeper.* He remembered her dorm room in college; so many clothes, books and papers strewn about that most days he couldn't see the carpet.

"How about Italian food?" he asked, as she reappeared fussing with a necklace.

"Sounds wonderful. What else do you have in mind?" She wrestled with the clasp.

Jack ignored the innuendo. "How about good conversation?" Waiting for an answer, he danced fingers across the shade of a lamp that set on an end table within arm's reach, feeling the linen-like texture.

"Come on now. You can't fool me," she said. "Are you sure you wouldn't like to talk about flights of fantasy... or anything else that might make Walter Middy cry bullshit?"

"If it happens to come up in conversation would I go on the clock?"

She laughed. "You can't afford me." She looked down at the necklace clasp.

"I was wondering about that. I only have fifty bucks and—"

"I'm referring to my professional fee, dummy, not the date." Her eyes crossed as she attempted to slide one tiny ring into the opening of another on the necklace.

"Oh. Sorry."

Her chest was bare above well-tanned breasts that almost spilled from a blouse with top buttons left unfastened. "Look, if it's a choice between that and staring at each other, then... yeah, let's talk about it." She became distracted. Her brow pulled down over crossed eyes. "Don't just stand there. Help me with this damned necklace."

Stepping behind her, perfume tickled his nostrils as he reached around her neck brushing the tops of her shoulders. Despite noble intention, his eyes panned down over her shoulder to an ample bosom that wasn't very well concealed behind a sheer blouse. He saw her bra through the silky material of the cream colored top that hung over hip-hugging black pants with billowy legs. The pants and top had a glossy sheen. She balanced the whole package on stiletto heels.

His heart thumped in his chest. When he started to feel its beat in his head, he had to look away. Rapidly concentrating testosterone threatened his calm as his fingers fumbled with the clasp. His good sense began wafting away.

Necklace clasped, he leaned in and full-well meant to kiss her on the neck. Lucidity smacked him in the face. He snapped back. He needed a cold shower, but that wasn't going to happen.

The trip to the restaurant helped rein in lust as they shared information about old friends and their whereabouts. Why he had not bought a new car resurfaced as a topic three times during the short drive. She refused to believe it was a money issue, preferring to think that Jack had some unnatural affection for that smoking piece of rolling junk. But mostly sentences that began with *Do you remember when…* remained the main topic of conversation. Eventually though, the conversation veered off into a place he didn't want to be.

"Your marriages? What happened to them?"

On that question, he clammed up and sat quiet, unwilling to go into specifics and said only, "Incompatibility."

She pressed for specifics, but he offered only generic answers that explained nothing. After a time, he tired of the interrogation. "Look, if it were a subject I wanted to talk about, I'd still be married. Stop with the questions already."

"Okay. No need to snap at me."

"Sorry." Not the way he wanted to cut it off but, for once, directness worked. Maybe that meant he'd be able to keep her at arm's length a while longer. She deserved the whole story. But that'd be valuable energy spent for nothing—a tale best saved for another time.

The hostess guided them through a crowded restaurant, negotiating narrow passages between tables. He slid sideways when necessary to keep up with the young girl charged with seating incoming guests. Waiters, waitresses and patrons streamed through the crowded trails and appeared much like ants in a mound. There was nothing intimate about the setting; the room was large and open. Sound reverberated amplifying noise even more. It was a party atmosphere, nothing at all romantic about it. Not a bad thing by his reasoning. But he wondered how fruitful a conversation would be if he had to yell across the table.

"Why haven't you called before today?" she asked, raising her voice as she dropped into a chair with a decided lack of finesse.

"Did it slip your mind that I was married five out of the last eight years?" He paused and shrugged. "I suppose I should have called after my last divorce." He bent at the waist and craned around to look her in the eye. "Forgive me?"

"That's better. It has been a long time… over a year I think, since—"

"I know. But even a failed marriage takes a while to get over."

"I'll let you have that one." She fingered the rim of her water glass.

Nikki's intentions for the evening were clear, every word carefully wrapped in desire. Her social life during those years between college and the present piqued his curiosity. "My turn. Eight years and you've never been serious about anyone? That's a little hard to believe."

"Serious? Yes. Married? Hell no!" She squirmed and sighed. "I finally came to realize it was a case of falling in love with the idea of being in love. There was no one who could hold my interest. But that didn't keep me from taking test drives." She flashed uncharacteristic shyness and, he thought, a touch of sadness, too. Barely above a whisper, she said, "I lived pretty fast and loose for a time."

"Not a concern." He waved off the comment and sipped his water. "We all do when we're young."

"Hell, there was no one who could even hold my attention during a first date much less later interest." Her face transformed, now sporting an impish grin. "But you have my attention. Would you like my interest?"

Nothing particularly clever came to him. But she did have his interest. *It sure wouldn't take much to fall into those chestnut brown eyes.* He blew a breath through pursed lips.

The waiter brought the wine and poured two glasses full. "Will there be anything else right now?"

Addressing the young man indirectly, still looking at Nikki, "Don't go too far with that wine bottle, son. We'll be needing more soon… very soon." The comment was as much for her benefit as the waiter's.

The young man grinned, bowed slightly, shot Jack a knowing glance, backed up a step, and turned to walk away.

Jack almost smiled at the lad because his assumption of what was going on between he and Nikki happened to be dead wrong.

He thought on her comment: *Her attention and her interest, huh?* "Right now, Ms. Endicott, I must respond by saying that's an answer best saved for another time." Overly formal maybe, but this was the best way to diffuse the issue without throwing cold water on the conversation. He needed a committed ally—a partner in solving life-altering riddles. A fine line existed between full partner and romance; a girl and a guy with chemistry, working close—a balancing act that would make even a circus performer lightheaded.

"Fair enough… for now," she said. "Tell me about your brother, Kyle. I don't remember his name coming up before our conversation in my office this afternoon."

Jack's tension drained away. He wanted to thank her for getting his head out of a sexual rut. But if she knew that's what she'd done, the conversation wouldn't have taken such a dramatic turn because that rut was big enough for two. "Kyle was my younger brother, but I never really knew him very well. After Mom died, Oscar was tried, convicted and sent to prison. Kyle and I were put in a boys' home, but I was older, so we were treated differently. My time around him was limited. He lived in a different cottage."

"What about Oscar? What became of him?"

"Don't know. Don't give a damn. Still in prison I guess. "Alive or dead… I really don't care."

True to his word, the waiter returned with the wine bottle, topped off their glasses, and took orders for dinner. It was comical watching the young man. The boy had a preconceived notion that Jack must be plying Nikki with alcohol to get into her pants. Each time he returned with the wine bottle he checked her sobriety.

Nikki's eyes followed the waiter as he walked away, her eyes squarely on his ass in those black slacks. Nonetheless, she stayed on track. "But Kyle and you remained on the same campus at the home, right?"

"Stayed together? No. But I did see him often." Her questions took his mind to that time many years ago. Poignant memories gave him pause. He took a moment to think and sip wine. "Kyle had been an infant in foster care with various families off and on outside the home. I stayed with the older boys on campus. For some reason I never did go into foster care… probably too old and not cute enough. Kyle does have killer dimples. Back in the day, those pudgy cheeks put that boy in demand."

"They didn't know what they were missing. Did they?" She sipped wine and shot him a come-hither look.

"I don't know about that." He shook his head, embarrassed. "Anyway, once this pattern established it seemed he was always with a different family and away from the home for extended periods."

"Were you capable of keeping an eye on him?"

"Sure. I suppose I should have been thankful. But I was young and stupid and didn't recognize it as a blessing."

Jack welcomed her questions, recognizing them for what they were; she had slipped into her psychoanalyst persona. She wasn't prying. It was just all those years of analyzing patients coming out. It was good, even though her queries led away from the real problem; he realized she had to come to the conclusion on her own that his childhood had no bearing on the spooky things happening to him. Confidence swelled. If he continued forthright and truthful, advice should follow.

"Is Kyle a healthy happy individual right now?"

"Not sure. He lives on the west coast. We drifted apart. I haven't talked to him in about a year. He had a new wife, Cary, and a child on the way at that time."

A tipsy customer walked behind Nikki's chair and bumped it. She smiled up at him. Otherwise she paid it no mind. "Let's discuss the times your consciousness alters. Your last account ended with the episode on the interstate. What happened next?"

Jack stared at a meaningless spot on the tablecloth. Even though her question was at the heart of the reason for this date, he suddenly wondered how deeply he wanted to delve into it in a noisy crowded restaurant. He enjoyed the date and sort of wanted the conversation to remain light. Besides, the rosy glow of the wine may have been the source of her interest. She certainly didn't want to hear about it earlier. Wine happened to be the only difference.

He looked up at her. What he saw put his mind at ease. Nikki emulated his moves. She pushed her plate back and pulled her wine glass in close, all the while maintaining eye contact. She appeared ready to hear the story. Inebriated or not, it was a start. He figured he'd better not waste such an opportunity and thought he'd go for it and see where it led. Settling back, he began.

"It was only a couple of days after that episode on the interstate. Following much thought and introspection, I became convinced to put it out of my mind, to forget it, write it off as a random psychotic event. Therefore, I wasn't prepared for what came next.

"It'd been one of those days that I couldn't do anything right. I didn't care to look back as I left The Journal after work. The straightest route to my apartment didn't get me there soon enough. Thinking the way I wanted, dressing the way I wanted and drinking whatever I wanted was my only focus. I felt compelled to reclaim my life, at least for the evening.

"If I'd gotten one more asinine order... one more idiotic project that day, I'm certain I would've choked the shit out of someone... starting with my editor, Gus Landau. No doubt about it, I was primed and pumped. I was *that* pissed off at the world.

"The first good thing to happen that day was my best friend, my dog Buddy, greeting me at the door. That little guy has a marvelous calming effect, especially on days like that. I poured a bowl of dog food for him and a glass of straight gin for myself.

"My only goal was to crash on the couch and watch television. But even that seemed like too much effort. Tossing the remote control aside, I dropped onto the sofa and sprawled with my head back and my eyes closed. I stroked Buddy's belly. And, then, I let my mind go. In retrospect, that may have been the wrong thing to do.

"An image of Kyle appeared in my mind's-eye; not a dreamlike image but a vision defined in great detail. He stood in front of an unfamiliar house—head slumped forward. He appeared distraught. Marveling at the vision's clarity, I, at first, studied it with amusement, as it played on the screen that was my closed eyelids.

"Suddenly, the temperature in the room dropped, or so I thought. At the time, I wasn't sure about that because it was an indirect sensation. My eyes and my head remained on that vision. I know now that it did drop, dramatically.

"I felt Buddy fidget beneath my hand. Then he whimpered.

"When I raised my head and opened my eyes the image of my brother did not disappear. Instead, it became greatly enhanced, ringed with soft white light, as though I were seeing it through a kind of tunnel vision, although everything in my living room was still visible. I wasn't frightened. I suppose I had fatigue and a bad attitude to thank for that. The fear of earlier episodes had been replaced by curiosity. I rose. Unlike that first time, I wanted to understand what it was I saw.

"The scene continued to unfold as a balding, middle-aged man slung the front door of the house open, banging into the wall behind him and rebounding with enough force to hit him on the butt before he exited the house. It must have made one hell of a racket but I didn't hear it. The guy was agitated... not just a little miffed but royally pissed about something. He charged into the yard and confronted Kyle. Judging by Kyle's appearance he was still in his teens. Although the house was unfamiliar, the angry man I recognized. He and his wife were the last family Kyle lived with before going out on his own.

"By this time, Buddy paced in a nervous circle on the sofa, whimpering nonstop. In a slow calculated way, I advanced toward the glowing ring of light, gingerly extending my right hand toward the image. As my hand broke the plane of what I believed to be a vision, the fingers became obscured, as though beneath a thin layer of water. From the instant my fingertips breeched that barrier it was no longer a little cool in the room. I was hit with a chill that took my breath. I shuddered... then came dizziness. I stumbled slightly, jerking my hand away back-stepping until my legs touched the sofa.

"Buddy pawed my leg and whined. I became fascinated. An analytical eye replaced fear. The little dog's eyes were fixed on the scene playing out in front of us. But how could that be if it was *my* vision—*my* imagination? The dog whined, followed its tail in a circle, stopped, looked at the scene, and repeated the process over and over.

"That's when it occurred to me, Buddy could help prove or disprove what we both witnessed. My little friend was about to help me figure out if I was los-ing my mind. I picked him up. He dug his claws into my arm, poking his nose in my armpit. I cradled him. I drew a breath, deep and long, as if about to plunge into icy water. I took three giant steps directly into the eerie image.

"On the third step, extreme dizziness accompanied the chill. I closed my eyes. When I opened them, what I experienced scared holy hell out of me.

"The soft glow enveloping me had vanished, so had the chill. Bright sunlight assaulted my eyes. I squinted against its sudden intrusion and felt a warm summer-like breeze brush my face. As vision cleared, I saw that I stood in the front yard of that unfamiliar house, still holding Buddy in my arms. It no longer was a holographic movie playing out in a haze in front of me. I was there. It was *not* a God damn vision! I stood in that place at that time... wherever the place was and whatever the time had been.

"Kyle cowered in front of the man.

"The son-of-a-bitch snatched up a leaf rake leaning against the house, flipped it over and threatened my brother with the handle of it. His face distorted with rage. Kyle threw up his arms. 'No, no!' he shouted. 'Please don't! I'm sorry!' Falling to his knees, he covered his head.

"The man raised the rake high about to hit Kyle with it.

"I dropped Buddy to the ground. 'Hey you!' I yelled and ran to intercept the man. 'You'd better not hit him, you crazy bastard!'

"The old man turned his anger on me, driving the handle of the rake into my stomach. Air left my lungs in a violent rush.

"In retrospect, it was an important learning lesson. I most certainly could be seen, heard and feel pain. As the impact threw me forward, gasping for air, I dropped to my knees and over on all fours, clutching double fists full of grass. The thought struck me: What the hell is going on? Why am I here? And where the hell is *here*? They were all the same questions I had asked before and destined to get the same answer—none.

"Buddy's warm tongue lapped at my cheek. He whimpered. My attention turned to him.

When that happened, the chill returned. But it only lasted a fraction of a second. The bright light of day dimmed. That happened to be my only warning before I found myself, once again, in my living room. No white light, no chill, no brother, and no angry man—nothing out of the ordinary, except that I was still in a crouch trying to catch my breath.

"I yanked up my shirt. There it was; a bloody red welt on my stomach where the rake hit me. I touched it. It stung. I smeared the small amount of blood between my thumb and fingers. I had trouble believing that it had happened, still do. But there was no denying the smear of blood and grass on my fingers.

"I lost trust of my senses. At that point I began searching for reasons to believe I was crazy. If what I experienced was genuine then that was much scarier to contemplate. Crazy I could deal with. They have pills for that.

"Only then did I turn to look at Buddy curled up and cowering at the end of the sofa, shivering. The mark on my belly and Buddy's agitation seemed to rule out insanity, but I still need confirmation of that."

Jack again connected with Nikki. "That's where you come in. I need you. In you lies hope that an answer can be found that doesn't include life in a padded room. While still on the floor nursing that injury, I remember thinking: Being insane is the saner explanation. And, damn it, Nik! That's... that's just crazy."

With no finesse whatsoever, Nikki lifted her wine glass and gulped down the last two swallows. "I have a feeling you're going to be a high-maintenance friend."

CHAPTER 4

Nikki didn't interrupt once. That was good. Chin in hand; she'd stared the whole time he told the story. Varying facial expressions indicated she stayed with the story and wasn't daydreaming. Such detail would be of no value if she lost focus and drifted into thoughts of a roll in the hay.

When he finished telling everything he remembered and emerged from concentration, the noise and crowd of the restaurant suddenly became irritating. There wasn't an empty table or booth anywhere. A crush of people near the door waited to be seated.

Nikki followed his glance toward the throng near the door waiting for a table. "That was fascinating," she said. The patronizing smile was gone. The timbre of her words rang honest to Jack.

He wasn't certain whether to trust his instinct, remaining wary of what might actually be on her mind. But, his powers of divining intent had become muddled by wine. He wondered if she considered making that phone call to have him institutionalized. If she would have excused herself to the ladies' room, that might have been the clincher. Instead, she sat and seemed to be assimilating information without comment.

Even that short silence became unbearable. "Look, it's still early and there's an article I need to research. You were kind enough to let me look in on your career, in a manner of speaking. How about going with me on an interview for a story? I hadn't planned on doing it this evening and haven't made an appointment, but maybe the guy's available. Want to give it a shot?"

"Sure."

"If he isn't home, no big deal. I'll just do it another time. If he is, what the heck, maybe you can develop a sense of who I've become since college."

"A real news story, huh? Something interesting?"

He shrugged. "Don't know. Probably not. Are you still sure?"

A passerby bumped his shoulder, reminding him of congestion in the restaurant. "Sorry buddy," he said, patting Jack on the shoulder.

Smiling up at him, Jack just waved him on.

"Yeah, I'm still sure but don't keep me in suspense. Who is it?" she asked.

He fumbled through his pockets. "He's a psychic… or… something like that. The way I understand it, he's helping the police solve crimes. Don't know if he still is or not. But they're giving him credit for playing a role in solving a couple of mysteries that had them stumped."

Searching every pocket, he finally found it wrapped within a number of crumpled notes in his hip pocket. "Here it is." Pulling it out, along with a wad of others, he read, "Arthur Wainwright," and dropped the slip to the tabletop and pecked it with a finger. "According to this address, he doesn't live far from here. I'm not at all familiar with that area though. I don't have reason to go into that neighborhood often, a bit too ritzy."

"It's amazing you're able to find anything with that paper and pocket filing system." She knocked back the last swallow of wine. "Let's go. It might be fun. Besides, it's too early for a date to end."

It could have been his imagination, but her sudden mood change indicated she might be relieved to do something other than listen to his odd story. He also sensed she preferred a quieter environment. A night of passion could have been her goal. Then again, maybe what he sensed was his own thinly masked desire. He tossed his last fifty dollars on the table to settle the check.

"Lead on, Jack Dane, investigative reporter extraordinaire." Her volume was clearly enhanced by wine.

"I hate to douse the glowing image you seem to be developing... " he said, pulling her chair out, "... but I'm a feature writer, nothing as intriguing as investigative reporter. I've been assigned to write a story about the man's psychic abilities. The actual crimes he supposedly helped solve are assigned to hard news reporters at The Journal. I only handle the human interest side. The lay term for it is *fluff*." He glanced and grinned.

She seemed to ignore the self-deprecating opinion. He offered a hand to guide her off the chair to her feet. "Always the gentleman." She smiled, reached for his hand and held it tighter than necessary as she rose.

Threading the narrow aisles through the restaurant, they headed for the exit. He hadn't realized how claustrophobic he was until he broke through the crowd at the front door of the popular eatery. The air seemed easier to breathe. He fumbled for the keys to unlock the passenger-side car door.

"I really would have thought you would've given your car a name by now, something like Old Blue or Lizzy. Isn't that what guys normally do when their rides get this old?"

He opened the door. An unexpected squawk and groan came from the hinges. Nikki fell into the seat laughing. "Ol' Blue Lizzy is talkin' to ya."

She grabbed his arm and feigned fear. "Maybe she's talking to *me*. Could she be jealous? Maybe she's pissed. Will she hurt me? I don't think she liked my comment."

With a sheepish head bob, Jack refused to respond. It mortified him that he'd ushered such a classy well-dressed woman into such a dilapidated vehicle. "Okay that's enough. As soon as I get promoted up to middle class, I'll—"

"Oh, stop it. I was joking."

He closed her door, walked around, and slid into the driver's seat. She continued chuckling softly. "Let's go Clark Kent." She put a hand on his knee. "I know you're only living this way to protect your true identity. I understand." She crinkled her nose and whispered, "I'll keep your secret." She slid next to him on the old-style bench seat.

Concerns at the beginning of the evening faded. He and Nikki became comfortable with one another all over again. Like two high school kids on a first date, they laughed and exchanged barbs over a mutual inability to get directions straight.

Jack wandered through the neighborhood he knew to be the right one. Winding streets, circles and cul de sacs proved confounding. Finally, he turned onto a dead end street and another narrow poorly marked street intersected it to the right about a hundred feet in. The street sign appeared to have been hit by a car and tilted forty-five degrees. According to the damaged sign, this was it—the street Wainwright lived on. "Well. I'll be darned. I guess I'm not the unluckiest guy in the world after all."

Nikki slapped his arm. "Shut up and turn. We're almost there."

Steering onto the narrow street, it curved left behind the row of houses in front of it then angled away. Jack had only driven about five hundred yards when the street abruptly ended.

Straight ahead, he saw a pair of massive brick columns supporting a heavy iron gate. Mounted to one of the columns was a concrete placard with a number on it—Wainwright's address. The street turned out to be the private driveway to his home.

Awestruck by the wealth he saw framed within the headlights, Jack became impressed with the ivy-covered iron fence, resembling spears welded to rails. The headlights accentuated ghostly shadows cast by huge gnarled limbs of oak trees overhanging the fence on either side of the gate, looking like protective arms of giants. The branches seemed to warn them to go away. It was unsettling and he was inclined to take the hint.

The gate began opening even before the car had come to a complete stop. He eased on through. "Wow. Either this guy is a very good psychic or he has another source of income," he said, glancing at Nikki.

Her lips parted, as she studied the statuary lining the long driveway, some mostly hidden by tangled vines and encrusted with patches of lichen. "It looks like all this has been around for a long time."

It could have been the garishness, but he became inclined not to cut this guy any slack. Jack developed a snap opinion that he wouldn't like him or his lifestyle.

He rolled over a dip in the driveway. The old car rattled and squeaked. That softened the hardening impression somewhat; reminding him that jealousy might play a role in his leap to judgment. But he remained firm in the conviction that this guy, the owner of all this... crap, would have to prove himself before he'd consider writing an article that even remotely resembled serious journalism.

The scene unfolding before them needed only the addition of two flesh eating guard dogs to be complete. And that suddenly seemed possible. His searching eyes now included looking out for big dogs.

The car rolled to a stop near the front door of a sprawling vine-covered mansion, everything bigger than necessary.

"How come I have the feeling there should be a small shrine or graven image that we should kneel to before we ring the doorbell?" she asked.

"It's funny how you're thoughts migrated to a religious view point about this place. The *Adam's Family* popped into my head. But I suppose it does look sort of like a medieval church."

They walked up four weathered rock steps to face an intimidating set of well-aged hardwood double-doors, the largest he'd ever seen on a private residence. The carvings on the twin oak behemoths standing roughly nine feet were clearly cut by hand. It was a coat of arms, half on each door that, when closed, completed it. It had been intricately detailed—a magnificent sight.

Jack suddenly felt insignificant. He had to keep his head in the game and save the awe for another time. He owed Gus a good story, whether it happened tonight or he had to come back another time. But his editor wasn't the reason he'd chosen tonight to come. He'd blown all available cash on dinner and couldn't afford to take Nikki anyplace else. Otherwise, he would have taken her to a bar or a club like a normal guy would have.

As he rang the bell, he leaned sideways toward Nikki. "The name Wainwright sort of fits a place—"

"Hold on, Jack, I'll be right down," a voice called out from an open window overhead.

Jack snapped a look upward.

So did Nikki. "I thought you hadn't met or talked to this guy."

Still looking up to the open window, "I haven't. Maybe Gus, my boss, told him I'd be calling or coming by." He shook it off. "Besides, he's likely playing a little I-know-who-you-are game with us... you know, to establish credibility."

Jack quickly developed an assumption of Wainwright's appearance having more to do with the look of the real estate than intuition. Wainwright would be the type to wear silk smoking jackets, sip brandy, sport a pencil-thin mustache, immaculately groomed and generally exude wealth, probably a disgustingly blatant display of it. He continued leaning toward a disdainful attitude about a man he envisioned looking like Errol Flynn but with a condescending smirk like George W. Bush.

One side of the large double doors swung open with a deep groaning squeak. And there stood an astonishing sight. His initial assumption was, perhaps, a servant, maybe a gardener or handyman.

"Come in, come in," the man said robustly, accompanied by a joyful hand-clap. It's so nice to finally meet you Mr. Dane. And this must be your companion, Ms. Endicott. Nikki I believe." He spoke fast and crisp. He seemed quite sure of himself.

Nikki hesitated, glanced sidelong at Jack and extended her hand, clearly shocked to hear her name come out of the mouth of a man unknown to her minutes before. She whispered sideways into his ear, "This is weird." She smiled. "But it should be fun."

"Allow me to introduce myself," he said in a high-pitched friendly way. "I'm Arthur Wainwright and I—"

"Mr. Wainwright, how do you know who we are? I didn't call or talk to you beforehand. And what did you mean by, 'finally meet you'?"

He ignored the question, maintaining a childlike appearance accompanied by an innocent grin. "It took you a while to get here. I'm sorry you had trouble finding this place. But it's still quite early. I'll fix drinks then we'll relax and have a nice chat."

Nikki's brow pulled down as she glanced to Jack, stepping in and standing closer to him. He sensed her discomfort. But, it must have been clinical curiosity that drove her on.

Wainwright led the way down a long, dimly lighted hallway toward a sturdy, intricately carved door, no less ornate than the front door, just smaller. All the while, he chatted nonstop about weather and other things of equal disinterest. The air inside the house felt damp and musty, indicating he seldom, if ever, opened it up to outside air. It had a cave-like feel. As Jack made observations, focus remained on a growing list of questions. The still-developing truth was already contrary to expectations.

Dressed less than casual, Wainwright wore a gray sweatshirt, the sleeves removed entirely. Apparently, he used dull scissors judging by the ragged look. He sported a green peace symbol tattoo on his upper right arm. The tail of the shirt hung over short and loose fitting khaki pants. The wiggling toes of his over-sized feet danced on the soles of a pair of well-worn sandals. It appeared that this was a normal look for him, judging by his obvious comfort level with strangers. He was as tall as Jack, maybe an inch taller, and very thin. His hair was mostly gray, shoulder-length and thinning. It appeared not to have been touched by a comb or brush in several days, bringing to mind an aging surfer or hippy.

He and Nikki followed the old guy into a large room decorated with enough oak to have cost the lives of several trees. The high ceilings, arched windows and rolling ladders attached to high rails along floor-to-ceiling bookshelves suggested a library crammed with books, papers and maps. But it was in total disarray. The cool odor of dust hung in the air.

Stopping at a chest that may have been an antique dry sink covered with partially emptied liquor bottles, he spun to face them standing next to the makeshift bar. "What'll you have?"

Noticing a Beefeaters bottle with a couple of shots left in it, "A gin and tonic will be fine." He looked to Nikki. "How about you?"

"Me, too," she said, "with a squeeze of lime, if you have it."

As Wainwright searched for the ingredients, Jack began. "Mr. Wainwright, I'm sure it doesn't come as a surprise that my curiosity has piqued. How did you know our names and the trouble we had finding this place?"

"I know more about you two than just your names and that you have a problem with directions." He licked a drop of lime juice from his fingertip with a smack. "Especially you, Mr. Dane."

"Call me Jack."

"Thank you. You can keep calling me Mr. Wainwright." He grinned a stupid grin.

Nikki squawked a laugh but quickly covered her mouth.

Jack offered her a measured look and only hinted a smile. It seemed that Nikki and this character would be getting along just fine.

"Well," he said, handing us our drinks and ushering us to nearby wingback chairs, "as I was reading the original article in your paper about my assisting the police, it occurred to me, this was a human interest story that would probably capture attention. Of course that's very logical, not mysterious at all." He bent and shoved a pile of papers off into the floor from the seat of a chair and gestured for Nikki to sit, pointing Jack toward another. "As I turned the page and saw your picture above an unrelated single column article—well, let's say that was the first time I met you."

"'Met me'? What do you mean? I've never seen you before."

"Please, let me tell you about myself before I give a direct answer to that question, otherwise you might dismiss me as insane. On second thought, you may anyway." He shoved aside a couple of books on the floor in front of him so he could cross his legs. "I believe you've had concerns lately that people may have cause to look at you that way."

"But how—"

He tossed a hand up. "Hold on. Don't ask more questions before I get the others answered. If you don't let me tell the whole story you'll leave this evening with questions still unanswered." He grinned and cleared his throat. "I've been blessed with an ability that is neither deserved nor earned, but I have it. There was certainly a time I tried to make it go away. Let me tell you I certainly thought life was terribly unfair back then." He shrugged and rolled his eyes. "Ah, sweet ignorance of youth. I was so stupid. We waste most of our youth. You know that?"

Jack frowned when Wainwright's story began a merry prance down a rabbit trail away from the subject.

Wainwright must have noticed. "Ahem. Sorry about that. Now, where was I? Oh yeah. Even a major force of will couldn't stop what had begun in my life." His happy-go-lucky expression segued into a serious look, but it didn't seem sincere.

As Wainwright fell silent for a moment, Jack thought: *Staying serious might be a major problem for this guy. Maybe he's incapable of seriousness.* He leaned back and prepared to hear a long story. He looked to see Nikki bring a hand up and rest two fingers against her lips in an attentive pose.

The old guy looked at Jack with a strange expression, like he'd just heard a joke and squelched a laugh. "First of all," Wainwright said, "It's fortunate I was blessed with a considerable amount of family money, the sole heir to a rather large estate. That afforded me the opportunity to figure out what I wanted to do with my life with no concern about income. I'm a product of the sixties when Flower Power, LSD and pot were the order of the day." He proudly pointed to the peace symbol tattoo.

So that's the look he's going for, hippy, not surfer dude.

Again, the old guy had the look of a man who'd just heard something humorous. "When I first began having episodes," he said, "I paid them little heed. I thought they were drug-induced deliriums. Sometime later, curiosity heightened when I realized I didn't recognize any of the people and only a few of the places in these, so-called, hallucinations." He pushed his hands into the air and shrugged. "It was a time when chemically induced altered states were popular and common. I can claim to have been around many indulging groups at one time or another."

"I'll bet in the sixties a lady didn't have to wait to be asked," Nikki said.

"Asked what?" Jack asked without thinking.

Wainwright answered with a smile, while tapping the tip of his nose with a finger.

Nikki returned the smile and held her drink in the manner of a toast.

Geez, they're already developing private jokes.

Wainwright looked at Jack, grinned and took a sip. He wriggled into a more comfortable repose, as the soft cushions of the chair parted for his lanky frame. "The first time I took a vision seriously it had been several days since I had dropped acid, took a drag off a joint or even had a drink of alcohol. I was disgustingly sober!" He paused and his thoughts clearly took a serious turn. "The vision hit me like cold water in the face. The image was from the perspective of standing on a sidewalk in front of a row of houses. I looked to my right down the street to a line of parked cars against the curb. I recognized it right away as my own street, about half a block down from my rented house. I saw a young woman and a child of about six. The woman had her head out of sight in the trunk of her car getting sacks of groceries out. The young boy bolted between that car and another, heading toward a busy street." He stopped talking and took a drink.

Jack flipped a hand into the air. "That's it? That's all there was to the vision?"

"I'm getting to it. As quickly as the vision appeared, it disappeared. I was about to dismiss the episode as an acid flashback or something like that. I continued my mission to find scrambled eggs and pancakes. As I walked down the street I developed an eerie feeling of having done the exact same thing before. I stopped dead in my tracks. I looked around and realized I was standing in the same spot I had seen when I witnessed those events in the vision only seconds before. Directly ahead toward the end of the block it unfolded all over again. That time it wasn't just a vision. A car pulled up to the curb, a young woman jumped out and walked around to the trunk. At about the same time, a young boy jumped out and ran in front of the car to grab something that had rolled out when he opened the door. I heard him say, 'Wait a minute Momma and I'll help.' His attention split between his mother and the object of his chase and not on the busy street. He was about to step in front of oncoming traffic. I shouted, 'Lady watch out for your kid!' Her head snapped up. She took a couple of quick steps from behind her car into the street. The fast approaching vehicle swerved to miss her, thereby missing the child at the other end of the car."

Wainwright abruptly stopped talking and visibly shuddered. "I get a cold chill every time I remember that episode. The child would have been killed had I not screamed."

"You're sure of that?" Jack asked.

A somber look painted his face. "In the vision I saw him die."

Wainwright possessed an innate sense of drama, a flair for story telling that proved captivating. So much so, Jack hadn't taken a single note. Intense concentration showed that his mind was in that time and in that place. The detail he offered was astonishing. Several seconds passed before the old guy rejoined the present once his telling of the story finished.

Re-emerging, he smiled. "And, you might ask; how does a committed hippy, vowing to be eternally irresponsible, handle something like this? Well, I'll tell you. I turned around and headed back to my rent house and broke the seal on a brand new bottle of scotch."

Jack shook his head. His expression hinted disgust.

"What?"

"Don't pay any attention to him," Nikki said. "Jack can be a fuddy-duddy."

"It seemed like the right thing to do at the time," he said.

"So, you weren't born with this ability?" Nikki asked.

"Heavens no." Wainwright chuckled and stopped abruptly, stabbing the air with a finger. "But, you know what? I *can't* say for sure that I *wasn't* born with it. Although, I can say with absolute certainty that I wasn't aware of it until I reached adulthood."

Wainwright's eccentricities were making things less uncomfortable. Curiosity grew. It was early, plenty of time to satisfy inquisitiveness as long as Wainwright was willing to talk. Jack ceased worrying about Nikki becoming bored and settled back, gin and tonic in hand, ready for more. It was better than a movie and a lot cheaper. It occurred to Jack that this eccentric old man with an amazing ability just might serve a purpose in helping understand his own problem.

"Although I have hundreds of stories that may, or may not, interest you," he said, "I'd better skip ahead to contemporary times, so I might fit all this information into a single evening. Besides, I've kept you waiting for an answer to your question long enough." Wainwright's expressiveness proved fascinating. He seemed so eager and excited by everything he said. "That first day, when I saw your picture in the newspaper, I got a flash vision of a man in distress—a man I came to understand is your brother. The surroundings I witnessed were bleak, a large body of water, full of death. I could almost smell the stench and disease it held. You, dear boy, did smell it and were frantically swimming to catch him before he made it to the other shore. I saw that the farther he swam, the happier he was. In that instant, I knew you should not, could not and would not, catch him."

Jack's jaw slackened, his lips parted, and his mouth fell open. He couldn't speak, just made a guttural noise, alerting Nikki.

"Who else did you tell that story to, besides me?" she whispered.

"No one."

Wainwright chuckled. "Ms. Endicott, don't be too hard on your boyfriend. Your trust should remain intact. You're the only one he has knowingly shared that story with."

Nikki nodded but agreement remained guarded. She had just begun to learn things that never appeared in any of those textbooks in that bookcase behind her desk. Smugness that she had a firm grasp on most all human behaviors vanished.

Jack, on the other hand, had never been self-assured, even before all this crap began. Now this; with each bit of information shared by Wainwright, knowledge he shouldn't have had, unnerved Jack more.

Wainwright nodded. "Yessiree, from that day until now, you've been a regular visitor into my thoughts. Every time you've witnessed or visited other times and places, I've seen it through you."

"You mean you were there?"

"No, I simply witnessed the events." He thoughtfully stroked his chin. "When the two of you showed up this evening, my little display of precognition about your names and trip over here was necessary to establish my ability as real."

"That's what we thought."

"But it was also to establish the fact that I'm not as crazy as I look." He giggled. "I'm probably not quite right in the head by societal norms even without such an ability." He waved off that possible perception with dancing fingertips as if to say that's neither here nor there. Wainwright seemed to keep himself amused. "I'm now coming down to the main point. You, Jack Dane, have abilities I do not possess... deeper and more complex."

"I don't understand."

"I know you don't. Here's the truth of it. I'll try not to short-circuit your brain. We are conscious of and live in only one level of reality. There is past, present and future, of course. But, also, there exists multiple dimensions within each one of these layers of time. Picture a cliff face where strata of sediment deposited horizontally and stacked vertically become successive layers of the same rock. Each layer expands horizontally forever, creating dimensional considerations."

Jack listened, but the story took such concentration that he forgot all about taking notes.

Wainwright went on to explain that within each of those layers or dimensions, there are multiple pasts, presents and futures, creating an intricate web of possible realities—each one as genuine as the moment in which we now live and are aware of. He described his abilities as seeing the past, present and future within our current perception of reality—a single layer of that rock. He used the term reality interchangeably with dimension and said that until he met Jack his visions were limited to the past, present and future, and only from one vantage point—the present. He said that until he became aware of Jack, he couldn't see into those other dimensions—realities. But now, as long as Jack provided the window, he could.

"Jack," he said, "You've given me access to other times within other dimensions to witness. I emphasize *witness* because you have the ability to move with ease between this reality and another. It's awesome! You seem unrestricted by time once you've arrived in those other dimensions, almost like a universal chess game in which moving in a straight line isn't always necessary. You can move from time to time within any dimension you choose to travel to."

Jack sat in stunned silence, muddle-headed. His mind boggled under the suffocating amount of information that simply could not be processed or comprehended within the confines of a single conversation. Nonetheless, Wainwright kept laying it out.

"It's not clear to you yet what it's all about," he said, "but it will be in time. I hope to learn right along with you. As you learn the limits of your power, it's vital you also learn how to control it."

Control it? How could something be controlled with no notion where it came from, how it manifested, or even why it chose this time to begin? Wainwright said that the next dimensional layer, up from the one we exist in, is another physical plane, just like this one, with one major exception. It is a crossover realm, from the physical to the spiritual. People who die see this place, and only from a personal perspective—different for everyone depending on how they lived their lives and how they view death. He told them that Jack had moved his physical body to an alternate reality on two occasions, once within our own physical plane at a point in time many years ago. This was the episode with Jack's brother confronted by his stepfather. The other time was in that world a level up from ours at some point in the future. That level, he went on to explain, was more than a vision; it was a place, a destination, as real as the three them sitting in that room. Jack had the ability to get there and exist within it, along with many other planes—different vertical layers of life itself, sandwiching past, present and future within each layer. The most extraordinary thing Wainwright said was that Jack had the capability to place his physical body in other times, past or future, within all these layers—realities. According to what he said, there were no barriers, no limitations, moving into, away from, or within these worlds.

"In the simplest terms," Wainwright concluded, "time, space and dimension provide no more resistance for you than stepping up onto a curb once you learn to harness the power you already possess." Satisfaction settled on his face. He'd explained it all.

Jack went numb and stayed that way—more questions became unimportant, as did the interview. Should he believe what he heard? Did he even have the capacity to believe it? The overwhelming amount of information demanded suspension of so much disbelief that it left him short of breath. Suddenly, he felt the need to get out. Wainwright's house, as large as it was, suffocated him.

Nikki pulled him to his feet and looked into his eyes, as any good clinical diagnostician might, and concluded the obvious. "Mr. Wainwright, thank you for the drink and an interesting evening. I'm afraid that fascination doesn't touch what Jack's feeling right now. So, if you'll please excuse us... "

As he escorted them to the door, Jack turned and mumbled, "Mr. Wainwright, I—"

"I was joking about the 'Mister Wainwright' thing... call me Arthur."

Jack retained no memory of the trip between Wainwright's mansion and Nikki's apartment, remembering only that she had given him a hug at her front door and spent a few seconds searching his eyes for… something. Even brain-fried, he noticed that she worried about him. But he was in no state of mind to appreciate it and left her standing under the soft yellow glow of the porch light over the front door of her apartment.

Somehow, he made it home, uncertain of the time or retaining any memory of getting out of the car and walking to his front door. His mind remained a stew of disjointed thoughts.

Nikki called within seconds of his unlocking the door to make sure he'd made it safely. Afterwards, he couldn't recall what he'd told her. His mind had derailed. His future somehow seemed even murkier.

The next morning, Wainwright called him at the newspaper. "Please trust me. Let me answer your questions and, if I can't, let's explore them together until we discover answers."

Jack made a mental note to make good on that offer. There'd be questions come up that he'd still be too uninformed to even think of until faced with them. If he could depend on the old guy as a guide through this maze of weirdness and maybe lean on Nikki some, too, maybe he could learn to cope with it. He sure as hell didn't want to cultivate it.

CHAPTER 5

Two days passed. Talk of alternate realities and dimensions with Arthur Wainwright didn't seem real. Had it happened? Even that experience became questionable. Jack's head remained in a whirl from which he couldn't seem to emerge. Questions spun to the center of his brain into a vacuum that left room for nothing else. There just wasn't enough comprehension space between his ears to handle complexity of that magnitude.

Mundane daily tasks may have been a lot of things, but difficult shouldn't have been one of them—simple chores became an exercise in focus. He functioned in a zombie-like trance. Everything he'd ever done in the past or planned to do in the future lost relevance, reduced to inconsequential tripe, nothing more than leftovers from a life that didn't exist anymore. The world according to Dane had been razed, leaving behind ashes of an incomplete life. His world shrank, narrowing to a search for answers about the new direction of life. If all the answers fell from the sky into his lap today that still wouldn't insure understanding. Arthur Wainwright proved that. He provided plenty of answers except one for the most important question: Why?

What the hell is the truth anyway? Nothing matters anymore—work, parties, friends—none of it. He tried to reestablish a semblance of order, conformance to a standard of living dissipating at an accelerated pace. Even basic survival seemed pointless, even frivolous.

It was as if he were going on a trip and given a deadline but no destination. Now he found himself racing flat out in a rush but had no idea where he went. Desperation gnawed at him, but for what reason and to do what? Thinking on it: *Time, dimensions, life and death and a so-called power to move within these realms. Realms?* Even the word seemed ghostlike and spooky.

To ponder it ripped him into three different viewpoints: Learn to cope with the episodes as they occurred but, otherwise, ignore them. Discover the extent of the power and use it for some universal good. Or, finally, skip through life unbelieving and wait to wake up from this God-awful nightmare of surreal bullshit.

Saturday morning Jack sat in his kitchen in his underwear eating Cheerios, milk dribbling down his chin. He considered elements of things Wainwright had said. Problem was, he saw the whole confusing picture and wanted a single answer—everything all at once—easy to comprehend. Conclusions about anything wouldn't be forthcoming over a bowl of cold cereal.

Buddy didn't mind his disheveled appearance as long as a cereal nugget came flying his way occasionally. As he sat on the floor beside Jack, panting, sweeping the floor with a wagging tail, it provided a calming effect, always had. Now, the little pooch had become the only normal thing left. A jostle of his hairy head, a playful mauling of his paunch little body or simply watching him fan the floor with that hyperactive tail; it kept things in a simpler perspective.

"Ol' Bud, I need to pull myself together." He shoved a spoonful of cereal in his mouth, spraying a little milk when he said, "I wonder if Nikki would be jealous of you as a rival therapist?"

In truth, Nikki had no fear of that. However, the relationship had meandering parameters. Attempting to find help through her had already complicated things. It had to be true, judging by the fluttery little tingle behind his belly button every time he thought about her. At the same time, a small voice in the back of his head kept whispering, "Not now... not ever." That voice remained in its infancy and those were the only words it knew. He figured the source to be obvious; two failed marriages didn't bode well to try for a third. That had to have been where that little voice was born. Part of him wanted it, alone and lonely most of the time with only Buddy's company.

Working on an answer to the Nikki dilemma had to be a priority. It just happened to be close to the bottom of that list at the moment. But the question kept surfacing: *Why am I so scared of romantic involvement with her?*

Emerging from weighty problems, he turned to lighter thoughts—things familiar and less complicated. Things ordinary and comfortable like a well-worn pair of slippers. Saturdays were reserved for hygienic endeavors—a single-guy thing—a day set aside to straighten the apartment, do dishes, laundry, and all things that didn't get done the other six days of the week. It usually took most of Saturday to take care of six days worth of mess. A shower should provide necessary motivation to begin the monotony—drudgery he welcomed.

Slipping from his boxers as he walked to the bathroom, Jack grabbed his toothbrush from its holder, pasted it and brushed the foul taste from his mouth as he allowed the running water in the shower stall to heat the entire room. Steam billowed. He pulled in deep breaths of the sweet dampness. While brushing, he noticed the small paunch on his belly and sucked it in. The mirror lied. It said he wasn't overweight. Jack knew better; that marshmallow of a love handle was the truth of it. He chose, instead, to concentrate on a more appealing asset, a thick head of dark hair. As his mouth foamed with toothpaste, the phone rang. Aggravated and feeling cheated out of this moment, he hurried to the front room and clumsily picked up the phone.

"Hey Big Guy," Nikki chirped, "How would you like the privilege of buying me dinner tonight?"

He sputtered and gurgled, making a few other wet noises.

"Now that's the most unusual sound for heavy breathing I've ever heard."

He leaned over and spat toothpaste into a vase next to the phone. "It's the latest thing in obscenities," he said, ignoring the innuendo. "Even fashionable, I'd say. How'd ya like it?"

"Ooh, I'm tingling. I have to ask… and be truthful; what are you wearing right now?"

Jack looked down at his naked body. "A smile." He pinched the bridge of his nose, drawn into the banter but in no mood for it. But all it took was that pause and the briefest silence for a tingle to set in, followed by an awakening of another testosterone driven response. Her comment may have been offered as humorous, but as he looked down, what he saw was no joke, almost as though he had no control. Annoyance vanished. "Dinner'd be great, if you don't mind fast food under five dollars. If it were anyone but you, I'd be embarrassed to admit it, but I'm broke… flat busted… nada and… well, that should be enough to clue you."

"Hmm. Okay. Then we move on to plan B. I'll see you at my place at seven and I'll cook dinner."

"When did you learn how to cook? I didn't think you could boil water without scorching the pot."

"Hey, that's cruel… "

I'll be damned. She's pouting. He heard it in her tone and was taken aback by it, thinking she was impervious to sarcasm, judging by the way she dished it out.

"…And you're hovering on the verge of flat-out crude. You… you weenie!"

There it was—the lack of sincerity. For almost a full second, he really thought she might be losing her touch, that the years had matured her. Maybe they had, just not around him. She whined but it was melodramatic and disingenuous. He sighed. *I should have known.* Although not surprising, he hoped that someday she'd show a vulnerable side. But for the moment she didn't. So goes the game. "You're right. That was crass and uncalled for… you poor little thing."

"Oh shut up."

"We'll call that one a draw. Can I bring anything?"

"If all you have is five dollars, bring the best five dollar bottle of wine you can find. If it's no good, we can always use it for salad dressing."

"And you have the audacity to say that I'm cruel?"

All he heard was a quick chortle, a click and a dial tone. His mood took a turn for the better.

The person answering Nikki's apartment door was certainly not the sultry vixen of two nights ago. The vulnerability he sought came in the form of an expressive mask covering a beautiful face. She yanked the door open and, in a single motion, turned to run in the opposite direction. "Come in. Sit down. Whatever." He saw her frantic side. It amused him.

The sound of things sizzling and bubbling came from the kitchen along with the faint odor of something burnt. "Is everything okay? Something I can do, maybe?"

She disappeared through the door into the kitchen. "No. I told you I was going to cook and that's what I'm doing. You can open that bottle of wine in your hand though. I need a glass... now."

Jack stepped into the kitchen and marveled at the sight. Nikki was over-dressed in a low-cut, off-the-shoulder black dress, hugging her tall, curvaceous body, all perched atop high heel black patent-leather shoes. She wore a full apron spattered with oil and food over her front. The view of her backside, as she hovered over the countertop range, was appealing, but it was the sight of her conducting a symphony of boiling and bubbling pots and pans that enamored him most. Judging by the manic way she waved that wooden spoon, it was more punk rock than classical. She was definitely out of her element.

Opening a drawer, he fumbled around among sharp utensils for a corkscrew.

She glanced away from the cooking chore. "Not there." She pointed with a dripping spoon. "Look in that drawer."

Bottle decorked, he poured two glasses full. She eagerly accepted the wine and gulped it, never taking her eyes from the range top.

"I hope the wine helps. You look out of control."

She finally looked back. "Ya think."

"A wee bit." He kissed her shoulder and rubbed it in with his thumb.

She smiled and moaned softly. Gooseflesh came up on her bare shoulder.

Jack put his glass down and massaged her shoulders. "Thanks for going through all this trouble."

"What trouble?"

He snickered. "Surely you jest."

"Shut up."

His smile wilted away. "More importantly, the effort you're putting into it." The implication of the comment went farther than a compliment to a novice trying to cook. He wanted to tell her how touched he was by her willingness to stay close despite his odd behavior and weird stories.

The muscles in her neck and shoulders relaxed. She offered a contented smile. "Man does not live by breakfast cereal alone, you know."

How did you know I ate breakfast cereal this morning?"

"I didn't. It's just the stereotypical single man's breakfast." She shrugged and glanced back at him. "Behaviors are my business. Remember?"

"You're one smart chick. You know that?"

"Yep."

"It's your turn to shut up." He resumed massaging her shoulders.

"Seriously," she said, "I just felt you needed good food and companionship."

"True." He suddenly realized that he was becoming overly comfortable and had to remind himself that he could only afford a casual friendship for now. He patted her shoulders a final time and backed away.

As it turned out, Nikki had no reason to worry about the quality of dinner. The asparagus with cheese sauce, the chops, and the salad were all top rate.

Afterwards, quick work was made of dirty dishes, and they moved into the living room. He studied the surroundings with a critical eye. The decor could have been considered modern. It was uncluttered. He assumed nothing had been purchased from discount stores. His knowledge of art wouldn't fill a thimble, but the artwork and sculptures appeared to be original works. He figured she wouldn't know what the inside of Pottery Barn looked like. There was no television in the room. "Hey, what if I want to watch a game tonight on television?"

"In that case, Stud, you'd be out of luck."

"Seriously, why don't you have a television? It seems unusual for an American home these days."

"It's an aversion to network news programs, even some movies, and other entertainment programming. It was a conscious decision not to allow mass media to determine how I view life or the world."

"Did I hit a nerve?"

"Sorry. But, ya know what? We're so inundated with reporters, commentators and news anchors who not only want to give us the news but also mold our opinions of it. And don't even get me started on Madison Avenue glitz designed to create a lifestyle and sell it to us; worse yet, charge us by the month for the rest of our lives for it."

"Excuse me, but isn't it a little strange you're telling me this? You know, because of where I work?"

"Maybe a little." She retrieved her wine and sipped. "I don't apologize for it though. I have enough regrets without some jerk on television I don't even know trying to tell me what's right and what's wrong in the world then watch a commercial that tells me my brand of butter is inferior."

Jack saw a side of her he hadn't known before. In college, his interest in this woman had been defined by testosterone; how long it might take on any given evening trying to get her into bed. Now he was getting to know the woman, not just her parts. But there was a story in her lifestyle that made him believe that once her opinion had gelled on any given subject, it would be cast in stone and absolutely unalterable—something he'd have to be careful about but could be helpful later.

She spun on her heels and dropped onto the sofa. "Come sit beside me and I'll show you what I really think of you, Mr. Journalist."

Unsure where she was going with it, uneasiness stuttered his step. The sound of the invitation was clearly steeped in sexuality.

"Get over here and sit down," she demanded.

With knee-jerk hesitation, he sat next to her, feeling like a high school kid around a friend's oversexed mother.

"Turn around."

He turned his back to her, and she began rubbing his neck and shoulders. "I suppose I owe you this for what I'm sure you thought was an attack on the source of your livelihood," she said in a breathy whisper, chin resting on his shoulder.

After a time, his eyes drooped, and then closed. He relaxed, really letting go, and went lightheaded and tingled, but it wasn't a sexual rush. A chill hit him. It intensified quickly, stripping the warmth from Nikki's hands. An image of the boyhood version of brother, Kyle, popped into his head—a bedroom setting. He couldn't determine where or whose bedroom it was.

Nikki yanked her hands away. "What the hell is that?"

He opened his eyes and saw the scene that had been in his mind now floating in front of his face bathed in a soft white light. Everything beyond the scene in Nikki's living room still remained perfectly visible right through it.

He slowly turned toward Nikki, her eyes transfixed at a point in front of him. "Can you see that?" he whispered, as if it might be scare away if he spoke louder.

"Yes," she hissed. "What the hell is it?"

Jack's breathing quickened. He became excited and scared of what they witnessed together—anxious about what Nikki may think. He had to stay calm and objective. He needed her as an eyewitness. He didn't want to lose her or the vision until some determination of its origin could be made.

Nikki pulled away in a panic. She froze. Her posture indicated she was ready to bolt for the door. Digging her heels into the carpet, she propelled backwards on her buttocks one shove at a time, all the while, never taking her eyes from the unfolding scenario in front of them. One second, she seemed ready to leap up, get away, and then a second later become enthralled with what she saw.

Hitting the far armrest on the sofa, she abruptly stopped sliding. "Where did it go?"

Jack glanced back and saw in her darting eyes that she no longer saw what he did. "Can't you see it?"

"No, but there's a weird glow around you." Her voice was thready.

"There is?" For the first time, he noticed that the soft white light not only surrounded the ghostly scene but enveloped his body as well. That's when it occurred to him that the glow was the connection that his physical body made with that time and place—wherever that time and place happened to be. He had to attempt to understand what created it, what held it in place, and what ended it. For some reason, Nikki's presence emboldened him to explore, even though she wasn't exactly the picture of serenity. "Nikki," he said, voice low and even, "Don't panic. Slide back in my direction."

"Not on your life, fella. This is absolutely too freakin' weird."

"We have an opportunity to study something that only a few people in the entire world believe exists. Yet, there it is, right in front of us."

She swallowed hard. He heard the gulp and glanced back.

She closed her eyes, breathing fast and shallow. "Okay," she said and began scooting toward him but had only moved a couple of inches before stopping. "I can't do it."

"Come on. I'm right here with you."

"I —I don't have the courage." The whine was reminiscent of a scolded child. This time there was no insinuation of melodrama. The whimper came as a product of terror.

Slowly, he held out a hand to her as a calming gesture that everything would be okay.

"Give me a second," she said, attempting to even her breathing. She began sliding towards him, inching closer. She stopped abruptly. "There it is."

He saw that the vision continued, and he looked back and offered a reassuring nod. Perspiration glowed as color drained from her face. A surge of admiration raced through him. Although in a cold sweat and eyes wide, she fought the urge to panic. For some inexplicable reason that glimmer of courage, though tainted, kept him focused on what needed to be done.

"Stand up with me and move in close enough for your body to touch mine. Can you do that?"

"All right," she stammered and stood at the same speed he did. Once standing, she poked her index fingers in two of his rear belt loops. "Jack," she whispered, "The air... it's so... so cold."

He stepped forward. "Stay close." Nausea washed over him, forcing his eyes to shut tight.

She jerked him to a standstill. "Stop, stop. I'm getting sick to my stomach. I think I'm going to puke."

In the span of time it took for his eyes to blink, the air temperature changed. The ambient smell changed, too, as the transition completed in a single beat of his heart. Eyes opening, he saw that they stood in the same bedroom with that young adult version of his brother, but recessed within the shadow of a closet door. Jack turned his head in slow motion and with equal slowness put a finger to his lips. She nodded but it was hesitating. She dug fingernails into the soft roll of his waist.

The sound of the bedroom door snagged his attention away from the brief pain of her nails. He backed up, pushing both of them deeper into the shadows.

A middle-aged man whom he recognized as his brother's foster dad, burst into the room cursing, a rolling verbal assault. Kyle ignored him and continued examining album covers. The man looked crazy and dangerous.

"Get off your lazy ass!" the man shouted, red faced and slobbering. "I've told you at least a dozen times to get those leaves raked!"

Kyle didn't respond, as if the man weren't even in the room.

"Are you deaf, you little son-of-a-bitch?" he ranted. "This is the last warning you'll get before I beat you senseless!"

"Get me out of here," Nikki hissed. "Get me out of here now." Her nails clawed into the tender skin of his waist.

Jack turned his head slightly but didn't break eye contact with the drama in the making before them. "Shh." The pain from her grip threatened his ability to remain quiet and still. So, he peeled her fingers off him and turned ever so slowly to face her so as not to be noticed. He placed hands on both sides of her face and pulled it into his chest to keep her quiet.

The movement was excessive. They were noticed. The confrontation ceased. They both looked to where he and Nikki stood. As contentious as that relationship plainly was, it was clear that they had the same thought at the same time; how did two strangers get inside the bedroom and what are they doing here? The old man's surprised look hardened into anger.

Suddenly, Jack was swarmed with regret for having pulled Nikki into this, fearing they were about to be attacked. Wrapping his arms around her, he closed his eyes and hugged her. "I'm sorry."

In the time it took to whisper it, the room temperature and light changed. Having experienced it once already, it lacked the shock this time. Although he once again failed to see the transition, they had returned to her apartment.

A couple of nights ago, at Wainwright's place, Nikki had gazed analytically into his eyes. Now, Jack found it necessary to return the favor. He looked into hers and saw naked fear in darting pupils. He refused to let her go until reason returned to those beautiful brown eyes. But it wasn't just for her. He needed this moment, too.

CHAPTER 6

The morning sun streamed through the large arched window of Wainwright's home at a severe angle. Dust particles danced within the beam.

"When transition begins, anyone standing close, within your aural sphere, their aura is consumed by yours and brought up to match your frequency. Then that person will become a part of whatever you are experiencing. The energy you project becomes a vehicle, a bubble if you will, that a person can climbed into and go along," Arthur said.

"What's an aura?"

Arthur recoiled. He frowned, holding a profound look of shock.

Jack suddenly felt more than a little stupid by the old man's silent reaction to his question. With a sheepish grin, "I take it you're not referring to my beaming personality."

"My goodness, man, for a newspaper reporter you don't seem very well read," he said while waving a, you've-been-naughty finger. "Tell me, have you ever wondered why your career doesn't seem to be going anywhere?"

Jack let the comment slide. But, sadly, the answer would have been yes.

"The aura is an energy emanation surrounding all of us. Every human is encircled by energy that radiates but cannot be seen without special equipment or special talent. The unique frequency of each individual produces color variations. We all possess our own uniqueness in that way, different colors in each one of us, just as everyone's personality is different. No two people have exactly the same color. Furthermore, the color is never consistent even within the individual. Mood and health dictate hue at any given moment. For example, when someone says they're feeling *blue*, it's more than a euphemism; it's a lower vibration created by waning energy. On the other hand, if someone is considered *bright*, that too has significance beyond descriptive. Those people are vibrating at a faster frequency, producing a richer, sharper and, yes, a brighter aura."

"If the aura is color, how come we can't see it?"

"Some people can, but they are a select group with God-given talent. But you must understand that the slowest of these vibrations move very fast. Even the deepest and gloomiest of colors still vibrate beyond the visual range of the average human. Animals can sense the aura. That's why your dog knows when you're sad, or mad, or happy. You don't have to say anything or act a certain way. He just knows… because of your aura."

This idiosyncratic human sparked a flame of admiration. The old guy spoke with eloquence and precision in detailing the experience, without having been there. But bloated cynicism kept admiration from flaming too high. Jack still had not hit a point of unfettered faith in what he was being told. "If you can't do the things I'm capable of, how is it that you know all this in such fine detail and with such conviction?"

"Trust and an open mind is what I'm asking of you for now," he said. "Specifics of what I know and how I learned it will be divulged as it becomes necessary. Please don't concern yourself with that for now. If I shared it, it would only overwhelm you and not even be important at this point. I want you to develop a clear understanding of what's happening to you. I believe it's more important you realize what it is you're blessed with. As for me… I'm a story that can wait."

Jack nodded. "Okay," he said, drawing out the word. "I guess I can do that."

Wainwright and this palatial but dank home went together like peas in a pod. It was a perfect symbiosis; Wainwright, a highly intelligent and articulate man yet eccentric with physical characteristics of a bum—the house, an elegant awe-inspiring structure neglected and in disrepair. He and his surroundings were a perfect match.

Having received acceptance from Jack of his explanation, the old guy brightened. It seemed to fuel his mood. His voice went up an octave. "And the soft white glow you achieved indicates a vibration high enough to pierce space and time. The only people I'm aware of that have the ability to display this type of aura are a few shamans, monks and other religious people, not newspaper feature writers living in obscurity in the heartland of America, for God's sake." He laughed. "It's a birthright. It cannot be learned, although some people spend a lifetime learning to master it."

Listening intently to every word, even inflection, Jack remained clueless about what it all meant. Why had he been blessed, or maybe cursed, with it? Short on patience and long on frustration, "What does it mean? What the hell does it all mean? That's what I want to know."

Wainwright leaned back, dropping his elbows on the armrests and propped his chin on his fingertips. With pursed lips, he lifted and fixed a gaze to a point over and behind Jack's head for a couple of seconds. "Are you a religious man? Do you believe in God?"

"Sort of."

"Explain 'sort of'."

"Since my brother and I were abused as children and spent most of our childhood in a boys' home we were certainly around it a lot. Going to church was mandatory at the home. As children, we didn't have a choice. It was thrust upon us. That 'sort of' just means that I stepped away from it once I no longer remained under the domineering thumbs of the administrators of that home."

He paused. It hit him that he was embarrassed by an admitted lack of religious affiliation. "It was difficult to believe in a god, given the circumstances. The home's major funding came from religious organizations. At the time, I was certain that salvation wasn't the foremost reason we were herded into buses and taken to church twice a week. Even then hypocrisy angered me."

Arthur seemed saddened. A wrinkle formed on his brow.

Jack quickly added, "That's not to say it didn't have an impact on me. It did. Part of me relates to the spiritual, although I haven't practiced it in years." He expected Wainwright to put a voice to that expression on his face. He didn't. "How's the depth of my religious faith germane?"

"Are you aware of all the books and stories about people who die and go into The Light?"

"Sure. It's common folklore."

He leaned forward. "It's more than folklore, friend. That soft white glow that develops around you is a lesser version of *that* Light… a *vastly* dimmer version, mind you."

On that comment, Jack sat back hard and wondered about the gravity of what the old man had just told him. It was so far beyond his comprehension that it sounded absurd.

He stood, turned, and walked toward the door. "I'm in need of a big glass of orange juice. How about you?"

"That'd be great." Still contemplating the light thing, he remained a long way from getting his mind around the concept and how he was related to it.

Arthur, true to his word, had remained available to answer questions. It was early, not yet seven o'clock Sunday morning. Jack had been at the mansion over half an hour dumping details of his latest encounter with the teenaged version of his brother and foster father while Nikki stood at his side.

After returning her home last night, Jack had gone to his apartment and straight to bed. But sleep was light and fitful. His mind raced most of the night—in and out of sleep, plagued by confusion to romantic fascination. At the base of it was concern for Nikki whom he hoped would develop some objectivity. She might not be able to cope with it. But he couldn't blame her if she ran, never to return. He refused to believe that he might not see her again but had to consider it a possibility after what he'd put her through.

Earlier, he thought he had no recourse but come to Wainwright. He needed to talk about it. It wasn't just Nikki scared by it all. The time fast approached that it wouldn't matter where the truth led, as long as the process of dealing with it could begin. It had yet to come together in his head just how perfect a choice the old man was. The old guy had thrown the door open and seemed excited to see Jack on his doorstep after having been disturbed from a sound sleep. He greeted Jack with that trademark grin and swollen red eyes.

Wainwright reappeared in the cluttered library. "Here ya go." He extended a juice glass towards him. "I see a question in your eyes."

Jack gulped the juice, realizing how thirsty he was. As thoughts and questions formed, he gazed into the half-emptied glass before setting it on a side table. He sprang to his feet. "I can understand the aura and light thing, but how is it possible to physically move from place to place and time to time?"

"I can talk on the subject but only in the broadest sense. I know only a few details. There are great thinkers that have hypothesized, correctly so in my opinion, that time is just an extremely high frequency. You know, like radio and light waves, vibrating within unique ranges to produce distinctive signatures."

"Is that why I've always heard, if man can exceed the speed of light, breaking the time barrier is next?"

He clapped his hands. "You're beginning to catch on."

Jack wanted to call him a wise-ass but didn't, in fact said nothing.

"There's another theory that's compatible with the frequency thing. A quark may not the smallest unit of an atom. If so, it's possible all these realities exist simultaneously, just different configurations. Thousands of variations of your life and mine may be happening at this very instant, and they're all just as real as our conversation is right now, occupying the same space we are, just dimensionally different. Because, my boy, those tiniest units that make the quarks that comprise atoms that form the molecules that make the cells that result in the man are arranged slightly different in each of these unique and totally separate dimensions; so different in fact that there is no crossover, no interference from one dimension to the next... even though all are occupying the same space. Heaven only knows how many dimensional layers there are."

Laced with grins and giggles, it was difficult to watch such flippancy and still believe this doofus knew what he was talking about. It was irksome, but Jack attempted to see it from Wainwright's point of view. These subjects were as common for him as last Sunday's football game to the rest of us. He spoke of theories as if absolute truths. *Am I arrogant enough to believe that what's happening to me is more sane than his theories?*

Wainwright grinned.

Jack wondered why? That's when it finally struck home. *That old son-of-a-bitch is reading my thoughts!*

Arthur's grin widened further, his body rocking with a stifled snicker. "One thing needs to be clarified," he said, allowing his slender frame to sink back into the softness of the chair. "It's a popular misconception that the frequency of time is a short step up from the speed of light. This of course depends upon your belief that time is a super high frequency, as I do. Add all the frequencies together up to the speed of light, and that wouldn't touch the difference between light and the frequency speed of time." Pausing, he struck a contemplative pose staring down at a pile of books on the floor so askew they might topple. Although his sense of humor sometimes became irritating, this serious look didn't suit him at all. *He looks like he's getting ready to tell a dirty joke in a monastery.*

"Great analogy." He didn't even look up when he said it.

"Great anal…? I'll be damned. You *are* reading my thoughts, aren't you?"

He laughed. "That's who I am and what I do. Have you forgotten that's the reason you came to see me in the first place?"

Heat of embarrassment rose in Jack's face. "I'm sorry. I didn't mean—"

"It really is easy to forget that I know what's on your mind. Don't worry. Your thoughts have been flattering compared to some of those detectives I've worked with who refused to believe even after the crimes were solved."

I sat back hard. "Mr. Wainwright, I… I apologize."

"There is absolutely no reason to apologize, and for heaven's sake quit calling me Mr. Wainwright. My name is Arthur."

He paused and took on a somber look. "I hoped we might become friends. I haven't had much luck over the years with that, the ability sort of gets in the way."

Jack nodded amiably but was also analyzing what he'd been thinking. Unfortunately, there'd been many unflattering thoughts about Arthur, but he remembered nothing specific. And now that he knew the old guy always knew what was on his mind he purposely thought: *The guy is just freakin' weird.*

Arthur locked eyes with Jack, and he nodded and smiled. Arthur said nothing, just sighed.

"The difference," he continued, "between the frequency of light and the vibration rate of time can roughly be compared to the speed of a snail and that of a diving falcon. This may help you visualize it, although still a woefully inadequate comparison. If you consider this, then you're capable of assessing the awesome power your mind generates. To take that a step further, The Light that people go into after death is many, many multiples of the power you are generating. I don't think there is a number high enough to give it comprehensive clarity." He rolled his eyes and laughed. "I can only imagine the string of zeroes on such a number."

"Are my thoughts triggering these episodes?"

"Indeed. But beyond that it's how you're thinking. *What* you are thinking only precipitates the way in which the thoughts come together. Thoughts begin the process, but it's your heart that is the key." He tapped his chest. "The heart, Jack… the heart. Once the thought is solid, it initiates physical recomposition at the sub-atomic level. Vibration hits a certain speed then the heart takes over and shoots it to that unimaginable level. Love, hate, anger, sadness… all the things that make us who we are is the genesis of that power."

"Getting my mind around this is… hell, it's nearly impossible."

"It might be best if you not try to understand it. But it's important you believe and accept it. Embrace it. Otherwise, there'll come a day I'll have the unenviable task of scraping your sanity off the sidewalk. This is your life. You can't get a prescription from the doctor to make it go away. It's not a sickness so there can't be a cure."

He took a swig of orange juice and snapped forward in his chair. "One other thing; your ability to move into that physical realm that is a crossover to the spiritual world is virtually the same thing as physically moving within the time arc. The only difference is what you happen to be concentrating on. Time and dimension are just different strata of the same rock. Don't ever forget that. There is precious little difference between them. If we had the sensitivity to do so, we could see these places and people that are occupying the same space as we are at this very instant."

"You mean like ghosts?"

"If that's what it takes to make it easier to understand… then yes." His eyes followed a ray of sunshine coming through the window that had moved a little higher as the sun made its daily trip up the sky. "Always remember, you control it. You can start it and you can stop it. It's all controlled by your mind and the power of your heart. It's an extraordinary blessing, not a curse. Your mind is the steering wheel but it's your heart that is the engine."

An uncomfortable knot tightened. Jack didn't welcome or want these abilities. If what Arthur had told him was true, and he had no reason not to believe it, this had the potential of doing great damage. "Do you mean the possibilities of what I could accomplish would be virtually endless?"

"Well… yes. But you must also know there is a popular belief that if you interact with people and events of the past. You will change the future, somewhat like the rippling effect of a stone hitting the water."

"Now, that's something I *am* aware of."

"Hah! If you believe it then you're absolutely wrong."

"What?"

"Just because it's a popular belief doesn't make it so," he said with a wave, sweeping the whole notion aside. "If you project your physical body into a *present or future* event, you most certainly will be seen, known and remembered. On top of this, you *can* alter events of the future from that point forward just by your presence."

Rising and pacing along a straight seam in the worn carpet, Arthur stopped, interrupting that streaming ray of morning sun. "You must always be aware that the past has already transpired. Your presence will in no way change it. In fact, while you are in the past you'll be able to interact with people you encounter of that time. They in turn will see, feel and communicate with you. You'll be in their time one hundred percent. But the moment you leave, there'll be absolutely no memory of you having been there. All events you have affected or altered in any way will revert to the natural order of occurrence. You cannot change history because you can't change the past, no matter what you do while in that time."

"If I kill someone in the past, won't they be dead? I mean really dead?" Won't all children born to them disappear?"

"Jack," he said, "I'm not being philosophical. I'm conveying hard truth. Forget everything you think you know and all the popular science fiction stories you've ever heard. Don't ever, ever forget, no matter where you are in space or when you are in time it is *your personal present reality.* You cannot change the course of a past event. Should you kill someone, they will only be dead as long as your presence continues to alter that state. Then poof, it all reverts back once you leave. But listen well and remember this; the people you interact with can harm you and change *your* future because it will be your present—subject to change. You could even be killed. Your corpse will evaporate into the basic building blocks of all things. There will be no memory of you in what had been your own time. Nikki will have no memory of you; Mr. Landau, your editor, will never know you existed… everyone you've ever come in contact with will have memories wiped clean because if you screw up and get killed in the past, you will have never existed in any future time. Your murderer will never know he killed you or that you were even there—no memory of the episode at all. You just cease to exist… period."

Jack attempted to speak but couldn't. He sat dumbfounded, feeling stupid and small, watching Arthur drink orange juice. The old guy seemed so at ease with all this crap.

He belched. "Besides, it's not allowed," he finally said wiping a drop from his chin.

"What's not allowed?"

"Changing past events. It's a Divine No-No."

Even if I had money, I don't think I could pay this man to stay serious.

He slapped a knee and bellowed. "Money doesn't mean much to me."

Jack let his head fall until his chin met his chest, flushing once again with embarrassment. It was becoming clear that warding off thoughts or trying not to think about anything at all around Arthur would be virtually impossible. He'd better become accustomed to many more embarrassing moments if he hung around this guy. That's when it occurred to him that he didn't even have to be around him. He was tuned in regardless. But why? What motive did the old guy have for trailing his life so closely? Questions kept piling up faster than answers were coming in.

CHAPTER 7

Although a reluctant student, Jack's hesitance didn't deter Wainwright's willingness to act as a guide. Fortunately, the old guy had plenty of patience. Compassion for Jack's malaise came tempered by excitement that he'd found a local with such ability and the opportunity to study it first-hand. Exhilaration went over the top each time they discussed the possibilities and consequences. Jack saw it as an annoyance, but the old man plainly viewed the episodes as adventures that he not only wanted to know about but be smack-dab in the middle of. If he indeed used mind altering drugs in his younger days, Wainwright's behavior had to be the result of a form of brain damage—then again maybe not. But the way he acted would be better suited to a ten-year-old at Disney World. Could it be that he'd always been this way? The old guy seemed to be on a high that had no end.

Although he had no plan to embrace this curse, Jack developed a smidgen of curiosity. It became an infectious maze that had many twists and turns. He began to wonder what was waiting around each corner. Sometimes, he felt off-balance—like a toddler in a way—discovering the world all over again, learning how to live in it. Unlike the youngster though, he remained torn between wanting to know and resistant to finding out. It became Arthur's duty to convince him that he needed the information. Jack refused to give in and accept that his lifelong belief system had a big hole blown in it.

He didn't make it easy for the old guy. As friendly and accepting as Arthur was over Jack's on-again-off-again desire to know, cracks began showing in his patience. What a teacher he would've made; an individual with his level of self-control and perseverance was rare and he was certainly determined to stay the course through a mind-numbing multi-tiered chess game. That might explain his excitement; for him it was a game. Each time an assumption was proven correct his eyes twinkled. He'd giggle, clap his hands and dance around. He fascinated Jack as much as Jack's ability fascinated him. The only difference happened to be that Arthur found all this bullshit amusing.

All other riddles about the man aside, his presence made the problem easier to cope with and better understood. To cope with and understand it was one thing but to embrace it was quite another. To Jack, it was if he'd been afflicted with a terminal illness, eager to discover how fast it was going to kill him.

Traveling to strange places utilizing an even stranger mode of transportation seemed like black magic. Fear was the enemy—time and space the battlefield. Somehow, he had to come to terms with it, at least accept it as part of who he had become. He refused to believe, though, that it was here to stay.

The date with Nikki, the initial meeting with Arthur, and the conversation with him Sunday morning added up to a wild weekend. He wanted to make Nikki part of the discovery process. But how could he keep her calm and objective if he couldn't keep his own emotions in check? She experienced too much too soon.

"Don't ever lose sight of her," Arthur had said to him before leaving the old man's house Sunday. "She's your soul mate."

Soul mate. What the hell is that anyway? Soul mate is just an overused label that sweethearts use when they cuddle. He didn't think of Nikki as his sweetheart. Confused, he came to believe that it simply meant she might be of some help. Nikki and Arthur should be kept a part of this journey; Arthur for motivation and knowledge and Nikki to keep him grounded when strangeness stole away good sense—the mentor and the nurturer.

As unusual as it seemed, Jack craved the ordinary and longed for the mundane. Taking care of everyday business seemed like a vacation. On that Monday, it revolved around a paycheck.

The thought of playing hooky from work appealed to him but was out of the question. It occurred to him that he had promised to write a feature article about Arthur. But other than a little background on his pot smoking days, he possessed insufficient information. The lengthy conversations had nothing to do with solving those murders, his abilities or his background. A few stories to prove his credibility had been the only personal information shared. Fascinating stuff, and to an extent useable, but he knew nothing about what Arthur went through to close the cases on two murders. The only ace was that Gus had not given him a deadline.

Jack arrived at the paper and double-timed into the building keeping his head down as he did. Going unnoticed was the only way to go. He didn't want to speak to anyone because that'd catch the ear of the elf-with-an-attitude. Gus reminded him of the Keebler Elf out of costume with a Sergeant Carter voice. He glided through the maze of cubicles in the direction of his workstation, avoiding eye contact with anyone. He didn't consider himself unfriendly; he just had no desire to engage in conversation. At that point, he wanted to avoid Gus's anger. That's all. His step chopped fast and straight as he bee-lined to his desk.

He heard a cheerful, "Good Morning" from Dora, a woman near retirement that seemed happier every morning. It was sickeningly syrupy.

He mumbled as he breezed by, "Mornin'." *Getting closer to the day you can chuck this job, eh, Dora?*

In spite of his best efforts, the trip across the expansive and noisy room was interrupted by that raspy voice. "Dane!" Gus peered over a cubicle partition, like a Kilroy-was-here cartoon but with an added visual of that cigar spinning between his cheek and teeth.

Jack stopped abruptly; certain that he must have appeared lobotomized lacking the drool. "Yes sir?"

"You can run but you can't hide, son. Where's the article you promised on our local soothsayer." He held out his open hand over the top of the cubicle glass like he actually expected Jack to trot over and lay the copy in his chubby palm.

"You wanted that today?" He tried to act sincere.

"No, I thought we might put it in the freakin' Christmas edition! Of course I want it today."

"I thought you may have wanted it for one of the weekend editions since you didn't mention a deadline Friday."

"I didn't give you a deadline?" He scratched his chin and calmed. The rotating unlit cigar in his mouth slowed to a stop and drooped. Silence was fleeting. "Okay, have it done by deadline tomorrow. We'll put it in the Wednesday edition. That day is shaping up to be light anyway."

The simple truth worked without having to provide an explanation. But luck could only stretch so far. He whipped his chair out and plopped into it, wheeling it under the keyboard at his computer terminal.

He picked up the phone to call Arthur. While he waited for an answer, the paycheck was top of mind. He needed it yesterday. If the article didn't get done, this payday and all future checks from this place of employment might vanish.

"Good morning, Jack." a shrill cheery voice announced over the phone even before he had a chance to say hello. "I trust you're better rested this morning."

Hesitatingly, he said, "I'm not sure about that. But thanks for asking." By now, he should have been accustomed to Arthur's strange little way of knowing things, like who's on the phone before anyone speaks. But it still came as a surprise. "You know, Arthur, it dawned on me that I've learned a lot about *me*, but I hardly know anything about *you*. That was the purpose I went to see you in the first place. I need information for the article."

"Would you like to play a game?"

That one seemingly innocuous question ignited frustration. Jack rolled his eyes and huffed. "I don't have time. I have to get this story done pronto. I'm pretty sure my job depends on it."

Arthur's inclination to frivolity and unearned wealth made it a difficult concept for him to grasp. He had nothing in his life to compare it to, so making a living was the same as speaking a foreign language to him—meaning the game was more important than Jack's paycheck.

"Aw, come on. We have a great opportunity to cultivate your psychic perception. It'll be fun, you'll get all the information you need and you'll get your article done much quicker than if you ask questions that you already know the answers to."

"Know the answers to? Are you out of your mind? I hardly know you at all."

"Don't kid yourself. You know me." He laughed. "If you take time to ask questions, jot down answers, compile it then type it into a word processor, you'll have wasted an exorbitant amount of time." He took an exaggerated draw of air because he'd said it in a single breath. To Arthur, the game was afoot. "I promise you'll get it done quicker. You have my personal guarantee. What do you say?"

Jack sighed and angrily swiped his forehead with the heel of his hand. "Okay, okay. Just get on with it. I have to get this written."

"Good. Listen close because this is a complicated set of instructions you must follow to the letter." His tone was serious. He paused long.

Jack clutched the pencil tighter, pressing it to a reporter's notebook. "I'm ready."

"Hang up the phone and begin typing."

Almost on its own, the pencil went flying across the desk. "What the hell are you talking about? The interview never happened. I have no notes. That instruction is asinine!"

"Calm down. You can perceive thoughts as easily as I can read yours. People like us have no need for verbal communication. But if you continue to doubt and disbelieve, it'll never develop."

He was too cheerful in the face of annoyance. That peeved Jack more—not so much with the information, but with the way he chose to say it. It was a pastime to him. He loved it.

"You've got to realize it, believe in it, and then practice it," he said.

This is too bizarre.

"Only to the disbeliever," Arthur replied to the unspoken thought. "It's time you moved into the believer column."

"What if the article turns out to be gibberish with no substance?"

"Am I the only one with faith here?"

Goofiness aside, it was a good question. One Jack had no answer for except, "Apparently."

Jack mumbled an acerbic goodbye, hung up and turned to his keyboard. Hands lying lifeless in his lap, he stared at the blinking cursor on the blank screen thinking how crazy it seemed, and how much crazier he was for going along with such a hare-brained scheme. It occurred to him that there was some background mentally tucked away—not much but a little, maybe enough to get started. *I'll write about his college days, embellishing and fabricating to fill out my word count.* He began pounding keys. *This should wipe the smile off that old fart's face.* He typed, and kept typing, caring little about the words flowing from his fingers. *I'll give this guy a background that'll make him cringe, and then tell him that I don't give a damn what he thinks, I'm going to publish it.*

After two hours of typing, proofreading and editing, the article was complete—the best fiction he'd ever written. He thought about that. It was the only fiction he'd ever written. And, now, it was time to call Arthur.

As usual, Arthur snatched up the phone and began talking with that bubbly exuberance. "How do you think it turned out?"

Strange how he chose to frame that question, since it was make believe. *Why is he asking what I think? He's the one that should be concerned.* "It's pretty good short fiction I suppose. Do you have e-mail?"

"Of course. Send it over."

As he jotted the email address on a scrap of paper, "You realize, don't you, regardless how incorrect it is, I'm going to submit it for publication as written." A wry smile stretched his face. He felt wicked—the first time since meeting the old guy that he believed himself in control. The tiny rush of power felt good. "Let me tell you, Arthur, it's harsh. Makes you look pretty darned irresponsible. After all, I just did what you told me to do. Right? I have a deadline to keep you know. Are you still sure you want to read it?"

"Sure. I was honest with you. You're just being honest with me."

Jack hoped to hear nervous hesitation but didn't. Arthur just kept up that silly cheerfulness.

Hanging up the phone, he sauntered to the coffee pot and poured a cup, sitting in his chair and leaned far back, fingers laced behind his head, feet up on the desk. His eyes drifted from the steaming cup on the desk to the ceiling and absently counted acoustic tiles, unable to keep from thinking cruel thoughts. He snickered. *And he thought he had me hoodwinked.* "Humph."

Five minutes passed, and the phone rang. Jack snatched up the receiver but didn't yet have it to his ear when he heard the excited voice.

"It's excellent. This is great journalism."

With a lazy grin and a shake of the head, "Correction, it's excellent writing, not journalism." The smile began to droop. He grew uneasy, pulling his feet from the desk and sitting upright. "What about the parts I fabricated?"

"There is no fiction in this article. It's all true."

"Bullshit!" Realizing the volume put into the profanity, he glanced and saw heads popping up from behind cubicle walls. He sank down and fell forward onto his elbows on the desk. In a much quieter voice, but no less intense, "Come on, Arthur—"

"All true, every word."

"Are you telling me that... all those things happened? What about that detailed account of your vacation in Seattle when you were thirty-two?"

"True."

"What about sitting intoxicated on a high balcony?"

"True."

"Come on, Arthur. I... I can't believe that. Those events are products of a fertile imagination. Do you expect me to believe you were about to pass out and fall off a balcony when the mysterious appearance of an Oriental holy man arrived in time to save you? For God's sake, that's the stuff fantasy novels are made of." He pounded his forehead with the phone. "No one's going to believe it. I wrote it and I don't believe it."

Arthur not only addressed the concerns, he picked up the story and continued it. "The oriental gentleman's name is Maigo. He's a friend, mentor and personal guide. How do you think I came by all this knowledge? I didn't just glean it from the cosmos." He laughed. "Maigo pops in occasionally for a visit."

"Pops?"

"You heard right... pops. Maigo discovered my abilities when I was young and confused—just as you are now. That day in Seattle, I didn't care if I fell or not. In fact, I would've jumped if he hadn't shown up. My grasp on reality was shot. Or, so I thought. I figured that I had turned into a raving lunatic from drugs and had destroyed my ability to differentiate between fantasy and reality. I wasn't prepared to live that way the rest of my life."

"I have a hard time believing you, of all people, didn't embrace it right away. Now you're telling me you would have rather committed suicide then live on like that?"

"Yep."

"What changed?"

"Maigo. Bless his little Asian heart. The first thing he asked of me was that I quit drinking and doing drugs. I quit the drugs."

"I don't understand. I never heard a voice, not even a mental image of you. All I did was dream up a story and put it in print, pulling it right out of my imagination."

"What you're referring to as 'imagination' is pieces of information I sent telepathically. Of course, the actual composition of the information was all you. I had nothing to do with how you wrote it. Everything in the article is true... even the finest details."

Amazement tended to be a matter of course these days. Jack mumbled that he'd call later and hung up, staring at the article glowing on the monitor. Confused or not, he'd beaten the deadline by a full day.

CHAPTER 8

Jack hadn't heard from Nikki and the week neared an end. Since reconnecting, he thought of her often. The urge to talk to her became strong. The time had come to get a handle on where she stood as an ally and confidant. He paced through his apartment, tentative about calling, convinced that bothering her at work would not be appreciated. *Maybe I'm too strange to suit her taste.* If the situation had been reversed, he felt certain he would have bugged out on her. He didn't consider himself paranoid over never seeing her again, just practical. She had good reason to run and not look back.

He considered waiting until after she'd left work, later in the evening perhaps. But, if he should do that, what if he caught her with some guy? Jealous twinges nipped at him even after simple consideration of the possibility. He chose to believe that she'd been buried in work leaving her exhausted in the evenings, spending quiet time alone. Jack suffered from the deadly duo—arrogance and ego. He had possessive leanings when he thought of her. She'd become an ever-increasing part of his shrinking universe, regardless what she may have thought about it. It was midweek. He finally gave in and dialed her number.

The pool secretary said, "I'm sorry Mr. Dane, but Ms. Endicott is not in the office at the moment."

He detected hesitance in her voice. "Thanks, I'll try later."

"That might be best, sir."

He hung up, conflicted about trying again. After joining him in that unearthly adventure, he figured she might be screening her calls, maybe afraid if she got back with him she'd be shot off somewhere—to another time or neighboring dimension.

He had another pressing issue to deal with and that was to locate his brother, the perfect distraction to force his head from the new rut Nikki inadvertently carved in his overworked mind.

An unusually strong feeling settled in the pit of his stomach when thoughts swung away from Nikki to Kyle. He hadn't talked to his brother in over a year. He became sore that Kyle hadn't called him. But he hadn't called Kyle either. Setting aside petty thoughts on whose negligence carried the most weight, he decided to make the call. Procrastination on two fronts had brought him to late Friday afternoon without accomplishing anything.

He guessed that Kyle should be off work, allowing for the two hour earlier time difference on the west coast, and might be a good time to catch him at home before making evening plans. Preparing to make the call as if it were his own evening out, he fed Buddy and threw together a bowl of leftover chips and a few stale crackers, popped the top of a small can of bean dip and called it a meal—the healthy vegetarian alternative. Had he cared to delve into it, the bulging roll around his waist came as a direct result of such stupid justifications. After hunger had been vanquished, he opened a bottle of wine and poured a glass brim-full.

Looking down at his little friend's wagging tail, it eased anxieties. "Someday, Ol' Bud, I'm gonna buy the good vino, the ten-buck-a-bottle stuff. Who knows? I might even buy a new car. What do you think of that?" Just the tone elicited a muffled woof, as the dog followed him. The little canine did a happy dance around his feet and the tap, tap, tap of nails on hard vinyl of the kitchen floor created genuine rhythm.

"Right now I need to find a phone number," he told the dog, as he rummaged through drawers, canisters and piles of papers scattered throughout the apartment. He remembered writing it down somewhere, once upon a time. "Humph. Well, ain't that just like me?" He chuckled.

Searching every stuffed cranny, amusement vanished and turned to aggravation by the amount of useless notes and memos he kept for no good reason, spilling from every box and container, even flagging from between books on the shelf. All those odd bits of information, yet he couldn't find Kyle's phone number anywhere.

As a last resort he booted up the computer, logged on to the Internet and found him listed in Coos Bay, Oregon. Even alone, a wave of embarrassment washed over him that he had to find his only sibling in the same manner someone might go about looking for an old classmate.

Heading for his favorite spot on the sofa, cordless phone in one hand and wine glass in the other, the phone rang. It startled him. He almost dropped it and clumsily found the talk button. "H'lo."

"Hey, big guy, I didn't make any plans for tonight. How about you?"

"Nikki. I thought you might not want to see me anymore."

"The thought crossed my mind more than once this week. The cold truth is I'm bored senseless. How about it? Any plans?"

"Don't you realize a man of the world, as I happen to be, has a date every night?"

She laughed. "Good to know you don't have anything to do." Guardedly, she said, "Right?"

He allowed her to dangle for a few seconds. "Nah. I don't have anything to do." It felt good talking to her again.

"Hey, if I buy a bottle of wine and come to your place, would you promise not to fire me off into some distant galaxy?"

"Is that cynicism I hear?"

"Hell, I thought it was pretty much in your face."

He let the crack slide. "I had the phone in my hand when you called. I was about to call Kyle and find out if he and his family are okay."

"Do you want me to wait until you've had a chance to talk to him?"

"Come on over. I think I prefer that you be with me when I talk to him. I'm feeling a little weird about it. I'll wait until you get here."

"You know," she said, "a girl might think a fella was getting serious if he wanted to introduce her to his family. Sort of... romantic... don't you think?"

"This is not exactly Sunday dinner with the Cleavers."

"See? What you just said... you're cynical, too." The phone clicked. She always needed to have the last word.

He finished the first glass of wine and on the way to the kitchen for another when the bell rang. Opening the door, there stood Nikki, lovely as ever. She had come directly from her office dressed in a business-like navy blue suit. She wore conservative medium heels. Nikki stood tall by most standards at five-eight. In those heels, he could look her straight in the eye. Feeling a wine glow, gazing into those brown eyes intoxicated him even more. *Whew. Settle down boy.*

Not waiting for an invitation, she breezed by, kicking off her shoes, clearly assuming an invitation to be a needless formality. "I hope you don't mind if I make myself comfortable."

He smiled and followed. "Please do." Having been sipping wine a bit too long when she arrived, he couldn't pull his eyes away from that fine looking rear-end of hers and didn't want to. It danced seductively as she glided across the room.

Whirling around, she poked a long fingernail in the center of his chest. "All right, pal, let's get something straight. I've thought so much this week about your weirdness that getting paperwork done was almost impossible. I couldn't concentrate on a damned thing, for God's sake."

"Is that why you didn't take my call?"

She poked his chest again. "Of course."

Glaring at the accusing finger, he frowned, as it painfully gouged his sternum.

"I still don't count myself among the believers, but it's difficult to disbelieve when I was in the middle of it with you. There still must be some explanation other than mystical hocus pocus better suited to graphic novels."

"I don't disagree. But what's your point?"

"The point is, Bucko, this crap scares hell out of me. But curiosity to know more is almost as strong." She smiled and draped a hand over his shoulder.

"Another fine point to be made is that I kinda like havin' ya back in my life, Jacky."

She hadn't called him Jacky since college and she's the only one that ever did. A nostalgic twinge dampened his eyes. Her rant had been nothing more than a blustery precursor to willingness to participate in his quest for knowledge. But would there be a string attached? She made it sound as if there might be. "Well, Nik, does that little speech mean I now have a partner exploring this... this *thing*?"

"Sure," she said, with a toss of her head, "My summer just wouldn't seem complete without a little magic."

His eyebrow went up. "Magic, huh?"

He poured wine and they sat close together on the sofa. He snatched Kyle's phone number from the end table and dialed. His brother didn't recognize the voice. It saddened Jack but didn't surprise him. "This is Jack... your brother. Remember me?"

"Well, I'll be damned," Kyle said. "This is certainly a shock. Where're you calling from?"

"I'm still here in Springfield. I never saw the need to move."

"If it hadn't been for Cary, I'd probably still be there, too."

"Didn't you live someplace else last year?"

"Roseburg. That's not far from here though. Cary's parents retired and we moved to Coos Bay to take over a small grocery store that's been in her family for a couple of generations. At the time it seemed like a better idea than breaking my back in the logging industry..." He paused abruptly, as if he wanted to say something else, but held back.

"Well, did it turn out to be a better idea?"

"The jury's still out. Logging has suffered. People are moving away looking for jobs elsewhere. The grocery business is off. With a daughter not even a year old and Cary expecting another child, our income has to go up, not down."

Jack felt responsible, blaming himself for not having stayed in touch. "Kyle, if I had the power or the money—"

"No, no Jack, don't misunderstand. I'm not asking for help and I'm certainly not the type to take it if you offered it."

"As long as you know you can depend on me in a clutch."

"Thanks. That means a lot."

Suddenly, his own difficulties seemed miniscule knowing that he likely only heard a fraction of the troubles Kyle faced. His brother couldn't know that he'd already sensed problems. Kyle needed to stay focused on the family—wife Cary, niece Melissa, and the baby on the way. He didn't need to be worrying about anything else. Jack's mind went into overdrive trying to think of ways to dance around the issue and learn what he needed to without obligating his brother. "Hey, bro, do you remember that girl I dated for a couple of years when I was in college?"

"I'm not sure that I do."

"Her name was Nikki. Nikki Endicott."

"Oh yeah, now I remember... Ms. Mouth. I recall how she acted like the boss of you, those few times I spoke to her on the phone when she was looking for you."

Jack laughed.

Nikki shook his elbow. "What'd he say? What'd he say?"

He looked at her but responded to Kyle. "Yeah, and *Ms. Mouth* is sitting right here."

She hit him on the shoulder, leaned close to the phone and in a loud voice, "Hey, Brat. I don't even know you."

Jack welcomed the mood-lightening interlude, making it easier to transition back to a serious subject. "Kyle, that last foster family you lived with; what were their names?"

"Butch and Audrey Jones, why?"

Kyle's tone indicated Jack may have veered into a touchy subject. He thought it best to tread lightly. "It's just that I saw a man that strongly resembled him. I thought it may have been him and I couldn't remember his name."

"Not likely. Audrey passed away in the spring and Butch moved out here. He's really turning into a pest, calling incessantly and trying to convince me that I owe him for all the money he and Audrey spent on me when I lived with them."

"He's harassing and stalking you? That's not just being a pest, Kyle. That's extortion... plain and simple."

"Oh well, it's nothing to lose sleep over. I keep blowin' him off. He's always been that way... just a little stranger now. That's all. I guess he might be losing it." He paused. "It's nothing to worry about though."

"Are you sure?"

"No worries."

Kyle's words didn't match the worried tone. The image Jack had seen of Butch Jones clearly showed a man capable of uncontrollable rage. "Be careful, Kyle."

"Sure. Why are you so concerned about Butch? You never knew him."

"Just call it brotherly intuition. I'm developing a bad feeling about that guy."

"Don't worry. I'll be fine."

"I'd better go, but you need to call me sometimes, too. Give Cary and Melissa my love. By the way, teach Melissa to say Uncle Jack."

"Take care." He hung up.

He reluctantly pulled the phone away from his ear, letting it dangle between fingertips. Details had been few, but enough to provide a chilling intuitive feeling when Kyle spoke of trouble with his foster father and what Jack already knew about the man. From what he witnessed, it wouldn't take much for Butch Jones' over-the-top temper to turn murderous. His gaze came away from the wall. He turned to Nikki. "There's something terribly wrong and that old man is playing a major role in it. I'm sure of it."

She pulled the phone from between his fingers and reached across to lay it on the table. "I think you'd better have a talk with Arthur. If you become agitated, no telling what might happen… or where or when you might end up. I don't want you triggering an ill-timed episode."

No doubt, had she not offered the advice, he would have stewed on possibilities, getting worked up and, possibly, creating something he couldn't control. But even as he looked at it objectively, instincts warned him that time was wasting. Some unseen force had begun pushing him to act, and soon. *How the hell do I do that impartially?*

Arthur had told him, "Trust your instincts because they run much deeper than intuition."

Did this odd feeling about Kyle mean anything? It might but, then again, maybe not. He growled and shook his head. *No, I have to believe. He's my brother.*

Aside from being the lone sibling, Kyle fathered his only other living blood relative on earth, Melissa. Soon, her unborn brother or sister would join her. That weighted the obligation in favor of acting to prevent a catastrophe, whatever it might turn out to be. Arthur Wainwright might be right about intuitive feelings being so much more. He wondered about altering a course of events that might create the very thing he wanted to avert. *What the hell should I do?*

He saw that Nikki had tensed, becoming uneasy that he might react regardless of assurance to the contrary. He leaned back, sipped wine and decided that using her as a sounding board might be the next best thing to action—no edicts, no demands, no snap decisions. They spent the remainder of the evening talking. She quizzed him about family life, his relationship with Kyle, and what he knew about Kyle's life in that last foster home. It proved therapeutic. He needed that; someone to listen and show an interest, no matter how disjointed his thoughts were. It showed a level of seriousness and, at the same time, proved she was one hell of a therapist.

Three times he paused to call Arthur, but the old guy was either not home or not answering. On the final call, Jack left a recorded message that he needed to speak to him right away. Slipping the phone into its cradle, a tingling sensation swept over him, suddenly thinking he'd already talked to Arthur and, perhaps, had forgotten the conversation until that instant. He remembered, or thought he did, that Arthur would be out of town until tomorrow evening, at which time Jack should be at his house at seven o'clock. It took a moment, but Jack came to the conclusion that he hadn't spoken with Arthur at all. But how could he have obtained that information? It just suddenly was there in his head.

He didn't mention it to Nikki. He knew there'd be plenty of strange things that she'd witness in the coming weeks that he might not be able to protect her from. *It might be better to keep a few things to myself.*

CHAPTER 9

Bolting upright in bed, Jack woke Saturday morning to booming thunder that rumbled off into the distance. He was muddle-headed thinking it might be something more serious than a thunderstorm. Clarity finally caught up. Releasing a held breath in a huff, he collapsed back, covering his head with a pillow and tried to ignore the noise that sounded as though he were beneath a bridge while a train passed overhead. Eventually, he gave up on the extra winks and rolled to face the bedroom window. Through a slit in the curtains above, he saw lightning spread web-like tentacles across the northwestern sky. He stared— too sleepy to care. Eyelids remained heavy, eyes bleary.

It looked as though Springfield was due welcome relief from the summer heat. It was blasphemous in the nation's heartland to speak badly of moisture during the summer. Plans could wait until the parched earth had had its fill. He yawned, sat up and parted the curtains just as a flash flickered across his face. The extended yawn ended with a throaty roar as he placed bare feet on cool floor tiles. *Okay, we need rain. But does it have to screw up my day?* "Oh well."

The aggravation of changing weather proved brief. It crossed his mind that Nikki had indeed become a partner and confidant. A smile stretched his sleepy, still-awakening face—optimism to start the day with. Life suddenly seemed manageable. Maybe things would turn out okay after all.

But a sense of gloom about Kyle colored those thoughts. *Why do I feel so damned apprehensive? I'm not sure anything is wrong.* Not only did a sense of foreboding settle in but also a strange feeling that he'd already failed at something.

I refuse to let these feelings have their way with me today. "Be gone with you." He fanned his arms like Merlin casting a spell. He placed a closed fist to his mouth, blew into it and opened it into the air as if releasing the bad feeling to fly away. *My imagination is running away with me. That's all… just running away.*

Now fully awake, he sprang to his feet, placed hands on hips, and performed torso twists, bending to touch his toes, or at least extend hands in that direction. The floor got a little farther from his fingertips every morning. Still, it didn't inspire him to do more.

He planned to visit with Arthur, as Nikki had suggested. As eccentric as Wainwright was, he'd be a good mentor—adept at helping navigate a maze that, as yet, had no basis in fact. Doubts lingered about the old man but one thing had become abundantly clear; without the old guy's help it would be like swatting mosquitoes in the dark while the pests sucked the energy right out of him.

Today would become the first day of a life's journey fraught with danger yet fascinating. Today, this precise point in his life would forever alter how he viewed the world. He knew this—just damn well did, but had no clue why so certain. Jack had never been religious but this so-called gift could not be a genetic anomaly. No drug, no surgical procedure and no incantation could create it. So, where did it come from? God? If so, why?

The nature of it required a slant in thinking toward the religious. It might make it easier to digest. A basis for faith had been laid. This thing seemed more spiritual than scientific anyway. It seemed something, or someone, not of this earth had designs on testing him for some purpose. And, clearly, it hadn't gotten underway yet. His skin crawled when he considered the down side—black magic. Why would that be any less believable? But the question arose: If it was an evil curse, who did it? And to what end? He was beginning to feel trapped in a fantasy world and had to pull his thinking out of that muck. Finally, he dismissed the black magic thing as too scary to even contemplate. But to believe God was responsible, then not so much. *Maybe God does exist.*

The day went well, going about weekly chores—a wonderfully mindless exercise. The weather deteriorated further. The guy on television said an approaching cool front would keep rain in the area all day and might become severe by sunset. It looked like a stormy night coming. Since Arthur expected him and Nikki at seven, Jack pushed up the schedule so they'd not be driving across town in stormy weather. The one sure thing in this plan-becoming was that it'd be impossible to surprise Arthur by arriving early. *He'll know when I know what I plan to do.* He chuckled and went about his business.

Later, after returning to his apartment from the grocery store, the last chore of the day, he showered and changed clothes. He saw no reason to dress beyond a favorite pair of faded blue jeans, red t-shirt and jogging shoes that he never jogged in. It appeared he might spend time in the rain anyway. Taking note of the sky as he left the apartment, the look of it made a drenching seem inescapable. It looked as the squall line would be arriving on time. The drive to Nikki's apartment was made quickly. He raced the weather, even passing a police car. The two local cops didn't even notice, clearly more interested in the darkening sky.

He trotted to her door and knocked. She immediately flung it open. Each time he saw her in different clothes, he was captivated all over again. She wore a white blouse buttoned up the front, tucked into a pair of snug and beltless designer jeans. Below that she had on white canvas deck shoes. Her hair was in a long ponytail revealing large, dangling silver hoop earrings. Those earrings and that dark hair, with a well-conditioned sheen, set off a beautiful face. She appeared ready for anything except the Governor's Ball. Although dressed and ready, she scolded him for arriving early as if she were embarrassed about being ready on time. It must have been a woman thing. They were out the door and on the way to Arthur's house.

A few freakishly large raindrops fell as they wheeled into Arthur's driveway. It escalated fast, falling heavier on the approach to the mansion. Jack sped up, trying to beat the downpour coming. Dark gray cloud-to-ground streaks a few hundred yards away moved in. It appeared that it might arrive about the same time they planned to get out of the car. *Murphy's freakin' law!*

He braked hard near the front door of the mansion. "Hurry, Nik. It's only going to get harder. Looking like a Chinese fire drill and less like a planned dash to the shelter of the portico, they ran flat-out zigzagging like that would somehow keep them drier.

The door swung open. There stood Wainwright wearing a God-awful Hawaiian shirt about two sizes too large hanging loose over baggy cargo shorts. Those shorts revealed skinny legs and bony knees, but well tanned ending at large shoeless feet. The picture implied a mad scientist visiting the set of a beach party movie, or maybe the Shire's tallest Hobbit trying to look cool.

"Come in, come in," he said. "Hurry kids before you get any wetter. Isn't this rain magnificent?"

"I suppose so... as long as a funnel doesn't drop out of those clouds." Jack shook accumulated drops from his dark hair, reminding him that he was about two weeks overdue for a haircut. It hung over the tips of his ears. He wiped dampness from his face.

"Like Maigo once said—"

"Maigo? Who's that?" Nikki asked. She daubed her face gently with a long shirtsleeve, trying to preserve the makeup.

"Maigo is an Asian friend of mine, also my guide and instructor into all things metaphysical."

Following Arthur down the hall, Jack placed fingertips lightly on Nikki's forearm and whispered, "You see, even Arthur needs someone to show him the way occasionally."

"So true," he said, again demonstrating nothing thought or said got past him. "Maigo once said 'life without surprises would be lifeless.' This was his explanation of why psychics, seers and soothsayers are not allowed to see everything."

They walked behind Arthur and, as he spoke, Jack's other hand brushed a tread on the stairs that rose beside them. His fingers came away dust covered. He brushed it away as they passed through the now-familiar door into the library. Jack headed for a chair and so did Nikki. "Okay," he said, looking up at their still-standing host. "So, you don't care if a funnel drops and destroys property and people? Is that it?"

"The point is, friend, I wouldn't wish a tornado on anyone, but if it happens... it happens. Then we'll deal with it."

Nikki nodded and shrugged tacit acceptance of the oversimplified wisdom.

Arthur clapped his hands and said in a lively voice, "Well, we don't need to be wasting time philosophizing. We have important work to do." His more childlike persona bubbled up fast.

"So, you're aware?"

"Oh yes. Through you, I've seen a future event that you've only sensed. I do wish you'd open up your mind and see these things for yourself." He paused. "Maybe in time, you'll—"

"Focus Arthur. What have you seen?"

"I'm afraid a man… your brother I believe, will have an attempt made on his life by an elderly man who did not appear mentally stable."

Jack jumped to his feet, prepared to fly into action. "That elderly man is Butch Jones, his foster father! I'm sure of it." He paced to and fro in choppy steps when it occurred to him that he had no notion what to do about it.

"Calm down. Remember what I told you…" he said, gesturing Jack back to his seat. "…Should we do nothing, this vision will be the future. It will come to pass. But, since it's a future event, we have the unique opportunity to *possibly* effect a change." He stabbed the air with a finger. "I repeat, *possibly*. Your brother's future doesn't necessarily need to end in tragedy."

"What do we need to do?"

"I saw the event. It was a shooting with a small caliber pistol. I saw it through your subconscious." He dropped into the chair across from them. "This means somewhere below the conscious level, you know the exact time this is going to take place."

"Do you think it would be best to confront the old man?" He fidgeted. "Maybe we can thwart his attempt before the demented son-of-a-bitch has a chance to act. Whaddaya think?"

"Honestly, this is virgin territory for me, too." He stared at his wiggling toes—hands on his knees drumming his fingers. "I see these events and aware how it all works, but my abilities stop there. You, compadre, can affect the change because of a rare ability to move freely into, among, and out of many planes of existence. Keep in mind this time and place we're now standing in is only one of those planes."

He tapped his lips with a finger, rose and paced among sparse furnishings that exuded neglected elegance. Although questions hung ominously, like those storm clouds outside, it didn't seem prudent to interrupt whatever plan the old guy might be putting together. Arthur meandered in a big circle through the library, so lost in thought he appeared to have forgotten there were other people in the room. He straightened a book on a shelf, although many others remained askew. He drifted toward a world globe and wiped dust from it although a dusty film covered everything else around it. His actions were independent of whatever was on his mind.

Nikki rose and moved next to where Jack sat, uncomfortable and nervous as the intensity of the thunderstorm swelled into violent rumbles and a howling gale. Standing so near, he suddenly realized just how creepy the surroundings must have appeared to her at that moment. The natural coolness of this spacious room, the noisy wind outside, the lightning visible through the window and the unnatural reason they happened to be in Arthur's house.

Arthur whirled around. "I think I've given birth to a plan."

Nikki giggled, shaded by nervousness. "You seem to have endured the labor pains with no ill effects."

Arthur laughed.

Jack frowned and rolled his eyes. "Okay, what's the plan? Do I need to buy a bullet-proof vest?"

"No, nothing like that." He returned to his chair and sat. "I believe we need only to observe for now. This may allow time to pull from your subconscious the exact time this would-be tragedy is going to take place."

"That's all you have?" The lack of depth annoyed him. "What the hell do you mean 'just observe'?" He slid aggressively to the edge of his seat. "Aren't we sure this is going to happen?"

"Absolutely. If we do nothing, it will, but—"

"Damn it, man!" Jack slapped his forehead with the heel of his hand and slung a wild gesture in Arthur's direction. "There are no buts! Observing is doing nothing. And doing nothing is not an option. Are we going to sit idle and watch him be shot?" He suddenly had second thoughts about Arthur. The old bastard may well have been just as crazy as originally thought.

"Jack," Arthur said in a fatherly way, "Calm down. Hear me out. As far as I can determine, the only sure way to stop this from becoming inevitable is to murder Butch Jones right now. Are you prepared to do that?"

"No, but—"

"Another idea," he added without taking a breath as he slid forward to match Jack's posture, "would be to tell Oregon authorities that I had a vision and you sensed that your brother was going to be shot at some undetermined point in the future. Does this sound like something you'd believe if you were a cop?"

"Well… no…" The murkiness of his wisdom began to clear. Jack slid back in the chair.

Despite eccentricities, he and Nikki discovered intelligence in the man most of the world wouldn't recognize if they did witness it. Jack's trust in him ratcheted up. Still, he couldn't get past thinking the old man might be insane.

CHAPTER 10

The storm outside Arthur's home raged. Jack watched the old guy quietly thinking about the dilemma they faced. Nikki remained quiet, too, but judging by the closed body language, hugging herself and legs crossed, her thoughts may have been a little darker than Wainwright's. Jack gave Arthur time to sort through his thoughts. So, he let his mind drift to other things.

As careers go, his job as a feature reporter for a local rag could be a mind-wasting expenditure of time—the bi-weekly paycheck the only upside. The job at The Journal was the result of career indecision solely to keep groceries and dog food coming in while he waited for fortune to find him. Now he looked back and wondered why his confidence had been so high in that regard. Did he sense something about his future that included wealth? Regardless how he felt about the job, he believed himself a capable reporter and writer.

His take on the art of living might occasionally change, but he always maintained an easygoing approach in spite of where mood took him. Most days he could describe his life as a thick layer of monotony smeared like peanut butter over a deep base of dull—unaware that he wasn't happy. And that's the way of it, until all this mind-bending crap began.

Now he felt caged. Whether a man walks into prison or is thrown in against his will, once the door is slammed and locked, he's trapped either way. Now that he thought about his life and career, Jack resented having been made aware of his aimless drift into the future. He longed for a return to blissful ignorance.

Short on cash, the dead end job was on his mind because of what Arthur had said, "Pay attention to those odd feelings because it's more than simple intuition." Maybe the passive confidence that wealth would find him was a byproduct of this so-called talent—maybe he subliminally realized it long ago.

The musing was idle because his career didn't matter under the present circumstances. Everything had changed. Dull no longer defined him. Life barreled along with such velocity he felt he needed to be hanging on to something. For all their combined intelligence, Arthur and Nikki had no more idea than he did about how far he could take this thing. The difference was, they wanted to find out—he didn't.

He wondered if a mental illness existed in which a person was aware of being out of control yet couldn't stop it and woke every morning terrified to still be in their own skin. He wouldn't go so far as to describe himself as terrified, but he became uneasy every morning once he remembered what he could do.

A mind-boggling amount has been written and publicized regarding psychics, mediums, time and dimensions. His interest in all of it had grown exponentially in recent days. Up until he met Arthur, it never crossed his mind—filed in a wee part of his brain along with science fiction, religious myth, fantasies, fairies, leprechauns, ghosts, goblins, mummies, zombies and folklore.

Jack understood why devotees of any spiritual discipline might want to remain under the radar, drawing no attention—believers as a matter of quiet faith. But to a small town middle-America boy, raised in a conservative redneck quasi-Christian environment, all of this was like stepping directly into a B-movie and he was the freakin' star and hadn't been given a script.

Before Arthur had clammed up to think things through, the three of them had been discussing plans, but kept coming up with more questions than answers. The best idea was little more than an experiment in which a window into Butch Johnson's world to observe his actions would be attempted.

That made Nikki nervous. It wasn't cool enough to cause that kind of shivering. Her catty sense of humor vanished. Jack quickly missed her tart-tongued sarcasm. Nikki just wasn't herself without it. Maybe she steeled resolve to face the madness yet to come. Jack chose to believe that and look upon her nervousness as positive. He sat in the large wingback chair, lightning flashing through a tall arched window without curtains in Arthur Wainwright's mansion.

Arthur appeared ominous, as harsh high-contrast light threw blinking dark shadows across his sharp slender features. Since he wasn't smiling at the moment, he looked evil. He finally began to emerge from his ponderings.

"Jack, during those times images formed, what were you thinking?"

"Nothing in particular. Pictures just formed that spawned a thought, usually about my brother."

"Images first then came the thoughts?"

"Yeah, I guess that's right. But general agitation over unrelated things tended to precede the images."

"What I want you to do is close your eyes and create a mind's-eye image of Kyle's *foster father*."

As Nikki sat in the chair next to him, he wriggled down and relaxed. After scant seconds, a montage of mental imagery swirled, recollections of Butch Johnson at the center. He remembered nothing important or relevant, so all memories were snippets of someone he really never knew. No single thing emerged to guide him into a locked-in and clear mental image.

"I sense your psychic energy increasing," Arthur whispered.

Images of the man continued coming in bits and pieces. He tried narrowing his focus but couldn't. Childhood memories of the man were just too vague.

"The vibrations leveled off and faded," Arthur said.

After a few more seconds, Jack opened his eyes to the same thing he saw before they closed, a scary-looking Arthur Wainwright with lightning flashes streaking across his face, no milky white glow, no chill. "What am I doing wrong?"

Nikki appeared relieved. She sighed and fell back into her chair. Her arms remained tightly folded, occasionally rubbing one shoulder or the other. One leg draped over the other and that foot spiraled around to hook behind the leg.

She didn't have to say a word to realize she wasn't at all certain she wanted him to succeed in conjuring another episode. He wondered where the breaking point on her courage lay.

"I just happened to think," Arthur said, wagging a long slender finger, "the previous times you saw Butch Johnson was a by-product of other thoughts in which your brother was the central figure. Kyle was the first image you saw. Right?"

"Right."

He paced once in a tight circle. "It's possible your abilities cannot, at this point of your development, access anyone other than family. Is Kyle your only living full-blood family member?"

"Yeah."

Arthur grinned. "Okay then… let's go with that.

"So, are you saying Kyle by virtue of being blood kin is the key or, possibly, the only reason?"

"Don't know yet, just a theory. But if not the main reason, he must have been the catalyst." Arthur turned away briefly and whirled back. "The more I think about this, it makes sense. Consider this: Siblings have a lifelong connection as the result of a common birth, both coming from the same genetic blend. This is true in all families. But, add a dash of strange, a pinch of absurd, and a generous helping of conflict to the family soup and… voila! We have a mind connection beyond normal boundaries." Arthur flashed a grin. Confidence and humor collided.

Nikki chuckled. Her amusement seemed to be out of courtesy. Nonetheless, the poor humor eased her anxieties. She relaxed a bit. Her arms came unfolded and now lay on the armrests of her chair.

"It makes sense," Arthur said. "You had an untapped natural ability but circumstances forced an issue whether you wanted it to surface or not."

"I'm still in the dark about how I caused it… you know… to make it start up in the first place."

"You, my friend, probably did nothing." His fascination and voice moved into a higher range. "That's what I mean by a *family* connection. Your ability may be your birthright. Your brother is troubled beyond anything he's experienced before, and that turmoil found its way to you. It's logical. He dialed, and you answered but neither of you outwardly attempted to communicate. You're detecting the disturbed mental waves he's emitting… or vibrations if you prefer, and the frequency of that agitation was like him rubbing a magic lamp. You're the lamp." Arthur's voice stepped up another octave. "Who knows? You may be your brother's Genii and he inadvertently called you up. And, like a Genii, you didn't have any say over when or where it happened."

Nikki frowned. "I keep trying to rationalize this from a psychological standpoint. I can't. It doesn't make sense. None of my textbooks cover this stuff."

Jack nodded. "Good point. Arthur, does documentation exist on any of this?" Or, are you just putting on a show of theory?"

"Well… yeah. It makes a wonderfully intriguing story. Don't you think?"

Jack didn't know whether to kick him or kiss him. His quirky little jaunts off into clown town always seemed ill timed. He slid forward to the edge of the chair. "Come on, Arthur, focus."

Arthur stopped grinning. "Sorry." He drummed his lips with fingertips for a moment. "Although these abilities are well known by small groups worldwide, documentation is scarce since it would be looked upon by the general population as fictitious anyway. That means the trial and error method is necessary and we need to determine your personal limitations. I'm afraid that even with a guidebook we'd still be feeling our way along. No two humans are exactly alike and just as personalities vary, so do abilities among the exceptional."

Jack rose and turned to face the large arched glass and the light display offered up beyond the curtainless window by the thunderstorm. "I think I can comprehend sensitivity to a family member's disturbed brain waves, that's common among twin siblings and between mothers and their children, but I still don't understand how the visual then physical connection is made." A loud clap of thunder rattled the window. Jack returned to his chair, and the three of them in unison moved chairs closer together, like pioneers circling the wagons.

"The best way I can think of to explain the process when the link is formed is by way of an analogy," Arthur said. "But first, let me set it up: Let's say you detect his vibrations. It's just an uneasy feeling you can't quite put your finger on. You may not even be conscious of those vibrations, but a quick mental image pops into your head without even having a thought of him beforehand."

"That's exactly how it happens."

"But his thought patterns are not strong enough to do anything more than create a subliminal connection, tenuous at best. You perceive it only as intuition." Arthur rose to again pace before us. While looking to the ceiling, he said, "But your mind is different. You absorb vibrations and strengthen them like… well, like an electrical transformer changes a weak incoming electrical current before sending it on down the line. This is what takes it to the next level. It begins by connecting then matching the incoming frequency. Your ability intensifies it to maintain and strengthen the link. For you this connection is not just a mind thing... it only begins that way. It's the mind/heart connection that creates a highway, a portal, a bridge, a way for you to get from here to there. Strong enough to walk on, man! The vibrations are that fast and that dense. Your heart takes over and the exponential rise into an even higher frequency range begins, until the speed of it hits that point the white light is created."

Standing straight, he again paced. His thoughtful meandering took him to the hearth of a large fireplace. There, he absently traced the design of a carved fleur-de-lis on the mantle with a fingertip.

After a few seconds to absorb the idea, Jack wrung his hands. "That makes a scary amount of sense. Even scarier is that I think I know where you're going with this."

"Good. Then I'll move on. Now for the analogy: Let's say you're standing on a beach watching the surf. But it's not water. It's thoughts coming at you in waves. Your mind establishes a connection with the energy of that rolling surf. The power of your heart begins to tighten those waves closer and closer until the separation between them is indistinguishable, forcing them higher into a single large tidal wave. Now you've created a frequency high enough, tight enough, and strong enough to support the mass of a human body. Then it becomes a simple matter of grabbing your surfboard and riding the waves."

Jack shook his head and offered an indulgent grin. "Only you would tell it that way. You're a piece of work. You know that?"

He shrugged. "Of course. Furthermore, just like in surfing, the waves move in directions you cannot change, nor can you alter the wake left behind, but you certainly can dictate where the wake is going. As you become more adept at riding them, you'll learn how to steer to destinations of your choosing in the time and space of whomever you have a mental connection with."

"Are you capable of any of this?"

"My mind generates vibrations only strong enough to view events, past, present and future." He returned to his chair and dropped. "Unfortunately, I'm confined to our present physical dimension. Quite literally, I don't have the heart for it. As I have explained before, everyone on earth vibrates at different levels, in different ranges. This is what determines the color of your personal aura. The only advantage I have over you is a certain mastery and knowledge of my limitations. Plus, Maigo my spiritual guide has taught me awareness of other disciplines. This is how I'm able to speak with some authority on things I personally have never experienced."

Nikki took an exaggerated breath and blew it out through circled lips. "Well guys, don't you think it's about time to quit talking and start doing?"

He slapped his bony knees. "Quite right."

Jack saw that she still rubbed dimpled gooseflesh on her arms, but apparently had become eager to get on with it, to dive in and get the shock over with. He offered a reassuring smile. If that's the way she wanted it, so be it. "Let's do it."

"Remember," Arthur cautioned, "if you physically put yourself and anyone moving with you into a past event, you and they can be harmed or even killed but you *can't change* what has already transpired. Don't be tempted to stop or alter something you'll ultimately have no control over. Conversely," he quickly added, pausing for dramatic effect, "this is not at all true of a current or future event. You *can* change the course of events that are occurring presently, or have not happened yet, and you *will be* remembered as someone who popped in and disappeared. This could screw up someone's head for the rest of their lives. It's best to remain out of sight if at all possible."

"I'll try to remember."

"Stay cool. Be slow to react to things you see and hear if you feel compelled to react at all."

Jack began relaxing, leaning back and allowing his head to sink into the soft cushion of the wingback chair. He concentrated on breathing deep and even. After a moment the sound of it seemed as loud as air being forced through a pipe.

Nikki moved behind his chair and stood next to Arthur. "Whatever happens, I'm with you," she whispered.

As Jack's eyes closed, he was aware of lightning flashes coming through the window.

"Now," Arthur began in low monotone, "think about that last conversation you had with Kyle. Concentrate on the part when your suspicion hit a high point."

Jack took a breath and released a measured exhale. "Okay." Thoughts immediately went to that phone call.

Arthur became excited but still spoke in hushed tones. "You're doing great."

As Arthur said it, Jack felt the temperature drop. A chill swept over him. He detected a flash of lightning. But, it wasn't a flash at all. Instead, it was a constant glare pressing his eyelids.

"Oh shit," Nikki hissed. Her nails dug into Jack's shoulder.

He opened his eyes to see the same image as was in his thought, projected in front of them. Kyle stood by the phone, holding the receiver to an ear with his right hand, the left hand resting on his hip.

"You've done it. For the first time, you've directed a thought at a specific event in another time and another space, accessing it with your mind and the power of your heart."

Nikki's fingernails gouged his shoulder, but he was only peripherally aware of it.

"Can you hear what Kyle is saying?"

It wasn't until Arthur asked the question that Jack realized Kyle's lips were moving. "No. I can't."

"We must join the vision in that time and space to determine what is happening."

Nikki loosened her grip, as though she had finally accepted that her senses were not playing tricks. In nervous vibrato, she said, "Do we all go, or just Jack?"

"We can all go," he said, rubbing the friction of building excitement between his palms. His childlike persona was taking over. "You must direct your thoughts toward the doorway in that darkened far corner of the room. Wherever your mind is focused, that's where we'll end up. We must not be seen. Since this is a past event, it's for our protection, not Kyle's. We don't want to panic him into grabbing a gun and shooting us, or… something like that." Arthur patted Jack's shoulder. "Let's go."

Arthur and Nikki stepped around the chair, flanking him. Jack rose slowly because, as yet, it wasn't clear what might break the link with the image suspended in the air before them bathed in that soft white light. He didn't want to lose it. Arthur and Nikki huddled at his back, bodies touching.

Arthur gently patted his shoulder. "Are you focused?"

Jack directed all mental energy toward the dark corner of that room where the dream-like scene took place—a moving picture contained within a transparent glow.

The three, surrounded by the same circle of light, stepped forward. Nausea swept over him after only three steps.

"The queasiness is our bodies reacting to changes at the sub-atomic level," Arthur said. "It should only last until we've arrived in that time and space."

The temperature changed. The transitional light disappeared. Different smells became apparent and the air temperature was drier and warmer than in Arthur's study. Jack saw that he succeeded in guiding them to a doorway in a bedroom facing the living room. The place he'd focused his attention on—the exact spot. Bright sunlight beamed in tight focused rays from every crack in the drawn curtains giving them advantage of deep shadows where they stood off to the side.

"Shh. Don't move," Arthur said in a breathy whisper.

Nikki held Jack's upper arm with both hands from behind and peaked around at Kyle with the phone to his ear.

Kyle said, "Butch and Audrey Jones. Why?" After a pause, Kyle pinched the top of his nose furrowed his brow and responded, "That's not likely. Audrey passed away back in the spring and Butch moved out here. He's really turning into a pest. He keeps calling, trying to convince me that I owe him for all the money he and Audrey spent on me when I was living with them."

Watching his brother tugged his heart. At the same time it was creepy witnessing a phone conversation he'd had with his brother yesterday. He successfully had transported himself and two others over a thousand miles from Arthur's mansion to a point in time twenty-four hours before. He couldn't afford to dwell on it—not at the moment. He had to concentrate on a tragedy that hadn't happened yet and figure out what it would be and then how to prevent it. He now had the opportunity to witness nuances of Kyle's side of the conversation that might provide clues.

Kyle said, "Melissa," followed quickly by, "I promise I will. See ya."

He recognized the end of the conversation. Beyond this moment, he had no knowledge of events. Now, he saw what had happened after he'd hung up the phone.

A pregnant woman entered the room. It must have been Cary. She walked into view holding a toddler in pink overalls, Melissa.

"Should I have told him about the assault warrant on Butch?" Kyle asked her.

It seemed obvious whatever he grappled with clouded his judgment. He needed confirmation that he'd done the right thing. He turned to face her.

Cary considered the question. "No," she said and paused. "No, I don't think so. It's probably better he doesn't know. Maybe the police will find the old man tonight or tomorrow and you can tell your brother the story afterwards. There's no use worrying him. We don't even know if we have reason to worry."

"I'm sure your right... as usual." He sighed with a faint smile. He took a quarter turn in Jack's direction, just far enough to reveal a large bandage on his cheek with a swollen bruise radiating upward from beneath it and disappearing in his hairline.

Jack flinched. *That old sonofabitch has already attacked him.* He ground his teeth.

"Beans," Arthur whispered.

"What are you talking about?" Jack hissed through clenched teeth, as his face went from rubicund to crimson.

"Just think about beans, that's all... just beans."

A wave of nausea swept over him. They were back at their starting point, the study in Arthur's house.

"Beans!" He spun belligerently to face Arthur. "What the hell does that have to do with anything?"

"Absolutely nothing. You needed to break your concentration on *that* moment and *that* place," Arthur said with an easy shrug as he sat down. "You lost objectivity. Strong emotion can be your worst enemy." He looked to Nikki. "And ours. When you began thinking about beans and tried to determine its significance you couldn't make the correlation. That became our ticket home."

The storm raged outside. The formidable structure, that was Arthur's home, all but eliminated concern over its violent power. It was noisy and occasionally made rafters groan high overhead, but there was safety in the massive stone and beamed structure.

Jack tried to digest what had happened. It was his first taste of traveling to a different time purposely. A glance at his watch indicated they had certainly spent time standing in Kyle's house. But it was within a different time frame. The clock on the fireplace mantle of Arthur's library was now five minutes behind the time on his watch. They were five minutes older than the library clock indicated. The true passage of personal time would have to be marked by the timepiece he wore. It was odd to think that he could live out his life in another time while using only the fraction of a second in his own time. At the very least, it could mean a very long Saturday evening.

"You know, a girl really has to have a strong constitution to be your friend." Nikki scooped up his hand. "Tell me, does it make your head ache to think that hard?" She winked.

It seemed the short hiatus on caustic humor was over. Her wit and presence comforted him as he looked into her eyes, cupping her hand and feeling the buzz of a romantic connection. It turned into an awkward moment. It wasn't the time. Jack cleared his throat, looked elsewhere, dropped her hand, and walked away.

"The next step," Arthur said, "is to determine the point in time Mr. Johnson might consider ideal for an attack. Do either of you have ideas to share?"

Nikki raised a hand, like a schoolgirl looking for recognition.

"Go ahead. Please share."

At first timid, she said, "I think it's important to remember that even though the old man is deranged, his ability make a detailed plan could actually be sharpened beyond normal limits for the same reasons he is deviant in other ways." As she spoke, professional confidence grew. "You see, sometimes a mental deficiency in one area creates an advanced capacity in another. Under no circumstance can we underestimate his ability to choose the ideal time and place. And, for God's sake, we certainly can't misjudge the slick precision he might be able to employ to carry out his plan."

"Excellent point," Arthur said.

"Since we heard Kyle say that an assault warrant had been issued, wouldn't it be safe to assume the police are watching the house?" Jack asked.

"Yeah, that's right," she said. "So if Kyle and his family stay indoors until Monday, they'll probably be all right until then."

"Well... maybe. But even if he has someone to work the store over the weekend, he'll still have to go to work Monday morning."

"I think that's the time we should be concerned with," Arthur said. "He'll probably be safe this weekend. And he'll probably be okay driving to the store Monday morning, too."

Nikki frowned. "I'm not so sure about being safe enroute to work."

"You may be right. Don't know for sure. But logic dictates consideration of the outstanding warrant. Johnson's license number will have been distributed to every policeman in the county by then. It's reasonable to believe he'd be stopped on sight; inference being Kyle would be safe at least until he made it to the store."

"If what you're saying should turn out true," she said, "the old man might find a hiding place near the store and wait to surprise him there."

Arthur spun away, hands clasped to his back. He struck a somewhat melodramatic pose, eyes focused on a cobweb laced through a high chandelier, waving gently with the slightest push of air. "The next step, kids, is for us to help determine what thoughts Jack must have that will take us to that specific point in the future."

"I've never seen the store Kyle and Cary inherited. How do I concentrate on something I've never seen?"

"I think if your connection happens to be with your brother's thoughts, then you should concentrate on him, his livelihood, and Monday morning," she said. "You might get a picture of the store through him. Kyle is your portal. It would seem you can't do this without him, without that family connection."

Arthur clapped his hands. "Bravo! I couldn't have stated it better myself. Now we have to see if it's possible for Jack to put those thoughts together in a way that will access it."

Jack's cynicism came back. He couldn't understand how to develop a mental image of something he'd never seen.

Arthur wagged an accusing finger. "No negative thoughts. You must be confident or failure will be a self-fulfilling prophecy."

"What are you talking about?" she asked.

"His faith is wavering," he said.

"Humph." *You're a lot more perceptive than I am,* Jack thought.

"Yes. I know," he said.

Nikki looked at Jack and back to Arthur. "What the hell are you two talking about? That disjointed conversation made no sense at all."

Jack felt obligated to come to her defense. "It's okay. Don't forget, he reads minds. I can't hide anything from this guy."

"True." Arthur grinned and tapped the end of his nose with a fingertip. "Now back to business. Just moments ago you accomplished it by directing thoughts to a specific place and time. The only difference now is that your focus should be forward, not back."

"That makes sense." He let his head fall back in the chair preparing to conjure a mental picture.

"Think of Kyle. Keep asking yourself: Where is the store? How will it appear Monday morning? You must attempt to channel it from Kyle's perspective." Arthur's voice trailed off, leaving it quiet in the room.

Jack closed his eyes.

The only sound was an occasional creak caused by gusting winds.

During a moment when there was no sound at all an image of Kyle appeared in his mind. The chill set in. He opened his eyes to a white glow surrounding a transparent scenario projected just ahead. Both travel partners moved in close, blending with the aura within the light so they could study the vision, too.

"That doesn't look like a grocery store," Nikki said.

The door of the building abruptly opened. Kyle appeared beside Cary. She held Melissa.

"That must be Kyle's house," Arthur said. "Yes, there's an outside view of that large window the light was streaming through during our visit. The house must face west."

Nikki relaxed and stepped back. "How could you be thinking of a grocery store and get a house?"

"I'm not sure. I just tried to think of Kyle and going to work."

"Your thoughts must be specific," Arthur said. "Don't think about him *going* to work, but *at* work. You must break the link with this connection and try again."

Jack turned his back on the vision, but it just moved one-hundred-eighty degrees and remained visible directly ahead of him in the opposite direction. Kyle was getting in his car, waving at Cary.

"Jack, think of something else."

He moved a step or two in Nikki's direction and put a hand on each cheek. The glow faded away. The chill was replaced with the natural warmth of the room, maybe a few degrees warmer in that space between the two of them.

Nikki grabbed his hand and patted it patronizingly. "Now I know what I'm good for, a distraction."

"I can always depend on you to break the silence."

Arthur giggled. "It looks like your job in this adventure is assured, Nikki."

She arrogantly flipped her hair. "I think I can adequately fill the role." She paused for show. "Okay. I accept. It'll be my job to distract and break silences. Obviously, my years of training and professional expertise will be of little value."

"Let's get back to what I need to do to get this right."

"You, dear boy, just need to be specific in your thoughts." He put his palms together, as if praying. But it was a plea for specificity. "If you want to see a grocery store, think grocery store. Of course, your brother will still need to be the central figure."

Nikki moved around to get in his face. "Get it right, Stud." She poked her index fingers in his two front belt loops and yanked him close.

He stared dumbly. *This mind thing is crazy. Here I am, a mental giant of some sort and I can't direct a simple thought.*

"Think about it," Arthur said, "even though it wasn't exactly what we were looking for, you conjured a vision of a future event. We saw something that would not be happening for over one full day."

That notion sobered Jack and brought a sudden end to self-deprecation.

Nikki moved her hands from belt loops to his chest, gently guiding him backwards into the chair. He sat down. This time, he drew a mental picture of Kyle and superimposed that image over a building and everything began happening much quicker than before. The chill and then the glow hit within seconds of his butt hitting the chair.

"Jesus, Jack!" She jumped back.

Arthur became excited. "You did that so quick I didn't even detect the rise in energy first." Apparently he didn't see the need to be quiet and soothing in tone any longer.

The store didn't appear the way Jack thought it would, barely larger than a convenience store. He expected a supermarket. It was something between those extremes—a small grocery store set in an older neighborhood on a tree-lined street. Jack guessed most of their customers were within walking distance. The exterior was horizontal clapboard siding with puckered and peeling white paint in need of repair in spots. The roof was faded red corrugated metal with occasional rust streaks. The sign over the front display window was the odd exception. It appeared relatively new with big round Coca Cola emblems on each end. In bold block letters it read: K & C Grocery and Market. He assumed that stood for Kyle and Cary. Hand-painted posters on white butcher paper adorned the display window touting specials. There was a homey look to it. It was no wonder Kyle struggled to make a go of it. It seemed idyllic and worth the effort.

"In a residential area like that, there are many fences, shrubs, trees and houses. The old man could be hiding anywhere," Nikki said.

"Arthur, do you think it's necessary we be in a specific place or position to return safely to our present time and place?"

"No. There are no portals, warps, cracks or anything like that. We'll be in that time and place as long as you want us to be. Once your mind returns to this room, in this house, on this night, then we will return with you. It makes no difference if we're standing by that grocery store or at the bottom of a river. All that counts is where your head is at, so to speak."

"What if we become separated?"

"That might be a problem."

"It makes sense," Nikki said. "If it's necessary we're close enough to touch you to get there, then it's logical that we must be just as close to get back."

"Right," Arthur said. "If we're wandering through that neighborhood searching for the old man, Jack doesn't need to know where we are, but we certainly need to know where he is and be able to get near him quick in order to return with him. Simply put, Ms. Endicott, he's our ride home."

"It's time. Let's go look for a demented old man," she said. As she moved in close to Jack, Arthur did the same.

A few quick steps, a flash of light, quickly passing nausea, and they opened their eyes to a gray day. Mist floated in the air—typical for the Pacific Northwest. They stood by a backyard fence. Jack saw the small grocery store about fifty feet away on this quiet, tree-lined street. Birds sat in the quasi-protection of nearby trees singing as though it was sunny—a comfortable Norman Rockwell look to it all.

Arthur pointed to the limited parking area around the store. "I believe if he's hiding nearby, the old man will be quite close to wherever Kyle parks his car. I don't think it'll be necessary to lose sight of each other, so let's not." He shot us both a warning glance. "This is for our safety, of course."

"Yeah, don't you dare get out of my sight," she said, slapping Jack's arm. She looked around. "There's an alley right over there running down the center of this block behind the store. I bet your brother parks behind it. Customer parking is pretty limited up front. Don't you think that'd be the best place to begin a search?"

Jack nodded agreement. "I'll cut straight through to the alley behind this fence. Arthur, why don't you walk left to the intersection, entering the alley on the other side of that house? Nikki you take off to the right, go around the store and into the alley from that direction. But don't dawdle; keep moving so the time we'll be out of sight of one another will be brief. We'll make a broad sweeping circle toward the store and meet there."

Nikki gave a quick salute and started toward the store while Arthur walked away in the opposite direction, both moving slow and deliberate, scanning the area for anything out of the ordinary.

In the meantime, Jack cut toward the alley beside the fence, adjacent to the store's parking lot. Walking along and searching, he thought on Arthur's warning not to lose sight of each other but he couldn't see any other way to get this done. That's when it happened. He saw the man he'd come to know as Butch. "Hey you!"

The older man stiffened and began walking away, as he held a stare on Jack.

"Wait a minute. I just want to talk to you."

He began running toward the cross street at the end of the block. Jack tried not to lose sight of him.

Johnson turned in the direction Arthur should have been coming from, but Jack couldn't see him, just Johnson reacting to his friend's presence. Jack picked up the pace and ran harder trying to catch up.

The guy abruptly turned and sprinted across the street.

As soon as Butch Johnson bolted, Jack knew beyond doubt the worst of his fears would be coming true. His brother's life was indeed in danger. He thought of nothing else. "Stop! I just want to ask you some questions!" He ran flat-out after him into the street.

That's when he heard Arthur. "Jack! Look out!"

His head snapped back in time to see a car heading toward him, going into a dead skid.

Jack leaped. But the evasive act came late. The bumper clipped his ankle and he landed on the hood of the car banging his head hard. The pain was intense.

He rolled off the hood, landing on his feet just as the car came to a complete stop. He saw Arthur running in his direction.

His head began to spin. He became dizzy. Vision blurred. His knees buckled and he went down.

Arthur knelt beside him and slid a hand under his head. As the world faded to black, the last thing he heard was Arthur saying, "Don't lose consciousness. Stay with me."

CHAPTER 11

Jack woke to the hollow sound of his own breathing. *Why am I flat on my back? What happened?*

"Can you hear me?"

The question seemed to come from far away and meant for someone else.

"Jack, are you okay?"

Jack? The name was unfamiliar. Something cool and damp brushed over and pressed his cheek, swiping his forehead. It felt good, almost sensual. He became excited as the vision of a woman floated through his awakening mind—tall, slender, with long dark hair. A familiar face, but whose was it?

"Wake up, Jack. Are you in pain?" The voice quite suddenly seemed closer.

Light slaps smacked each of his cheeks. He opened his eyes. As vision cleared, it was not the face he expected to see. Instead, he looked into a not-so-attractive male face coming into focus. Memories flooded in—but not all.

Arthur soothed his face as he lay on the floor.

Jack panicked and tried to sit up but fell back when a sharp pain bolted up his back into his head like a jolt of electricity had collided with the top of his skull. It nauseated him.

"Where does it hurt? Is anything broken?"

Jack rolled his head back and forth. "I don't think so." Another shooting pain streaked. He groaned. "But I have a helluva headache."

Arthur slid a hand under his head while gripping his upper arm with the other and lifted.

Other than the headache, he felt no other pain. He came on up to sit, stretching his neck, shrugging, rotating his shoulders one way and then the other. Every move slow and calculated, he began paying attention to the remainder of his body. Things seemed to be attached the way God intended. Rolling over on hands and knees, he pushed up off the floor.

Once on his feet, a sharp pain stabbed his ankle. He wobbled on rubbery legs and fell into a chair. "Ouch, ouch, ouch." He rubbed it and performed a fingertip examination. The ankle didn't feel broken, just bruised. *I suppose that's where the car bumper caught me.* Car? "Nikki!" He leaped up, hopping in a circle, looking about. "Where's Nikki?"

Arthur didn't answer right away. He said, "Sorry, dude, she's still in Coos Bay... Monday morning."

"Crap!" He fell back into the chair. A head rush squeezed his eyes shut. "We tried so hard to prevent it and it happened anyway." He slammed the back of his head into the chair and pounded the armrests. "God damn it! It was my fault… my stupid carelessness!"

"No time to be hard on yourself. We have to do what we can to get her back. And when I say back, I don't just mean to this location… but to this time… our time."

"What'll we do?"

He didn't answer just stared—eyes lifeless—almost catatonic.

"Damn it, man, don't just stand there! Talk to me!"

Uncharacteristic seriousness straightened his lips and set his jaw. He stepped forward as if he might need to restrain Jack. "We'll accomplish nothing if you panic. You need to be focused and settled more than ever."

Given a moment to think, it occurred to him that the old guy was right. Acting while agitated as he was could only end badly. "Okay." He forced breathing back into normal range. "What do I have to do to get her back?"

"First, understand what we're dealing with. Remember when I said that it's impossible to change the course of an event that has already happened, a past event?"

"Yeah. So?"

"This is true of people you encounter in a past event, but I'm not at all sure about this for those of us doing the traveling. Although she's trapped in the future, paradoxically, the episode that left her behind is in *your* past."

He drove a fist into the chair. "You're confusing me!" He remained at the fringes of control.

"Nikki is over thirty hours ahead of our present time. The physical distance doesn't matter. Do you understand that much?"

"Of course," he said, almost whining.

"I know it's difficult to understand, but we have a paradox to deal with. If you happen to access that time again through Kyle's consciousness, you'll be in his time and space. This means past, present or future, it will only be Kyle's universe that exists. Nikki was not and is not part of that universe, just a visitor, courtesy of you. She was in your bubble of influence. That no longer exists for her in that future time. If we go back she won't be within your bubble, your aura. And she wasn't part of that time to begin with—"

"I don't like the sound of that."

"And you shouldn't." He held his hands to his back as he attempted finding words to explain something that contradicted universal laws. "Let's say you and Nikki go to a party and you introduce her to a friend." He drummed his lips with two fingers for a moment and came back around to look Jack in the eye.

"Prior to the introduction she did not exist to that person, nor he to her. Now apply that logic to the current situation. Through the power of your mind and strength of your heart, Nikki was introduced to a time and place that would have been inaccessible any other way. As long as the host... that's you... was there with her she was fine, part of your world as you visited another. Once the accident rendered you unconscious and the connection with that time and space was severed, you returned without her. At that instant, she ceased to exist."

"Are you telling me Nikki is just so much cosmic dust?"

"I'm not sure, but I don't think even that much would be true," Arthur said as gently as he could. "There's no evidence in that future of her existence at all... because she never was. Even in the here and now, the only place she exists is in the memories of those who knew her. It's like remembering a shared dream; the dream itself is real, the vision is real, the feeling it leaves behind is real, but the content is not. As far as laws of matter are concerned, she never existed, then or now... I think."

Hands balling into fists, Jack's agitation rose.

Arthur stepped in and held his wrists. "Look, it's entirely up to you to make her exist again so we can bring her back. I believe she still can be a reality but only in the here and now and *only if* we can retrieve her. I'm confident that you have the power of will to make her exist again in that future time and place. I know it's a heavy burden, but without you, she no longer exists."

Jack's hands relaxed and Arthur released his wrists.

The old guy stepped away and paced the room occasionally stopping and gazing at inconsequential things, as if he might find answers in a dusty corner. "This is certainly no time to gloss over hard truth," he finally said. "If we fail, Nikki becomes just another missing person, never to be seen or heard from again, leaving a nasty cloud of suspicion hanging over our heads since we will have been the last to have had contact with her. The truth would forever remain between you, me and God. And, for heaven's sake, we couldn't be honest about it; they'd issue matching strait jackets."

Talk of paradoxes and contradictions threatened to blow off the top of Jack's aching head. He needed clarity but only got *ifs* and *buts*. Arthur's explanation made some sense, but offered no promise of success. He suddenly realized that Nikki had become part of this as a result of his selfishness and this was no time for a self-pity side trip. "I've heard enough. Let's get to it."

"Hold on," Arthur said, waving him down. "There's more that needs to be understood. If you're able to access the same scenario then join it even a split-second *prior* to the time we returned here then that puts you in *her past*. I fear that you will have seemingly reconstructed her, able to interact with her and everything will seem normal except when you return to this house and this time again; you might do it without her. It's divinely forbidden to change the course of history, even if the difference is only the time span of an eye-blink. History is history, whether it's a single second or an eon. I'm only guessing, but we'd better assume that includes a personal past event you construct in the future. We need to treat this as if the law is true in this case, too. I'm just not certain if it applies to someone from our time visiting a future time—"

"That's enough. If you keep explaining it, I'll be so confused I won't remember my own name."

"Sorry. It's difficult to simplify it."

"So, I'm going to put myself and Nikki's existence in your hands. But one last question: Are you saying that if we fail this time a second chance might not be an option?"

He nodded. "I think that's right. Even though you can effect change by interacting with future events, Nikki is not of the future," he said. "She is of our time. It's all about you, Jack. You are the host and must go get your guest."

Jack shuddered at the enormity of responsibility and just how fragile this plan seemed. "Oh God."

"Stay in control, my friend. Can you do it?"

Jack didn't answer.

Arthur placed a hand on his forearm and shook it. "Can you do it?"

Perspiration dampened his face. He wanted to yell, *Hell yes!* But it came out, "I think so."

No psychic ability necessary, the old guy read the apprehension as if he were a Dick and Jane primer.

After agonizing seconds, Jack found his wavering bravado and offered affirmation by nodding.

"Listen carefully. Thus far you've accessed other times and dimensional planes *only* through your brother, becoming one with his personal universe, past, present and future. This time…" He paused.

Jack saw his own uncertainty reflected in that aging face. Becoming unnerved, Jack hadn't seen this side of him. "'This time'… what? Spit it out."

"This time you must become one with the personal universe of Nikki Endicott. There is no alternative. You must synchronize your soul with every quark, every atom… everything that made Nikki Endicott a living creature and pull it all back together."

"But, that's… that's impossible. Isn't it?"

"Only if you believe it is," he said. "We discussed the family connection but that doesn't necessarily mean your ability is limited to it. It may have just made it easier. Now's the time to find out because I don't really know."

"I wish you wouldn't sound so unsure. I need your optimism."

"Sorry. Weak moment. Truth is, if we believe it and visualize it, it'll happen."

Out of all the complicated explanations Arthur attempted, it was that short cliché on faith that drove it home—the encouraging but simple answer he sought all along. "You're right. Failure is only assured if I don't try. I now have two missions; saving Kyle cannot happen without Nikki at my side."

Arthur's warmth returned at the same rate Jack's confidence did. "It couldn't be called an adventure without a little of the unknown and a dash of danger."

"Is there anything different I need to do to make it happen correctly?"

"I'm not certain," he said, "but I'm of the opinion you must generate the same passion for seeing her as you just expressed over the possibility of losing her, you know, a feeling of what she means to you. You do like her, don't you?"

Eyes closed, Jack almost grinned. "All things are possible," he mumbled.

"Let your mind go. Think only of Nikki's image then examine every detail." Arthur spoke in hypnotic monotone.

Even before Arthur had finished the sentence, Nikki's delightfully tart humor came to mind. He saw her smiling and laughing. Her hands clasped in front, she bounced on her toes as a little girl might, anxious to be photographed on Easter morning. She wore those unbelted jeans with that snug fitting white blouse tucked into them. Her long auburn hair bound in a ponytail revealing oversized silver hoop earrings. Instead of a chill, there came unexpected warmth traveling from his feet to his head.

"Pure love," Arthur whispered.

A buzz in Jack's eyes transformed into a full-body tingle and the more familiar chill came. For the first time, he opened his eyes wide and witnessed the transition in detail. It happened slower than before, deliberately. The room blurred. A hazy white glow appeared as boiling mist, stabilizing as a translucent picture appearing from an opening created by a receding wave of haze at its center. Nikki ran toward Jack's unconscious body lying sprawled in the street. Arthur's future self knelt beside him, lifting his head.

Preparing to step into it, Jack rose. Arthur grabbed his arm. "Not yet. We've been back in our own time for about twelve minutes. All we can do is observe for at least that long."

"But if we wait twelve minutes, won't she still be twelve minutes ahead of us?"

"Nikki's time stream ceased, yours continued. That puts her twelve minutes in your past. The sequence of events that we are witnessing is only transpiring because you are willing them to exist. You're now constructing the missing twelve minutes. Our time stream in the here and now is not progressing, as long as your vibrations remain constant while we stay within this sphere of light."

A lateral glance confirmed it; a bolt of lightning through the window of Arthur's library had frozen in the sky, a marker of proof.

"You and I continue aging. Our personal time streams go on, but Nikki is not a split second older than she was when we disappeared from there to return here. What I'm witnessing and you are doing is creating a past for her, twelve minutes long. It's imperative we don't go there until it becomes, what would have been, her present then Nikki's soul will synchronize with yours in a common time frame. Only then will she instantly become twelve minutes older. This, I pray, is the way it will work."

Arthur sat close as they watched the driver of the car hit the garbage cans that spun away like bowling pins when she swerved to avoid hitting him. Once stopped, she threw open the door and bounded out fast for an elderly woman. She ran around behind the car searching the street but saw nothing. He and Arthur had vanished. The poor woman wandered from sidewalk, to gutter, to street, and back, looking for the man she was certain she'd hit. She frantically ran back to her car, trotted around it again and, again, looked beneath it. There was no more to see the second time. This would leave a scar on her, all because he lost objectivity at a crucial moment.

Nikki came running and appeared from beside a backyard fence, clear panic on her face. She realized she had been left behind.

Seven minutes had passed.

Nikki turned away from the site of the accident, meandering back into the alley, pausing every couple of steps, plainly trying to piece together a plan. Finally she stopped, faced the fence beside her and rested her forehead against one of the wooden pickets, arms dangling loose at her sides. There she remained for a couple of minutes.

Now ten minutes had passed.

Nikki straightened and began walking toward the rear of the grocery store, but indecisive movement suggested she had no specific plan on what she'd do when she got there.

Eleven minutes had passed.

She reached for the doorknob but stopped, holding her hand inches from it. It seemed she might be wondering if going inside would be wise.

Jack became itchy, wanting to be there and allay her fear, to hold her, to assure her that everything was going to be okay.

Twelve minutes had passed.

Arthur held his finger in the air. As he let it fall forward, he whispered, "Let's go get your girl."

Slipping into the vision with only the slightest queasiness, a scream began abruptly, like a phonograph needle dropped on a record album. The arrival startled her.

She ran to Jack, leaping into his arms, wrapping her legs around his waist. She shivered and cried. With arms around his neck, she nearly choked him. Jack didn't stop her. He let her get it out. Finally, she regained her wits and relaxed her legs, standing on the tips of her toes. She pulled her face back and looked into his eyes with tears streaming down her face. That thankful dreamy look soured fast. Planting hands on his chest, she shoved him back and slapped him. "Don't you ever do that again, you sonofabitch!"

He reached for his stinging cheek. "It's great to see you, too," he said as a smile came up.

"Before we become too excited by this rescue," Arthur said, "we still have a major test facing us. Let's not forget, we guessed at how much time would be needed."

Nikki's eyes darted between them. "Needed for what?"

"If we arrived in this time and place too early—even by the smallest margin, say a second or two—then… take my word for it, it wouldn't be a good thing," he said. "You may not go back with us. In fact, it's pointless to talk about it until we do get back. Another try may not be an option."

The color drained from her face. "That sucks."

Jack slipped an arm around her. "Let's go home."

"It's time." Arthur grabbed Jack's other arm. "Let's go."

The thought of a yellow brick road, a tin man, a scarecrow and a young girl in a gingham dress crossed his mind, he being Dorothy. And, instead of ruby slippers, he wore a pair of jogging shoes that only hinted at having been white at some point.

The absurd thought served a useful purpose. It broke the mind connection with that time and place. As they transported back, Jack kept his attention on Nikki. His knees wobbled and his heart skipped a beat while in the process. Once again, they were back in Springfield in that musty library Arthur called a study.

Nikki was with them. They had successfully brought her home.

Less than an hour had passed but for them over two, evidenced by the difference in time between Jack's watch and the library clock on the mantle. Most of Saturday evening still lay ahead. Jack suddenly discovered he had a new annoyance. He couldn't get the song *Somewhere Over The Rainbow* out of his head. He rubbed the purple lump on the left side of his skull. He made a mental note to be more careful in the future—anyone's future.

Arthur gave him a couple of aspirin, as Nikki stood behind his chair. She massaged his shoulders. Staying close was not unusual but now it seemed tinged with paranoia, as though she feared he might disappear again. He glanced up and smiled when her hands left him. "Don't stop. That feels great."

"Don't worry. I'm not through with you yet." Her hands went from his shoulders to his neck. She thumbed circles at the base of his skull.

He needed these quiet moments to let the ache in his head and sting in his ankle subside. Her hands were magic. The aspirin helped.

She leaned over, touching her cheek to his. "Better?"

He felt her warm breath. "I'll live. How about you?"

"I'm shaking. But I sure have a right to."

"I feel it in your hands." He paused. "I hope you believe that no one was more scared than me about what happened."

She moved around the chair to face him, making a show of pulling her brow down to an angry slant. "I have beautiful beachfront property in Arizona for your purchase consideration, too."

Arthur sat sprawled, legs wide apart. He dozed. Watching air puff his cheeks as he snored softly, Jack realized how energetic the old guy was for a man his age. *There's no way I could be doing any of this without you—you crazy old fart.*

He snorted and smacked his lips. "I know," he mumbled.

A ground-shaking boom followed a brilliant flash. The lingering rumble reminded him that a thunderstorm still wreaked havoc outside.

He stood and took tentative steps. The ankle seemed fine, except for a small point of sharp pain when he applied pressure a certain way. Shuffling toward the window, he remained cautious, not wanting to spiral into a heap from a sudden stabbing pain.

She offered a hand. "Are you all right?" She walked alongside.

"Yeah, I just want to check on the storm." Limping across the room, he dodged dusty piles of books, magazines and papers. *With all his wealth, why doesn't he hire a full-time housekeeper?* Stopping at a large window arched over its top, he glanced back at the old guy. In that sleeping face, he saw understanding of his thoughts yet the old man's eyes remained closed.

Nikki approached the window like an acrophobic would a steep cliff.

"Scared of storms?"

"Of course."

Gazing out as the electrical display danced across his face, he watched the storm rage. Hailstones bounced off the grass. Others shattered on the stone and concrete surfaces. Trees bowed to the storm's power. Broken branches lay scattered about. But, at this moment, even the fury of nature seemed unimportant.

Another force trumped it—his ability to correct a future event that had not yet occurred. These things were difficult to comprehend, even as they were happening. His brother would be killed in a couple of days, and he had a single chance to prevent it—a homerun or a strikeout. He'd only be getting one swing. The fine hair rose up on his neck.

Fretting wouldn't accomplish anything. But that didn't stop frightening possibilities from pounding his brain. Worry flowed through him—unable to stop it or stem it. So far, he hadn't been a shining example of how to remain calm and focused. Arthur's words, "If you believe it and visualize it, it'll happen," rang in his ears, although faith to back it remained infantile.

Nikki came to stand at his side and nudged him. "A penny for your thoughts."

He glanced sideways. "I'm not sure they're worth it." He continued watching the storm.

"Okay. But mine are," she said. "Offer me some pocket change for *my* thoughts?"

"Well, I—"

"How does the storm look?" Arthur asked.

"Still raging," Jack said. "I bet there's property damage galore by morning. A storm like this should—"

"Hey, Bucko." Nikki slapped him on the butt for allowing attention to be so easily diverted. "Let's get back to my thoughts."

Arthur snickered. "It looks as though you two might be creating your own storm." He yawned and stretched.

Jack shrugged. "A stiff breeze at best."

Nikki turned her nose up. She huffed and looked out the window, pretending to ignore the sarcasm.

As alluring as she was, his head was stuck in another rut. "We need to go back and try again to stop the old man, or do you think we might be able to notify the authorities and let them foil his plans?"

Arthur vigorously rubbed his face. "I wish it were that simple." He massaged his reddened eyes. "Time is on Johnson's side. If we notify local authorities in Coos Bay tonight, we wouldn't be able to credibly explain any of it. Besides, Kyle is under a protective watch already... the assault charge against Mister Johnson, you know." He sighed. "But we already know how much good that'll do without intervention."

Jack probed the lump on the side of his head. "My point exactly."

"Sorry. If I could think of an idea that didn't include us going back there, I'd be laying it out for your consideration this very instant."

"Damn it!" *How many people on the face of this planet have to deal with crap like this?*

"Never forget," Arthur said, rushing to his side. "You're not alone. There are two people in this room that have trusted you with their lives. Don't make it be for nothing."

"You know," Nikki told Arthur, "you enjoy acting a little crazy, but you're not really, are you?"

He stiffened. "Of course I am. And what do you mean by, 'a little'? I'm as loony as they come... " He hooked his thumbs into an imaginary vest, "... and darned proud of it."

Jack almost laughed, but an image of Kyle popped into his head when a sudden pang of guilt hit him for allowing a moment of levity. With no effort or warning the chill hit.

Nikki gasped.

Arthur frowned quizzically. "Dude... you're getting good at this."

The scene was the busy street, just beyond the alley. He didn't want to be in that location again. It already held a bad memory.

"I don't know exactly where the old man ran. My focus was on you at the time," Arthur said.

"I do," Nikki offered. "Unfortunately, I couldn't see you two, but I saw Johnson run behind that vacant dilapidated service station on the corner."

Jack nodded. "Since he's determined to get at Kyle, he'll likely stay there. When we stopped chasing him, he probably didn't want to get any farther from the store than that. If he's anywhere else, it'd be closer not farther away."

"We have to make sure we're looking at the same general time frame as the last time we were there," Arthur cautioned.

"Look. There's the car that hit Jack. She's just now pulling away from the scene."

"How in the world was I able to rejoin this scenario so impeccably well-timed?"

"Your subconscious did all the work. You meant to return where you left off." He tapped his nose with a fingertip. "I told you that you had the power. It really didn't matter whether you were thinking about that specifically or not."

"Is everyone ready?"

Nikki sucked in a large breath. "You bet."

"Let's do it," Arthur said.

They were in that time and space in a blink, feeling the sudden ambient shift to a cool morning mist. Once again, they were a thousand miles from home in the day after tomorrow.

"Okay guys, topping my short list of ground rules is: Watch out for the traffic."

Nikki popped his arm with a soft fist. "Just listen to you, Bucko."

"Seriously, let's stay in a tighter pattern. If anything happens we can get back together quickly. Also, whoever gets to him first, don't try to subdue him, just talk to him until the other two get there."

They walked in the same direction, fanning wider as they approached the overgrown corner building. Judging by the appearance, the old neighborhood gas station had not served a useful function in thirty or forty years. A tree with a trunk about eighteen inches in diameter grew out from under the concrete slab foundation, breaking it into heaving pieces. It was collapsing the exterior wall but the destruction could be measured in decades. It'd probably be a few more years before it actually brought the wall and that side of the roof down altogether. The structure was of no value. It should have been demolished years ago.

The patterned sweep brought Arthur close. Jack said, "It worries me that we may inadvertently do something to alter a course of events unrelated to what we need to accomplish."

Arthur patted his back. "A noble concern, but you must understand that there's an Omnipresence that just will not allow you to change a master plan. The simple fact that we're here indicates this was all preordained as appropriate before you ever had the thought to do it. But don't ask me why. You'll have to meet your Maker to get that answer. The way events ripple in time, what we do today may not have anything to do with His ultimate purpose. On the other hand, it may be setting in motion something that will happen years or even centuries from now as part of His plan. We just can't know until He's ready."

Jack shook his head. "Do you just enjoy boggling my mind? That doesn't do a thing to keep me focused. It's having the opposite effect."

The old guy offered a mischievous grin. After walking some distance farther, he glanced sideways. "Neither I nor any human being on the planet can give you answers for what we are doing... nor, why it's you that is capable of doing it. Someday it'll be made clear to you."

They continued walking. "So, there's a strong spiritual control of all this and not so much a scientific consequence."

"Don't ever attempt to separate religion from science. Always remember, science is nothing more than mankind discovering with the physical senses what religions have known to be true through faith for centuries."

"It's good to know I can't mess things up."

"Jack!" Arthur stopped abruptly. "You weren't paying attention. You *can* mess things up. You *can* alter a series of future events resulting in a fatal catastrophe. But if it should happen, it just means it did not conflict with an ultimate master plan and was allowed. That's all. No more no less."

Jack slowly resumed walking, dumbfounded that Arthur would drop it on him like that at such a sensitive time.

Nikki walked faster, now some distance ahead, not interested in hearing the conversation. For obvious reasons she glanced back frequently. She waved the two of them forward, urging them on. "Hurry up," she hissed, stabbing the air with an excited finger. "There's someone crouching behind that gangling lilac bush over there."

Jack caught up to her. He craned his neck this way and that until he caught sight of what she saw. "I'm going around the building and come up from behind it," he said, not taking his eyes from the bush at the rear of the listing overgrown structure.

"All right, but don't do anything stupid," she said.

He turned and took a single step. She grabbed his wrist and yanked him to standstill. "And, for Christ's sake don't be out of sight long. I don't trust you."

He nodded and trotted off. Pain in his ankle lessened as he worked it. Turning the corner on the backside of the building, he saw the old man sitting on his heels. He was not in the exact location Nikki had assumed. Crouching low, the guy kept his eyes in the direction of Arthur and Nikki. He obviously saw them. They had not spotted him, whereas he had not seen Jack.

He cut a breath short when he saw an automatic pistol on the ground near the old man. That was enough for him to slow his pace, realizing that he only had a couple of seconds to decide what to do before the guy noticed him.

Arthur and Nikki were in danger. Jack had no alternative. Like a sprinter out of the blocks, he sped to get to the old man before he had a chance to react.

The other two saw Jack's sudden desperate move and froze.

The old man snapped his head around to see where they looked. That's when he saw Jack and sprang up to run, only to realize he'd left the gun on the ground.

As the old man reached for it, Jack went airborne to tackle him but couldn't prevent him from snatching the firearm up and swinging it into his face. The blow was a grinding cheek slap that sent him reeling.

Capitalizing on the few seconds it bought, the old man took off running with the astounding agility of a man half his age.

Jack rolled around on the ground momentarily dazed. By the time he sat up, his two friends had arrived. He waved them off. "I'm fine. Where'd Johnson go?"

"He's running toward the store waving that damned gun!" Nikki cried.

"Shit! What have I done?" Dizzy, he rolled over on all fours and tried to get up. He felt hands on each arm pulling him up awkwardly. He ripped his arms from their grasps and stumbled down the street in the direction of the store. As he did, his head cleared. He pushed the pace to a jog as equilibrium returned, kicked it up to an all out sprint. After about fifty feet a siren blast shocked him to a standstill.

Two officers screeched to a stop and jumped out of a police cruiser. One stood back with an open palm resting on the grip of his holstered pistol. The other approached cautiously. "Is there a problem, sir?" the lead officer asked.

"Yes, there's a problem!" he bellowed. "There's an old man with a mental condition on his way to kill Kyle Dane!"

"Could I see identification, sir?"

"Would you quit asking stupid questions and get someone inside that store?" He waited only a second for a reply. "Now, damn it!"

The other officer unsnapped the leather constraint on his pistol.

Arthur and Nikki trotted to his side. Breathless, Arthur jumped in to cool the situation. "Officers, this man is Jack Dane, brother of the gentleman that owns that grocery store over there. You must trust us for the sake of expediency; his brother is in grave danger."

"We'll do what we need to do," the officer said. "First, I need identification from all three of you."

Jack tried to stay in control but failed. Without another word, he spun in the direction of the store and ran. The commands to stop were wasted. Feet hitting the pavement behind him indicated he didn't have a sufficient lead.

The front double door of the grocery store came into view, but no sign of Johnson.

Believing he'd already gone inside, Jack went airborne, jumping and then sliding on his buttocks across the hood of a parked car near the front door of the store.

Two rapid gunshots sounded off from inside.

With no care for safety, he burst through the door, scoping the unfamiliar layout, jerking his head side to side, trying to determine where the shots had come from. In a visual sweep, his eyes stopped on Kyle, teetering sideways, clutching his shirt with both hands. Blood oozed from between the fingers of a fist clenched over his chest, surprise and pain frozen on his face. Kyle dropped to his knees and onto his face.

From the rear of the store, Jack heard a terrified scream and turned to see Cary racing from the stock room toward Kyle.

Johnson stood totally inanimate still pointing the gun at Jack's brother. His expression told it all—a man just beginning to understand that he had done something wrong. He waved the gun toward Jack and to Cary. The old man clearly didn't know what to do next but understood perfectly what he'd done.

Anguished, she shouted, "You crazy old sonofabitch! You've killed my husband!"

Johnson looked as though he had just regained consciousness, not realizing where he was or what he was doing. He looked at Jack, eyes blinking like a frightened child, his face a mix of anger, sadness and fear. He looked at the gun, as though it were in someone else's hand and examined it. And his expression went bland. He opened his mouth, inserted the muzzle, and pulled the trigger. A spray of fluid and tissue followed the blast.

Cary screamed, grabbing for her ears.

He crumpled onto the floor, no longer a threat.

Cary and Jack converged at the same time over Kyle.

The four pursuers burst through the door into the store. Rolling him over, Jack noticed Kyle's chest rose and fell but bloody bubbles gurgled from it—alive, but barely.

Shoving him aside, Cary fell to the floor over her husband. She scooped Kyle's head up and hugged him, sobbing, repeating his name over and over. His eyes fluttered opened, this time showing no pain.

Tears rolled down Jack's face as he looked down on them both.

A weak smile came up on his face as Kyle looked up at Cary, "Have I told you... today... that... I love you?" he asked. The words came at a price.

She said nothing and smoothed his hair back, gently rocking, as tears streaked her cheeks. Kyle swallowed. His swimming eyes shifted and focused. Jack saw recognition in them. "Big brother? If I'd known you were coming—"

"Don't talk, Kyle. We'll get help." He clenched his teeth to keep from sobbing.

Cary looked up. "You're Jack?"

He nodded. She reached and squeezed Jack's forearm.

"This is great," Kyle whispered. "Two of my favorite people right here... together... right now." His drew a breath. His body convulsed. Air came out in a lifeless wheeze.

CHAPTER 12

Numbed by grief, Jack was muddleheaded but, within that gloom, a growing urge to run and not look back had been set into motion. He didn't belong in that place or that time and now sought by the police. The longer he stayed, chances increased that questions would arise that he wouldn't be able to answer.

Andy and Barney over there, guns drawn, just wouldn't understand. But what they thought didn't concern him as much as the affect on Cary. She hunkered over Kyle's body grief stricken. Jack didn't want to add the burdensome riddle of his presence to her problems. Mentally and physically fragile, she had become strained to the limit. Her pregnancy could even be at risk.

To stand and walk away took more strength than he possessed. Knowing it necessary made no difference. His knees buckled and he went back down on his first attempt to rise. Grief pressed him and kept him on the floor next to Kyle. He simply wanted to stay with his sister-in-law and cry with her, to console her. The circumstances of his presence made that illogical. He glanced back and saw questions building in the officers just then beginning to animate. Any moment, he'd be in the hot seat about how he knew what was going to happen.

Although there was nothing extraordinary about Coos Bay, Oregon, his way of getting there was. An explanation to Cary would have to wait for another time. A conversation covering many hours would be necessary before he could even begin to make sense of it for her. But he'd have to wait until the clock the rest of the world lived by caught up. He could call or come back and do the right thing by her and his dead brother.

He had to come to terms with the fact that his brother would remain alive for two more days once he returned to his time, but there wouldn't be a damned thing he could do to prevent his death—no second chances. He'd struck out.

Finally, he rose. He had no choice but leave Kyle's lifeless body in the arms of his grieving widow and go back with friends to where they'd come from.

His companions moved in, one on each side. He stumbled—his body racked by convulsive sobs. He tried offering gratitude but choked on every word. He found comfort in the calm support as they assisted him away.

Reluctantly, he stepped back, unable to turn away from Kyle, knowing this would be the last time he'd ever see him. Although saying nothing, Cary's expression made it clear she had questions. But she wouldn't understand even if he had the time or strength to invest. Arthur had proven that with his lengthy complicated explanations that only confused him. How could he explain it to Cary in a few short minutes?

"What are you doing here?" Cary asked in a strained voice. "How did you get here?"

Pulling away from Arthur and Nikki's hands, he dropped back to the floor on his knees, sitting on his heels and pulling her bloodied left hand off Kyle's chest. He squeezed it affectionately. "Cary, this is not the way I wanted to meet you. I know you have questions." His chest heaved from a contained sob. "I promise you'll have answers to all your questions, but they must wait for another time." The words choked off. "Kyle was my only sibling. Now, you, Melissa and your unborn baby are my only family. I'll never again be so distant from you. I swear it. I'll keep you in my life and never be far away… ever again." He had no more to offer.

Cary nodded, retrieving her hand and returned it to Kyle's chest. Grief quickly pulled her under. She folded and cried. She and her children deserved the whole truth. But if he'd tried, she'd forevermore have looked on him as no saner than Butch Johnson.

Arthur put a hand on his shoulder as he returned to his feet. Nikki held his hand between hers.

Turning slightly, he saw the two officers. They appeared to be absorbing details, mapping a crime scene.

Anger replaced grief and rumbled deep inside. He sought someone or something to blame. *Those pompous idiots robbed us of time. They killed Kyle, the bastards!*

One radioed for emergency assistance. The other stepped over to look at Johnson's body. The officer's glance was cursory, realizing the old man was beyond help. He knelt opposite Cary and checked Kyle's vitals. He straightened, pursed his lips and tipped his cap to the back of his head.

What the hell do you expect? The heat in Jack's face rose. He flushed red with rage, fast approaching an eruption. He trembled. Choking the life out of those Mayberry hicks seemed like a plan. No one else should have to lose their life to backwoods arrogance.

Arthur leaned in close. "Careful," he said in a low voice. "It's imperative we bow out quietly and we need to do it now."

"We have to come back and try again."

"We can't."

"What do mean, 'we can't'?"

Arthur pulled him away from the others so he could talk. "Remember, we've yet to experience Monday in our own space but we're in another time and space. You know that. Your brother's death is now in your personal past."

"But we've got to try!"

"Even if we left and came back and *succeeded* on a second attempt, events would revert to how they happened from your personal historical perspective. It would be just as you witnessed it moments ago."

"That has to be a theory. We need to test it. If Kyle is alive in our time and this is the future, we still have the opportunity to change it without hocus pocus. Right? I can fly out here and try it the old fashioned way."

"You've created a paradox. This is the future, but it is *now* in your past and you're divinely forbidden from changing history. It'll happen the same way as we just witnessed. You wouldn't be able to save Kyle, but it might do irreparable damage to Cary's mental health. You simply can't occupy the same space at the same time with yourself. It might compound her grief next time because she'd have a double sense of loss and believe you had something to do with it and not know why. Déjà vu. Ever heard the word?"

Jack nodded.

"As it stands, you have a credible excuse for bowing out—giving her time to grieve. She's not looking at us. This is the perfect time to leave."

Though Jack refused the logic, Nikki clearly understood. She pressed close to his side, shedding tears of her own. "You did your best. To change destiny was only a remote possibility from the beginning."

Like a heavy flywheel under power of attained speed, unlikely to slow down without great force, anger built and multiplied. Fury heaped upon frustration in layers. Regardless what they said, Jack was headed for a cataclysmic eruption.

"Grab hold of his arm, Nikki, and hang on. We're going on a trip whether we want to or not. It'll be like a slingshot."

They back-pedaled toward the front door pulling him with them but had only taken a few steps when the chill hit.

Nikki flinched.

He felt no reaction from Arthur.

A brilliant white glow flashed and washed out the entire view of the small grocery store. A solid beam shot out from the left side of his chest with laser-like precision and doubled back slamming into the three of them. This time no picture appeared, just a massive flood of light opened like a giant mouth swallowing them whole. It was incredibly bright—yet, surprisingly, not uncomfortable on the eyes.

The scene developing was still forming as they were hurled toward it. He didn't recognize it. It didn't matter. He didn't care. Glancing back, he saw the officers stunned, as they shrank away at unimaginable speed. One of the pair talked on his radio and stopped abruptly holding out an open palm, apparently intending to issue a don't-move order.

Cary didn't turn again. He was thankful she didn't see them flash out of her store. She didn't need a reason for emotions to be stretched in a different direction. But it couldn't have pleased him more that he'd just given those two cops reason to question their sanity, hoping that every day the rest of their lives they remembered how tragedy resulted from a moment of arrogant procrastination. Memory of the departure should provide them a constant lifelong reminder of that.

Transition was abrupt, nausea barely more than a stomach twinge. Suddenly, he saw that they stood abreast in yet another world but had no clue where. For a time he didn't care to look around. Grief ground him down, clutching his shirt with both hands because tightness in his chest cut deep. *If this is a broken heart, I don't ever want to feel it again.*

The sun burned white hot, the air dry. They stood in the midst of a desert, somewhere and in some time—as yet unrecognizable. He turned around.

"I don't like it here," Nikki said, scoping the surroundings. "There's something about this place that's filling me with anxiety." Despite sweltering heat she shivered. Her face glowed with perspiration, as did Arthur's.

Arthur scratched his head through unruly hair. "It appears this place was recently a lush forest with tall trees and thick grasses. All the vegetation is still here but dead." Like Nikki, he turned a full circle examining all within view. "There's no green anywhere. In fact, I don't see anything living as far as I can see."

"I don't think I want to be here," she whispered, as though speaking louder might invite something frightening.

Raising his head, wiping tears from puffy red eyes, he looked at what lay before them. In addition to heat, the air hung heavy, stale and foul smelling. "This is it," he said.

"This is what?" she asked.

Stretching out before them lay a large body of water—calm, muddy red and strewn with dead trees and brush. The only movement happened to be the wake of a swimmer far out and moving fast away from them. "That's Kyle."

Nikki looked puzzled. "I don't understand. What are we watching? What is this place?"

"Everyone's image of death is different," Arthur told her. "You and I are blessed with an extremely rare opportunity. We're standing in the physical manifestation of Jack's image of dying and death. This is a dimension that ties the physical world to the spiritual. How we are viewing it right now is through Jack. It's a creation of his mind, the way he views life after death. We are quite literally seeing death through Jack's eyes."

She shuddered.

He placed fingertips on her forearm. "Don't fear it. Whether you're conscious of it or not you have your own mental picture of what this place should look like and there'll come a day you'll see it. I suggest, now that you've seen Jack's version, yours will be similar."

She smiled out of courtesy, clearly not amused.

"I'm engaging in guesswork," Arthur continued, "but I believe I understand the symbolism. The canine carcass stretched across that limb over there represents a violent end at the hand of man. It's a dog because Jack loves dogs. The lake represents death in the broad sense, the passing away, evidenced by the dead vegetation and littering of bones. Kyle is swimming because it symbolizes a personal unassisted mode of transportation to accomplish the transition. We're all born alone and we'll all die alone; that's the inference. He's moving from the physical to the eternally spiritual. We're watching it happen."

"Once Kyle makes it to the other shore does that signify a permanent transition?" She looked to Arthur. "When he climbs out of the water over there then that's... death?" She whispered the word.

"From the moment Kyle was shot, he was cast into this lake and began his swim. As life leaches from his body, we're watching life drain away, symbolized by the crossing, watching the progression from life to death. Once he arrives on the other side, then that will have been the instant of his last breath, which we've already seen. He'll forever be at peace with the universe—paradise."

Nikki faced Arthur. "I'm having trouble comprehending the scope of this. It's... it's huge."

"This is a glorious thing and would stretch any mortal's comprehension."

They watched silently for a time.

Jack remained speechless, gaining strength and insight from their conversation, although his eyes remained fixed on the ever widening wake and shrinking figure moving through the water. Unlike the first time he'd been in this place, it was now obvious; Kyle's destination would be infinitely better than where he was. Jack regretted that Kyle had to leave his family behind. Otherwise, desire to stop him was no longer an issue. Instead, he quietly wished a blessing on his journey. Somehow, knowing what he knew and watching it objectively, he came to terms with it. As Kyle reached the other side, the beautifully serene picture again appeared. One he since learned to be his impression of paradise.

He noticed his friends looking at it with wonder. After a short while, it was time to go. With arms spread wide, he gathered his friends in. Their foreheads touched. There was no talking. His only thought was of their time and their own infinitesimal space in the universe and how much he wanted to be there with these two people. The chill and nausea came and went in a blink. Once again, they were in the cluttered surroundings of the library in Arthur's mansion.

Drained of energy, the three of them found chairs and collapsed.

A brilliant bolt of lightning reminded Jack that a storm still hammered the world outside this house—their world. It seemed as though it had been going on for hours. In truth, it had scarcely been an hour. To realize they had aged over six times the passage of real time made exhaustion justifiable.

"Would either of you care to join me for a drink?"

A gin and tonic," Jack said. "Don't waste too much tonic water."

Arthur headed for the bottle-cluttered antique chest he used to store liquor. "What about you, Nikki?"

Almost incoherently, she said "Sounds good. Same here."

He watched Arthur play mixologist as he mulled events of the evening, attempting to think analytically. He couldn't help playing the *what if* game. "Arthur, do you think there's any possibility that our presence created the circumstances that resulted in Kyle's death?"

He didn't answer right away.

It was a loaded question and unfair to lay such an encumbrance of proof on him like that. It had not occurred to him that however Arthur chose to answer would be a no-win.

"I believe," he began as he measured a drink, "Nikki was right when she told you it was destiny and would have happened if we had not been there anyway. Now, it's a future event we know will take place no matter what we do or say. It hurts me that you had to go through all this and not be able to change the outcome."

"Do you really think that's the truth of it? Or is it theory?"

"There's no manual to explain what the three of us experienced, or the limits of what you're capable of. It's only the shared experiences of a handful of people on earth that form the dos and don'ts. We must reason based on experience. Even the word *fact* may have no relevance. Never forget even without such phenomenal abilities, facts are subject to change, but truths are eternal."

"So, destiny is destiny and it would have happened whether we were in that time and space or not?"

"Not necessarily. I do believe we had a one-shot opportunity. We must use one of your previous experiences as proof that you did not create the circumstances that ended in tragedy. You and your dog Buddy traveled to that dimension bridging life and death once before. It was just as real the first time as the second. You tried to stop him. The old man had killed Kyle then, too. The circumstances may have been altered by our presence, but it was the same result." He turned away from his drink-making duties. "Incidentally, you came very close to death when you went after him in that first encounter. If you would've swum any farther, death would have sucked you in."

The afterthought was sobering but, at the moment, unimportant. "It's difficult to sit here knowing that he's alive right now but will be dead Monday morning."

"I'm sorry," he said. "It's a paradox and totally unavoidable. Should you physically fly out to Coos Bay and try again, you'd unwittingly create the exact circumstances that you've already experienced. It's a future event for the rest of the world, but it's historical for you and cannot be changed by you. I fear if you tried, your mental health might be compromised."

Clumsily, he picked up all three drinks, delivering Jack's first and stepping towards Nikki.

"You know, there's another aspect to all this, Jack," she said, taking the glass. "These strange abilities of yours could lead to a new life's calling." She took a sip, savoring it, and held the glass in her lap.

Arthur nodded agreement before she'd offered the comment.

"It crossed my mind," he said, looking at their distorted images through the bottom of his drink glass. "There are a couple of problems with it though." He took another quick gulp.

"Care to share?" she asked.

There was comfort in knowing her light-heart was intact as she attempted to lessen his sadness. "You want enlightenment?"

He set the drink aside.

"Okay. As I see it, it's a dangerous problem that I don't know my limitations in this mind-heart thing that we're delving into in a willy-nilly fashion. This lack of understanding, more succinctly the lack of control, could cause more harm than good. Hell, I vaporized you without even trying."

Nikki's expression implied she realized she chose a bad time lighten Jack's mood. "I'm sure Arthur and Maigo would provide the necessary education to solve that problem," she said, "That is, if you'll ask for it and then open yourself to suggestions."

Arthur listened, sipping his drink. Although he contributed nothing for either side, he did pull his chair in close to better hear. He sat chin in hand.

"Don't you think that's possible?" Nikki asked him.

"Yes," Arthur said, "I do."

It was apparent a case was being built Jack couldn't win. But he held an ace and played it. "There's another minor detail I need to mention... "

"And what might that be?" she asked.

"I don't want to." He spoke in a slow exaggeration, forming each word carefully.

"Checkmate," Arthur said in monotone with a straight face.

"Come on, Jack—"

"All I want to do is play with my dog, write weak watered-down feature articles for a not-so-well-known newspaper and work for a guy who would as soon choke the crap out of me as look at me. I want to get back in shape. Maybe I'll take up tennis or golf. There are many things I'd rather do, ordinary things... very ordinary things! Got that?"

With a sweeping gesture, "Don't you care what you might offer the world with that God-given talent?"

Finally, he said, "Do you guys realize how much this sounds like the argument of a married couple?" Arthur asked.

Jack glared.

Nikki smiled.

He snorted a loud exhale. "Okay. I'll tell you what I'm going to do... "

"Please do."

"I'm going to take a breather from this—this surreal bullshit—and be an ordinary guy for a while." He came to his feet, aggressively placing his nose inches from hers. "My abilities, I assume, are with me for a lifetime. So, regardless of personal desires, these episodes might occur anyway. Why waste valuable chunks of my life trying to develop something that'll pop up again whether I want it to or not. Sure, I want to understand and know more about it. I just don't want to cultivate it."

She didn't back down, stepping in until the tip of her nose almost touched his. "Get to the point."

"The point is: If it happens... it happens. But I'll not be embarking on a search for wrongs to right or good deeds to do. I'm not, and don't want to be, Superman. I don't even own a suitable cape!"

Her frown faded. She grabbed him by the ears and kissed his forehead. "That's good enough for now," she said. "And while I'm waiting for your good sense to kick in, can we play together?"

"If you don't mind being in line behind my dog."

CHAPTER 13

Jack raked a dry tongue across the roof of his mouth. He felt as if he'd been drugged. Pains provided a not-too-subtle reminder of what he'd put himself through the evening before as he emerged from a fitful night's sleep. His cheekbone ached from the smack of that pistol. The ankle was swollen to twice its normal size and his head pounded from a quick introduction to a fast moving car. Resting and healing topped the priority list.

Through squinting eyes, he noticed the clock beside the bed showed eight-forty-seven, much later than he normally slept, even for a Sunday. Light streamed around the gaps in the draped windows. The storm had passed sometime during the night. He appreciated waking to a sunny morning. It seemed to promise a good day.

Pushing up to sit on the edge of the bed, he hurt in places that had caused no problems yesterday. Once his feet were on the floor, that was far enough for a time, needing a moment for his brain to shift into a higher gear. He scratched his head and yawned. Then came experimental stretching—a bend here, a twist there, and a moment to think about it. "Humph." It seemed manageable.

The slow motion aerobics roused Buddy. The little pooch scampered into the bedroom and dove into his lap. The point of standing eluded him; he had nowhere to go and nothing to do—very appealing. He smiled. Buddy got all his attention. The dog buried a cold wet nose between Jack's naked legs, fanning a breeze over bare skin with a wagging tail.

"Hey friend," he said, scratching the dog's ear, "It may have only been a single Saturday evening but it sure seemed a lot longer." He stopped and thought about it. "Well, enough of that...you're the important one here. I need to spend quality time with you. You know that, Buddy Bear?"

Movement in the living room caught his ear, and he remembered that Nikki had come home with him and slept on the sofa. Lewd references indicated she believed that *play with his dog* might be a sexual euphemism. If so, she wanted in on it, feigning fear of the storm in order to invite herself in for the night. He had been too tired to make an issue of it or be polite about it. He tossed her a pillow and a blanket pointed at the couch barely breaking stride on his way to the bedroom. It put the issue of what he meant aside without explanation.

Buddy whimpered and pulled his nose from Jack's lap. "Hungry? All right, but I can't do it as long as you're in my lap."

He rose in a slow measured way, steadying on the lamp table. Sharp ankle pain straightened him, but after a few tentative steps he discovered that his full weight on it was possible—confident that by afternoon the limp would be gone.

The thought of a hot shower beckoned. On the way, he shucked boxers and t-shirt, stopping at the vanity to shave and brush his teeth. He winced at his reflection in the mirror. "Whew. Nasty bruises ya got there, Mister Dane." He shook his head at the battered guy looking back, but the haggard appearance just wasn't that big of a deal.

Buddy poked his head around the bathroom door and whined.

"Damn, Buddy. I'm sorry. I've already forgotten I promised to feed you." He hurriedly walked through the living room into the kitchen, having already forgotten something else—Nikki—just one more thing to slip his mind. When he realized it, he froze, hoping she remained asleep. As bad luck would have it, she lay wide awake.

"Mornin', Jack," came a singsong greeting.

Somewhat panicked, he whirled around. On her back on the sofa, blanket up to her neck, she had her fingers laced beneath her head.

He stood in the kitchen doorway dumbfounded, staring to where she'd spent the night. Her devilish half-grin made him painfully aware of his naked-ness. Modestly looking away was clearly not her intention. Instead, she drank in the view, eyes traveling up and down his length. He must have appeared mentally retarded.

Regaining sense of the situation, he frantically searched for something to cover himself with—larger than his two inadequate hands. He noticed the cookie jar. Snatching it from the countertop near the doorway, he covered the source of his embarrassment. Nikki's wicked expression turned into a smirk and then a snicker.

He'd covered his groin with a ceramic Pillsbury Doughboy.

"I have the strongest desire to come over there and kiss that little fat guy," she said.

He opened his mouth to speak.

She cut him off. "Being caught with my hand in the cookie jar doesn't seem like such a bad thing at the moment."

Mortification heaped upon embarrassment. He stepped into the living room toward her and slid sideways into the bedroom, refusing to offer a profile.

Humor aside, he remained concerned that Nikki was becoming too famil-iar fast. Episodes like this didn't help matters. Due to events of the previous few days, she had come to know almost every important detail of his life. But what did he know about her—roots, childhood, choice of profession, family and many other things?

Intimacy with her was fast becoming a negligible point. He wasn't sure anymore if romance would jeopardize the semi-professional alliance in navigating the limits of his so-called talents. Still, something inside him prevented him from taking the relationship to that level. Besides, once rolling, he might not have the strength to stop it if he later determined it a mistake. As murky as his feelings towards Nikki were, one thing was abundantly clear—that train was already on the track and building a head of steam.

A little voice far in the back of his head kept whispering, "It can't happen, now or ever." He needed Nikki. More than that, he wanted her. Aside from that nagging voice, practical reasons for not beginning a romantic relationship was a baffling conundrum.

He finished the morning ritual, now sitting on the edge of the bed putting socks and shoes on, while Nikki hummed a tune in the shower.

It seemed the only two things in his head were thoughts of her and that other one—the more somber thing that he wanted to banish from his mind altogether. Against his will, his head sunk into a sad rut. Tomorrow his brother would be murdered. He could do nothing to prevent it. Even to the point of developing a headache, he still couldn't put it out of his mind. But he kept trying.

The humming stopped abruptly. "Hey, Jacky, you left me a wet towel. Where do you keep the clean ones?"

He leaped up and headed for the linen closet. He wondered if there might be more than one reason she wanted to spend the night. *What if she thinks I shouldn't be left alone until after midday Monday?* He opened the bathroom door a crack. "Here ya go."

"Thanks."

Was her presence merely a professional thing? He became determined to prove that he could return to a normal life without psychoanalytic intervention.

As the day progressed, the gruesomeness of yesterday shrank to the recesses of his mind. Sunday turned out to be a good day.

Jack woke Monday morning emotionally galvanized, thankful to Nikki for having done a great job of keeping him occupied yesterday.

After taking care of Buddy's needs, Jack left the apartment and walked briskly to his car. The daily adventure that his old car provided kick-started his mood for the day and what it was going to be like. Silly maybe, but the car laid the groundwork for how a day would go. It started right away. "Oh yeah, baby. You da machine!" He patted the dashboard.

When the car cranked easily, it was the omen he sought—another good day lay ahead. He loved that old car. He just didn't know why. Sort of like his dog, he guessed. The dog and the car were his babies. With a clank, a clunk and a rattle, he was off to the newspaper.

Breezing through the front door of The Journal, past the receptionist, and right on into the cubicle filled room of reporters and editors, he took a moment to scan the area. He didn't see Gus roaming about. He looked to the glass wall where the editor's office was—not there either—another promising sign to start the day.

People scurried about—deadlines to be met. Bustling activity filled the expansive office in a buzz of indistinguishable conversations. He walked straight for his workstation and noticed by the blinking light on the phone that he had a voice mail. He punched in the code and a mechanical voice said, "You have... three...new messages." He stabbed the button with a pencil eraser. An elderly woman thanked and congratulated him for a story he barely remembered writing. The second was a co-worker asking about some obscure detail of another article he'd written for a story that the man had been researching. The final message was from Arthur. "Jack, I've already called Mister Landau and told him that I have follow-up information for your article about me. Meet me at Nikki's office at ten o'clock."

Jack deleted the message just as Gus's face appeared over the top of his cubicle. "Dane, that psychic fella called and said he had more information that might make good reading. Call him and get another interview." He turned to walk away. "Oh, by the way," he added in that grating voice, "Good morning." He spun around and away he went.

Jack's lips pressed into a thin straight line. He slapped the desk; Arthur presumptuously conspired to have him close to keep an eye on him. Arthur, and Nikki too, treated him like a child afraid of the dark. *Who the hell do they think they are?* He'd worked hard not to wallow in Kyle's death and certain that was what Arthur's message was about. The inevitability of it had been occupying an increasingly smaller place in his mind—until now. They had no right shining a spotlight on the ugly episode.

He pushed away from the desk and sprang up. Heat rose in his face. He marched towards the exit and his car.

Flinging open the door to the parking garage, it slammed the wall. Stepping into the concrete maze that stunk of gasoline and diesel fumes and echoing every click of his heels, he barely noticed the morning air, already heavy with heat—but cooler than his attitude. He grabbed the door handle of his car, jerked it open and slid into the driver's seat, slammed the door and jammed the key into the ignition.

"Damn it! Those two have no right to..." He stopped talking, saving the tirade for a face-to-face encounter with them both. Fuming, he wrung his hands over the top of the steering wheel. He weaved in and out, cutting people off and hearing an occasional honk from an irate motorist. He didn't care. They didn't matter.

Tires squealed as he negotiated a dangerous turn into the parking lot at Nikki's office complex, narrowly missing a luxury car, to the horror of its driver.

A speed bump threw the front wheels into the air, crashing down with a thunk and rattles. Another shuddered the old car. Finally, he slowed. In a fast maneuver, he was in a parking space, out of the car and enroute to Nikki's office, walking faster than most people jog.

Instead of waiting for the elevator, he took the stairs two at a time heading for that large waiting area where the pool secretary/receptionist sat guarding a suite of offices including Nikki's. He charged by her desk so fast, loose papers took flight and drifted to the floor.

"Can I help you, sir?" she said as he breezed by.

She came out of her chair, trotted to catch up, and followed him. "Sir, can I help—"

"No! There's no damned way on earth that you could be of help to me."

Before she could follow up with more words of constraint, he reached the door to Nikki's office and shoved it open. He locked onto her across the room, behind her desk, looking serious and businesslike, the fingers of both hands laced together atop it. She had transformed from the casual weekender to a professional, wearing a fashionable suit with dark silken hair draping her shoulders.

Arthur sat across the desk from her; his back towards Jack but turned to face him when the door flung open. Both watched but neither said a thing. Clearly, his presence had been orchestrated because neither showed surprise nor startled by the noisy entrance.

The receptionist stood beside him, but not too close, as though afraid of assault. Nikki waved her off. "It'll be okay. Please close the door behind you."

The receptionist hesitated. "Shall I call security?"

"No thank you. We'll be fine."

Still reluctant, the young woman backed out and closed the door.

Jack tore into them. "What the hell are you two trying to pull? Do you have any idea how I've fought to keep this whole mess off my mind?"

No answer.

"Well, do you?" he shouted.

Neither seemed ready to address the question.

"Damn it all! I don't need you two planning my life for me behind my back, creating reasons to counsel me, console me, or… whatever the hell it is you're trying to pull!"

Nikki rose and with slow even voice, "Please Jack, stop and think about your reaction, how you're sounding. Your anger is part of the grieving process. Can't you see that? Grief is spewing out of you right now. You may not have realized that you sought a reason to explode... but you did. We knew that. We also knew you needed to get it out and it might as well be among friends aware of your loss. God knows, you couldn't tell anyone else about it."

"That's crazy talk! I was dealing with it until this game was set in motion."

"This isn't a game." Her reply was quick and firm. "I could tell yesterday you worked hard at ignoring it. Denial like that is dangerous. Think about it. If someone at your work triggered that pent up rage you could have injured, even killed, someone without meaning to, maybe even that grumpy boss."

He wanted to hit something, white-knuckling the back of a chair. Then it happened. Unchecked heartache poured out before he realized anger had indeed turned back to grief. It flowed like vomit. He slung the chair into the wall. "I killed my brother! God almighty, I killed him!" His face exploded in anguish. "Please God... take me, too." His voice trailed as he slumped over. "Take me, too," he mumbled. Sorrow pressed him to his knees.

"Jack, it's time you met someone," Arthur said, barely above a whisper.

Although expressionless, Nikki's sympathetic eyes watered.

But, at that moment, he didn't care about anything except his brother. He heard Arthur's words, but they rang hollow.

The familiar milky white glow developed in the room, but it wasn't of his doing. It faded and a small slender man appeared from it, distinctly Asian with delicate features, almost feminine, gray at the temples with almond eyes and a kind face. An odd aspect was what he wore. He looked like a smaller Oriental version of Arthur, wearing sandals, wrinkled shorts, topped with a loose fitting, brightly colored shirt.

Jack turned to Arthur. "What's this all about?"

Arthur came out of his chair. "Remember when I told you about the man responsible for helping me understand my abilities?"

Jack nodded and pressed fingertips into his aching temples. "So?"

"I'd like you to meet Maigo."

"We're sorry for tricking you," Nikki said as she sat down. "It scared us to think what you might do, and we were convinced you wouldn't come any other way."

He calmed. "You're right. I wouldn't have."

"Try to understand," she said. "Going to the newspaper was out of the question."

The small man stepped towards him. He stopped directly in front of Jack and nodded, partially bowing, saying nothing. His confident manner left no doubt he was taking charge.

Nikki remained in her chair, but Arthur faced Maigo and Jack. Palms together, Arthur placed fingertips to his lips as if praying. "Gentlemen, this is a tremendous honor. Two of the most extraordinary humans I've ever known in the same room at the same time." Snapping a glance at Nikki, "Excuse me, *three* of the most extraordinary individuals."

Nikki mouthed, "Thank you."

"So I finally meet you, Mr. Dane." Maigo's first words were soft, almost childlike.

"Finally?"

"I've been in tune with Arthur's thoughts for years and you've occupied most of them in recent days."

Jack remained in the throes of grief; so much so that he couldn't ask what should have been obvious questions about the man's presence. Maigo accepted the duty of explaining. "Mr. Dane, there are countless wonders in the universe. If we were to move to the far limits of imagination, we could not even see the beginning of these divinely inspired wonders."

Jack stared at the odd looking little man with only loose coherence.

"The recorded miracles in the Bible, the Koran and other writings seem fantastic to the nonbeliever. Over centuries these wondrous events have inspired faith. To be a believer of anything begins with faith. I implore you to believe in yourself, Mr. Dane. Faith in what and who you are is the well from which all belief springs. Give it time. Confidence will come. Your presence on earth is a gift with divine purpose. We're human. Therefore, we are shackled by earthly limitations. It takes each and every person on earth to fill the colors of the spectrum called the human race. Each human is here by plan and purpose. For reasons still unknown, there are those blessed with unusual and far-reaching abilities. You are one. I am one. There are only a few true Radiant Hearts on earth. You and I share that distinction."

"Radiant Hearts?"

"A simple label for a human that can exceed usual human capacity normally reserved for the unseen universe. Reasons why a small group worldwide possesses such talents will not be answered until that time comes when the Almighty deems it appropriate. Arthur cannot answer that question, nor can I. No one can. But in the end it will be made clear. Of that, we are sure."

Arthur listened. Nikki appeared engrossed, too. As for Jack, it remained a struggle to pay attention, much less ponder such revelations.

Maigo continued, "These things I speak of may be difficult to understand, given your state of mind. In time, infinite clarity will be yours. A path has been chosen for you, possibly for the purpose of enriching the lives of others. I can't say."

As Jack listened, he pressed the heels of his hands into swollen eyelids. His head ached. "How can I enrich anyone when I can't even save a family member?"

"Mr. Dane, it's time to show you something. Stand next to me," the little man said with an inviting gesture. "Ms. Endicott, Arthur, you're welcome to join us."

As they stood in a loose huddle, the chill came and the milky white glow increased in an even, deliberate manner, amplifying to a radiance that should have hurt the eyes but didn't. The brilliance faded and all that was visible were the four of them, standing in featureless black limbo—a void, in which Jack couldn't detect near or far limits. All he saw were his three partners as clearly as he did when they stood in Nikki's office. "Where are we?" he whispered, trying to focus on something aside from their bodies.

Maigo smiled for the first time, opening his arms in an expansive gesture. "You have been to this place twice."

Skeptically, he said, "I don't think so." The comment seemed absurd since he couldn't see anything to base the memory of a previous visit on.

"The first time you were in this place was when you tried to stop your brother from passing over. The second time was when you merely watched in resignation with Arthur and Ms. Endicott."

"If that's so, where's the dirty lake, the dead trees, the hot sunshine?"

Maigo clasped his hands together behind him. "The human mind is a magnificent creation. When it does not understand something, it paints a picture using familiar objects. This is how we cope with death. We know it exists and we know it's inevitable, but it's nothing we can visualize as mortals. So, the mind fabricates a picture. The first time I visited this place, it was a treeless prairie, isolated high on a plateau during a driving rainstorm. I was drenched and sought clues. It was the product of my mind... a scene that I could wrap my mind around though at a loss for where I stood. I saw it as lonely isolation; the storm represented gloom. In the years since, I have come to understand that death is no more than a transition from the physical to the spiritual, no imagery necessary. We stand in that place."

Maigo turned to face the same direction they did, into the still featureless void. As soon as his back was to them an opening appeared, and the white glow spilled from within it—in the center stood Kyle.

Jack sucked in a quick breath preparing to speak but Kyle shook his head. "Jack," he said, "I've come to understand everything. It's simple yet profound. You'll know it someday, too. Brother, I'm at peace. What happened to me was one tiny piece of a puzzle you can't yet imagine—a step closer to a universal answer, pieces that have been falling into place since the beginning of time. You'll understand in due course, but don't mourn my passing, just know that my path was preordained, as yours is now. Trust in those friends with you now. Their hearts are pure and selected for you. You are a Radiant Heart. Embrace it."

As Kyle spoke, tears dried on Jack's cheeks. He understood. There was no way for any mortal to grasp the depth of His plan. Kyle's basic message became clear; there was no fault to be dealt and carried no burden of blame—what happened was meant to be. And, he had been granted a great blessing, hearing it directly from his brother's mouth.

The entire ordeal had been an initiation into a world destined to become part of him. Drawn into a purpose he didn't understand, except that now he clearly saw that he was never meant to stop that murder, just given the opportunity to try, a learning experience. But for what purpose, he didn't know. It could have been a crash course, preparing him for something on a grander scale.

Kyle's final words were simple. "Love is the only constant." He disappeared. The light receded. The opening shrank and vanished, leaving the void as it had been, without beginning and without end.

Maigo took Jack's hand into his, and then Arthur's. In turn, Arthur scooped up Nikki's hand. In the blink of an eye, only the three of them were back in Nikki's office. Maigo was gone.

Nikki threw her arms around his neck, letting go pretense of formality. She looked him over and smiled. "Welcome back."

Feeling the heat of judging eyes, he became fidgety feeling an increasing obligation to speak. "Why in the world would a spiritual intellect, a mental giant like Maigo, be dressed like that?"

Arthur bounced his eyebrows. "A good teacher never stops learning. Maigo may have taught me a lot, but I taught him how to do it comfortably."

Jack wrapped Nikki in a bear hug. "Now that I have you, I think I might just hang on to you." He rested his chin on her shoulder. *But where do we go from here?*

She pulled back and rested her nose against his. "Why do I have this odd feeling that this isn't over?"

"Don't tell me you're having strange intuitive feelings, too."

"A big difference, dear, is that my intuition is normal, yours isn't."

"That's a mighty big assumption Ms. Endicott… that you're normal, I mean."

CHAPTER 14

The year following Kyle's death was uneventful, insofar as the episodes were concerned. But Gus Landau, his editor and boss at The Journal, remained cranky and difficult to please. Nonetheless, Jack rediscovered his rut and blissfully fell into it, facing the grumpy old geezer everyday with a smile.

Humdrum felt good—cozy, safe and predictable. He flowed with it. Although Nikki and Arthur provided some pressure to explore his gift, it was the ordinary life he embraced and, by his reckoning, excelled at it. He kicked himself for ever having wanted to break out of it. When adventure did find him, he discovered that it wasn't for him. Jack lived the life he wanted, not seeking nor wanting surprises.

Acceptance of Kyle's death as unavoidable came slowly, but it did come and he moved on. The more time he put between that unearthly series of events and the present provided ample opportunities to pause and wonder if it had even been real. Was it a strange and twisted nightmare? Had he genuinely been thrust into a world of metaphysical extremes? If it had not been for friends convincing him otherwise, he probably would have written it off as a mental breakdown.

Following Kyle's death, he sought excuses for not seeing Nikki and Arthur too often. When the three of them were together the conversation digressed to contentious debate. He loved them, but he didn't want to be Christopher Columbus of the supernatural. Leave it be—that's all he wanted—like a sleeping dragon chained to a distant corner of his mind.

Huge gaps in his knowledge of Arthur's past frequently gave him pause. He knew only enough to form an opinion. Arthur had been a rebellious child of the sixties, or so his story went—overindulging in drugs and alcohol, born into wealth, yet shunning the pretentious life. This explained why his mansion was a place to live, nothing more and clothing to cover his body—no purpose beyond that. Material wealth had no hold on the man. The old guy discovered in Jack something money couldn't buy and coincidentally paralleled his keenest interest. Jack assumed whatever his net worth had been in the beginning had not changed, maybe even increased, because he spent nearly nothing.

He'd known Nikki for nearly ten years and Arthur for only one, and although lacking in knowledge of Arthur's background, he knew less about hers—almost nothing. He didn't even know if she had siblings or not. She never volunteered information, and he never asked.

He had become curious. He thought it strange that she never referenced her past. It's not that she lied; she never said anything about it. He wondered why not.

The other big question: why was he compelled to keep pushing her away? It was that old romantic bugaboo—an oddity that he'd eventually have to confront. Wouldn't it make sense to simply allow the attraction take a natural course? His feelings for her were intense at times—far beyond a brotherly kind of love. But how could he know if he didn't explore it? Like a small child scared of the boogey man, he pulled symbolic covers over his head so he wouldn't have to see what lay out there in the dark. Why?

He'd endured a dreary winter and it wasn't quite over yet. A touch of cabin fever kept him pacing. Entertainment duties fell too often on his little dog, Buddy—simply too much for one pooch to handle. Jack had never been good at keeping himself entertained. He needed stimuli and wondered where he might look for it. "Hey Buddy Bear, I'm bored. What can I do about that?"

It had been days since he saw the sun. The sky remained bleak. Nonstop Pacific fronts swept one after the other across the Great Plains. Weeks settled into predictable patterns—boredom a byproduct. On this particular day monotony had finally ground him down. For the first time in weeks status quo wouldn't do. He wanted a break from routine—an anxious feeling in his gut he blamed on the weather. Was it more than weather-induced anxiety? He remembered Arthur's advice not to overlook anxious feelings, because they'd always be more than simple uneasiness in his case. He chose to ignore it.

All he thought about was the last good time he had had and longed for another. His mind flicked back and it replayed: That time, too, he'd been like a caged animal circling its compound seeking a way out of the doldrums. It had been just over a month ago when Arthur called on a whim and invited him to dinner, promising a lavish meal complete with wine. He'd expected all the stuffiness that comes with expensive restaurants—waiters in starched uniforms and linen napkins. The truth was far different. The evening consisted of chicken fried steaks at a truck stop out on the Interstate and Arthur brought the wine. It matched the setting; screw top, off-brand, right from the bottom shelf at the grocery store. Jack discovered, to Arthur, that was a treat. Truck stop food was his favorite. The way he dressed, lived and his food preference were homogenous to an odd but predictable personality. He should have known what the old guy had in store for him. That night, they shared laughs and bad wine. He learned a little more about the enigmatic old man but it was just enough to raise more questions.

As for Nikki, he stayed in contact on a regular basis—a game of trading phone calls. If he called her twice in a row, he'd roundly chastise her for having to. On the other hand, she'd do the same. They shared lunch a few times; although he took that curious extra bit of care to avoid socializing one-on-one in the evening, realizing that if he did he'd likely drag her to the bedroom. It was on his mind often. Each time he found himself close to her, his libido developed a life of its own. It was getting harder to pull away. Cracks in his willpower surfaced. She read it and played it.

He decided to call both of them and try to get a small party lined up to counter the winter blahs.

His old apartment had become unbearably small. Plus, the landlord changed the policy on pets. If that idiot believed a cramped apartment was more important than a best friend, he was out of his mind. This old house in a quiet neighborhood served his purpose just fine. He'd furnished it with odds and ends from flea markets and second hand stores. Some might call it ratty. He called it shabby-chic.

The last time the three of them had gotten together it turned into an uncomfortable confrontation. That evening, he was on the hot seat most of the evening.

Gouging a pull in the worn pile of the carpet with a bare toe, fingers dancing on the table near the phone, he questioned whether he truly wanted them over. In the end, the answer was yes. He dialed Arthur first. He'd be the easiest to talk to, particularly since the old guy would already know the reason for the call. He might even be on his way to the phone before it started ringing. He heard that irritating electronic noise followed by a recorded message: *The number you have dialed is no longer a working number. Please check the number and dial again.* Maybe he hit a wrong digit. It startled him when the phone rang mere seconds after he'd broken the connection.

"Jack," Arthur said in that high cheerful voice. "How are you? Thanks for calling. Sure I'd love to get together with you and Nikki tonight. Would you—"

"Whoa. Back up a second. Has your phone been disconnected?"

"Well… yes. Darnedest thing, I was no more than a single month late with payment and, wham! The scoundrels cut my service. Can you believe that? I get no respect, none whatsoever, I tell ya." The words may have been serious but the Rodney Daingerfield impersonation practically screamed "Who cares!"

Jack snickered and tapped the phone receiver to his head. "You have more money than most third world countries. How could you let phone service be disconnected?"

"Money." He let out an exaggerated groan. "Having it is such a pain. Would you care to take this ghastly burden from me?"

"Be very careful what you say and especially to whom you say it. Someone might believe you. That kind of talk could be dangerous in the wrong company."

"Isn't living life on the edge exhilarating?"

"On the edge, huh? I'll let you know when I get there, but don't expect it anytime soon. All I want you to do with your money is pick up the check for dinner tonight and maybe a bottle or two of good wine for the three of us if I can talk Nikki into coming, too."

"Say no more."

"I will say one more thing."

"Anything."

"When I say dinner and wine, I don't mean chicken fried steak and that screw-top stuff."

He laughed.

Even with all his oddities he was a gem. Arthur gave his cellular number and Jack hoped he'd keep up payment on that or he might have to develop that telepathic thing after all. It occurred to him that Arthur might crave little things, like hearing human voices not just reading thoughts all the time.

Hesitation about getting the threesome together became a non-issue. He dialed Nikki's apartment. No answer. He ended the call and sat for a moment wondering where she might be. Maybe she was in the shower or something like that. He redialed. "Hello, Endicott residence," a gruff male voice announced with a decidedly country drawl. A sudden flush of embarrassment filled him. Instinct screamed to slam the phone down, but he held on. He heard a faint female voice, "I'll take it." Seconds later, "Hello."

"Nikki?"

"Yes."

He heard uncertainty in her greeting.

"I'm sorry. I didn't realize you had company. I'll call back another time."

"Jack? Is that you?" She paused. In a sultry voice she said, "There's no reason to be embarrassed, just because you caught me in the middle of… well, let's just say I'm not finished, and leave it at that. Shall we? You know," she said in a breathy Anna Nicole sort of way, "there's plenty of room for one more over here. Another set of hands would be magnificent."

He twisted in his seat wanting to end the conversation. She had no intention of letting him off easy. "That's disgusting! How could you even consider something like that? You should be—"

She laughed. "Whoa boy! Don't leap to conclusions." She kept laughing.

"What's so funny?"

"All morning I've had rubber gloves on and up to my elbows in really nasty looking black stuff in the oven."

"Come on, do you expect me to believe that? You don't cook."

"I expect you to believe it *because* I don't cook. Every time I put something in the oven, it bubbles over and turns into disgusting black burnt stuff in the bottom of my expensive oven; an appliance, I might add, I should be barred from using."

"Even if I did believe you, why didn't you answer the phone to begin with? Who is that guy?"

"That guy is Rusty Allbritton, the complex maintenance supervisor. He's trying to stop a leak under my kitchen sink."

"A leak?"

"Yeah."

"Oh."

"And the reason I didn't answer the phone the first time was because it stopped ringing before I had the gloves off. The second time you dialed, Rusty offered to answer it. Is there anything else I might clarify for you?"

"Uh… "

"Before you start your apology, ask me out tonight. That should be apology enough thank you very much."

"Done."

"That was easy enough. How about seven o'clock?"

"Done."

"I must be on a roll. How about we live together?"

He hung up.

CHAPTER 15

Jack sat in his living room on the old sofa, legs stretched, ankles crossed, reclining with fingers laced behind his head. He focused on a point near the ceiling where the wallpaper had lost its grip, now in a decades-long descent down the wall. The house was only new to him and bore marks of many occupants over forty years, maybe a few ghosts, too. But, as he chose to believe, the place dripped of character. Defects in the old house became integral to his comfort zone. Thoughts of remodeling verged on blasphemous.

The faded drooping wallpaper may have been where his gaze was but his focus shifted. His mind drifted—migrating to things universal. As usual, he pondered and philosophized dead-ends.

He grappled with mankind's misplaced priorities. Technology produced computers, e-mail, even cellular phones that can now do things that large computers could not only a few years ago and an endless array of other wonders yet to come—gadgets that served more to tear the world apart than bring it together. These things had become excuses to eliminate the warmth of one-on-one communication—becoming extinct as fast as the advance of technology itself.

The unusual ability lay within him to bridge different times and different dimensions, both simultaneously on occasion, making the notion of modern communication an important consideration for him personally. When he called someone using the radiant heart, or they called him, it was a means to see, touch and feel—to be there with them—no time too distant, no place too far. If it was a phone he compared himself with; it was one he feared dialing. Still, it made more sense than gadgets that kept people apart and offered only an illusion of closeness. As he considered it, the question became: would he have capitalized on an opportunity to see his brother a last time before his death, if he didn't have the power to just pop into his world? It was an earthly question applied to an otherworldly episode, just another philosophical riddle. That list grew.

"Jack," Nikki called out.

Startled, he turned to see her standing in the doorway to the kitchen, beautifully backlit by the harsh light coming from a bare light bulb in the other room. She wore those tight khaki pants well and had a certain little-girl look. She tossed her head from side to side with a beautiful smile. He suddenly had need of a deep breath.

"I know you have an unusually powerful mind," she said, "But I have a feeling the wallpaper will still be peeling when you're finished staring at it."

He smiled, but his expression said, *Screw you.* All those rabbit-trailing contemplations began with the simple thought of appreciation that Nikki and Arthur had come for an evening of friendly closeness not at all common anymore.

"Do you mind if we turn up the heat in here?" Nikki hugged herself and rubbed her arms.

"Why ask my permission? You're always trying to turn up the heat." He paused. "Oh... you meant the thermostat?"

Dropping her chin, she glared from beneath a perturbed wrinkle between her eyebrows. "Watch it, buster. You're skating on thin ice."

Arthur walked from the kitchen through the doorway past her and appeared in the living room holding a small cutting board doing double-duty as a serving tray holding three glasses of wine. Nikki fell into step behind him.

Jack adjusted the thermostat and spun around to get back to the wine, which had suddenly become the center of attention. His friends claimed squatter's rights on each end of the sofa. He headed for a nearby chair. "This is so much better than a crowded and noisy restaurant."

Nikki took a sip and looked around. "How come you haven't invited us over to your new place before now?" She kept looking about as if she might really be interested.

He figured she was just being polite—then again maybe not. It was Nikki that said it, after all. "This is my home, but surely you can tell it's not going to be featured in any home decorating magazine." Feelings of financial inadequacy came easy around these two.

"You worry too much about things like that," she said and turned to Arthur with a wink, "Besides, Jack needed a place resembling his car to complement his lifestyle. He'll probably christen this place with a name soon."

Jack toasted her wit but offered no smile and no comment.

"Really Jack," Arthur said, "a little paint, some wallpaper, maybe an exterminator and this house'll be perfect."

"How can I ignore such stellar advice?" He waggled a finger at the old guy. "Don't forget, I've seen your place and it's not that much different than mine, just a helluva a lot bigger." He swung a glass in Arthur's direction. "A toast to you, too, sir."

After a pause and a few hits from the wine, Nikki broke the silence. "Well, how have things been lately? Anything... interesting?"

"What do you mean by *interesting*?"

"You know what I mean."

Arthur leaned forward—elbows on knees. "It's possible he can't induce them. Although he has the ability, he may not have the will. The only reason it happened before was because of a strong emotional genetic link. Family connections are powerful you know."

"What about when you guys popped out and left me behind in Oregon."

"True," Arthur said, rubbing his chin. "That did prove it was possible outside the family circle. You must realize though just how deep his guilt feelings were."

"Guilt! That's all it was to you, Bucko, a guilty feeling?"

"Don't jump to conclusions," Arthur said. "It just happened to begin with guilt for, you know, letting you get out of sight."

Jack took a gulp. "Great save." His head buzzed. "I celebrate your wisdom with another drink." He turned the glass up and finished it.

Nikki's nose turned slightly up. "I hope you realize that that explanation doesn't cut it."

Jack waved her off. "Arthur, you did call for dinner to be delivered to *this* address, right? I'm drunker than I should be, and I think it'll only get worse without something in my stomach. Because, frankly dear friends, I don't plan on stopping." He toasted them with an empty glass, sprang up and went to the kitchen for a refill.

"Don't worry. It'll be here soon."

The wine began to affect Jack's mood. The combination of friends and alcohol relaxed him. He became reflective. "I have no idea why, but I've been virtually consumed with anxious feelings all week." His speech slurred. "I'll sit for a while, jump up and start pacing, antsy for no reason. It's difficult to explain, but when this sensation comes over me, I feel that I should be someplace doing something but can't get a handle on where that is or what should be done when I get there." He rose and stumbled slightly. The long suppressed need to know resurfaced. He wanted to connect it to some event, place, or person and thought maybe this was the right forum for input. He snickered. *What am I thinking? It's the only forum.* And, he just happened to be drunk enough to invite opinions.

Swaying slightly, he stood facing them as they sat on each end of the sofa. He inadvertently sloshed wine but didn't want to put it down. It dripped from his hand as he caught the drops with his tongue, noticing his attentive audience. He took another drink. "It's as if I'm pulled along without knowing where I'm headed." His eyes darted between them. They appeared confused. "For example, I walked away from The Journal the other day with a note pad and raced for my car. Guys, I walked as if I knew where I was going, paper and pen in hand. Instinct drove me to get going... that I had a job waiting to be done. I even felt deadline pressure. I walked all the way to my car before I realized I had nowhere to go. Weird, huh?"

He noticed exchanged glances. "What are those looks for?"

"You still believe you're normal, with the occasional strange feeling attributable to a vitamin deficiency or something," she said, "but lover boy, you're not. Don't worry though. That's a good thing in your case."

Arthur moved to the edge of his seat. "I don't mean to make it seem as though we're ganging up on you, but she's dead-on."

"Come on guys. I don't want to—"

"Hear me out," Arthur said.

He sighed. "I prefer to be at least partially inebriated first."

Nikki chuckled. "I think the ship has sailed on *partially*."

Swirling the small amount of wine remaining in his glass, he tossed down the last swallow.

Arthur shrugged. "What would a party be without a drunk?" He appeared cartoon-like with that uncombed gray mop that looked like a firecracker went off on top of his head and then there was that baggy shirt and cargo pants.

"We have a consensus," she announced. "It's agreed by all present that you may get as drunk as you like."

With no further comment, Jack headed for the kitchen where the wine bottle beckoned. It seemed to call his name often. He may have been focused on the bottle, but his body drifted left. His shoulder caught the edge of the doorjamb, knocking him to a standstill. For show, thinking he could cleverly conceal drunkenness, he examined the jamb where a door had hung sometime in the past, paying particular attention to worn paint, an empty hinge mortise and paint-encrusted screw holes. He fingered one, pretending to care.

She grinned.

"I should get that fixed someday, huh?"

Arthur didn't wait for his return. "Jack, do you remember the little game we played when you wrote your first article about my work?"

Even as alcohol worked on cognition, the memory of that strange experience Arthur chose to call a game caused him to stop and remember. He shook his head. "Yeah… I do. I still have great difficulty believing you telepathically sent me all that information." He rejoined them with a brim-full glass, listing sideways as his butt searched for the seat.

"It's all true, but that's not my reason for the question." He ran fingers through his hair, or tried to.

If you want that hair to lay, you'll need something more than fingers. Axle grease, maybe?

Arthur grinned but said nothing about what he surely read in Jack's thoughts. "The point I'm trying to make is to trust your instincts. If you're confident in what your body and mind are telling you, you'll open your soul to a whole new world of insights and knowledge."

The more Arthur stayed on subject and spoke of it, the more he took on that excited youthful persona. These things intrigued the old guy. For some guys, it was the Super Bowl. For Arthur Wainwright, a simple conversation about things metaphysical did the trick. "Take note of that anxious feeling, my friend. There's something going on beneath the surface. A connection is being attempted. If I were a betting man, my money would be on another family member."

"I haven't done anything or thought anything to make that happen."

"What makes you think you need to be doing something? It may be that someone is trying to connect with you for their reasons, not yours." Arthur paced in a tight circle as his hypothesis developed.

"Even so, the only living relatives I have are Kyle's widow, Cary, and her two daughters. Those two nieces are my only living blood relatives." Cary had given birth to another daughter two months after Kyle was murdered. She named the baby Kyra.

Arthur shrugged. "What makes you think the family member I'm referring to is living?"

Jack had been prepared to continue the debate until Arthur said that. Now, he had nothing. Someone in his lineage possibly trying to contact him put a stop to his fledgling expertise on the subject. A measure of sobriety had just been slapped into him. He didn't like it. "Are you suggesting I have ancestors that have the same ability I do?"

"Yes!" he exclaimed, slapping his knee. "Or, perhaps you have an ancestor that knew someone who possessed the same talent."

"Jesus, Arthur." Jack stood and walked to the kitchen and returned with a freshly uncorked bottle. "I see you're determined to sober me up."

Nikki sat wide-eyed, appearing to love the conversation almost as much as Arthur loved talking, joining in only to address Jack's opinion of sobriety. "Sober is a long way from where you are right now. We need to get rice and something stir-fried in you soon or this party may end with you drooling face down on the floor."

Facial muscles refusing to cooperate, he fashioned a look of disapproval. Otherwise, he ignored the comment. "I know nothing of my ancestry."

"Doesn't matter," Arthur said. "Family links will always be strong, regardless how thin the blood has gotten over the years... or decades... or even centuries. You don't need to know a name or recognize a face, you just have to have an intense desire to connect with family—you to them or them to you, and only a general sense of time and place."

That had not been a concept considered until this moment. Could there be others—possibly many others—with the same radiant heart thing? It came as a stunning shock that a connection might be made by someone who may have died many years ago—maybe centuries, attempting a contact prior to their demise in that other time. The relevance of time vanished. "Any suggestions why someone might be trying?"

"That's something only a solid link will tell you. There's no way to know who it might be, much less the reason for it or from what time and place it's coming from. But I can offer a guess."

"Please do."

"Whoever is attempting to contact you is probably deeply troubled and only hoping someone in their lineage has the ability to receive the message. That would be you. But you have to accept it. Otherwise, it'll remain an anxious feeling, nothing more, and you'll never know what it's about."

Although nonchalant about it, Arthur's guesses had a way of being accurate. His insights made Jack uneasy. Recent fretful feelings thought to be boredom had quite suddenly become complicated. He threw his head back. *I don't think I want this to be happening to me again.*

The front door rattled with three hard knocks. The food had arrived. Nikki opened and arranged small carryout containers on the rickety coffee table in front of the sofa. Hunger pushed manners to a back burner.

Jack attempted eating sweet and sour pork chunks with chopsticks.

Arthur and Nikki chuckled at his performance with the utensils.

In his haze, he heard snickers and laughter, but it didn't seem real, nothing did. All he knew was that it took an incredible amount of concentration just to eat. He was determined to make those chopsticks work regardless what they thought about it. Finally he gave up and began stabbing the meat with a single stick. Even that didn't come easy. He realized then that he had achieved what he sought, inebriation—total and unequivocal.

CHAPTER 16

Jack swirled a gravelly tongue around a dry mouth. Rancid breath drifted in warm wet puffs up his nostrils. Opening his eyes didn't seem worth the effort. He did wonder, though, if it was still morning. A pounding head and a stomach refusing to settle robbed him of concern about much else because those thoughts took fleeting spins around his head and sickened him. The mother of all hangovers affected every part of his body. When he tried opening his eyes, it felt as though someone had taped quarters to the lids.

Another cold front raced through Springfield on its way south. The copper strip of weather seal around the north facing back door buzzed intermittently with particularly hard gusts—a mournful sound at just the right pitch to aggravate queasiness.

Extending an arm up to the window above his bed, he parted the faded and drooping curtains with the tips of his fingers. A spider scampered from the encroachment of a hand on its web in the fabric folds.

Broken clouds scudded across the sky, leaving hope that sunshine might hang around for a while. A few hours of clear skies would be nice. With every gust, the lifeless tree outside the window raked the trim along the roofline. The paint had been peeled away by months of relentless rubbing. *What next, the wood under the paint?* He vowed to cut back the tree and paint the trim—someday.

Releasing the curtain, it fell back and the mental note he'd just made disappeared almost as fast. Dust from the curtain drifted into his eyes and open mouth. He spat and rolled over, threwing the blanket off and feeling the cold radiating through the closed window to his nearly naked body. "Brrr!"

Buddy heard the commotion and came running. Untrimmed nails pecking on the vinyl floor in the kitchen announced the dog's journey to the bedroom; he scampered in, jumping about, happy tongue wagging and, before Jack could prevent it, jumped onto the bed and stroked Jack's face with that long wet tongue."

Although apprehensive and uncertain how the aching head would react to the stupidity of overindulgence the night before, he didn't stop the little dog from rousing him. That was one of his daily chores after all. An attempt to sit up confirmed the fear; his head pounded with every heartbeat. "Oh, Buddy," he muttered, "Every time I have too much to drink I say never again and now here I sit. How stupid am I?"

Head cocked to one side and ears perked, the eager pooch appeared determined to understand.

The dog was convenient to blame. "If you were truly my best friend you would've bitten my ankle when you saw me drinking too much."

The self-serving analysis made the concussive head pain worse. Cosmic revenge? He pressed his temples until the discomfort overrode that of the hangover. He hung his head. His rancid mouth tasted like someone had had a foot parked in it all night. *How much of that stuff did I drink?* The wind wailed and moaned, as it continued gusting. The old house creaked—steeped in loneliness and did nothing to cheer him.

Prancing behind him on the bed, Buddy seemed to know that he'd feel better if he stood and moved around. The dog stuck a cold wet noise in his armpit, whimpered and jumped to the floor and ran, sliding to a stop at the bedroom door. A muffled woof quivered his hairy little body. That's when he performed his let's-get-it-going dance.

Moving slowly, Jack took the cue but tried not to aggravate a skull that housed a brain in need of gentle care. It shifted like sludge with each head tilt. Summoning his body parts, it took a concerted effort by all four limbs, but he finally stood.

As he passed a mirror the reflection shocked him—a scary sight for sure, but not worth lingering over. He didn't know his hair could go in that many different directions. When he turned the corner into the kitchen Buddy shuttled from Jack's feet to his food bowl. "Okay, okay. I'm moving as fast as I can." He squatted, so that that liquid mush he called a brain wouldn't tip. He poured dog food into the bowl.

He rinsed two-day old grounds from the coffeemaker and put a fresh pot on to drip. He sat with a thud, pulling himself in close to the table, eyes fixed on that ten-dollar made-in-China coffeemaker. Starting without coffee was out of the question. Filled cup finally in hand, chunks of time passed as he drifted into catatonia lasting several minutes at a time—not thinking, just staring and sipping.

A gust of wind rattled the back door.

Buddy let it be known that it was time for his walk. Jack turned up the final swallow of tepid brew. Once around the block might do more for him than the dog. Buddy knew it—smart dog. He pushed back and rose, doing so with utmost care. Dizziness passed. *A cold blast in the face; that should fix me right up.* Suddenly, the warm air pumped out by the central heating unit inside the house seemed suffocating.

He finished dressing and grabbed the heaviest coat with a hood from the closet next to the front door and snatched Buddy's leash from the umbrella stand next to it. Man and dog stepped into the bracing morning air. It took Jack's breath. The strong wind stung his face.

Buddy didn't have that reaction. Exhilaration overcame the dog, and he shot out at full speed on short legs across the front yard. Jack didn't have the heart to contain such enthusiasm and allowed Buddy to run unleashed. The little dog cut a zigzag, as he scurried up the block.

The icy wind forced measured breaths to prevent nipping his nose. He flipped the hood over his head and pulled the drawstring until only the eyes remained uncovered.

Buddy clearly enjoyed the romp—running, jumping, spinning. He chased his tail and suddenly stopped, catching sight of an airborne plastic grocery sack. The dog scampered off to chase that for a while. Doing a dipsy doodle in the wind, it lifted high into the air and drifted into the street as it descended, almost close enough for Buddy to snatch it with his teeth… but not quite. He jumped at it repeatedly.

Jack's heart skipped when he saw that Buddy remained focused only on the diving and darting bag. There wasn't time to shout his name. Jack heard the sickening thud of a car bumper connect with his tiny body and a loud yelp. Squealing tires came afterwards. The driver obviously hadn't seen him in time, leaving his best friend on his side, motionless in the street. The only detectable movement was his curly coat whipping in the wind.

Jack ran, dropping to his knees near the dog. He lifted the furry head with one hand, as blood from Buddy's open mouth oozed between his fingers.

The elderly driver came to stand over them, shaken, apologizing as he wrung his hands. Jack didn't hear what the old man had to say and didn't give a damn anyway. He lifted his little friend, clutching the dog to his chest and wept.

The biting cold lost significance. Another kind of chill swept over him that had nothing to do with winter. Without checking to see what might be appearing before him, he looked to the sky and railed, "Not now! For Christ's sake, give me peace!"

The old man abruptly stopped talking and backed away.

Jack staggered to his feet with Buddy in his arms and ran toward the house.

The old man called after him, resuming unheeded appeals to help.

Without slowing, he burst through the unlocked front door and gently laid Buddy's lifeless body on a braided oval rug in the front room. He fell to his knees beside the dog, disbelieving what had happened.

The chill returned.

A dull white glow developed around his body, the first in over a year. But there was something different about it. It was unlike previous episodes—not as intense. After scant seconds, a much brighter light bloomed across the room, sending a broadening beam to blend with his dimmer glow that now deepened and surrounded him. His dull glow intensified to match the brilliance of the other. He didn't start it, therefore, couldn't stop it.

Grief deadened normal feelings that he had come to associate with these episodes, not the least of which were fear and wonder. He could not have cared less at the moment what might appear before him. He sat back on his heels, hoping the uninvited and unappreciated intrusion would be quick and go away soon, so he might get back to mourning. He looked at the still developing images as a child might look at a preacher near the end of a long Sunday sermon.

When the image cleared, curiosity went over the top—sense of wonder restored.

CHAPTER 17

Long ago, Jack relinquished reasons to question things he saw as real. It had to be genuine, but from where and when? He observed and developed no opinions. He rubbed his eyes just to make sure it didn't disappear. It didn't. He could ponder his sanity later if need be. There was an upside to his grief; this episode didn't frighten him in the slightest.

An unusually dark-skinned young man of small stature stood facing him. His expression was one of extreme agitation and hinted fear—hate and anger could be in that mix, too. The young man appeared tense, arm and leg muscles twitching. In front of the boy, kneeling, an older man sat, apparently of the same race. Streaks of black ran through very long gray hair. Their faces, even on the younger one, were ruddy, weathered to a deep red. The glow faded but the two remained in the room.

The old one was in the midst of a rhythmic chant, rocking side to side even as he first appeared in the room. He continued the mantra but settled back and sat cross-legged on the floor, arms draped over knees, hands hanging loose. The younger one spun in knee-jerk fashion taking in a view of the living room. The surroundings awed him but his features never softened. He was clearly on a mission.

The old one seemed to be the catalyst for the event. He kept his eyes closed. Jack figured the chant kept his thoughts on this time and space to maintain the connection. The young one not only examined his surroundings, he took off and ran a step this way then that, looking behind everything tall enough to conceal a person. It appeared as though he expected someone to leap out and attack them.

The yellowish garb they wore bore crude markings of various colors and may have been nineteenth century Native American. Although decorated differently, they both wore breechclout, leggings and moccasins, all made from varying colors and thickness of animal hides. The older one continued the melodic hum, rising and falling in time with his gentle sway. The younger one finally stopped and faced Jack. He'd now become the boy's focus.

The young man stepped forward aggressively speaking in an unfamiliar choppy guttural language. Jack shrugged apologetically and offered his friendliest I-don't-know-what-you're-talking-about face. Then English came to him. But it wasn't a voice. The young one's voice, the strange language, remained audible. But the English was a direct translation sent telepathically by the old one.

"We beg your forgiveness of our intrusion at this time of your great sorrow, but it was only now, as grief opened your mind to universal truths that your radiant heart allowed us in." As the old one communicated, the audible rhythm of his chant provided background. "My time with you is short. I am old. My concentration is weak. Please allow me to explain without interruption. The young one is known to The People as Brave Child." He gestured in a slow fatherly way to the boy who retreated back to stand next to the old man. "He is called this because he was the first of The People to create a bond with the light skins near a place they call Laguna Rica."

In his present state of mind, Jack didn't trust his memory to adequately retain what was said. Without taking his eyes from the old one, he fumbled across his chest until his fingers found the small spiral bound notepad and ballpoint pen he carried in his shirt pocket, the habit of a reporter. He began scribbling.

"Brave Child comes from a group of The People known as *Those Who Turn Back.*"

The young one saw the ongoing unspoken communication. Impatient wonder kept his nervous eyes bouncing between the old one and Jack.

"Brave Child comes from a region to the south," the old one continued. "I am of the *Antelopes.* We are The People of the North. Brave Child sought my help to determine if there might be a radiant heart in his future bloodline. We now know that one exists… you. There may be others, but you are the only one ready to receive me, and he must depend on you to hear his plea and fulfill his wish. The eternal honor of Those Who Turn Back and the Antelopes now rests with you. Their souls will wander, tethered by lies. Only truth can break the shackles forged from the fires of deceit that will allow them to join their ancestors. The truth must be recorded, just as you are doing now."

It was disconcertingly clear; taking notes had not been exclusively Jack's idea. There was no time to consider it. Thoughts continued streaming and filling his mind.

"Brave Child sought to take a girl of the light skins as his life mate, but a violent act by the Antelope leader known as Black Horse caused Brave Child to be shunned and no longer considered a friend of their people. Black Horse attacked and killed the light skins in anger over the slaughter of the buffalo. All of The People are being held accountable for the desperate and ill-timed actions of the renegade Black Horse and his misguided followers. Brave Child hardly knew him. But that did not matter to the light skins."

Jack wrote fast but keeping up with the volume of detail was difficult. He wondered why the old one thought it all had to be laid out so quickly. Why couldn't he slow down and allow time to record it accurately? He had to focus to stay up with the old man's barrage of information. He shook off a cramp in his hand and persevered.

"Brave Child knows his life in the physical is short. He will be passing into eternity soon. The light skins are moving from village to village exterminating

The People. He knows, as I do, that we will not survive the coming attack on our home. It is imperative the world knows that harmony existed between our two very different peoples. The actions of a few have dictated the course of many, creating a cloud of division that never should have happened." He paused, weakening fast. The rhythm of his chant changed, slowed.

While waiting for him to continue, Jack let his hand rest on Buddy's head. With the old one's last statement, it became plain why he and the boy had to be intrusive, they were about to do battle and might not survive to try again.

"It is much more personal with Brave Child," the old one went on to tell him. "He wants a member of his bloodline to find ancestors of the light skin girl known as Beatrice, and tell them his love was genuine and will continue through death and beyond. She carried and bore his child. Brave Child will not see his offspring in this lifetime, and now will be crossing into the spirit world soon. He needs assurance this will be done. Will you help him know peace? Will you, as a radiant heart in his bloodline, do this?"

The old one's chant faded further, his movements became labored. The connection would soon be lost and, together, they'd vanish. Jack stopped writing and looked to the old man who repeated his plea with a simple gesture of upturned palms ready to receive a positive response.

The young one, who he now knew as Brave Child, appeared agitated, apparently knowing, too, that time was running out.

He suspected there'd be times in the days to come he'd regret it, but a sense of obligation overcame him. He placed his right hand over his heart and nodded.

Brave Child's face softened. He clenched both fists and firmly placed them over his own heart, and then extended both hands, palms up.

Jack recognized it as a thank-you. The last thing he saw before they disappeared in a flash of light was the old one falling over with his knees drawn up.

Skepticism never took hold—probably because of his grief. He didn't question its validity. It occurred to him that it served a dual purpose. He came to realize, while gently stroking Buddy's lifeless head, how important it was to enter death at peace with the universe. The dog's life ended during a state of euphoria doing exactly what he wanted. He scooped up the hairy little body and smiled. His gaze lifted to a nondescript point on the wall and thought on what he'd learned. *I wonder if Buddy's death is a piece of that universal puzzle Kyle mentioned? If so, why does it have to be my family and friends that are catalysts? Am I somehow responsible for the course of human events?*

Regardless of the larger philosophical questions, Jack determined that Brave Child deserved no less than his pet—eternal peace in death. He hadn't figured out how, but his promise to compile and record the truth would be kept. First, he had to find out just what that truth was.

CHAPTER 18

Jack went about the unenviable task of having Buddy buried professionally by a pet cemetery. As cash strapped as he was, it didn't seem extravagant. Still, it sure wasn't the way he'd envisioned spending Sunday.

If there could only be one thing learned from the adventures of the previous year, Buddy had not ceased existing; just altered in such a way that he couldn't be part of Jack's life any longer. He couldn't be sure about that though; animals might be divinely looked upon differently than humans. Better to believe it and wait for that time when secrets of the universe would be made clear. Somewhere, he believed that Buddy still romped and played.

The day went fast. A hangover, anguish and the stress of new adventures loomed. It drained the little vigor he had. He had one last thing to do before this day ended—honor his friend by finishing the walk that had been tragically interrupted. Completing something they'd begun together would be a final tribute.

The long walk cleared his head. The wind had not let up all day and the temperature struggled into the forties but now was more invigorating than nuisance. The clouds of morning moved on and left behind brilliant late afternoon winter sunshine. Unfettered rays put the world in high contrast—shadows long, well defined and dark. His hands and cheeks numbed as he walked but didn't care.

Returning home, the quiet was unsettling—the old house large and hollow. Throwing his parka over the umbrella stand by the door, he started for the kitchen, thinking a cup of hot cocoa might quell pain and smooth over loneliness. As he sat at the fifties-vintage chrome and Formica table in the kitchen, hot mug in hand, staring at the steam rising from it, thoughts turned to those few minutes in the living room following the accident.

For the first time he attempted analyzing what he'd been told. *Did those two Native Americans have any idea where they were in the flow of time... or geographically, for that matter? Did they have any idea, or even cared what year they dropped in to? Maybe it was superfluous to their cause.* All he could be certain of was that they had come from long before his time on earth. A scant sense of the era they came from was all he had to go on. And only vague clues as to the part of the country they originated from.

Jack took good notes and managed to glean a few hints on where to begin researching what the old one shared. He had a promise to keep and figured he'd get started while opportunity permitted and the information fresh in his mind. A sense of urgency seized him—the same feeling as when pressured to have an article completed by deadline at The Journal. But how could that be? Those two guys had been dead for many decades. What could possibly be the rush to get it done now?

He became fascinated by the newfound knowledge that Native American blood flowed in his veins. He had no previous knowledge of his ancestry, but it might explain how he made it to forty with a thick head of dark hair.

Retrieving the notes, he focused on key elements and other bits of information that might be helpful. The first thing was the old man's references to tribal names. He had called his tribe *The People*. He said that *Brave Child* was a member of *Those Who Turn Back* and that he, the old one, was part of a group known as *The Antelopes*. Obviously, history books would call these tribes by their Native American names. But he received them by way of a telepathic English translation.

Since the old one helped *Brave Child*, it seemed safe to assume two different sects of the same tribe had been on a friendly basis and living in close proximity. *Where could that be?*

The old one referred to white settlers near a place called Laguna Rica. *Laguna Rica? That's a Spanish word.* It made sense; if a Native American used the Spanish name for a place, it likely bore the name prior to their occupation of the area. He thought about the possibility of the name having been changed later to bear a contemporary label—then again maybe not. Many places in the south and western part of the country retained the more romantic sounding Spanish names. Either way, it seemed rational to believe that the location was somewhere in the southern states, because of the strong Mexican influence along the border. But how far north should he search? Where should that line be? On that, he had no clue. For now, he figured it best to confine the search to the border states.

The phone rang. It startled him. On the way to answer it, he gulped down the last swig of cocoa, wiped his mouth on the sleeve of a flannel shirt he wore, and paused to notice the darkening sky through the kitchen window. Again, he was reminded how lonely the house had become, even more so now that darkness encroached. He offered a quick good-bye and good riddance to a harrowing day and snatched up the phone. "Hello."

"Jack," Arthur said, "I've been getting rather confusing signals from your direction. I thought I'd call and see if there is any foundation to these disconnected visions."

He stared at one of Buddy's squeaky toys on the floor and didn't respond, just chewed on the inside of a cheek trying to determine whether to burden him with all the crap that went on. *I really shouldn't trouble him with it.*

"Don't be silly," he said. "I want to be troubled with it."

"When am I going to learn? I can't hide anything from you." Jack eyes followed a small bug crawling in and out of a crack on the ceiling.

"Yes. When are you going to learn?" His voice moved into that high, light-hearted range.

"You first. What did you see in those visions? And, why didn't they make any sense?"

"Sometimes, my perception is somewhat distorted. I'm not sure why. It's closely akin to a dream when the mind pulls together a lot of small facts that don't seem to relate, but are put together in a single scenario anyway. The brain tries to make a coherent story out of it and, most times, it makes no sense on first examination."

"I think I know where this is going and you'll be surprised I'm sure."

"Maybe. Anyway, this potpourri of trivial tidbits will always relate to something, just not necessarily to each other. It usually makes for a bizarre dream. And that's sort of what happened today. I sensed a series of things, making for a vision I can't interpret."

"Let's hear specifics." Jack relaxed, beginning to believe this might be an entertaining distraction from the sadness and peculiarity of the day.

"This morning I climbed the ladder to that tall book case in the study. Remember the one?"

"Sure."

"I became curious… not sure why. Ever do that?"

"All the time, but don't get sidetracked."

"Sorry. I wanted to know what all those dusty books on the top shelf were. Recently I've wondered about the types of reading materials my parents left behind, but never cared enough to climb up there and look. So, I—"

"You're rabbit-trailing. Get to the point."

"You're right. That's neither here nor there. While I was on that ladder reaching for a book I had a vision of you holding a tomahawk in one hand and your dog in the other. You were crying. I lost interest in those books and climbed down. My feet no sooner hit the floor than I was struck with another. Your hair was long, below the shoulders, and you were dressed in pale leather pants of some sort, naked from the waist up. With that look, you'd have fit right in at Woodstock."

"Are you sure it was me and not someone shorter with a dark ruddy complexion?"

"Oh yes. It was you. Now that you mention it, though, your coloring did appear darker… but it was you. I'm sure of it."

"You're visions are making more sense than you realize."

"Stop gauging my ability and start filling me in."

Jack told the story. Arthur interrupted only once and that was when the part about Buddy's accident was shared. "I'm so sorry about your little friend." As the story came out, his fascination rose. Satisfying Arthur's curiosity did a marvelous job of taking Jack out of the quagmire of grief that kept sucking him back in all day.

After finishing the explanation of the visitation by two Native Americans, Arthur's visions came together. The old guy knew that he'd perceived Jack becoming aware of his heritage, by superimposing his face onto the body of Brave Child. Then, the old man saw the connection to Buddy's death—apparently too lazy to interpret for himself and calling Jack instead. That's when it struck him. *Why, you old goat. You were making an exercise out of this as an educational thing. You knew all along and just wanted me to practice interpreting visions.*

He snickered, having read that thought quite clearly. "Whew." Arthur said, "We really have a lot of research ahead of us."

"Are you saying you want to get involved in this?"

"I can't believe you're asking that question. Is there still some part of you that believes I wouldn't want to be involved… compadre?"

"Let me put it this way, have you ever made a promise to someone who's been dead for at least a century?"

"No." Arthur paused. "But that makes one very good reason why I want to be involved; it's absolutely fascinating!"

"Okay… you're in." The offer came tagged with hesitance but nothing like the flat out reluctance of last year. Strangely, he felt twinges of excitement and willing to take the lead.

CHAPTER 19

Jack explored the Internet, gaining an overview of nineteenth century Native Americans and worked from snippets of information provided by the Old One who had dropped into his living room out of the time stream. Being woefully under-educated on America's first inhabitants didn't surprise him. Jack couldn't sit in judgment of prejudices; he was as guilty as the worst offenders.

He focused on the southern tier of states. Historical fragments concerning the region surfaced randomly. So, he began a process of elimination. It seemed prudent to hone in on that part of the country Brave Child and the Old One were from, and the name of the tribe they belonged to in modern terminology. He knew neither. The only solid location name he had was Laguna Rica. But, that was only as solid as the time frame in which it was popularized. So far, no clues had come to light where it might be located.

He accessed libraries, public and university, in California, Arizona and New Mexico and discovered the word Laguna was quite common, but none pairing Laguna with Rica. Jack's grasp of Spanish was poor, although already surmising that *laguna* was the Spanish word for lagoon. According to his information, that word applied to any placid body of water. *Rica* translated as wealth. But was that name given because of what Spaniards or what Native Americans thought of it? It seemed reasonable to assume that the location might be along a coastline. Bays and lagoons dot those regions and rich with food sources, or so he believed Native Americans would think. Since it was a Spanish name, though, maybe the potential was for areas of monetary wealth, gold, silver, or other things considered valuable a couple of hundred years ago. Maybe it was in close proximity to a mining area. As he thought on it, it seemed logical that wealth at that time could have been interpreted more by abundance of necessities than any form of currency—game, fish, building materials. The latter seemed to make more sense. This assumption dropped interior southwestern states low on the priority list. Large areas of this part of the United States are sparse on timber, plus, fishing would have been virtually nil, and even good hunting of game wouldn't be very good in drier climes.

California had a long coastline. He checked there first. But after a few hours, nothing held promise. Moving on, he turned to the other likely locale, states bordering the Gulf of Mexico. The first two that came to mind were Texas and Florida, due to coastline length. Texas won the coin flip to research first.

It occurred to him that Nikki had taken an advanced Spanish class in college, remembering incessant complaints about it during their time in school.

Although unsure there'd be anything she could contribute, he still welcomed the reason to call her—as weak as it was. She could serve as his sounding board. This time, if a man answered, he vowed to remain cool. Luckily, she answered. "Hey Nik. What's goin' on?"

"Hey… you," she replied in a somber tone. "Arthur called and told me what happened to Buddy. I know how dear he was to you."

"Thanks. That means a lot."

"I wanted to call earlier, but I didn't know when would be the best time. I bet I had the phone in my hand half a dozen times and too scared to dial. I was afraid of catching you at a bad time."

"For future reference, a call from you anytime under any circumstances would be a good time. I think I've come to terms with it, just sad, that's all." He paused. "I thought we'd reached a point you didn't need a reason to call."

He heard a sharp draw of air. He detected sarcasm building. She obviously started to, but cut it off. After a pause, "Arthur told me you had a visit."

"Yeah. Apparently I'm of Native American descent. Quirky, huh?"

"I want details."

He collapsed onto the sofa wincing at jab by an errant spring on his bony butt. Squirming a bit, he prepared for a lengthy commentary. At the same time, he made yet another mental note: *I need a new sofa.* All these remodeling notes jammed a cranial filing cabinet to the bursting point.

He explained the episode, including the research thus far. After a half hour, the story came full circle to the reason he'd made the call in the first place. "If you have no more questions then I need your help in a translation of something I was told by the Old One."

"I'm not so sure I'll be of much help translating Indian."

"First of all, now that I know him to be family, they're not Indians, they're Native Americans. Got that? I'm reasonably certain they never saw India."

"Oops."

"Secondly, it's a Spanish word, not Native American. Besides, even if it had been some Indian dialect, I have no idea which tribe." He abruptly went silent. A word he now labeled as racist had just tumbled from his mouth automatically. All his life they had been *Indians* and, like everyone else, he placed them in a container, so to speak, and the rest of the world in a huge assortment of other ethnic containers, all based on skin color, ideologies, and cultures. For years, he'd compartmentalized to a vulgar degree. Now aware that he was of Native American lineage, all the characterizations had become different—disgusting. He had to set aside philosophical meanderings for now and get on with the task at hand.

"Go on," she said. "What's the Spanish word?"

"The word is *rica.* To be precise the entire name is Laguna Rica."

After a quiet moment of nothing more than a hum on the open phone line, "I believe rica means rich or wealth and laguna is a body of water, maybe a bay or a lake. Couldn't you have gotten that translation online?"

"I did. But I wanted to call you. It was a good excuse." He paused. "So, it must have been a place the Spaniards saw as valuable or believed Native Americans viewed as worthwhile. But why?"

"The first thing that comes to mind is gold," she said. "Spanish explorers were always looking for gold. But, I suppose, it could've been something less common to Spaniards. It might have been something quite ordinary by their standards but very important to native cultures. Maybe the fishing was good or there was something else they considered valuable; you know… some type of bounty… something that that particular place held in abundance."

"You're a pretty darned good detective. Ya know that?"

"Are you patronizing me?" At the other end of the phone line, he couldn't see her but visualized the raised eyebrow. "If you want me to be your Dr. Watson, watch the tone Bucko."

"Okay, we have gold and good fishing on the table." He shifted his weight to avoid another poke from that broken sofa spring. Unfortunately, it settled easily dead center, between the cheeks. He winced. "Ouch!"

"Are you okay?"

"It's nothing… just another pain in my ass."

"Are you calling me—?"

"Never mind. How about the name? Do you think it survived into contemporary times?"

"Maybe," she said, "Or possibly a translation of it."

"Have an example for me?"

"Well, Rich Bay or Rich Lagoon for example. It could also be a variation such as Golden Bay. You know, something like that."

"There is another possibility," he added in a low voice.

"Oh?"

"The name, or any variation, has not been used in over a hundred years. Worse yet, the body of water may no longer exist… if it were ever a body of water at all."

"Those might be possibilities but also a defeatist's way of looking at it. If you think like that, this search is over before it starts. Save those for bottom-of-the-barrel last resorts."

He sighed. "You're right. I'm tired. This has been a long and stressful day. I've been deep in thought, too much and too long. I don't want to think about it anymore tonight. Maybe I can find time to work on it tomorrow at The Journal." He yawned.

"You sound like a man in need of a back rub. Would you like me to come over and take care of that for you?"

He said nothing but smiled at the offer.

"I know I can help you relax," she cooed. "Really."

He sat legs fully extended and crossed, head back, eyes closed, grinning. "I'll give you a rain check on that."

"'Rain check' is just another way of saying yes, no, maybe, never... all at the same time."

"I guess that's right. But in this case ambiguous is good. I think I'll leave it that way." He kept his eyes shut. Smile wilting, it occurred to him that he really didn't want to keep her at arm's length anymore. He ached for her. He sat up straight and shook off the tingle worming its way from belly button to crotch. *I have to keep this status quo. I can't let it happen. I can't let us happen. But why?*

CHAPTER 20

The research on Native Americans seemed promising. The Journal, by its nature, proved conducive to fact-finding. Unfortunately, professional considerations required attention, too. Jack promised Gus Landau an original piece if given the opportunity to write something other than fluff. With breathing space, he knew that writing well would come and that he could perform as well as any writer at the paper. His only problem was, and always had been, he'd become too good at a job no one else wanted, trapping him in a dead end job.

Gus had been coming at him with a nonstop barrage of deadenders, wanting newsy spins but none had a thing to do with newsworthiness—usually at the not-so-gentle urging of front office suits that held the advertising guns. Gus noticed how jaded he'd become. Jack read it in the stumpy old man's expression. Clearly, his grump of a boss had become bent on helping, but in his own cantankerous way.

"Dane," he said as he stormed by his desk. "Do you think I could interrupt your daydreaming long enough to get some work out of you?" His gruff voice and that foul smelling cigar arrived before he did around the corner of the cubicle.

"I've been meaning to talk to you about an expense account, boss. I'd like to research a project that might yield a multi-part article, but it may require travel… limited… only a few hundred miles."

"An expense account? Are you out of your mind? This isn't New York. Crap, boy, we can barely afford coffee and toilet paper."

Gus was old-school. That meant somewhere beneath the surface an article that had everything to do with pleasing only the readership might spark his interest. Gus may have been old and noisy, but he was also a reporter at heart. Jack saw the twinkle in his eyes even as he complained about expense money. *I know what your concerns are. So, chew on it for a moment. Then tell me what I want to hear.*

Jack wanted to be sympathetic with Gus about his budgetary problems but too much rode on getting the information. The article had been bait and important to Gus, but Jack's mission topped the priority list. "So, The Journal isn't willing to invest in a good story? Is that what you're saying, Gus?" The innocence in his voice may have been overdone a bit.

"I didn't say that," Gus growled, chewing even faster on that unlit cigar. "Giving you an expense account and investing in a good story aren't interchangeable ideas. It could turn out like… well, like pouring water into a parched crack in the earth. That might be especially true in your case. Sometimes, you act like a parched crack, you know that, Dane?" He spat tobacco pulp in the wastebasket.

Jack glanced at the little brown wad atop a pile of papers in his trashcan. He frowned. It was disgusting. *I think Gus is on the ropes and knows it.* "Getting a quality story takes time and research, boss. Both need to be funded somehow." He wanted to sound firm, but whiny was more like it. "If I'm to remain a feature writer, let me write something that subscribers actually *want* to read. Whaddaya say?"

Brow furrowed, Gus searched for insincerity, looking Jack up and down. He stroked gray stubble on the turkey waddle under his chin with the backs of his fingers. He yanked the cigar butt from between his lips and pointed it at Jack. "Here's an idea that might get you covered and be justifiable to those yahoos in accounting. We've got to stay politically correct on this." He marched to and fro, inches in front of Jack. "Let's say you take a week-long vacation and, because you love your work so much, you research and write a fabulous article while you're away that we *coincidentally* print." He stopped abruptly and held a finger near the end of Jack's nose. "I don't mean weak, watered down fluff either." He continued pacing. "I mean something with balls, something with legs." He pumped the air with a fat little fist that appeared as though he had a cigar growing from between the fingers. "By God, I want it so damned good that people will still be talking about it a week after they've read it. Got that, Dane? A week! It has to have depth, something that takes at least three issues to get it all in. Understand?"

He clasped hands together behind him, offering nothing to amend the old man's spiel. Gus had taken the cue. Why not let him run with it? His attitude leaned favorably. Even a misplaced expression might screw it up.

"Now about the expenses," Gus said." Remember, for reasons of political correctness, this is all to be coincidental so I can slide it by our business manager. Got that? Coincidental. You just happen to keep a scrupulous accounting of all your expenses, receipts, mileage and that sort of thing. Once the article is published, I'll requisition reimbursement money, and I'll not only pay you for the week and cover your expenses, I'll pay you an additional week's salary as a bonus, or give you another week's paid vacation… your choice."

Jack scrunched his face and sucked air between his teeth. "I'm not sure I have enough available cash to cover expenses until I'm reimbursed."

"Don't press your luck, Dane," he snapped. "Besides, if I don't like the piece and we don't use it, you can put ketchup on those expenses and eat 'em. Got that?"

"Still a paid vacation, right?"

"Sure. That would have been true anyway. Go have a good time." He made a show of poking that nasty cigar butt in the corner his mouth, shifting it to the other side with his tongue, his way of saying the conversation is over.

Jack smiled patronizingly. "How could I not jump at an opportunity like that?"

On that comment, the elf with an attitude spun and disappeared in search of other dragons to tease.

Jack worked to complete five days worth of menial chores in advance. This might move his career out of the dead-end column, all the while taking care of personal business. It seemed promising.

A sudden nervous flutter took his breath. "What the…" It came on quick. He gently rubbed his stomach, huffing through circled lips, hoping it didn't escalate to full-blown nausea. That was strange. He looked at his stomach as if it belonged to someone else. *Where did that roller coaster rush come from?* Could it have been uneasiness where this discovery quest might lead, or something more mundane; like nervousness about his airtight promise to Gus to deliver a top-notch three-parter? Neither reason seemed important enough to cause such a strong sensation. What could be so all-fired important that could bring on a sudden breath-robbing moment? *What the hell is this little gloomy feeling all about?*

It was after seven o'clock that Monday evening before finally wrapping up chores at the paper and making the remainder of the day his own.

The money thing had become worrisome, but only because he didn't have any. A couple of hundred dollars in a checking account was the sum of his worldly wealth. He had no choice but ask Arthur—pride be damned. He had to get this trip funded and rationalized that if Arthur wanted to be an integral part of all this then he'd want to pay his own way and maybe Jack's, too. If all went well, reimbursement would come later anyway.

The ride home seemed extraordinarily long. Darkness and cold biting wind contributed to loneliness. He thought about that odd sudden rush while still at work—one that turned into a sense of gloom. He'd almost gotten home when something came over him and suddenly home seemed like the wrong place to be.

Without hesitation he turned away from his street and set a course across town to Arthur's place. Up until he acted, going to Arthur's hadn't even crossed his mind. Evenings had always been a one-man show, seldom uncomfortable about it and most often preferring it, but not tonight.

As he approached Arthur's mansion uneasiness lifted. He wheeled into the driveway, scarcely slowing. As usual, the gate was open upon arrival. Arthur's estate appeared foreboding on this February night. From the front gate, the long driveway that meandered through the woods was mostly hidden from the street. After taking a couple of winding turns, the mansion appeared straight ahead, backlit by a full moon, creating a ghostly sight. A production company in search of an appropriate setting for a horror flick might consider it perfect.

At the end of the approach, nearing the huge house, he circled in front of two statues overgrown with dormant weeds and vines. In an empty fountain dried leaves whipped in tight spirals playing chase in the moonlight. Vines draped over the top tier of successively larger bowls down to the fountain's empty pool. As the cold wind gusted, dangling vines waved to the racing leaves, cheering them on.

He drove close to the portico and killed the engine. Throwing open the door, he heard the hinges talk back with that familiar groan and pop. "Yep, I need a new car," he muttered, as a blast of frigid February wind brought tears to his eyes. He pulled his coat collar high, shrugging it up to protect numbing ears, stuffing his hands deep into the pockets, trotting up onto the porch and to big double doors.

The front door to the mansion sounded its own creaky hinges, echoing back from within the cavernous structure. Blocking dim light, Arthur stood with his hands clasped together. "Hurry, my boy, don't stand out in this cold a second longer."

"I bet temperatures stay in the teens all night." Jack blew warmth into cupped hands as he hurried through the open door.

"My goodness, it's cold. It's a long-pants kind of night out there."

Jack noticed and realized that it was only the third time he'd seen Arthur in anything other than baggy cargo shorts—the night he and Nikki met him, the night Jack got so drunk and now. He smiled, remembering the night they met. Those pants were short enough to have been confused with knickers. Tonight, the long pants he wore were the lower half of a sweat suit. Over that he still wore a short sleeved Hawaiian shirt. Everything in that place smacked of great wealth, except for Arthur's wardrobe; that could be measured in pocket change.

"So you did manage to get time off to do your research," Arthur said.

Something else he shouldn't have known, but did. "Yeah, I wanted to come by and see if you'd like to join me in this discovery quest."

"Just waiting for an invitation offered aloud and formally. It'll be great fun. I'll take care of expenses since you were kind enough to invite me along."

Sometimes, it was a good thing that he knew all this stuff beforehand; a request for money was unnecessary. "I appreciate the offer and accept, but this isn't a handout. Look at it as an investment in my writing ability and—"

"I know, I know." He waved off the concern. "You'll write a fabulous story, and your editor will throw money at you to cover expenses. When that happens I expect to be reimbursed. And I want every dime of it in cheap wine and chicken fried steaks." He flashed a crazy grin and turned that long slender nose up in a mock show of self-importance. "Come on." He walked lively to his favorite room—the library. There'd be no more talk about money.

Passing the staircase, Jack wondered briefly what the upper floors looked liked. He'd never seen them but fantasized that there was probably a room up there ideal for writing the great American novel. Maybe a room with a great view through one of those large arched windows. It brought the wisp of a smile when it crossed his mind that Arthur probably hadn't seen the upper floors in weeks, maybe months.

"Care for something to drink?"

"Anything but wine." He watched Arthur snatch up a bottle of gin and one of tonic water. mixing two strong drinks. Jack took a big sip and savored the taste. "Have you had a chance to think about our phone conversation?"

Arthur gestured him to a nearby chair. "More than that, I've been reading and consulting with Maigo. Bless his Asian heart, he offers such valuable direction. My good friend told me the shamans of several of the Great Plains tribes were adept at invoking the radiant heart… "

"Shamans?"

"Better known as medicine men. The elderly gentleman you saw was probably one. Every tribe had a spiritual guide and healer, much like a community doctor in modern cultures."

"I'm thinking Texas may hold the key to our search. But I can't be certain why I do."

He waved an accusing finger and clucked his tongue. "Jack, Jack, Jack. When are you going to trust your instincts?"

It still seemed foreign that every hunch could be an embryonic psychic insight trying to weasel in.

"I may not be connected to the worldwide web," he went on, "but I do have one of the most valuable tools of those seeking enlightenment."

"What's that, your psychic ability?"

"That too. But I'm referring to my library card." Arthur pointed to a pile of books on a nearby table.

With heaps of papers and books lying about the room, another stack had not been noticed. But maybe it should've been; it was one pile not coated with a fine layer of dust.

Grabbing the open book from atop the stack, he dropped into his chair and flipped through a couple of pages. "Ah, here it is." He pecked the page with a finger. "I read about several of the tribes that inhabited the states of the Great Plains during the nineteenth century, Shoshone, Cherokee, Apache, Comanche and a few others. Then I saw something quite interesting. There was a sect of the Comanche known as the Quahadi Comanche. Would you like to guess what Quahadi means in their language?"

"I probably have a fifty-fifty chance on this one. It would have to be Antelope or Those Who Turn Back. I'll say, Antelope."

"Exactly."

"So, you found the information in that book?"

"No, I found it on the worldwide web. I'm just reading up on it here, that's all."

"You what?"

"Did I leave the impression I was computer illiterate? Sorry. All I meant was that I used the computer at the library and checked out the books." He grinned.

The old fart loved playing these games—to confuse and to clarify.

Arthur continued smiling as he pulled some printed pages from the center of the book. "In fairness, I've been reading in more detail about the Comanche people, but I found a concise piece from the library of the University of Texas online that may pinpoint what you're looking for."

"I'm all ears but—"

"I know, but you can't help it." His dark eyes sparkled with amusement. "It must be a genetic thing."

Jack cupped his ears and fingered them. "Too big? Really?" He narrowed his eyes to slits. "You've been hanging around Nikki Endicott too much. My ears are just right."

"It seems the Quahadi Comanche roamed an area that encompassed parts of southern Oklahoma, north central Texas and westward into a region called the southern plains." He lost the smile and became all business. "Today, the South Plains of Texas is a farming region around Lubbock, home of Texas Tech University. Go Red Raiders!"

Jack shook his head. "Moving right along… "

"Sorry about that. It's also referred to as the High Plains, because it's a plateau atop a sharp rise known as the Caprock… but that's neither here nor there. This is what's interesting; a brief uprising called the Staked Plains War. Not much of one mind you, except to those affected. But the reason for it was a Quahadi renegade chief known as Black Horse—"

"That's the chief the Old One spoke of."

"Black Horse did what he thought was right and received written permission from authorities at Fort Sill in modern day Lawton, Oklahoma to hunt buffalo on the high plains. When his group arrived in an area just north of modern day Lubbock, they discovered the wholesale slaughter of thousands of buffalo and assumed, rightfully so, that it had been the work of white hunters. Black

Horse even witnessed one of those buffalo massacres as he sat on his horse on a hillside below the Caprock. He became so enraged that he vowed to kill every white buffalo hunter he came in contact with. Black Horse and his renegade band of Quahadi Comanche plundered hide camps all over that part of Texas and did kill a few buffalo hunters as well."

"So, the Native Americans were justified."

"I think so. But people shouldn't have gotten killed over it. There's hardly ever justification for taking a human life."

Jack nodded. For years he'd unwittingly discriminated against this race of people, all the while proudly telling others he supported America's melting pot heritage. He grappled with how to become the person he professed to be. Doing a one-eighty was tough.

"Jack, are you still with me?" Arthur waved a hand in front of his face.

"Oh... yeah, go ahead."

"Black Horse and his band of renegades did not have a chance to continue the campaign for long. Word of his bloody shenanigans got back to authorities. Cavalry from Fort Sill, Oklahoma was assembled and sent to the High Plains of Texas to stop him. The initial attempt failed. It was a short battle at a place known as Yellow House Canyon. The contingent was too small to overtake the Quahadi. Sometime later, more soldiers from Fort Griffin were sent out to bring Black Horse in. That time, they were successful and arrested him and his renegade band after a brief skirmish near the site of Lubbock Lake. The outlaw band was taken back to the reservation."

Interesting stuff but Jack couldn't make the connection. He walked to a window offering a view of what must have been a beautiful garden at one time in the past, complete with Greek statues quietly guarding it under a moon bright enough to cast shadows. The tall undraped window framed the full moon beyond the trees. The view belied cold harshness of the night. Lacing fingers at his back, he stared. If this had all taken place in the northern part of the state, he had just been hurled back to square one. Where was Laguna Rica located? Independent of Arthur's research he'd come to believe it'd be found somewhere along the Gulf coast and that, now, was no longer an option. He spun back. "You've saved me valuable time. I thank you for that."

"No thanks necessary. This is fascinating. I would have begged to be a part of it if you hadn't asked." Arthur had that joyful look of a child with a new toy.

"I need to narrow my search. The name Laguna Rica is my only clue."

"I can offer one more bit of information that might help sharpen the focus... "

"What's that?" He yawned and glanced at his watch, aware of the late hour.

"The tribe of Comanche you referred to as Those Who Turned Back inhabited an area of north Texas referred to as the Cross Timbers, westward to the mountains of New Mexico." He rose, preparing to usher Jack out. "They were known as the Nokonis Comanche. The word nokonis means *those who turned back*. So, my friend, the logical place is somewhere between the Quahadis and the Nokonis. Now," Arthur said, putting an arm around his waist and pulling him toward the front door, "Go home and get in bed."

CHAPTER 21

Jack's enthusiasm crashed as he slid behind the wheel of his car to drive home. Out of the wind and closed inside the vehicle the shock of stinging cold became bearable. Uncontrollable yawning began.

He'd been drawn to the old guy's house this evening—an automatic response to loneliness, perhaps? If so, why? He hadn't even wanted to go but did. He followed the urge—end of story. But his exhausted mind refused to let the question lie unexplored. It bounced around like a skipping record album that repeated the question over and over. There'd be no answers forthcoming this night. His give-a-shit-factor had flat lined. Answers suddenly didn't matter. Sleep did. He dozed.

The car veered off the pavement into the gravel. Pebbles spraying the underside brought him back abruptly. He sat straight, shook his head and worked the muscles in his face until a rush of fresh blood circulated through his cheeks. He'd be home in less than ten minutes. *Just a little farther. Hang in there.* Sleep stalked him.

Eyelids heavy, he forced his head into a cognitive frame, mulling information acquired from Arthur. If he could put his mind to the task, it might ward off sleep until he made it home.

Although possible to invoke an image of the place he knew as Laguna Rica, he didn't know how to bring it about. The radiant heart was the key. But how is it triggered? Which emotion is necessary—anger, frustration, fear—what? Or, could it be intensity regardless of type. Maybe even a euphoric rush would bring it on. He didn't know.

The heater finally warmed, replacing cold air trapped inside the car. He ceased shivering.

It was unsettling to think that concentration was all it took to bring on the power. Once begun, he'd be thrust into a different year, possibly another century. The confidence to willingly make it happen remained a barrier he had yet to cross, especially alone.

So far, Arthur and Nikki had been holding off bugging him about it. Jack was convinced they didn't realize how out of control he felt over the, so-called, gift. *Gift? Hell, it's more of a hemorrhoid with a bow on it.* He snickered.

This time around, he had ample reason to step out front and deal with it—to find the courage to press on with or without their help. The fight was for confidence and his alone to wage. The simple truth of it was that they had more confidence in him than he had in himself—bottom line. He needed them.

Clutching the steering wheel tighter, he arched his aching back. Exhaustion prevented a comfortable compromise. Adding to discomfort, his eyes burned to the point of distraction, fluttering moisture back into them frequently. He stretched his neck hard right and then left. It ground and popped. Soreness eased.

The night may have been cold and windy, but it happened to be beautiful, with a crisp clear sky, light from the silvery-blue moon shone brightly, casting shadows, and splitting hues of blue and gray. Serenely glowing across the landscape, the moon was worthy of a long admiring gaze into the night. It was peaceful; the world was at rest—exactly where he should have been.

Warm air brushing his cheeks, he had both hands on top of the steering wheel, hunched into it while his mind drifted. *I wonder what the landscape around Laguna Rica looked like over a hundred years ago. Does it still look like it did? Or, is it paved over with a parking lot or, maybe, a huge complex of condominiums sits over it.* He repeated the name aloud, "Laguna Rica ... Laguna Rica," liking the way it rolled off his tongue. It had a soothing feel and sound.

The car drifted across the center stripe of the highway directly into the path of an oncoming vehicle. Suddenly aware, he cut the steering wheel hard right—too hard.

The car went into a sideways skid propelling it into a roll down a steep embankment into a ditch. As it tumbled, he was tossed like a rag doll, held in place by a seat belt. He no longer had control over his body or the vehicle. Time seemed to accelerate rapidly.

It froze.

A flash of white light exploded before him. It was brilliant, even through closed eyelids. When he opened them, he saw that he still sat as if in the driver's seat holding his left forearm defensively in front of his face, the right, which had been on the steering wheel, gripped nothing.

The steering wheel was gone. The car was gone. Overhead was a brilliant sun on a clear day. He sat in knee-high grass. Dropping hands into his lap, he straightened and stretched his neck to its full length and looked around. He saw a sea of grass, all the same height, to the limits of his vision in all directions. It moved and appeared as water would—rolling in waves with each gentle breeze. The air had an unusually sweet fresh scent.

He had no clue where he ended up, or even if he was still on the planet. He sat unmoving for a time. Twice before he'd put his feet on a solid surface that wasn't of this earth. *Does time and dimension shifting include interplanetary travel?* He didn't want to add that to so many other unanswered questions.

Rolling over onto hands and knees, he rose and dusted the seat of his pants. *Maybe I'm hallucinating because of a blow to the head.* So far, there was only one undeniable fact; he was no longer in his car rolling into a ditch and that's the last place he remembered being. Real or imagined, he stood in a different place, and it wasn't night anymore.

He patted himself searching for lacerations, bruises, or broken bones—nothing, not even a scratch. He examined the landscape. There was little to see except an endless expanse of tall, brown and lifeless clumps of grass, gently rolling in time with each fresh breeze. Nothing else—no houses, no trees, no roads—nothing. The only discernible feature, aside from the grass, was a gently rising knoll straight ahead and slightly right.

He drew a deep breath. Although the sun beamed warm against his face, he felt tiny embedded streamers of coolness. Squinting up at the sun in a cloudless blue sky, he walked toward the hill thinking God had him in the cross hairs. He absently looked to his feet, placing one in front of the other and wondered about it all: *Why did my dog die? Was his life sacrificed to further some universal game? Am I a minor player or instrumental in all this crap? Why did I meet two Native Americans that have been dead for more than a hundred years? And why have I suddenly found myself in an outpost of hell?* He looked to the sky, threw up his hands and sent up a simple prayer. "I changed my mind. I want my monotonous life back and all of this to go away. Okie dokie?"

Self-pity ended abruptly, as he reached the highest point of the gentle rise. Stretching out before him was a lake surrounded by short drop-offs, no more than fifteen to twenty feet high, broken only by deeply eroded washouts down to the lakebed. It was rocky, all jagged and whitish. It could have been some type of clay or caliche-like material. The only plant life was short and scrubby, confirming a semi-arid climate.

This seemed to be the rule for the entire perimeter, roughly round in shape, appearing less than a quarter mile across. It was difficult to judge size and distance. The sun's rays danced in the distance creating a mirage.

Jack stood on the edge of a ten-foot drop. At the bottom, sand stretched to the water's edge another hundred, or so, feet away. The water appeared odd. He needed a closer look.

Walking parallel to the short precipice toward a washout that presented a passable descent to the bottom, he stopped at its lip. It was steep but not straight down.

He skated sideways down the gravel to the bottom into soft sand and sank a couple of inches with every step, getting it in his shoes as he approached the water's edge. The water didn't react to the wind. There were no ripples, no waves—mostly gray with white streaks across the surface. Stepping to its edge, he knelt to discover a thin crusty, crystalline layer covering the entire surface as far as he could see and only about an inch deep beneath it. The glaze broke easily under the weight of a hand. After touching it, he tapped his tongue with a fingertip. It tasted brackish.

It occurred to him that he should be committing as much to memory as possible. This place might hold relevance to his research. For the first time since arriving, he seriously took note of the things he saw.

It was then that the cool breeze under a warm sun held potential significance. He looked to the top of the short drop-off above him and noticed tiny green shoots at the base of tall dead grass. He deduced it to be early spring.

A distant muffled sound caught his ear. He straightened and faced that direction, cupping his ears. It sounded like a human voice carried on the breeze. As the wind died so did the sound, leaving him to believe it had simply been the wind across his ears. But, as the wind picked up again, so did the sound. As he walked in that direction, a familiar rhythm established, like a song he couldn't quite remember.

Suddenly, he became aware he was alone and defenseless. He paused. He turned in a slow circle, searching for anything that didn't look right. With voices came concern for safety in this strange place. He was armed only with curiosity. That was enough to set his feet to moving again.

The volume increased and he accelerated the pace.

A short time later, he came upon an overhanging precipice with grass waving gently over its edge. It had weathered into a C-shape, creating natural protection from sun and rain. The sound seemed to be coming from below it.

He looked about and approached cautiously. Gliding past a clump of weeds, he saw a hole in the side of the inset dirt wall no more than three feet across. He hurried over and stood beside it.

Squatting down, settling gently upon bended knees, he peeked in. Just past the small entrance a chamber opened up, large enough for a grown man to stand.

There, in the glow of a torch suspended from a hole in the wall, an elderly Native American sat on his haunches humming a chant. Cool musty earth was laced with the pungent oily scent of the burning torch. A cloud of black smoke hung near the ceiling in the unventilated interior. Standing beside the old man was a much younger one, dressed in similar fashion. *My God! I'm here! I'm standing smack-dab in the middle of Laguna Rica!*

It felt as though a giant hand pressed all the air from his lungs. His heart skipped. His face heated. A buzz set up in his ears.

As the shock of it leveled off, he began to realize that he witnessed their efforts to connect with him prior to that morning they appeared in his living room in the days before Buddy was killed.

He jumped to his feet. Urgency to determine where he stood came over him. "Laguna Rica... Laguna Rica... Laguna Rica," he mumbled as he looked from side to side and then up and down, searching for clues, markers that might indicate where the hell he was in the United States.

He continued repeating the name until the thought shot through his mind that he had been in the middle of an incomplete car accident when thrust here. He didn't want to think about that. Not now. Not yet. But it was too late. That thought took over. He looked down to see the white glow enveloping his body, getting brighter fast.

A sudden force smashed squarely into his chest. The impact drew in his forearms protectively over his ribcage.

The brightening light suddenly exploded in brilliance. No analysis necessary, he was returning to his home space and time.

When it became possible to draw an uninterrupted breath, he opened his eyes to his own world—lying crumpled on the ceiling of his upside down car. He glanced up and saw the seat and steering wheel. The seatbelt buckle had broken, dropping him. But it apparently held long enough to prevent serious injuries.

He struggled upright. Something warm oozed down his face. He yanked the rear view mirror around, now between his legs, until he saw the shape of his head. In the moonlight, a trickle of blood was visible. He sourced it to a small cut in the hairline.

A female voice came within range, shouting, "Are you all right? Are you okay?"

Feeling a sudden misplaced sense of embarrassment, he crawled through the shattered passenger side window, emerging just as a woman appeared.

"Are you okay?" she asked, helping him to his feet.

Still unsteady, he leaned against the wreckage, "I think so. But, I'd better just stand here a moment until I'm sure."

"Let me call an ambulance for you."

"I don't think it's necessary," he said, fingering the blood trickle on his forehead. It occurred to him how incredibly nice this woman was. "But I appreciate the offer. Thank you." He stepped away from his upside down car and turned to check the damage. That idle promise he'd often made about buying a new car seemed closer than ever now. He'd just run out of reasons why he shouldn't buy one. "But if you have a cell phone and don't mind, I'd appreciate you calling a tow truck."

"I don't mind at all." She sighed, clearly relieved. As she walked away, "Come sit in my car. I'll stay until it arrives. It's too cold to stand out here."

She was right. It was damned cold. He hadn't realized it until she mentioned it. He slid into the big sport utility vehicle and closed the door. Shivering and watching her dial, he came to the conclusion that the most severe injury incurred was to his pride for nodding off and losing control.

After she made the call, he had the opportunity to visit with the late night angel of mercy. She deserved a thank-you beyond lip service. *I have to do something special for her someday soon.*

The tow truck arrived. After thanking her again, he waved goodbye and watched as she disappeared down the road into the night. His heart stuttered when he realized that he hadn't asked her name or where she was from.

Silently cursing the judgment lapse, he dumped hundred-year-old sand from both shoes and climbed into the cab of the wrecker.

CHAPTER 22

Steam curling from the coffee dampened Jack's nose as he cradled it in both hands to his lips. He took in the view through the small eye-level window in the front door of his house—his old car that should be on its way to be crushed and shredded, not parked in his driveway. But it was not so much the car as the reminder—a quick trip to Laguna Rica late last night—wherever and whenever that was. Aside from escaping the accident with his life and walking away intact, he had a lot to consider. He finally took that sip.

Ironically, the car didn't appear much worse than it did before the accident; a few new wrinkles plus an assortment of fresh scrapes and scratches; but all the windows were intact except for the front passenger-side. *That car in front of this house makes the perfect picture of poverty.* "Humph." He lived in crap and drove crap. He sighed. "Oh well…" Gulping coffee that had now gone tepid, he wondered what to do with that piece of junk.

It was after ten o'clock Tuesday morning, the first official day of a working vacation and not the way he would've chosen to begin it. He ached, still groggy. Soreness transformed into a sleep-robber overnight. The worst of his pain happened to be his chest—thrown into the steering wheel when the seatbelt broke. The older model car wasn't equipped with a shoulder harness, just the lap belt. So, it could have happened even before it broke. It'd been stupid negligence—no more, no less.

Suddenly, it occurred to him that he'd lived fifteen or twenty minutes within the span of an eye blink. *If this keeps happening, I won't just feel older than my years… I will be.*

A late model blue sedan pulled in behind his wrecked car, squealing to a stop. *Very nice.* He studied the sleek little number through the eyes of a shopper. *I wonder what the payments would be on a beauty like that?* He downed the last swallow of coffee.

Nikki wasted no time leaping out and bounding to the front porch. Jack yanked the door open before she knocked, startling her. She recoiled and stumbled backwards, nearly falling off the porch. "Let me guess," he said, "Arthur called you first thing this morning and told you I had been in an accident, bruised but otherwise okay. Am I right?"

"Yes! I'm damned angry you called him first!" She regained balance and advanced aggressively.

He may have started it and wanted to play the game but a hitch in his chest cut sarcasm short, like an ice pick plunged into his sternum. He gathered a fistful of shirt with one hand while sloshing the last drops from his cup in the other.

"You worthless piece of—"

"Whoa. Slow down." He abandoned the pain in favor of stopping a wild gesture in mid-air before the back of her hand connected with the side of his face. "If you make me drop and break my favorite cup, I certainly won't laugh about that."

Her nostrils flared. It seemed clear enough that anger masked injured pride.

He tentatively loosened the grip but didn't trust her to let go of her arm just yet. "Look, I didn't phone Arthur. The only call made since the accident was to a towing company, and someone else made that for me."

She pressed on, jerking the arm from his loosened grasp, belligerently planting hands on hips. "How do you explain Arthur knowing...?" The truth of it finally smacked her. That tight face dropped like a stroke victim, metamorphosing into remorse.

"It *is* amazing how the old guy knows these things. Isn't it?" He grinned.

She covered her face with both hands. "I've made a complete ass of myself."

"I prefer to think that you've made my aches and pains not so bad and brightened my day."

Keeping her hands up to hide embarrassment, she fell forward into his chest with her forehead.

He groaned. "Shit! That hurt."

She straightened. "Sorry. "What are your injuries?"

"Bruises, scratches and plenty of soreness... but the accident isn't important. The important thing is that I was there."

"You were where?"

"Laguna Rica. I was in that place for the equivalent of fifteen or twenty minutes in the instant my car rolled."

"Tell me about it. Where along the coast was it? Could you tell where you were? Was it Texas? Could you see surf from where you landed?"

"It could have been Texas, but nowhere near the coast. It was a broad tree-less prairie and Laguna Rica was not at all what I expected. It was a small lake with very little water in it. Even that was covered over with a salty mineral. It looked like thin ice."

Nikki's chameleon expression took another turn, this time astonishment.

"What's wrong? Why are you looking at me like I have boils exploding on my face?"

Her eyes darted back and forth as her mind obviously shifted into overdrive.

"What's the matter?"

She stammered and stuttered but, for some reason, she couldn't put a single word together.

"Come on girl, spit it out."

She closed her eyes, took a deep breath and started over. "Laguna Rica was so named because of the salt content." Her eyes remained large, as if she read from the page of a book. "It wasn't because of gold or anything we might consider precious today. The Indians used the salt to cure buffalo hides and meat. That's the reason Spanish explorers interpreted the location as valuable, hence the word *Rica*, or rich. Its known today as Rich Lake, located about twenty-five miles south of Lubbock, Texas. I'd be surprised if you could find many people in Lubbock who could even tell you how to get there."

"You've known this all along?"

"I've never known it by another name. Besides, it never seemed very important when I was growing up. I was thinking like you, that Laguna Rica was somewhere along the coast, someplace larger, not a small alkaline lake virtually hidden in cotton farming country on the South Plains of Texas for God's sake."

"What do you mean, 'I've never known it by another name'? You make it sound like a favorite family vacation spot. Why are you aware of it at all?" That now familiar tingle he'd come to associate with eye-opening information of great importance set in. "You're scaring me a little."

"Do you remember the day we met on campus?"

"How can I forget? I had a tray loaded with food in the Student Union cafeteria trying to get between crowded tables when I looked up and saw you coming. I remember that I'd been watching you and wanting to meet you, plotting a way to get an opportunity to say hello. At that moment I thought I'd found it. But you walked hell-bent-for-leather right past me. I didn't have a chance to speak. You blurted something rude and vaguely threatening. Something like, 'Out of my way, I have places to go, people to see and things to do… and you, Bubba, are in my way'."

Her eyes took on a somewhat distressed look as though touched. "All I remember is that I was rude and didn't care."

"I stood there spellbound that you spoke to me for the first time with solid eye contact. At the time, it didn't matter what you said, just that you said it to me. I did the hayseed aw-shucks-shuffle with the point of my toe because you spoke." His dreamy look went serious. "But what has that got to do with Rich Lake?"

"Bear with me."

He saw that the story would not come easily. Her expression showed signs of strain. "You deserve to know the whole story," she said, turning away. "There was no plan." Her demeanor spiraled down even more. "What you read as a plan was bad attitude and resentment… because of my parents. That day was less than two weeks after I'd had an abortion." She let that revelation hang. Finally, she glanced back.

The seriousness of it had suddenly become quite clear. He chose not to respond and just listen.

"My parents are staunch Southern Baptists. Still are… I think. If the church doors are unlocked, they're usually inside. The label ultra-conservative is grossly inadequate, but it'll have to do. It's a severe puritanical slant on living. They refuse discussion on lifestyles that don't emulate theirs. It's their shield against the world. They wield that view alongside the sword of hypocrisy. To them everything is right or wrong determined by deep biases. Growing up in that environment was hard, Jack, more difficult than you can imagine. I saw the world in shades of gray. My parents hammered me day and night with proselytizing bullshit; opinions by my way of thinking, facts by theirs. So, you can imagine, telling them I was pregnant was the most difficult thing I'd ever done. Their response created a rift that hasn't healed to this day."

She paused and after quiet seconds turned to face him. "I can't be sure it'll ever be okay between us."

Delving deeper into the story pained her. Even the passage of ten years hadn't been long enough. But she persevered in the telling of it and an hour later wound down.

"When I told my parents about the pregnancy everything they'd ever taught me went out the window because the problem shrank to saving face in the community. It was no longer about right or wrong. I was whisked out of town, the procedure done, and back on campus in two days. I haven't forgiven them for that. The day I passed you in the student union the physical and emotional wound was still raw."

Her story had taken a toll, shuffling across the floor as if dragging iron shackles and chains. She sat at the kitchen table and began tracing the pattern on the tablecloth with a fingertip. She said nothing more.

He sat, too, but remained uncertain what he might do or say. Maybe it'd be best to just continue the quiet support. He snaked a hand across the table and up over the back of hers and squeezed gently. The lengthy story had only been a precursor; the setup to what she intended to say all along.

"My mother and father live less than five miles from Rich Lake. I grew up on the cotton farm they still live on and continue to operate today. I hope you understand why I didn't remember that crummy little lake. I've been blocking that whole part of my life for years and anything that might remind me of it."

Astonishment swarmed Jack. It seemed unfathomable. But other events of late flashed before him. *With all that has happened, why should one more twist of fate be less believable? Is this, somehow, building toward those universal truths?*

"Jack," she said and scooted her chair back and rose. "It left more than just a psychological scar." She turned and leaned on the kitchen sink and fixed a gaze through the window to a tree in the backyard. "The procedure was botched. I'll never have children."

He joined her at the sink and put his arm around her waist.

Tears filled her eyes, spilled out and down her cheeks.

The tingle and shiver he experienced had just been explained. He finally understood her sarcasm and lack of serious relationships. He thought how knowing that wasn't necessary to the point of her story. It was something she wanted him to know. Why? There was a story behind her story. He was seen as more than a friend and potential sex partner. She thought in terms of a life together.

"I can't explain it," she said, "but somehow I know you're the catalyst I've needed to address this situation with my parents. Our estrangement has got to end. Maybe this is the time."

"Are you suggesting a road trip?"

She nodded. "I guess I am."

The ache in his chest reminded him that he had no car. "Concerning transportation—"

"You don't think taking your car is an option, do you?" Even before tears had dried, she forced a nervous smile and laughed.

CHAPTER 23

A trip to the Texas High Plains was about to take place. Jack had no idea what to do or what might happen once there, just necessary. Courtesy dictated that he allow Nikki ample time with Mister and Missus Endicott. His reason for going to the Endicott farm would have to wait until the green light came directly from her. Neither he nor Nikki could predict what to prepare for.

Maybe if he were comfortable with his gift and how to control it, he could jump forward and get a clue so they wouldn't walk in unprepared. As always, that little voice inside him said, "No." He just couldn't imagine why it did. He had no intention of trying it even if the gut feeling had said, "Go ahead. Give it a shot."

But uneasiness over how to handle things didn't change what needed to be done. Nikki had an old wound in need of healing; Jack had a long-dead relative in need of eternal peace. If there were dots to be connected, they would have to figure them out as they went. But the coincidence of converging at the same place for different reasons baffled Jack to distraction.

His curiosity had begun heating up about Laguna Rica, the Quahadi Comanche and the source of the Native American blood that flowed through him. Rich Lake, the modern name, held the key. He was sure of it. A relative that had been dead for over a century needed a mortal assist because Brave Child couldn't get it done himself.

Jack had hoped Arthur would spring for airline tickets. The old guy must have sensed that, because he explained his fear of flying. Jack didn't pursue it, reasoning that the drive might be good—time to think things through. Besides, Arthur was paying. So why complain?

Nikki had difficulty preparing for the trip—confidence slow to catch up to intent. Jack encouraged her. "They're your parents," he told her. "They'll love and accept you… no matter what." Still, self-doubt nipped at resolve. Primly manicured nails disappeared one nibble at a time.

Six o'clock Wednesday morning finally came. He dozed in and out all night, thankful for that much sleep.

Nikki left his place late and seemed wired, chattering as she walked to her car after one o'clock. Less than five hours was the most sleep she could have gotten. Her mind had raced with possibilities.

Arthur arrived early. While they waited, Jack filled him in on details the old guy was aware of. He'd developed a psychic sense of Nikki's situation but hadn't tried to interpret it knowing he'd be chatting about it soon enough.

Jack ran a hand over his hair. "It's weird... you know... this exhilaration running through me like an electrical current, yet stained with awkwardness."

Arthur shook his head. "Trust your instincts, Jack. What else can I say?" He smiled, but it wasn't a silly grin. There was sincerity in it. "Listen to your heart as well; it's talking to you and you're refusing to listen. A psychic message is trying to get through that thick resistant head of yours."

"Hey, I'm not fighting it."

With a dismissive wrist flip, "Yes you are."

Nikki pulled into the driveway behind the wrecked car fifteen minutes late, but he couldn't be upset. They were taking her car, and he was aware how little sleep she'd had. But, he couldn't resist. "Did that extra fifteen minutes of beauty sleep work?" he shouted from the front porch.

With equal timbre, she said, "Can the remarks and load your stuff. Let's hit the road."

His and Arthur's luggage had to be relegated to a small area off to one side of the trunk. Nikki appeared to have packed for a two-week cruise. As he struggled to get one suitcase and Arthur's duffle bag stuffed into a tiny corner, he muttered, "What the hell is all this crap?"

"What'd you say?" she asked.

"Nothing." He held the suitcase so it wouldn't pop out as he slammed the trunk lid shut.

Arthur dropped into the back seat. Jack slid in next to Nikki. "I noticed you seem to have given yourself a good choice of clothing options." He buckled the seat belt, double-checking the buckle.

She offered a crooked grin. "How about you... pack plenty of clean underwear?" She screwed up her nose.

He held off smiling until he'd turned his head.

On the Interstate, Nikki set the cruise control. The trip would be long. He estimated arrival at her parent's farm in about ten hours. After a time, Nikki and Arthur ran out of small talk. Jack was thankful. There was thinking to be done, and a quiet car made it easier. Mile after mile, his eyes followed the scenery to his right. His mind drifted. He dozed, his own snoring rousing him. Head lolling to the left, he saw Nikki staring.

She patted his knee. "Good nap?"

"I guess so." He yawned. "I don't remember feeling sleepy." He noticed the dark circles under her eyes. "Let me drive. You probably didn't get much sleep last night."

"You got that right." She stretched her neck side to side and exited into a rest area just off the highway. They switched places and were back on the Interstate in seconds. Nikki snuggled down in her seat, rolling to her side facing him. She pulled her knees up, closed her eyes and seconds later asleep.

Arthur snoozed, too. The old guy's mouth hung open, his tongue comically danced in his mouth each time he drew air.

Issues resurfaced. Questions replayed in an endless loop, going around and returning without solutions. Although a moot philosophical point, he became embarrassed by long held opinions. He could have been cast with the worst of bigots. Efforts by Native American groups to have mascots of sports teams changed had become a personal issue. Names such as Washington Redskins and Cleveland Indians now bothered him. *What if we called them the Washington Whiteskins, or Brownskins or Yellowskins or Blackskins...or any other color? Suddenly, it's offensive. Why not rename the Cleveland Indians and call them the Wasps or Anglos or Pollacks or Negroes... or some other ethnic label.*

As heat of anger rose, it began. He shuddered from the chill. The glow billowed like steam in front of his face. The highway and vehicles remained visible through the haze. Traffic remained light, providing no problem keeping an eye on both, the highway ahead and the vision unfolding. Although the sun beamed in hard from his left and should have washed out a view of anything else at that angle, the vision overpowered the sun's rays.

The scene unfolding was a panoramic view of Laguna Rica. Without watching his hands, he fumbled with the cruise control to get it set slower than the flow of traffic. As it was, there was only the occasional passing vehicle to deal with. He considered pulling off the road but knew that searching for an exit might create a breach, eliminating what he witnessed. He didn't want that. He wanted to see what story his mind had taken him to because he remained woefully short on facts. He kept driving and watched the vision simultaneously, glancing occasionally at the white line.

This time it was Laguna Rica from a broad all-seeing vantage point overlooking the landscape. It allowed a clear view of the cave where the Old One and Brave Child worked to make contact with him.

There was something new—something he hadn't seen before. Straight up the cliff face, fifteen feet above the cave entrance, a knoll concealed a village at the bottom of the slope on the other side, plainly visible from this angle, as if hovering above it. There, in full view, were eight classically constructed teepees, complete with hand painted pictures and symbols, as well as smoldering fires and horses hobbled and grazing nearby. Three crudely constructed racks held stretched hides, presumably buffalo, and centrally located. Anguished women, children and a few old men scurried about. The reason for such agitation remained unclear.

That's when a brown cloud swelling on the horizon beyond the village came into view. A number of riders on horseback—twenty, maybe thirty, fast approached and rode with savage intent. Faces became clear and bore looks of hatred. At that point Jack knew that he witnessed a deadly all-out charge on an unprotected village.

In seconds, the riders overtook the people like demons-possessed shooting everyone in sight. The few still moving were brutally hacked with large machete-like knives.

Three of the riders became distracted when they reined in horses near the top of the small precipice above the cave entrance. One gestured to the other two. The three forced mounts into a slide down a steep washout to the lakebed below.

The man that ordered the others to follow leaped from his horse and approached the cave opening. He dropped to a knee. Without turning to face the other two, he waved for them to dismount and join him. After gathering at the opening they rushed in and reappeared scant seconds later. One wiped a large knife on his breeches.

Jack didn't need to see inside to know what had happened. They killed the Old One and Brave Child. Knowing beforehand what had happened made it no less shocking. The sight of that madman casually cleaning fresh-spilled blood on his pant leg repulsed him. A mixture of sorrow, disgust and queasiness overwhelmed him. His throat constricted and a lump too large to swallow choked him.

A hand touched his.

The glow faded along with the vision.

He turned to Nikki. "Did you see that?" he asked.

She nodded. "The chill woke me. I saw it all. I kept an eye on the highway in case you became too involved."

"I've heard all my life how savage the white man had been on Native Americans during the westward expansion, but I had no idea... " He banged the steering wheel with both fists. "The slaughter of animals is handled with more compassion than that. I hope God damned them all to hell!"

"Remember, what you witnessed happened over a century ago. There's nothing you can do, or could have done, to change any of it. Try to keep it in perspective." She squeezed his knee. "There can never be justification for treating another human being that way. But you have to stay objective about it."

He couldn't let it go. His face turned crimson.

"Jack, please, you have to set it aside for now," she said. "Remember, you only saw it from one perspective."

After a time, breathing returned to within normal range. "I hate it when you make sense." He held a stern eye on her. "I want to be angry and you're taking that away from me."

"Oh really? Well I have a long list of ways to make you have a good day in spite of yourself." She looked straight ahead and turned her nose slightly up. "And that's the truth."

Had she not been there, he would have catapulted into another time. Should that have happened, the sudden return to the car might have turned out fatal. Invoking the radiant heart while driving could be harmful to their health; worse, he could've been shot or hacked to death by one of those big knives.

The remainder of the journey proved uneventful. The closer they came, the more he sensed an odd feeling of nearing home, although he'd never been to this part of Texas. He stopped referring to the map. As they left the south side of Lubbock, Arthur asked, "Do we take the exit ahead or go straight?"

"Straight," he blurted.

Nikki glanced. "How'd you know that?" Her expression softened. "Never mind."

He didn't know how he knew and couldn't have answered the question anyway. He glimpsed her looking back at Arthur and watched him in the rearview mirror wink at her. The old guy knew that it was a tug at the spiritual level.

Within half an hour of leaving Lubbock, they'd arrived at the Endicott farm and turned down a long heavily rutted dirt driveway off a graveled road that wasn't in much better shape. The approach to the house was bordered on both sides by long straight furrowed rows still void of crops since it was early March.

The house stood near a large corrugated metal building and a couple of smaller outbuildings. Two tractors parked next to an overhead diesel tank and various plow attachments set scattered about a large area beyond the smaller fenced enclosure around the house in which three large elm trees grew. It struck him as odd the trees not only looked stark against the featureless plains, they were huge. One alone cast its shade over the entire front yard. He rolled to a stop in front of the house, a large, freshly painted white stucco structure.

Nikki audibly gulped.

"Are you okay?" he asked.

"I think so. But this is scaring hell out of me."

"Anger I understand, but why would you be scared of your parents?"

"I'm not scared of *them*. I'm scared of *me*. I'm not sure I have enough self control."

"Then don't try to say anything... not yet anyway. Save the serious stuff for later. Ease back into it. For now just concentrate on redeveloping a comfort level with them."

"Good advice."

A tall slender woman, hair in a bun wearing a floral print dress stepped from inside the house onto the porch. She shaded her eyes with the flat of her hand looking towards Nikki's car. The resemblance was uncanny. He felt as though he looked into the face of Nikki thirty years from now. *Not bad... not bad at all.*

Although he and Arthur exited the car, too, they stayed back.

She took one step and stopped, unwilling to take the initiative.

Jack quickly stepped around the car and moved to her side. "Look, if you feel that you're about to say or do something you might regret, give me a sign and I'll step in." He placed a hand on the lower part of her back and applied gentle pressure for her to walk.

Arthur trotted to her other side, patted her on the shoulder and murmured something he couldn't hear.

"Thanks guys. You're the greatest." After a couple of deep breaths, she took off walking and then jogging.

Her mother did, too.

Nikki began running.

They came together in an emotional embrace. Both sobbed.

A tall bald man with a large belly pressing the bib of faded overalls came to the front door holding a piece of bread in his hand, his cheek stretched with a mouthful. He pushed the screen door open. Once he realized who it was, he tossed the scrap of bread toward an old dog napping a few feet away, dusted his hands on his pants and walked lively to join mother and daughter. The three stood in a tight triad all speaking at once. It appeared to be tearful and happy. All those years apart no longer mattered.

He and Arthur held back leaning against the front car fender, giving her the space she needed. After considerable time she motioned them over. The wait didn't matter. After all, what were a few extra minutes after she'd waited ten years? The approach was still handled with caution, not wanting to intrude on the reunion.

Hesitation dissolved with a big howdy from her father followed by a small flurry of handshakes to end awkward seconds. "You kids must be hungry," Mr. Endicott said. "We just sat down to supper when y'all pulled up. Come on in. We have plenty."

Awed by the amount of food, he assumed what he'd always heard about farm families was true: they may not be the wealthiest people, but they'll always be the best fed.

The conversation stayed light and friendly—even spirited at times with plenty of smiles and laughs. Jack had the opportunity to explain why he and Arthur had accompanied Nikki on the trip. Of course, he confined it to a simple explanation about research for the article. This was not an environment to be discussing the Radiant Heart connection.

Judging by the tone of the conversation, the elder Endicott's view of the world substantiated everything Nikki had shared. Nothing they said hinted of open-mindedness. Everything out of Mister Endicott's mouth was spoken as definitive fact but had to have been opinions. Just as Nikki had warned, yes or no, right or wrong all the way. He became certain if Mister Endicott should take issue with anything, they'd be asked to leave. Nikki was right; *ultra-conservative* didn't go far enough for these Southern Baptists. Jack envisioned Nikki as a young girl trying to discuss issues but rudely shutout for having an opposing opinion. Her days growing up had to have been frustrating—always seeing problems from both sides while they closed their minds to other viewpoints.

Even so, George and Minnie Endicott seemed eager to share food, house, and time with them. They were really quite nice in a quirky way.

After supper in the living room with a distinctive sixties look, the discussion turned to George's favorite subject, farming. He shared the farm's history, having been in the family for four generations. George referred to the largest of the trees in front of the house as having been planted by his great-grandmother. He laughed about it. "We actually take better care of that tree than we do our pets."

Missus Endicott brought in a stack of very old pictures—a few valuable tintype images. Holding the box of photos, Jack studied each one, passing it down the sofa to Nikki who shared with Arthur. Studying the images, he turned each one this way and that trying to obtain the best light to see detail, lingering on one tintype in particular.

"That picture shows my great grandmother, her sister and a family from the farm down the road. Their names were McKenzie," Mr. Endicott said. "In that picture were Mister and Missus McKenzie and their daughter. In those days one of the greatest sources of entertainment was visiting with neighbors. On that day they all came together to plant trees, one of which is that largest elm tree I just mentioned. It was sort of a ceremonial thing farmers did in those days as a sign of claiming one's rights to a piece of property. A punctuation mark on the Homesteading Act, so to speak."

Jack handed the photo to Mister Endicott. "Whose back is that to the camera? It appears to be a Native American."

"Certainly could've been," he said and gave it right back. "There was a group of Comanche Indians camped most of the year over by Rich Lake."

Hiding a burst of excitement Jack would have trouble explaining, he asked rather abruptly, "What was the name of that neighbor girl… the McKenzie girl? Do you know?"

Endicott seemed taken aback by the exuberance. "It wasn't recorded anywhere. I can't say."

He showed the picture to Nikki and whispered, "I think this is Beatrice and Brave Child."

As hard it was to contain the questions, Jack remained reserved and didn't dive into an all out interrogation. But an insatiable appetite for information had been whetted. He had to play it cool, uncertain what it might take to offend Mr. Endicott and didn't want to risk doing so until Nikki had taken care of her business with her parents. This man could easily be upset. Of that he was certain.

CHAPTER 24

Thursday morning dawned as Wednesday had ended, skies beautifully clear. Still in its infancy, spring had difficulty gaining the high ground. Northerly breezes again rolled over the Great Plains leaving behind a biting chill, but it was calm. The rising sun glistened off a light dusting of frost. Jack discovered that comfortable accommodations did not guarantee a good night's sleep. A picture had begun to form but it was by no means clear and that occupied his mind as he lay in the dark considering possibilities for hours, managing little more than a nap in the predawn hours. Now he fought to restart thinking processes, unable to shake grogginess.

The charm of this country setting came with tranquility—sublime quiet— a good thing. The lack of smelly petrochemical fumes made for sweet metallic smelling air on this frigid morning. Maybe there'd come a time later for deeper reflection on these simple pleasures.

The first clear thought of the day to give pause was that strange sensation of having come home as they approached the farm yesterday, although he'd never been here before. *Is this why I feel so at peace?* There was little to see except sunrises and sunsets. So, the beauty must come in the complex tapestry created by the people themselves. There had to be many stories to be told in this featureless country atop the Caprock on the Texas South Plains. Deep in his bones he knew this to be true—itself a riddle. One of those stories was his mission that he worked to piece together. He had to find out more about that tintype picture of a Native American standing alongside the Endicott's ancestors.

George and Minnie had obviously been out of bed for some time, judging by their industriousness. Shuffling on sleep-weakened legs into the kitchen, he saw Minnie working at a pursuit Nikki hadn't displayed an aptitude for—cooking. She had prepared a breakfast to rival any restaurant buffet. He didn't know he was hungry until he saw the food. Just the marvelous aroma gave him his first smile of the day.

Arthur woke to the food aromas but it was the noise of people preparing to meet the day that roused Nikki. She joined them to hover over the coffee pot like vultures coveting a carcass. Minnie shooed them out of the kitchen.

Sauntering towards the living room, "What was your take on the Native American in that picture we saw last night?" he asked Arthur in a low voice, after a sip from his coffee cup.

"It proved a connection between this family and the local Comanche tribe at that time," he whispered, "but, like you, I'm only speculating who it was, what it meant or why he was with them."

As Nikki moved in closer, Jack spoke to them both. "It may not be safe to be making assumptions yet. I don't know. But it seems reasonable that the McKenzie girl was Beatrice, Brave Child's love interest." His face took on a look of starry wonder. "Think about it; that would make her my great grandmother. Just imagine, Nik, how strange it is that this coincidence has brought both of us to the same place, a mere pinpoint on the planet, and how both lineages can be traced down to a single photographic image on tin taken over a hundred years ago. It… it boggles my mind. The odds against such a coincidence are monstrous."

"I've thought about that a lot, too." She hugged herself and rubbed her upper arms. "It's a type of eeriness I've never known."

Eager to learn, Jack planned a drive to Rich Lake after breakfast. The first goal was to find out how time had changed the landscape of Laguna Rica since his brief visit during the car crash episode.

Arthur's clothing, interesting as always, seemed woefully out of place. He wore the colorful Hawaiian shirt with garish lavender orchids on a yellow background, frayed cargo shorts and sandals. He could have been ready for a walk on a tropical beach, not over ground covered with light frost. "Good Lord, man, aren't you taking this dressing for comfort thing a bit far? It's cold out here! That get-up you have on can't be comfortable."

"It's a magnificent day!" He flared his nostrils and sucked in a patronizing breath of morning air. It whistled up his thin nose. He pounded his chest. "Absolutely stimulating."

Not as enthusiastic, Nikki complained, "Stimulating? Hell, it's numbing." She had on a t-shirt tucked into beltless jeans and one of her father's flannel shirts over it. It hung halfway to her knees. She wrapped it tight around her upper torso and walked fast and stiff, arms crossed over her breasts. "Let's get that car started and the heater going." Jack quickened his pace to stay up but not fast enough to suit her. "Now… chop-chop, tick tock!" she demanded, waving at her father when he came out of the house. He returned it with a hardy hand high over his head as he made a beeline for one of the tractors.

Jack and Arthur acknowledged the friendly gesture, too, tossing back casual waves. Jack fell into the driver's seat, started the car, dropped it into gear and wheeled it in a tight circle to point it toward the gravel road at the end of the long dirt driveway.

Another curious question Jack mulled as he took directions from Nikki was that he, oddly, didn't need to be told where Rich Lake was. But he kept that to himself.

Something hadn't seemed right about the elder Endicott's telling of the story last night, like he knew something more than he wished to discuss. His knowledge of details over a century removed was phenomenal. Either he filled in gaps with a vivid imagination or the stories handed down within the family were flawlessly detailed. When he pleaded ignorance, as Jack tried to discuss the closeness of the two cultures, Endicott's inflection indicated there might be more and, for whatever reason, willfully omitted it.

It was a quick drive to Rich Lake. A hasty inspection indicated the immediate area looked just as he remembered from the inadvertent visit and the vision he'd experienced in the car on the trip down. The major differences were tilled fields nearby and farmhouses dotting nearly flat terrain. The landscape remained rugged around the lakebed with short drop-offs and deep washouts. On the previous two occasions, he had not been directionally oriented, ending up near the cave only because that's where his thoughts were when the car went into a skid and rolled. But now, they might be on the opposite side of the lake for all he knew.

He realized that he'd need to be standing at the cave entrance before anything else would be familiar. Over the span of about hundred-thirty years the hills and washouts might appear the same in a general way but had shifted, leaving no identifiable feature to be recognized. The cave was the key. He had to find it. But he searched blind—no markers to guide the way. Time and erosion may have obliterated the hideout altogether, covering it over or filling it in. Sand at lakebed level was still deep and loose. He had been told windy days were more common than calm ones. That meant shifting sand over just a few weeks, much less a century-plus, could make a big difference in the appearance of the terrain.

The morning sun warmed the dry air rapidly and temperatures were pleasant by midmorning. They wandered around the edge of the lake for a couple of hours debating possibilities.

Near the north side of the salt encrusted expanse, Nikki took the lead and tried skating down a steep gully. It was too steep. She fell backwards onto her butt and slid to the sandy surface of the lakebed below. She stood, dusting herself off while he and Arthur discussed possible locations of the village.

Suddenly she shrieked and shouted, "Jack!"

Looking down, he saw she had startled a diamondback rattlesnake that sounded off. It was huge—maybe over six feet long and as big as Jack's arm. It coiled into a defensive posture—lifting a heart-shaped head licking the air.

She flinched.

The reptile hurriedly reared its head higher into a classic pose.

Terrified and whining, she fidgeted within easy striking distance.

"Shit," he muttered and then yelled, "Stand still! Don't try to run! Don't move at all." He literally felt blinding fear channeled directly to him from her.

Startling as that was he had no time to think about it. Raw horror robbed her of rational thinking. He feared that she might not heed the warning, listening to her terror instead. If she ran, she'd get two fangs below the knee.

Carefully, he climbed down the gully trying not to create a minor landslide or any disturbance that might result in panic by woman or snake. After touching down on the sandy bottom, he got his first good look at the frightened serpent. The rattle, as long as a man's thumb only wider, sounded like escaping steam from the pop-off valve of a boiler.

Color drained from Nikki's face. Beads of perspiration gathered on her forehead and had begun to stream.

"You're doin' great kiddo. Stand still. As long as you don't move, the snake won't feel threatened."

She didn't display understanding—eyes large, fixed and glazed over.

"Do you understand what I'm saying? Don't move at all until the snake realizes you mean it no harm. Blink if you hear what I'm saying."

Nikki's eyes moved as far left as they could in their sockets. She closed them for a second and opened them.

"Good." He judged it to be about four feet from her leg. It could have buried formidable fangs anywhere below the knee if she so much as twitched. She wouldn't have a chance to avoid it.

A weapon... I need a weapon. Searching the immediate area, he spotted a partially rotted cedar fence post. He glided laterally without taking his eyes from her or the snake, all the while summoning self-control. *Stay calm, Jack.* Even though the air remained cool, the morning sun reflected heat off the light colored sand. Sweat dampened his face and gathered on his lashes. He blinked it away. The post, almost as long as he was tall, had become flimsy with age. But it would have to do. He wrenched hands over the post like a baseball player firming his grip on a bat. If he couldn't divert the snake's attention, he might accidentally provoke it. He tried to think it through but no better solution than jabbing it came to mind.

"Do something," she hissed.

"I'm going to help you," he whispered, "but you have to do exactly as I say. Okay?"

She closed her eyes and offered a faint nod.

"First, take a deep breath. Hold to a thousand-one count then exhale... slow and quiet."

"What the hell is that—"

"Don't argue," he growled through clenched teeth. "Just do it."

She again closed her eyes. He saw her chest rise as she drew in a large breath, puckering slightly as she let it out in a measured way. When she did, her body relaxed.

"Good. Now, keep doing that and lower your head slowly forward in a very relaxed position without moving any other part of your body. Keep your eyes closed." The snake sensed something had changed, but continued to rattle. It uncoiled, slithering toward a dead tumbleweed. As it moved out of striking range, he said, "Start backing away, but do it in slow motion." He continued to speak in low and smooth tones. He walked to within six feet of the tumbleweed.

The reptile again took a defensive posture, coiling, rearing its head.

Before it had the chance to complete the ideal striking posture, he stabbed at the head with the post but missed. It struck at it, penetrating the wood with a fang. He yanked it back, jerking the snake dangerously close. Fortunately, it fell away, slithering along the vertical cliff face where the lakebed met the base, partially obscured by the tumbleweed. The threat had been neutralized and reason told him to walk away. Instead, he was compelled to move even closer. He took a final jab, trying to pin its head to the vertical wall of compacted earth behind it. Again he missed, poking the wall of dirt just above the sandy surface. It gave way at the bottom, exposing a fingernail shaped opening just above the ground.

The snake retreated into a crevice a safe distance away.

Adrenaline left him in a rush. He leaned on the post, feeling faint.

Nikki sank to her knees in the sand, composure still a few minutes away, as Arthur was just making his way down the washout. "Jack, Nikki. Are you two all right?" He slid on his backside to the bottom.

"Yeah, I'll be okay," Jack told him and turned to Nikki. "How about you?"

She daubed perspiration with the rolled sleeve of the oversized flannel shirt she wore. "I remembered every nightmare I've ever had about snakes, all at the same time." Clumsily she rose, brushing sand from her knees. "But yeah, I think I'm okay."

Arthur dropped in front of the newly exposed opening, crouching low, bony butt held high in the air. "You may have discovered something here."

"Really?"

The old guy cupped his eyes between his palms and peered into the dark hole. "I can only see a few feet, but it appears to get larger just a short way in." He scooped soft sand away from the entrance and stuck his head and shoulders inside. "My body is blocking the light." Pulling his head out of the opening, he sat back on his heels. "Do either of you have matches or a lighter?"

"No," she said, "but I do have a small flashlight on my key chain in the car."

Jack had already turned and began to trudge through the sand. "I'll get it."

By the time he returned, flashlight in hand, enough sand had been cleared for one person to crawl inside. Both were on hands and knees trying to see inside.

"What do you make of this?" Arthur asked, waiting for Jack to place the flashlight in his outstretched hand.

"Sorry. It's my discovery quest. I'm not about to put either of you in danger to satisfy my curiosity," he said. "If you'll excuse me, I must crawl into a dark hole in the ground now." He smirked.

Miffed, Nikki countered, "Very funny. What if that snake's mistress is down there and pissed off at you for emasculating her serpentine boy-toy?"

"Only you would put it that way." Falling to his knees, he wriggled between, pushing them aside, centering his body to the crescent shaped opening. The bright morning sun reflected off the white caliche vertical surface. He poked his head in and shined the weak flashlight beam but didn't see anything extraordinary.

Before moving on in, he straightened and patted Nikki's leg. "It may have sounded like a joke, but I'm serious about the danger. Stay back." He held the most forbidding look he could conjure. "This is not a request."

She sat back and pulled her knees up surrounding them with her arms, holding fast to belligerence that pressed her lips together tight and flat.

"Look, this is my deal. I don't want either one of you in danger over it."

She tossed a handful of sand downwind. "Oh all right. But be careful in there. For all we know, that might be sanctuary to all the relatives of that disgusting snake… or hairy spiders… or big black scorpions." She shuddered.

Falling forward on his belly, "Oh, for heaven's sake, get a grip." He began inching forward, arms straight out ahead of his body. The temperature dropped noticeably as he slithered through the opening. It was cool, damp and musty, bringing to mind a backyard cellar, at odds with the ambient air outside which was dry and sun-warmed.

He discovered, after only a short distance, it pitched downward and suddenly became steep. He crawled and slid down to a solid surface a few feet in. Now able to check it out with the keychain flashlight, he noticed this manmade cave was about five feet high and not quite that wide. Moving cautiously, bent at the waist, he studied crevices and blind spots for wildlife he might startle. Tool marks covered the walls and ceiling. The tunnel had been dug using small instruments, probably animal bones that gouged small amounts of dirt with each jab. The ceiling had black streaks indicating torches had come and gone regularly. Eight to ten feet from the entrance, the tunnel expanded into a roughly round room. Those smoke streaks led to black blobs on the ceiling above holes augered into the walls where torches had been held. The ceiling was barely high enough to stand.

A portion of the ceiling had collapsed, leaving a pile of dirt on the floor and a ragged place in the, otherwise, neatly hewn area above his head.

"What do you see?" Nikki called down. "Anything interesting?"

"Nothing that would astound the archaeological world." The examination didn't take long. There just wasn't that much to look at. He backed up to the pile of dirt that had fallen and sat on it. He picked up a handful of soil and tossed it against the wall. Although an interesting piece of history, this didn't appear to be what he sought. Who's to say there weren't scores of these shallow caves dug into these walls adjacent to the lakebed?

"I feel that you shouldn't give up just yet," Arthur said. "Take your time. Look closer." The old guy's body blocked the sunlight as he began to crawl inside.

Jack glanced around again. "There's nothing else to see, aside from evidence that this was manmade and frequently used at one time. But, I don't… "His fingers swept across something solid in the dirt beneath and between his legs where he'd been mindlessly running them through the loose soil. It felt symmetrical and smooth. Pushing away more dirt, the shape of a human skull emerged.

"What's the matter?" Nikki asked. "Come on, Jack, say something."

"It's okay. It seems there's something here to see after all."

Arthur joined him. "I bet we're the first humans to be in this place since that fateful day in 1877," he said coming to stand over Jack. "It appears undisturbed, just covered over by an act of nature."

After having sat in that dank, dark cave for a short time, gently fingering the bones beneath him, he shivered. It all had suddenly become very, very real. The visions, the strange visitation, the attack and slaughter could no longer be dismissed or even questioned. Skeletal remains of a distant relative and that of a kindly old man who'd tried to save the boy from eternal torment lay beneath a pile of rocky soil he sat upon.

"I want to see what you've found," Nikki called down.

Arthur knelt and swept more dirt away from the remains. "It looks like you've discovered what you came for."

"I guess I did."

Arthur continued removing soil and, as more dirt came away, the picture became clear what happened in those final moments so long ago. A cleaved area on the right temple of the Old One explained that death. Apparently, Brave Child had been killed first because of the neat, round hole in the forehead, just above and between the eyes, probably shot trying to defend the old man. Over a century later and the Old One still embraced Brave Child protectively, frozen in time.

Uncovering more could not add additional clarity. The story was complete. He fell back against the cave wall, deflated.

Arthur turned his attention to the hand-hewn walls, fingering the hundreds of neat gouges. "I suppose the army saw this as a necessary measure to prevent further attacks on white buffalo hunters."

"There's never justification for systematic annihilation of people! It's thinking like that that created the holocaust."

Arthur didn't respond, didn't even look back, just continued inspecting the tunnel walls.

When Jack took a second to think about it, he realized it had been offered as a salve for discontent, but no words could calm his despair.

"We have to be sensitive to fears we can't begin to comprehend today," Nikki said. "That act was the result of century-old thinking that may have been appropriate in those days. We're looking at a nineteenth century deed with twenty-first century eyes."

"Thank you, Dr. Endicott, for that sage bit of analysis, but I don't give a damn what century it is! Inhumanity to man is never the right thing to do… no matter how popular it happens to be!"

Realizing too late that it wasn't a time for philosophical musings, she didn't press the issue. "You're right." She put an arm around his waist.

She had no way of knowing his depth of feeling, nor did he. He didn't understand. Why did he care so much? It happened so long ago.

Arthur went back to inspecting the skeletal remains as the light from the flashlight began to dim.

Jack slipped away from Nikki's embrace to face the small spot of sunlight at the opening. "Let's go. There's nothing left to discover here."

CHAPTER 25

The promise to Brave Child had taken a step closer to fulfillment. Authentication was the necessary first step but the speed with which it was accomplished seemed otherworldly that it could have been done that fast. Maybe it was. Jack never stopped questioning such things but had become accepting of them. Regardless how it came about, the truth could no longer be questioned. The two Native Americans had indeed slipped the bonds of time to pay him a visit on a blustery cold winter day while he was in the throes of grief over the loss of his dog. The final seconds of their lives had been locked in time, preserved, waiting for him for over a century to serve as proof. All lingering doubt whistled away like shifting sand on the bed of Rich Lake. But it didn't answer all the riddles.

Part of him still wanted it all to go away—memory erased, waking at home, Buddy leaping on the bed helping greet the morning. On the upside, he'd reached a point that he compartmentalized it as an objective goal and not so much as mystical crap that scared hell out of him. His gift, his talent, his curse—whatever label fit best, was here to stay. He improved on keeping it in perspective.

Jack's attention shifted and moved to the next level. He had to know about the relationship the Endicott ancestors shared with their neighbors, the McKenzies. How did the local Quahadi Comanche tribe fit into that relationship? *Why do I feel anxious about getting this taken care of? What does it matter?* Still, he remained driven to push onward and step up the pace.

Not passing up an opportunity to quiz George Endicott, Jack caught him in his recliner reading the newspaper. "Pardon me…"

Endicott collapsed the paper into his lap.

"Our trip to Rich Lake yesterday set my mind reeling with questions that might add color to the article I'm working on, so would you mind answering a few more questions about life in this area in the 1870's?"

"I don't mind at all. Have a seat." He folded the paper and laid it aside. "It's an enjoyable challenge to recall stories passed down in my family." He put his recliner upright and slid forward to its edge slapping his knees. "What would you like to know?"

"I'd like to find out about the relationship between the local tribe of Comanche and the settlers. The proximity of the tribe's encampment suggests amiable coexistence. Could that be true? I mean the Comanche are believed to have been ruthless. From what I've learned so far, that reputation doesn't seem deserved."

George Endicott considered the question. As he did, Jack glanced over Endicott's shoulder into the kitchen. Nikki and her mother stood close, whispering, expressions solemn. They held hands. He wondered if Nikki had found courage to talk about the rift in their relationship. Whether or not she chose this time to do it, it was inevitable and the point of her visit.

"I suppose the best way to answer your question," Endicott said, lacing his fingers behind his head, "is to say a peaceful coexistence may have *appeared* to exist between the whites and reds, but cultures were vastly different. Tolerance remained low at all times, a mutual ongoing atmosphere of distrust."

Jack slid to the edge of the sofa. "So, am I to understand there was little interaction?"

"That's not what I meant. There were many dealings between that tribe and the local settlers specifically because of cultural differences. The Indians saw the settlers as a good source of tools they had no access to otherwise—hoes, rakes, pots, pans... that sort of thing. On the other hand, the Indians were the indigenous people. They possessed a wealth of knowledge the settlers valued. The Indians were experts on survival, even during times of harsh weather extremes. And I can tell you from experience that *harsh* is, sometimes, a tame way of describing winters around here." He let out a bellowing laugh. He settled, snuffed a quick breath and swiped across his nose with the back of his hand and continued. "They coexisted. They needed each other. But they didn't trust one another."

The picture puzzle seemed to be coming together, one crooked piece at a time. "What about some of the other early farmers, the McKenzie family for example. Is it possible some of the white settlers formed closer ties than others with the Native Americans? I'd like to know if there was a basis for an ideological connection beyond... you know... material necessities."

George Endicott stared at him, a look Jack couldn't interpret. He wondered if he'd said something to offend him.

"Mr. Dane," he said with an edge, "Indeed, there were liaisons between Whites and Reds, but that had more to do with unchecked carnal desires than ideologies."

Endicott's labeling of these two diverse cultures as "Whites and Reds" struck an inflammatory chord. The way *Reds* came out smacked of profanity, a demeaning remark that reduced a beautiful tapestry of cultural blending to the same level as opposing sides in a football scrimmage. The inflection spoke volumes about Endicott's view that Native Americans were lesser humans, existing only to service settlers' needs like livestock. Endicott clearly had the historical facts but no grasp on the heart and soul of the matter. He took a moment to breathe, under the guise of digesting Endicott's answer.

In a flash of enlightenment, the true nature of Brave Child's fear struck him. It had nothing to do with dying at the hands of white men but how future generations would view his people—scared that opinions would harden into historical fact and live on in infamy. The American government didn't understand Native Americans and didn't try. Comanche leaders like Black Horse didn't understand the Whites and didn't try. Acceptance and respect only existed in those places where they lived together and took time to learn one another's ways.

Jack had finally glimpsed the world through Brave Child's intelligent and perceptive eyes, one of the few in either of the two worlds in his day that had a true-pointing moral compass. The Comanche were more socially tolerant than history would have us believe. Even back then, the spin masters of government painted a different picture to benefit a select few. In all the years since, nothing has changed—politicians manipulate truth to selfish ends. It's what they do. Money, influence and power guide them. The greater good is an excuse, not the goal.

Suddenly Jack's contemplations shattered.

Nikki slammed a coffee cup on the countertop in the kitchen. "There are two things very wrong with that!" he heard her shout.

His mind snapped forward a century or so, startled. Something brewed in the kitchen between Nikki and her mother. She was angered by something Minnie had said.

George sprang to his feet, heading for the kitchen to enter the debate.

Nikki swung an arm in a wild gesture. "First of all, Mother, we took a human life. Secondly, it was for the poorest reason of all—appearances!"

Her mother clasped her hands together. "Please, Honey, this is a private family matter." She whispered even lower, "It doesn't concern anyone else. Let's keep it between us."

"And that's wrong, too. It did concern you two... once upon a time... but that's far in the past. Now it concerns *only me*. It's my life that has been totally screwed up beyond repair!" Nikki hardened. Her voice sank to a growl. "Beyond repair, Mother. Beyond repair. Is that so difficult to understand?"

"Listen to your mother, Nikki!" her father demanded. "This is not a matter for all prying ears to hear."

Nikki backed away a step, squaring off to them both. As she planted hands on her hips, it became evident she'd not be running from the fray. She slapped her thigh. "There ya go again." Her voice broke into a higher range. "Y'all are more concerned what people will think than what's right. I've kept this dirty little family secret for over ten years. It's all going to end right here... right now. I refuse to let it ruin the *rest* of my life!"

"Daughter!" her father bellowed, "if you insist on talking to us in that tone—"

"It's the last choice of tones I have, Daddy. Can't you understand that? You've listened to nothing I've ever said."

"Leave! Pack your things and get out of this house!" He pointed toward the door.

She took an aggressive stance and stepped forward, getting directly in his face. "Sure," she hissed, "that would make it simple for you. Wouldn't it? That way you both can keep right on denying the truth forever."

Jack watched from the sideline, wanting to show support for Nikki, but afraid of jeopardizing his reason for being there. If forced to leave, he could lose the only chance to complete what he'd come to do. But Nikki needed this time. She'd sat on it like an unpinned hand grenade for a decade.

"Please. I'm begging you," her mother sobbed. "Don't dredge all this up." Minnie clutched herself. She pulled her chin into her chest—the picture of a tortured person.

Nikki noticed the change, too, and saw that it tore her mother apart. She turned away long enough to force an objective frame of mind. "Look," she said in a calmer, but no less determined voice, "have either of you ever wondered why I'm not married?" She again faced them, eyes darting between them. "It's a simple matter of guilt."

She glanced in Jack's direction—the look meant for him. "If I wanted to get married, I'd have to disclose to my husband-to-be that if we wanted children we'd have to adopt. At some point I'd have to tell him why. The wedding would be off, maybe even before asked." Again she paused and looked to Jack as he stood in the living room near the kitchen door, watching. "I refuse to lie about it ever again. I've run from relationships so I wouldn't have to explain it. I'm here with the first people I've trusted enough to tell it to without fear of being judged."

George's expression looked as though he'd been slapped. "They know? You told them about it?"

Nikki leaned in to him and hissed, "Hell... yes." She held that posture for maximum effect.

George yielded and took a step back. With no sudden moves, Jack glided into the kitchen and stood beside Nikki in a quiet show of support but maintaining neutrality, making no eye contact so as not to inflame George or Minnie any more than they already were. But a glance at George's face was all it took to see that Nikki had indeed cracked that conservative exterior.

George Endicott began a metamorphosis, softening, changing from anger to sorrow. "Baby," he said in a low voice, "we only did what we thought was right. We knew you really wanted to finish college and you were in such a confused emotional state—"

"Don't even attempt to imply that it's a decision I would have made."

"But, Honey—"

"It was a decision made for me and imposed on me with absolutely no regard for what I thought about it."

"You have to understand…" His voice trailed off.

Without a word, Minnie interrupted by putting a hand on his forearm. He looked down at it and then into her eyes, an unspoken understanding that only comes to people after many years of living together. "You're right," George said. "There's no good reason for what we forced upon you."

As the room went silent, Jack relaxed, believing the Endicotts had been set on a path of healing—a very old wound that kept child and parents apart had been acknowledged and confronted—presumably settled. Jack drifted away to the living room.

"Do you think she can put all this behind her now?" Arthur whispered as they came together.

He glanced back and shrugged. "I don't know. I hope so."

Arthur offered a subtle headshake. "I for one believe it's not over yet."

This time, Jack shared the uneasiness but refused to lend it credibility by agreeing aloud. "Maybe it'll be all right." He looked to Nikki who'd stepped in closer to her parents and held their hands. "As long as it doesn't get swept away like before, this could be the foundation for coming to terms with it."

He watched Nikki comfort her parents after such a dressing down of them. Roles had reversed. She had become their guide. A warmth of admiration cloaked him, drawn to her courage, to her sexuality, to her… everything. With each passing day, he moved ever closer to becoming hopelessly entwined. The notion of spending a lifetime with her crossed his mind in an honest wholesome way. Nikki Endicott was everything a life partner should be—beautiful, courageous, intelligent, humorous—the embodiment of the total package.

But, like all the other times, small hairs on the back of his neck stood out as he thought this way. Why? Another mystery that had to be dealt with soon. He had to know what prevented thoughts of intimacy with her. *I think I'm falling in love.*

Wednesday morning came. The odd feeling he and Arthur shared about Nikki and her parents had not lessened even after sleeping on it. Still, Jack had other urgent business to complete, feeling pressed to accelerate his investigation. In fact, urgency had begun to pulse in his ears.

The morning ritual at the Endicott's was subdued. Maybe each of them had become busy building coping mechanisms. But even quiet smiles couldn't mask embers of dissention that still glowed.

George showed the least emotion. Nonetheless, her father avoided eye contact with his only child as he went about business, slapping up a protective wall around himself against emotional hurts, forcing his head to go elsewhere, thinking about other things. Minnie had a strange look. Jack became ill at ease with that vacant stare. "Keep a close eye on Mrs. Endicott," Arthur told him. "She's a bubbling cauldron of instability. There's blackness around her."

Nikki seemed drained. Each time she approached her mother, Minnie feigned a smile, maybe saying a word or two, going about her chores in a mindless way. That pleasant look Minnie dutifully plastered across her face hid something. The smile lied, her eyes didn't. Nikki sat on the arm of the chair beside Jack. "I'm worried about Mother."

"We just need to watch her until she works through her feelings." It didn't take psychic ability or psychoanalysis to know Minnie had gone to a dangerous psychological place. But he couldn't see an advantage by adding to Nikki's concern.

George came into the room and sat heavily in his chair near Nikki. "What are you kids talking about?"

Just planning our day," Nikki said.

"Mr. Endicott, would you be in the mood to continue our conversation about your ancestors?" Jack asked.

"I suppose. I'm in no mood to climb on that tractor just yet anyway." He laced his fingers together in his lap. "I'll answer what I can." He seemed appreciative to have something to take his mind off the family crisis.

"I believe we stopped as you were about to fill me in on the McKenzie family."

"Why are you so interested in the McKenzie family?"

"Just a reporter's hunch. That picture with the Endicott's and their neighbors, the McKenzie family, showed a young girl standing near a Native American with his back to the camera. Something about the way she looked at the boy indicated there may have been a relationship between them."

"Your hunch doesn't miss the mark too far." He sighed. "There was something between those two all right , but she wasn't the neighbor girl, she was my great-great aunt, my great-great grandmother's younger sister, Beatrice."

Nikki locked eyes with Jack.

He stopped breathing and his heart skipped a beat.

Her face flushed and her features froze in astonishment.

Misinterpreting the looks, "I know, I know," George said, "It's a disgusting skeleton in the Endicott closet. We still don't talk about it much even though we're removed a couple of generations from it."

Jack felt as though someone had kicked him in the stomach.

Nikki meandered away toward the far end of the house.

Nikki and I are of the same bloodline—distant cousins. A dizzying array of questions spun out. *Was this the reason when I accidentally left Nikki behind in Coos Bay it was possible to make the Radiant Heart connection? Did it mean we were right all along; a genetic link had to exist to invoke it?* The most crushing revelation was no longer a question, the reason he continually shied from romantic involvement. *Should it make a difference? She can't bear children. Even if she could, the kinship is so far removed it shouldn't matter.* But it did bother him—greatly.

"The family story passed down," George said, pulling Jack's attention back, "had Beatrice and that Indian boy growing up in close proximity. They played together and became comfortable in one another's world—the farming community of the white settlers for the Indian boy and the Comanche village for Beatrice."

Endicott's voice slipped into the background. The remainder of the story just didn't matter. He looked around for Nikki. She was gone. *What does she think about it?*

"As a simple point of interest," George said, "the local Comanche tribe didn't trust whites at all, but the young Indian boy had no fear. He mingled freely with the local settlers, earning him the name, translated into English, Brave Child. Local farmers viewed him as a novelty. He wasn't perceived as a threat and actually created a level of comfort between the races."

It was sheer force of will that Jack made notes on the tablet in his lap. His hand shook. Distracting images of Nikki kept pushing aside the elder Endicott's words.

"As Brave Child and Beatrice grew older they became inseparable," George went on. "One day my great-great grandmother broke the news to her parents that her younger sister, Beatrice, had gotten pregnant." George's voice took the tone of a preacher at a tent revival. "It was an abomination the Endicott family could not and did not tolerate. Brave Child was never welcomed or allowed to come on this farm again. Beatrice was explicitly forbidden to travel to the Comanche camp to see him. The way I understand it, she was told the only time any of the Endicott's would travel to that village again was to leave her baby for them to raise."

Jack pitied George Endicott for his narrow view of the world. So tightly focused was it, it never occurred to him this was exactly the same penalty he had imposed on his own daughter.

With a smug look and a dismissive gesture, "Well, as it turned out, Beatrice disappeared before the baby was born and was never heard from again."

Thank God she did. I wouldn't be hearing this story today if she hadn't. It didn't take Sherlock Holmes to deduce that Beatrice Endicott had given birth to his great-grandmother later that same year.

Endicott finally exhausted his knowledge, complete with editorial spin. Jack could keep digging but additional facts would've been superfluous.

Wise far beyond his short time on earth, Brave Child had known the attitude that drove him away from Beatrice had been a microcosm of the greater problem. Jack visualized him wandering in that world between life and death waiting for him to finish incomplete business in the here and now. Brave Child's troubled spirit needed release but, first, Jack had to write the story.

CHAPTER 26

The air around the Endicott's home crackled with strained emotions. Jack's were all over the road, too—from empathy to sadness, up to naked anger.

Arthur remained neutral and accepting of it all, as if he knew how this would turn out. Maybe he did. Still, even his normal exuberance had been dampened. He remained oddly calm.

Jack and Nikki were of the same bloodline—no debating that. But knowing it and believing it hadn't quite come together in Jack's head. Like watching Kyle swim across that putrid lake into paradise, he saw it, acknowledged it, yet refused to believe. The blood relationship was quite distant and she was still the girl he had developing designs on marrying. Should it matter? Neither Nikki nor Jack thought that it should hamper anything they wanted to do, even marry. But that argument fizzled because, even if they kept it a secret, they'd know. And it'd always be the monster in the room.

"You know," Jack told her, "if we'd never learned the truth, it's possible we would've married, adopted children and lived happily ever after."

She didn't respond to the comment bordering on flippancy. It became a head game; clouds of incest would forever hover over them. Nikki had other insecurities stemming from the still raw and festering argument with her parents. Confidence that the issue of her contentious relationship with them had been resolved seemed to sputter and misfire.

Jack saw the Endicott's as a family unit huddled together moving farther out on a cracking limb. This went beyond idle analogous musing; it had become a movie playing in an endless loop in his mind. Once seeded, he couldn't let it go. It concerned him that something dire should be interpreted from it.

"Pay attention to those uneasy feelings," Arthur had said countless times. But knowing the future scared him, especially in this case. None of it could be dismissed as anxiety born of sadness.

Shortly after the interview with him, George got on with his day, oblivious that he had said anything profound. To him it was just another day on the farm. Cranking up one of the monstrous tractors, black smoke billowed from the exhaust. He ground it into gear and bounced down a rutted turn row to continue getting ready for spring planting.

With tablet and pencil in hand, Jack stood on the front porch holding the screen door open. Warmth from the rising sun radiating through the cool morning air felt good. Stepping off the concrete porch, he walked to the edge of the yard and watched George tossed side to side as he drove the behemoth machine down the rough trail through the field on his way to a day of plowing.

Jack sought a place to write in solitude. He had to begin putting the story of Beatrice and Brave Child on paper. He stopped meandering around the front yard and decided a fading Adirondack chair under one of the huge elm trees was perfect and claimed squatter's rights.

Before sitting, he took a moment to study the big tree and marveled at how many seasons had passed since it was first put in the ground and wondered how many people had actually sat in its shade. It was easy to visualize children with different faces in different decades playing chase beneath its branches, using it for home base. *People come. People go. People live. People die. And so it goes.*

After knee-jerk starts and several wasted sheets of paper, he slammed the pencil on top of the tablet and stared across the farm toward the road fronting the property to the horizon beyond. Nikki invaded his thoughts, providing a constant distraction.

It was early afternoon, another beautiful March day on the high plains of Texas. The creaking screen door captured his attention. Minnie Endicott came outside. Her face was pale and bore a distant expression. She stared straight ahead. She looked out of place, dressed in a blue suit with low heels and even a hat and white gloves, as though ready for church or some other semi-formal function. Whatever her destination was, she obviously saw a need to look her best.

"It's a beautiful afternoon," he called out to her.

She didn't acknowledge the comment and walked on by.

"Are you going out?"

"I have something I must take care, something that should have been done long ago."

Although acting peculiar, the fact she was getting out seemed positive, walking around the house toward the detached garage.

When she disappeared from view, he refocused on the blank sheet of paper in his lap. He sighed and picked up the pencil with fresh resolve and began to write.

Approaching voices startled him. He looked up to see Nikki and Arthur coming into the front yard carrying on a quiet conversation. Arthur patted her on the back as he focused attention on Jack. "I thought it'd be a good idea to get outside and take our friend here for a walk. She needs a big ol' whiff of this clean air and a fresh perspective."

"Good idea. I'm sure I'll be right here when you get back." He reached for her hand. His palm slid across hers as she walked by. There was a reflective look about her, but she didn't seem sad. He was happy Arthur had taken it upon himself to walk with her.

They walked down the same turn row Endicott had driven down on the tractor—an excellent place for a long undisturbed walk. He watched them only long enough for the sound of whispery voices to fade and returned to his project and, in short order, lost himself in the composition of an article, determined to give Brave Child a twenty-first century voice. Bigotry and a century of false beliefs would soon be exposed. He hoped to be as eloquent of style as Brave Child was of thought.

Time passed.

Arthur's voice shocked him as he and Nikki reappeared.

"That was quick."

"What do you mean 'quick'? We've been gone for almost an hour," Nikki said, "I'm exhausted."

Arthur huffed. Sweat trickled down his temple. "I'm far too old to be walking that much without getting complaints from these old muscles."

A glance at the watch on his wrist proved them right. An hour had indeed slipped by. Disbelieving he was capable of such concentration, he checked the tablet on which the article took shape, realizing fourteen handwritten pages had been filled. "I've never had an hour go by so fast in my life."

Nikki began looking around. "Arthur told me he sensed something was wrong and thought we should get back." Her wandering eyes settled on Jack. "Have you seen Mother?"

"She left some time ago."

"I don't think so. The garage door is closed. If she were gone it'd be up."

"Sorry. I didn't realize she'd come back." It occurred to him that he hadn't noticed her leave in the first place.

For the first time, he saw the approach of a thunderstorm towering in a mushroom shape in the western sky not far away. It'd be causing a problem soon. He hoped it'd be trouble for someone else, someplace other than the Endicott farm. The seasons were about to begin the battle for dominance but Jack had no desire to be on the front lines.

Nikki looked in that direction, too, shielding her eyes from the sun, which was about to disappear behind the massive thunderhead. "Daddy won't stay out much longer on that tractor with a storm coming."

Jogging to the porch, leaping up onto it, she yanked the screen door open and shouted, "Mom. Are you in there?" Waiting a few seconds, getting no response, she trotted back. The worry wrinkle in her forehead was all the encouragement he and Arthur needed to join the search.

Jack looked around and pointed to the largest structure on the east side. "Nikki, why don't you check that barn? Arthur, how about you look around those two smaller storage buildings over there? In the meantime, I'll check the backyard and garage. She's probably just out working in the yard somewhere."

The sun disappeared behind the storm cloud about the same time thunder rumbled in the distance. He remembered what his mother had told him as a young child. "If you hear thunder, the storm is within ten miles." Its approach coupled with sudden anxiety quickened his step.

Throwing open the sagging gate to the aging wooden backyard fence, he began the search. "Mrs. Endicott," he shouted. The confined yard was neat with few places to hide. He stopped long enough to make a cursory inspection of the small metal storage building near the back door, but when his eyes fell on the garage he became uneasy.

He heard an engine idling and jumped from the porch, just as a flash of lightning lit up his peripheral vision. He ran toward the garage.

Grabbing the loose and rusting knob on the side door he turned it, opened the door in one motion and rushed inside.

Fumes from the car engine were heavy and foul, watering his eyes. He coughed and fought to regain clear vision. Noxious fumes burned his throat so he shielded his face with a shirtsleeve, trotted to the overhead door, heaved it up and threw it open to clear the air.

Mrs. Endicott sat low in the driver's seat, head lolled to the side, mouth agape. He was too late.

Walking on stiff nervous legs to the open car window, he reached in and turned the ignition key off and noticed a scrap of paper still clutched in her hand. Gingerly, he opened her fingers and removed it.

It was a note to Nikki. An ache pierced his heart as the words flowed beneath his eyes: "*Sweetheart, I beg your forgiveness. The pain you feel has haunted me for years and has now grown unbearable. I knew George's decision was wrong, yet I did nothing. I've made my peace with God and he knows this is simply an act of recompense. I hope you'll marry someday and have many children, against all odds. I love you. —Mom*"

A delayed clap of thunder followed a brilliant flash through the open bay door. Rain fell in large, widely spaced drops. At the same time, the tractor engine grew into a roar as it came to the fence gate nearest the garage. The engine died. As that noise died away, he heard voices between rumbles of thunder and knew that George would be bursting in, followed quickly by Nikki and Arthur. He hated the feeling of absolute helplessness to prevent what was about to happen.

"I don't know where she could be," Nikki's father was saying, as he came through the yard gate.

Nikki didn't follow her father through the gate at the side of the garage, seeing Jack through the open overhead door first. She noticed the look on his face.

Her trot turned into an all out sprint.

Jack felt it inappropriate to say anything.

"Oh my God!" she cried above the sound of thunder.

Trying to slow her would be futile; yet he reached for her arm as she ran by. It wasn't intended to stop her, only meant as a comforting touch by a friend. Seeing the ugly truth was inevitable.

Nikki spun away from the gruesome sight and ran directly into her father's arms as he came through the side door, her lips pursed and tightened until they turned white. She could hold it no longer and wailed, hugging him so hard he couldn't move. In clenched fists, she held wads of his blue chambray shirt at his back.

At first, George didn't appear to comprehend, as he held his daughter with one hand while stroking her hair with the other. Tears finally appeared in the big man's eyes. His lip quivered, and he broke.

The howling wind, the thunder and small hail on the tin roof combined to create a sound that resembled classical music rich with cymbals as he and Arthur quietly backed to the far side of the garage.

Nikki sobbed. George cried. They held one another in a way only a father and daughter could.

The fury of the storm, combined with grief, harmonized into a chilling arrangement Jack never wanted to hear again.

It was after ten o'clock by the time all arrangements had been taken care of. Time spent with the sheriff took the longest. He asked question after question, repeating many of them several times. He did his job, making certain that it had indeed been a suicide. It was a good thing he and Arthur had been there to take some of that burden off Nikki and her father.

The county coroner was called. He determined an inquest would not be necessary. A quick collaboration between the coroner and sheriff ended with an official pronouncement of suicide. Minnie Endicott was then taken to the funeral home.

Watching Nikki tore him apart. She cried for hours, assuming responsibility for what had happened, and nothing Jack said made any difference. A gentle hug and an occasional touch was all he had to offer.

George was strangely in control of his emotions, or so it appeared. He talked, hop scotching from one topic to the next—needing to get back in the field as soon as the ground dried after the drenching rain to wondering if he had enough shaving cream to last until Saturday. In all his mindless chatter, the one glaring omission was any mention of his wife.

Nikki weakened, drained of all pretense or desire to hold thoughts in check. It became plain what was coming, but Jack had no plan to prevent it.

George stood near a credenza busying his hands with a small screw on his reading glasses, mumbling something about needing self-locking screws so they'd stop loosening all the time.

Nikki approached her father, arms tightly wrapping herself against a perceived chill. "Daddy?" She let her head press against his chest. "Why did it have to happen?"

"Honey, your mother was a good woman. But she had a problem distinguishing right from wrong. She let emotions dictate actions and not God's will. I always pushed her into doing things the right way—God's way. Sometimes, she just couldn't distinguish what the right way was. She chose a dangerous path of guilt. What happened is nothing more than the Devil's work."

Nikki stiffened. She stood straight and backed away from him. Her expression deteriorated into hatred.

Her father could have done no worse than if he'd shoved a lit stick of dynamite in her mouth. "You arrogant ... self-righteous ... sonofabitch," Nikki growled with an almost supernatural intensity. She stepped back further, doubling her fists, grinding clenched teeth and glaring at her father.

As she shook uncontrollably, George stepped away in shock. His jaw slackened.

"When are you going to wake up from your pretentious idealized dream of the way life should be?" she shouted, charging him and pounding his chest with both fists. "Are you so cold-hearted it's impossible to drop the right-and-wrong bullshit long enough to mourn the death of your wife... my mother? What the hell is wrong with you?" She beat his chest with every raised inflection.

Jack and Arthur could no longer stand idly by, determining with only an exchange of glances that intervention was called for. They stepped to her side, gently pinning her arms to her sides.

George paid no attention to the efforts to restrain her, stupefied at the sudden and violent reaction.

Once she was not allowed to swing her fists, only then did she seem to realize just how out of control she'd become. Anger drained from her face. It was the first time the family resemblance became obvious. They bore the same expression at that moment.

Nikki attempted to speak but no more words came. She spun around and hugged Jack so tight he thought it'd take his breath.

Arthur stroked her hair.

George stumbled backwards, clumsily turning and walking into the hall leading to the bedrooms. "I only did what I thought was right," he muttered.

"I loved her. I did." As he disappeared through the bedroom door, he said, "Oh God, what have I done?"

Once her father left the room, Nikki's knees gave way.

Jack and Arthur helped her to the sofa and sat her down. Several quiet minutes passed.

A blast shattered the silence.

It came from the bedroom.

All three leaped up at the same time and ran to the bedroom door.

Arthur pushed it open.

Crowding together in the doorway, they stared.

On the bed lay George Endicott on his side, knees drawn up and facing them with a bullet hole in his temple, a growing bloodstain darkening the bedspread. A small .22 caliber handgun lay loosely in his open palm.

Nikki fainted.

Jack caught her before she collapsed and carried her to the front room, laying her on the sofa. She had no more tears to cry.

CHAPTER 27

At the onset of the Texas visit, Jack had merely hoped to learn enough for a good article. The reality quashed anything a wild imagination might produce. The truth turned out to be a nightmare, but it damn sure wasn't a dream. Answers to all his questions flew at him like buckshot from a shotgun blast. If the promise to Brave Child had not been made, there wouldn't have been this trip and no way to learn what he did. As it turned out everything, even those events over a hundred years ago, was linked and now as clear as his haggard reflection in the mirror, what transpired had been preordained just as Kyle had said. Still, there was no way to understand how this played into a universal plan, but everything that happened to the three of them must have added up to a single divine puzzle piece. Someday he'd know—but not yet.

Although all things had been made clear, Jack tingled with anxiety from the moment they discovered Endicott's body. He wondered what the following day might bring that imparted such foreboding and didn't look forward to it sensing the friendship he shared with Nikki and Arthur might change forever. Beyond that, he didn't know what to expect.

Nikki's grief drained her physically and emotionally. Fainting turned out to be a backhanded blessing. He mopped her forehead with a cool washcloth for over an hour. Finally, her breathing evened out. Without ever regaining consciousness, she'd fallen asleep. He retrieved a blanket from the hall closet, covered her and left her on the sofa.

For the longest time, he sat beside her and traced her face with a finger, intermittently stroking her cheeks with butterfly caresses using the backs of his fingers, compelled to drink in her beauty, to stay close, to create a lasting memory—almost desperate to do so. The compulsion was wrapped inside the ambiguous fear about the coming dawn.

He remained aware that when she woke, every word spoken to her would have to be weighed carefully because her mental state would be delicate. Simply staying close, holding her hand, or hugging her would not be enough. The time for quiet support would end. Intervention in a major way was coming and he'd play a part. But what the hell was it?

Arthur had taken the initiative to call the sheriff back out to the farm. Although eyebrows were raised, the coroner ruled the Endicott's violent deaths a double suicide. The interrogation, the note taking, and the ruling—all of it took considerable time. He and Arthur were done-in when the authorities finally left and George's body removed from the house. They stripped his bed and trashed the sheets and pillowcases as the final duty of a day rife with violent eye-opening change.

He checked on Nikki. She slept and had a beautifully calm look about her. He wanted to sit and gaze upon her face for a while longer but fatigue took him down.

He and Arthur managed a few hours sleep in one of the back bedrooms. From the instant his eyes closed until the morning sun pried the lids apart, it seemed like mere seconds. Even before fully awake, he'd already begun dreading the day. But he succumbed to the inevitable and rolled out of bed.

He sipped coffee, sitting in the living room in George's chair and watching Nikki sleep. The house seemed cold and empty—no good smells of things cooking, no voices, no life. In the span of two days, there had been a revelation of monumental consequence in Nikki's life, as well as in his, and two suicides.

Before he finished the first cup, Arthur joined him.

Lack of sleep worked against him in spite of the caffeine coursing his veins. Grogginess magnified sympathy.

This weakening state of mind was not lost to Arthur. He looked Jack up and down, studied his eyes, and how he gazed at Nikki as she slept.

Becoming aware of his not-so-welcome analytical gaze, Jack attempted to avoid eye contact. He didn't feel that it was the time or place for psychic experimentation and certainly wasn't in the mood to be the subject of his fascination.

Nikki's first awakening movement was to work moisture back into her mouth, followed by suspending her upper torso on elbow for a time, eyes still closed. She pushed herself upright. Working stiffness from the neck, she rubbed it, massaging closed eyes with the heels of both hands and stretched. As she lazily moved, Jack's desperation began to rise, wanting to do something for her. *What can I do? What, for Christ's sake? What?* It was as much his fault for everything that happened, and he shouldered responsibility willingly.

As a by-product of an association with him, she found cause and opportunity to air long-held grievances. Although she did break free of dark secrets and guilt, it came at too high of a price. In the end, it only traded one type of guilt for another—deeper, more devastating.

"Stay in control," Arthur warned.

"I understand what you're saying, but regardless, I'm responsible for this… for her. End of story."

"There's nothing you could have done to change what happened."

"I don't believe it. It was my selfish interests that brought us here. Nothing you can say will change that."

"At the very most you may have changed the timing of events not the outcome. All things happen for a reason; you and Nikki coming to this place at the same time was inevitable. It was meant for you to be with her when your relationship was discovered and to be close to her when tragedy struck. It was no random cosmic coincidence." Arthur offered a knowing look—one Jack had no desire to acknowledge although he'd come to terms with the universal aspects of what had transpired. Arthur continued, "You two were put on the same road at the same time for a purpose. We just can't say what that reason is right now. That's all."

"He's right," Nikki said. "The confrontation with Mom and Dad was inevitable. It would have happened some day whether you were around or not. You were bound by a promise and I'm a believer in how important pledges are. Promise made, promise kept; that's all there is to it. There's no way you could have known it would lead to my parents' house, for God's sake. Besides, it only speeded up... it didn't change... it couldn't have... oh hell." Nikki's valiant attempt to remain in control crumbled. She covered her face and, again, wept.

Her pain was unbearable to watch. Jack moved to her side and put a fingertip under her chin and raised her head so their eyes met and said the only thing he could. "Let me take away some of your pain." The entreaty had not cleared his lips when warmth flowed over him.

Nikki's watery puffy eyes widened. He glanced down to see a glow radiating from the left side of his chest directly to the left side of hers. He winced when her pain flowed into his heart. It was sharp. He snapped his teeth together, receiving exactly what he'd asked for.

Wrapping him in a tight hug, she whispered, "Thank you."

Suddenly, the white glow expanded to envelop the two of them. Arthur moved within the aura. The glow intensified. In the blink of an eye, a radiant blue-white ball of light appeared across the room connecting them, via a milky white beam.

Jack was the catalyst, yet he could not imagine what was about to transpire. His companions showed no fear, nor did he; knowing whatever was about to happen was in the control of a higher authority.

Images formed within the blue-white glow; a scene he recognized even before it had fully formed. It was that place bridging the physical world with the spiritual where the process of dying occurred. He saw dead trees, murky lifeless water and even the beautiful green forest on the other side, symbolic images of dying, death and eternity. The whole picture faded into a blackened void, now unnecessary imagery.

Inexplicably, Jack pulled his two companions in close and held them. The three squared shoulders to whatever might appear within an endless expanse of nothingness and boldly marched through the brilliant tunnel toward it. Their eyes opened to that different reality known only to a few. They stood in limbo looking into empty space—not darkness, yet black. It began to wrinkle and take shape. Human forms emerged. As the brilliance subsided, Jack recognized faces.

Standing next to a small and very young woman clothed in a long plain dress and a bonnet, was brother Kyle. Only after seeing Brave Child did it become clear that she was great-great grandmother, Beatrice.

Brave Child stepped to the forefront. "The gratitude I feel cannot be expressed adequately, but now peace is in our family. Thank you."

"Your gratitude is premature. The story is only partially complete and still unpublished."

"I am part of all things, past, present, and future and I see the complete river of time and know it has been done," Brave Child said. "All that you have accomplished has set into motion an irreversible course, although you are still navigating the river and have yet to experience it. But you will."

Jack recognized his mother's face in the group behind the trio. She smiled sweetly, but otherwise made no attempt to communicate. Beatrice held an open palm to her mouth and gently blew a kiss his way as she, Kyle, and Brave Child stepped aside and faded.

He glanced over at Nikki. Her mouth fell open when she saw her parents emerge as the other three returned to unrecognizable shapes in the background. The appearance of George and Minnie came accompanied by the sound of a distant drumbeat.

Nikki's surprise disappeared and her mournful appearance transformed to joy. Her face beamed, a glow radiated from it. The rhythmic beat grew stronger. She seemed to become mesmerized by the sight of her parents and began walking toward them, her step slow and hesitating.

The rise and fall of the beat had a familiar cadence. Suddenly, he realized it was not a drum at all, but a heartbeat. Nikki was losing herself to the moment as she gathered them both into a full embrace.

The sound of that beating heart had become loud. It reverberated.

He could not remain calm once it was clear that Nikki was making a choice with a never-ending consequence, but it only took a simple satisfied smile to stop him cold.

The beating heart that filled his ears stopped.

Joining her parents in facing the light, Nikki Endicott looked back no more.

Her radiant heart was born, as she stepped into eternity.

CHAPTER 28

The window beyond his computer monitor competed for his attention and finally won out. Work nearly completed, it now didn't seem so much distraction as a pleasant diversion. Having typed the final words, Jack Dane finally loosened demanding bonds of concentration on the text still on the screen. This second floor view compelled him to look and enjoy. His hands slid from the keyboard into his lap and he took time to gaze beyond the window framed in frost and give it the admiring look it deserved. A cold gray Texas day greeted him. Large, lazy snowflakes fluttered and drifted past the window at a slight angle—artwork in motion, beautiful. The flakes resembled large bits of shredded tissue paper dancing and gliding, in no hurry to make it to the ground. They floated into then out of view. Occasional wind gusts stole away the gentle glide of the flakes through the air, adding brief urgency.

It brought to mind a plastic shopping bag doing a dipsy doodle on a cold winter's day. The image of that small dog chasing it as vivid now as it was all those years ago, but time had softened the impact, now just another point of reflection. It occurred to him that, that otherwise meaningless bag flying through the air on a blustery winter day had been an important turning point ultimately resulting in the man he became.

"Humph." He shook his head and grinned at the profound absurdity—such a minor event creating a major course correction, setting off a chain of events that altered the lives of five people, the afterlife of one, and a dog.

His survey of the landscape broadened. Beyond the fascinating flakes dancing and darting near the window, he took in the entire view all at once. It brought to mind a painted landscape framed by the curtains. It would seem the artist captured a world at rest awaiting a future rebirth. In each brushstroke he saw peace.

His eyes settled on the abandoned farmhouse. It seemed to whisper acceptance of the way things were on this winter day, standing empty and deteriorating. The tail of a ragged curtain attempted escape through a broken window of the old Endicott home and lazily waved, reaching to be free. Dilapidated and empty farmhouses are scattered across the South Plains of Texas. This one attracts no special attention, just another building needing to be removed, making way for something new and better. Only he knew or cared about the true nature of its history. As long as breath was in him, it'd remain a monument to a time permanently etched into his memory.

Still entranced by the view through the window, he reached for the computer mouse without looking. Finally his eyes caught up, forced away from memories to find the icon to save this finished manuscript. He hit print. As the printer hummed and clicked to life, his attention returned to the interesting view through the frost-encrusted window and to things that shaped his life. Completion of the manuscript spawned an introspective look back.

This was the first book he'd written that could not be labeled non-fiction. Twenty-seven years and twelve books later, he found it necessary to switch to fiction. He smiled at the mere thought of the word.

He had become a sought-after regional authority on the life of the Great Plains Native-American tribes—research that began with a promise to a long-dead relative. That promise turned into a well-received work titled "A Truly Brave Child." a particularly difficult piece to write. Frequently, conjecture had to replace unequivocal fact. What he knew to be true was because he had been a part of it and saw it first-hand, but sourcing facts in a believable way was impossible. Nonetheless, it stood as the quintessential guide to regional events of that era.

Its commercial success allowed the purchase of the Endicott farm. He didn't have the heart to change it or the courage to sell it. It served as writing motivation over the years. But a day approached that a choice would have to be made; what he should do with the old house, outbuildings and all those rusting farm implements. For the present, he needed continued proof that it had not been some twisted dream. Without it, he might have slipped over the edge long ago, never totally believing his sanity was intact anyway.

He missed Nikki and Arthur terribly. The passing years had not reduced the ache to be with them. Each memory of their time together brought on a sentimental lump. If it had not been for Arthur he wouldn't have been able to pull his life together and move on after Nikki left. Once she'd walked out of his life, and hers, days turned to weeks and then to months as he mourned her absence, unable to function—impotent in the simple art of living day to day. To this day, Nikki remains listed as a missing person. But clouds of suspicion hung low over he and Arthur's heads for years because of George and Minnie's double suicide then, less than twenty four hours later, Nikki went missing. The authorities hounded them for over a year asking the same tiresome questions over and over. The case went cold and police finally seemed to give up, but even after all the years since, he was still listed as a person of interest in the case.

He only had Arthur for another three years after losing Nikki. Too many years of cheap wine and truck stop food took its toll. Relieved, even pleased, that when the time came, the old guy passed comfortably, going out with a smile. Even the weakness of his final moments couldn't dull his excitement about the adventure that lay ahead for him. The only thing Arthur wanted of this world in his final moments was that Jack held his hand as he slipped earthly bonds. As he took his last breath, Jack made certain the hand was firmly in his grasp and told him, "Safe journey, my Friend. Learn all you can and fill me in when I get there."

A day later, an attorney contacted him. He discovered the old fart had left him the entire Wainwright estate. Jack never shared with anyone that the will was dated nearly six months before he ever met the man. Shocking but certainly not surprising. How could it be? Arthur Wainwright knew much more than he ever shared. In retrospect, it punctuated an important fact; he knew the outcome of his association with Jack even before it began. *Who were you really, Arthur? Were you even of this earth? Or did you just drop in under orders from a higher power? Did you really die or were you simply reassigned?* Jack wondered if he could have been the personification of something greater—more spiritual perhaps. There'd come a day he'd know.

With the combined wealth from his writing and from Arthur's legacy, he built a house on this Texas farm duplicating the Springfield mansion. His favorite room happened to be this eastward facing second floor room. Arthur had taught him to appreciate each new day as a new adventure. To honor that advice, he chose to begin each day facing the dawn.

Again, he read the last few words of the just completed manuscript.

Awed by the sequence of events that brought him to this point, he shivered slightly. It had taken many years to gather in the courage to relive such profound friendships and put it in print. He knew the story would eventually need to be written. Urgency finally invaded every waking thought to get it done.

At times, his hands shook so badly he had to get up and walk away. Some memories were too vivid—pain becoming overwhelming all over again. Sometimes, he couldn't find words descriptive enough to define his depth of feeling on the subject—hardly ever speaking of his friends singularly. Nikki, Arthur and he were like family, only closer. The spiritual connection was indescribable.

A glance at his reflection in a corner of the window showed a man he didn't recognize, older than his years. A snowflake came dancing across it. The hair remained thick but heavily streaked with gray. Lines burrowed deep across the forehead, radiating from eyes that no longer twinkled. Instead, they sagged with age and drooped with exhaustion.

He stood to check the printer's progress. It continued to whir and click, printing page after page.

Many times in the past twenty-seven years he contemplated invoking the radiant heart—desire to see Nikki pushing him to the brink. But each time, he'd become filled with peace and the itch to make it happen would go away. It had to have been Nikki, or maybe Arthur, advising patience. The reunion would come soon enough.

Startled by the printer going silent, he noticed a flashing light on it, alerting the need to be reloaded with paper. Shuffling to a box on the floor, he bent at the waist and retrieved another ream. The arthritic back reminded him that he was no longer agile or young. Reminders of this were many and all too frequent. The paper slid easily into the printer. It whirred, clicked and hummed back to life.

He cocked his ear to a sudden unrecognizable noise. *It must be the wind.* The snowflakes now flew at a sharp angle across the window.

He realized how eccentric he seemed to the outside world and how illogical his lifestyle had become. It had to have appeared unusual that he had no relationships or friends. Very few people held his attention beyond the initial introduction. Going into public had become very unpleasant. He'd become a willing recluse, more comfortable living in the past with an increasingly narrow vision of the future, but didn't consider himself odd for it, just a lifestyle choice.

He glanced through the window as a gust of wind pushed against the house and noticed a tumbleweed zigzagging, bouncing across the barren field chased by snowflakes. The ground whitened as the wind became increasingly angry. *It looks like we're in for a big change?*

He turned away from the window and shuffled back to his desk chair. The brittleness of age gave gravity the edge. Grabbing both armrests, he lowered his body into the seat. A knifing pain sliced deep into his chest. He winced. It disappeared as fast as it came. He no longer listened to the language of his body, seeing it merely as a useful tool to carry his consciousness, sort of like an old car he once owned. It might have been ugly, but it took him where he needed to go—same thing for this decrepit old body.

Smiling, he leaned forward and focused failing eyes through bifocals perched on his nose at the page number coming out of the printer. Absently, he massaged the tightness in his chest. The pages continue to pile up in the tray. It wouldn't be long now.

The temperature in the room suddenly seemed to drop a few degrees. Perhaps the sight of snow and the sound of wind played tricks on his mind. The thermometer on the wall showed no change. A particularly hard gust slammed the house. Lights flickered and the printer stuttered and misfired. He grumbled, reset it, and pressed the resume button.

Many times over the years he had to press his own resume button. There had been far too many low points, misfires, and numerous times he'd needed something, or someone to get him going again. He no longer had that support—tether-free and drifting ever since, thus the lifestyle choice. What damned difference did it make if the world viewed him as eccentric? No reason to search for new friends when anything less than what he had would not be good enough.

There had been an upside to melancholy. His best writing always occurred during low cycles. Nikki would have analyzed it and told him why. In her absence, it remained a simple curiosity. Is there a connection between depression and creativity? It seemed to be an interesting question, maybe good enough for another book. He sighed. *That's a project for another day.*

The tightness in his chest now felt more like pressure pushing against him—no real concern.

Removing a stack of paper from the printer tray, he noticed that only a couple of pages remained to be printed. Leaning back in the chair, he became very tired. No surprise. He'd spent the entire day at this desk.

He reached for the left side of his chest to rub away another sharp pain. *That deviled ham must have given me a helluva case of indigestion.* He took a deep breath and grimaced until the pain subsided. It went away and he went back to work.

What should I title this book? Arthur called this ability the radiant heart because of harmonic vibrations that radiate as light under intense emotion. Maybe that should be the title, *The Radiant Heart* or *A Radiant Heart* or, maybe *Radiant Hearts.*

He wondered on occasion whether there were others in the world still alive that possessed the ability to move in time and space the way he could. Maybe if he called it *The Last Radiant Heart,* someone would come forth to share his or her ability and prove that Jack Dane was not the last. *To the remainder of the world it'll simply be a work of fiction. But to that one person out there it'll mean so much more. That's what I'll do.*

For years he'd kept an eye on his nieces, Melissa and Kyra, both now adults, thinking it might continue through one or both. They were the last of the Dane bloodline. But, he'd seen no evidence. True to the vow he gave to his sister-in-law over the dead body of his brother Kyle, Jack stayed close to her and the girls. Cary now had two teenage children by a different marriage.

Oxygen in the room suddenly seemed inadequate. He forced air deep into his lungs but it was becoming more difficult. The chest tightness felt like a heavy weight on it.

The printer stopped. He read the final words of the last page: *"...her radiant heart was born, as she stepped into eternity."* He removed and stacked them with the rest then fell back in his chair. He jotted his choice for a title on the cover page. The instant the pencil was laid upon the desk, a sudden crushing pain knocked the breath from him. The room began to spin.

The chill came quickly.

He glowed.

It brightened.

The pain became unbearable fast. He thought his entire body would explode.

The glow reversed and dizziness consumed him. His head spun as though whirling off his shoulders. He closed his eyes, clenched his teeth and rolled into the fetal position, falling out of the chair onto the floor. The only thought beyond pain was that his time had come.

As quick as it started, the pain stopped. Euphoria rushed from his toenails to the tips of his hair. He opened his eyes to see a body below, crumpled on the floor, realizing he stared at his own motionless, dying body. *How can I navigate this realm without a beating heart? Am I to be trapped here forever? Haunting this room?*

"Don't be ridiculous. That's what we're here for." The voice was wonderfully familiar.

Feeling off-balance, he spun about, almost slinging his body right out of the house—then stabilized to see Nikki. He felt her love flow over him.

Behind her stood Arthur, wearing that devious grin he knew so well. "Remember all our conversations about universal truths and that someday we'd know them?"

Jack nodded and approached them, smiling as he did.

"Then come on, man," he said excitedly, waving him over. He laughed. The boisterous sound of Arthur's voice had the ring of angels. "I have something to show you that I promise will be an eternal thrill. It'll knock your ethereal socks off."

A great peace swept over him as both friends extended their arms. The two-and-a-half-decade need to embrace them was about to be fulfilled. The two people who completed him drew him in, but it wasn't an embrace he felt. He was absorbed into them. The world he moved away from quickly became a sketchy memory. As the light swallowed them up, he realized there was nothing left to say, to write or do.

Loose the soul to regain all that's lost.
Step free of binding emotions.
Look back no more on a harnessed spirit.
The path traveled is done.
Wonders wait to be known.
Avail the heart to love.
Eternal dawns greet eager eyes.
Loose the soul to regain all that's lost.

-THE END-

BIBLIOGRAPHY

THE HANDBOOK OF TEXAS ONLINE, a joint project of the General Libraries at the University of Texas at Austin and the Texas State Historical association.

Gunnar Brune, SPRINGS OF TEXAS, Vol. 1 (Fort worth: Branch-Smith, 1981)

John R. Cook, THE BORDER AND THE BUFFALO: AN UNTOLD STORY OF THE SOUTHWEST PLAINS (Topeka, Kansas: Crane, 1907; rpt., New York: Citadel Press, 1967).

Lawrence L. Graves, ed., A HISTORY OF LUBBOCK (Lubbock: West Texas Museum Association, 1962).

William C. Griggs, "The Battle of Yellowhouse Canyons in 1877", West Texas Historical Association Year Book 51 (1975).

Herman Lehmann, NINE YEARS AMONG THE INDIANS (Austin: Von boeckmann-Jones, 1927; 3d ed., A NEW LOOK AT NINE YEARS WITH THE INDIANS, San Antonio: Lebco Graphics, 1985

Morris W. Foster, BEING Comanche: a social history of an American Indian community (Tucson: University of Arizona Press, 1991).

William T. Hagan, UNITED STATES-COMANCHE RELATIONS: THE RESERVATION YEARS (New Haven: Yale University Press, 1976; rpt., Norman: University of Oklahoma Press, 1990).

Thomas W. Kavanagh, COMANCHE PLITICAL HISTORY: AN ETHNOHISTORICAL PERSPECTIVE, 1706-1875 (Lincoln: University of Nebraska Press, 1995).

Rupert N. Richardson, THE COMANCHE BARRIER TO SOUTH PLAINS SETTLEMENT (Glendale, California: Clark, 1933; rpt., Millwood, New York: Kraus, 1973

Ernest Wallace and e. Adamson Hoebel, THE COMANCHES (Norman: University of Oklahoma Press, 1952).

DANIEL LANCE WRIGHT is a freelance writer and novelist born in Lubbock, Texas. Having spent the first 19 years of his life on a cotton farm on the South Plains and the next 32 in the television industry, Danny has seen the world from two distinctly different angles. This unique perspective adds depth when bringing together characters from divergent backgrounds in his stories. Mr. Wright's fiction has been recognized by the Panhandle Writers League in 2004, The Abilene Writers Guild in 2004, The Oklahoma Writers Federation in 2005 and 2006, Writer's Digest in 2007, and Art Affair in 2007. A lifelong Texan, Danny currently resides in Waco. Find out more at his website, www.daniellancewright.com.

ALSO IN PRINT FROM VIRTUAL TALES

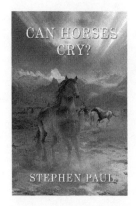

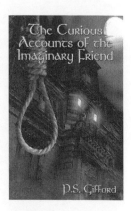

ALSO IN PRINT FROM VIRTUAL TALES

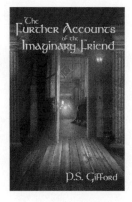

WWW.VIRTUALTALES.COM

Coming Soon from Virtual Tales

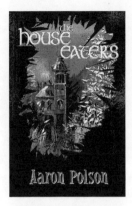

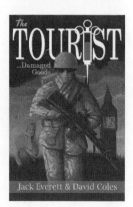

WWW.VIRTUALTALES.COM

Made in the USA
Charleston, SC
26 October 2010